TIM KEVAN practised as a barrister in London for ten years during which time he wrote or co-wrote ten law books and was a regular legal pundit for TV and radio. He is also the author of *Law and Disorder*, which was described by broadcaster Jeremy Vine as 'a wonderful, racing read – well drawn, smartly plotted and laugh out loud'. He is the co-author of *Why Lawyers Should Surf* (with Dr Michelle Tempest), which *The Times Online* described as 'a song for the modern age which could well become a cult classic'. He now lives by the sea in Braunton in North Devon where he surfs and continues to write the BabyBarista Blog for the *Guardian*. He is also the co-founder of two businesses, CPD Webinars and Law Brief Publishing. Brought up in Minehead in Somerset, he was educated at Cambridge University and was a scholar of the Middle Temple.

www.timkevan.com
timkevan.blogspot.com
www.babybarista.com
www.guardian.co.uk/babybarista

Law and Peace

TIM KEVAN

BLOOMSBURY

LONDON · BERLIN · NEW YORK · SYDNEY

First published in Great Britain 2011
This paperback edition published 2012

Copyright © 2011 by Tim Kevan
Illustrations © 2011 by Alex Williams

The moral right of the author has been asserted

Excerpt from *Animal Farm* by George Orwell (Copyright © George Orwell,
1945) reprinted by permission of Bill Hamilton as the Literary Executor of
the Estate of the Late Sonia Brownell Orwell and Secker & Warburg Ltd.

'Lord Finchley' by Hilaire Belloc from *More Peers* (© Hilaire Belloc 1911) is reproduced
by permission of PFD (www.pfd.co.uk) on behalf of The Estate of Hilaire Belloc.

Extract from 'Let Me Die a Young Man's Death' by Roger McGough from
The Mersey Sound (© Roger McGough 1967) is printed by permission of
United Agents (www.unitedagents.co.uk) on behalf of Roger McGough.

Bloomsbury Publishing, London, Berlin, New York and Sydney

50 Bedford Square, London WC1B 3DP

A CIP catalogue record for this book is available from the British Library

ISBN 978 1 4088 2175 6
10 9 8 7 6 5 4 3 2 1

Typeset by Hewer Text UK Ltd, Edinburgh

Printed in Great Britain by Clays Limited, St Ives plc

MIX
Paper from
responsible sources
FSC® C018072

www.bloomsbury.com/timkevan

For Michelle and my parents

The creatures outside looked from pig to man, and from man to pig, and from pig to man again; but already it was impossible to say which was which.

George Orwell, Animal Farm

Time is but the stream I go a-fishin in.

Henry David Thoreau, Walden

Contents

CAST

BabyBarista: A young Flashman meets Rumpole meets Francis Urquhart for the twenty-first century.

TopFirst: BabyB's former fellow pupil and, by the end of book one, his sworn enemy.

OldSmoothie: Think Peter Bowles in *To the Manor Born* and the Milk Tray Man, but not quite.

UpTights: BabyB's ex-pupilmistress. Insists on boundaries and personal space. Has 'issues'. Against him in the Moldy litigation.

OldRuin: How a barrister should be. Dumbledore meets Clarence, the angel in *It's a Wonderful Life*. BabyB's redemption.

Claire: BabyB's best friend and a barrister in another chambers. Think Scully from *X-Files*.

SlipperySlope: Solicitor who introduces BabyB to the dark arts of litigation and has a habit of misquoting from films.

Smutton: Brassy to UpTights's classy and yet still, somehow, sexy.

TheBoss: BabyB's ex-pupilmaster. Unscrupulous, spineless coward.

TopFlirt:	TopFirst's beautiful, bright fiancée.
BusyBody:	Barrister always up for a fight, particularly with OldSmoothie.
NurserySlope:	Solicitor who is Slippery's niece and apprentice.
TheBusker:	Barrister who is very laid back in his approach to both court and life, with the integrity and decency of OldRuin.
TheVamp:	Barrister in chambers and a walking *Carry On* film of an innuendo.
JudgeFetish:	Judge in the Moldy litigation with a penchant for ladies in particular attire.
BigMouth:	Pompous Tory MP stuck on the back-benches like a piece of old chewing gum.
BrainWasher:	Hypnotist, mentalist, you name it.
ScandalMonger:	Ruthless PR guru who becomes one of BabyB's secret weapons.
HeadofChambers:	Well meaning, pompous and completely out of touch.
HeadClerk:	The real power in chambers. All seeing, all knowing.
ClichéClanger:	Solicitor with a colourful use of the English language.
TheCreep:	A jumped up little twerp who sucks up to the big beasts in chambers.
FanciesHimself:	Junior clerk who had a fling with BusyBody.

PROLOGUE

Saturday 29 September 2007
Year 2 (week 0): School reports

I stumbled across one of my old school reports today and was intrigued to see what my teacher had to say about me at the age of twelve:

'BabyBarista is always first out of the classroom and into the playground when the bell goes and then the last one to settle down afterwards. He is clearly bright and tends to finish set work much quicker than the other pupils although this does have the distinct disadvantage that he then starts to distract his friends with idle chat. Yet despite these minor difficulties he does seem to possess an unerring ability to remain just on the right side of the naughty line even if he sometimes avoids more serious trouble only by the seat of his pants. My concern is that as he gets older this is a boy who could literally go either way: up the ranks or off the rails.'

The report then concluded with the following remark: 'I would hate to see him in court one day.'

CHAPTER 1
OCTOBER: BigMouth

Sunday 30 September 2007
Year 2 (week 0): A tenant

'You made it BabyB, I always thought you would. Tenancy in a proper barristers' chambers. You need never worry again.'

My mother was congratulating me yet again as we had breakfast together this morning. Ha. If she'd been aware of even a small part of what really went on in the last twelve months she'd have known that only half of what she said was actually true. As well as double-crossing my first pupilmaster, who was eventually struck off, I also had a hand in scuppering many of the pupils who were competing with me for that prized tenancy. I stood by as Worrier was encouraged to bring a trumped-up sex discrimination claim. I made it appear that BusyBody had posted a damaging recording of HeadofChambers online. ThirdSix had his court papers swapped at the last minute. Oh, and then there was also the small matter of blackmailing my rival TopFirst, after he'd fallen for a honeytrap called Ginny.

But as TopFirst said last Friday when he started to put the pieces of the jigsaw together: 'I just want you to know that *I* know. I will never forget, BabyB. No one has ever beaten me at anything. I tell you now that in whatever career you manage to scrape together for yourself in the future, you'd better watch your back.'

I am a tenant, it's true, and now at least I might be able to help solve some of my mother's financial problems: problems that stem from the sacrifices she made to put me through university. But as for never needing to worry again, well that might just be a little premature.

Monday 1 October 2007
Year 2 (week 1): Lap of honour

My first day as a tenant and on the face of it at least, it's a job for life. It's now almost impossible for them to kick me out, which reminds me of the American saying that there are only two things that will kill a political career in Washington: being found with a dead girl or a live boy. I'm not sure what I'd have to do to be ejected from chambers but it'd have to be something pretty heinous. Although that's not to say it never happens. Look at TheBoss. After he was struck off last week he had to pack his things and clear out by Friday afternoon: departing in disgrace, his wig properly soiled, never to be used again. It makes me wonder what an old wig might be used for if not for court? Attached to a small metal stick, the rough horse hair would make for an extremely effective, albeit rather extravagant, loo brush.

As if to really rub salt into TheBoss's wounds, they've given me his old room in chambers to share with the lovely OldRuin, who still makes an occasional sortie into the old smoke. So today, with tenancy in the bag and after unceremoniously dumping my things on to the desk previously known as that belonging to TheBoss, I made my lap of honour around chambers, accepting the congratulations with great modesty and making much of the qualities of my fellow, less fortunate pupils, bless their little cotton socks. 'Terrible shame that we all couldn't have been taken on ... Indeed, I don't know how I was picked given the quality of the other candidates,' etcetera, etcetera, blah, blah, blah. The disingenuous sentiments I have spewed out today beat even those of TheCreep when he's sliming up to yet another QC.

But I can hardly tell them the truth. Imagine it: 'Yes, thank you very much. I agree that as the most devious, sly and downright sneaky of all the pupils I thoroughly deserved to be awarded tenancy. These qualities, I'm sure you will agree, will serve me well in our esteemed profession. Yes, my fellow tenants, whether you like to admit it or not, these are qualities you have not only encouraged with this ridiculous pupillage system but you have now also generously rewarded.'

No, if I'm going to get anywhere in this job, I will endeavour to do what the English excel at, and what I say will rarely be what I mean.

Tuesday 2 October 2007
Year 2 (week 1): JackCard

Met the four new pupils at chambers tea this afternoon. And if yesterday I was playing the hypocrite card, today I was playing a gold-embossed Jack. I'm alright and for the next twelve months they're not. One of them asked my advice on how to survive pupillage.

'Oh, it's easy. Really. Just keep your head down, don't cause any trouble and be nice to your fellow pupils.'

If he believes that then he doesn't deserve to be taken on in the first place. Then another one asked if I could offer any tips for working with his new pupilmistress, UpTights. I was starting to enjoy my new-found power.

'Give her extra-strong coffee in the morning. Make sure it's caffeinated whether she says so or not. She always responds to a good dose of caffeine.'

She most certainly does. Watching her usual manic state go into hyperdrive should certainly provide some sport. On a roll, I then introduced another pupil to OldSmoothie, the man who last year had made sure that everyone with the name Wayne or Shane was rejected on the basis that 'it wouldn't look good on the board'.

'OldSmoothie,' I said. 'May I introduce you to our new pupil Sharon?'

OldSmoothie's jaw visibly dropped but he just managed to keep it together enough to say, 'How d'you do?'

'Very well, thank you,' replied Sharon earnestly.

'O tempora, o mores,' whispered HeadofChambers, shaking his head. 'Oh what times. Oh what manners.'

A silence descended upon the room and knowing looks were exchanged. We all knew what was coming next and the wind (some might say hot air) was back in OldSmoothie's sails.

'Young lady,' he started, 'just because your name is Sharon and you are quite clearly from Birmingham does not mean that you may answer, "How do you do?" with the words "Very well, thank you". Do they teach you nothing at Bar School these days? Never again, understand? It's terribly non-U and barristers don't do non-U. Solicitors, now that's a different story. They can visit the toilet and have settees in their lounges as much as they like. But not barristers.' He paused. 'Do you understand?'

He may as well have been speaking double Dutch as far as poor Sharon was concerned. She stood there mute, presumably fearful that opening her mouth to say anything would harm her more than the rabbit-in-the-headlights look she was currently demonstrating so well.

'Do you understand?' repeated OldSmoothie slowly.

The pupil raised her eyebrows and nodded tentatively.

'So what do you answer?' boomed OldSmoothie, now aware that he had an audience.

Sharon's brow furrowed and for a moment I thought she might try to make a run for it – and on only her second day in chambers.

'Speak up,' said OldSmoothie. 'I can't hear you.'

The silence again fell, this time so heavily that it seemed to be almost crushing poor Sharon into the floor. Then OldSmoothie eased up and said somewhat theatrically, 'Well, let's give it a try. You give the greeting to me.'

This she could do and she put out her hand, saying, 'How d'you do?'

To which OldSmoothie replied, 'How d'you do?' and turned on his heels leaving the poor pupil utterly bewildered.

TheVamp and TheBusker moved over to offer words of consolation. TheVamp patted Sharon on her arm and said, 'I wouldn't worry. He's a fat old git with a chip on his shoulder, not just about women and class but about life in general. He's certainly not representative of chambers as a whole.'

'I really wouldn't worry at all,' said TheBusker kindly. 'Terrible time, pupillage. We all understand that, believe it or not.'

Sharon visibly relaxed and answered, 'To be honest I really didn't—'

She was interrupted by what can only be described as a 'harrumph' from the far side of the room. It was HeadofChambers.

'My dear,' he started. 'It's all very well being the subject of OldSmoothie's little games but really, some things are truly beyond the pale.'

Once more, Sharon's face returned to what seemed to be her default setting of bewilderment.

HeadofChambers didn't keep her waiting.

'"To be honest" is what a criminal says in the witness box. What a barrister should say is "to be frank".'

Welcome, for another crop of pupils, to the all-inclusive modern Bar.

Wednesday 3 October 2007
Year 2 (week 1): BigMouth

OldSmoothie was once again holding court this morning, this time in the clerks' room just as everyone was arriving. I'd heard him sounding off before about how he was best friends with a Tory MP from the shires who, it seems, is stuck to the backbenches like a piece of old chewing gum. I'll call him BigMouth. Apparently, said MP created big headlines in one of last Sunday's tabloids because he had paid for the services of a prostitute. Or, I should say, he had allegedly paid for her services. For this was the point of OldSmoothie's story.

'You see, he is very hard up for money and he wants to sue them. Naturally, I'll take it on a no win, no fee but I'm looking for a junior to do the leg work.'

Despite appearances, OldSmoothie is not stupid and this whole little performance was staged to whet the appetite of the junior members of chambers. Perhaps even to tender it out in a rather gentlemanly sort of way. Needless to say, first up to the crease was TheCreep, a jumped up little twerp who sucks up to the big beasts in chambers and struts around with erroneous self-importance. True to style he began to ooze: 'Ooh OldSmoothie, I think you're great and I'm so very clever,' etc., etc. But he was batted away to the boundary without much more than a flick of the wrist from OldSmoothie. TheCreep is definitely not his style. Next up was TheVamp who was a far more serious proposition for the old lech.

'You know,' I heard her whisper, throatily. 'Libel cases are by jury. You're going to need a team who appeal *directly* to the jury.'

She gave OldSmoothie a knowing look and didn't need to elaborate further. I realised that there was no way I was going to be able to compete against her today, but with an opportunity like this coming up in chambers, I've got to try and think of a way to get myself on the case.

By hook or by crook.

Thursday 4 October 2007
Year 2 (week 1): CopyCat

Before I could even say 'plot', never mind try to implement one, OldSmoothie announced today that TheVamp would be acting as his junior in the BigMouth libel case. The most high-profile case to come through the doors of chambers in years has been snatched from under my greedy little nose. However, they do have a problem. Neither OldSmoothie nor TheVamp have ever done any libel law in their lives. My problem is that neither have I. The difference is that they don't know this.

With that in mind, I popped over to the library and fished out a couple of random articles on libel law from the computer. I made sure they were unrelated to the issues in this actual case so that no one is likely to refer to them any time soon. I then copied and pasted them, substituting my own name for the author's. It's dastardly, I know, but hardly the wickedest thing in the world and, of course, it will only work thanks to the pompous fat one's own ignorance and laziness. So, off the articles went in an email to him suggesting he might find them useful.

I wait to see if he bites.

Friday 5 October 2007
Year 2 (week 1): Threats

An email came today:

Just to tell you that I now have a tenancy in the chambers my father went to after he'd finished with yours. Don't know why

I even bothered wasting my time with you bunch of losers. And for the avoidance of doubt BabyB, I meant exactly what I said last week. You will regret having crossed me. What's more, if I ever hear mention of the Ginny Tapes [the secret recording I made of him trying it on with a girl I'd hired, despite being engaged], the consequences will be even worse. I do not use these words lightly.

TopFirst

He reminded me a little of a pantomime villain, shaking his fist and screaming petulantly, 'I'll get you BabyB, if it's the last thing I do!' Well, talk to the gown 'cos the wig's not listening. Plus, I happen to know that the chambers he's been forced to join is renowned for taking on people who have been rejected elsewhere. It is what OldSmoothie would describe as 'hardly top drawer'. However, I have already learnt that I underestimate TopFirst at my peril. So I decided to answer him in robust fashion:

I don't know what on earth you are talking about but I do not appreciate being threatened. Should I hear anything like this again I shall consider passing it straight on not only to the Bar Standards Board but also to the police. In the meantime, despite your unsavoury remarks, please give my regards to your lovely fiancée and I send you my warmest congratulations on joining such a well-known chambers.

With everything that has been going on in chambers I still haven't been in touch with Claire since the night last week when we both found out that we had been given tenancy. To be honest, or rather 'to be frank', I think this is probably owing to the fact that that was also the night when we sealed our long-term friendship with a tentative first kiss. I still don't know whether it was just a drunken celebratory thing as far as Claire is concerned and I'd never really considered that she might like me in that way. For that matter I'm not exactly sure in what way I might like her. She's my best friend, and if we get this wrong our whole friendship might be ruined. So, to my shame, I've been too nervous to contact her since that evening and today I received a text message saying:

> Hey, BabyB. Hope you've had a good week. I've just been added to a big case in Leeds for the next two weeks so I'm off up there this evening. Would be lovely to catch up when I'm back.

This of course makes the whole situation about as clear as mud but at least it has the advantage of delaying the need to make any decisions.

Monday 8 October 2007
Year 2 (week 2): Blind leading the blind

Had a visit from OldSmoothie this morning.

'The problem, BabyB,' he explained, with his charmometer switched to full, 'is that BigMouth has asked me to present the case, and TheVamp will no doubt prove a hit with both judge and jury, but neither of us know anything about running a libel action.'

Which makes three of us, I thought to myself.

'In fact,' he went on, 'the only thing I can remember about the subject is the well-worn advice to authors wanting to reduce their risk of being sued when they base a character on someone they don't like.'

'Oh, what's that?' I asked innocently.

'Think about it. If there's going to be a case then the description in the book has to be such that it leads the reader to think it's that man in real life. With me so far?'

'Er, yes . . .'

'So, to avoid that, you just tell the author in question to describe the size of the character's manhood.'

'Oh.'

'I mean, who's going to sue claiming that the man with the small one is in fact them?'

Then he returned to BigMouth. 'And of course,' he continued, 'he'll struggle to get some real libel barristers on a no win, no fee as these cases are seen as just too risky.'

'But aren't there professional difficulties associated with doing something outside your area of expertise?' I enquired, reinforcing my own newly established position as a great authority on the intricacies of libel law.

'Oh, it's never stopped me, BabyB. One of the joys of the Bar is that you can wake up one morning knowing nothing about a subject and then by the next day be putting yourself out as an expert in it. However, it's always useful to have a junior who can provide a little guidance from time to time.'

So, the good news is that I'm on the case. The bad news is that I will probably be up all night drafting a note on some of the legal issues that may arise – particularly given the fact that I'm starting from scratch.

Tuesday 9 October 2007
Year 2 (week 2): The conference

Now don't get me wrong. I've got nothing against politicians. Well, nothing more than the average prejudice against those MPs who are corrupt or simply power-hungry. However, even after reminding yourself that as a breed they're all still human and maybe even have families, you may still struggle to actually *like* a fair number of them. That's not to say they're bad or ill-meaning, merely that very few of us have anything in common with them. But even allowing for the fact that MPs are most definitely a discriminated against minority, I defy anyone to find even an ounce of sympathy for our friend BigMouth. Or should I say, my new client, who I met today for the first time in conference. 'Met' is perhaps an overstatement. Even though I was the one who had done all the work, I basically served the coffee and then sat at the back of the room taking notes. These ended up being my thoughts on the great man, which were rude and unrepeatable. Honestly.

Suffice to say, my first impression of BigMouth was not a positive one. He just isn't a very nice man. He's arrogant, egotistical and completely lacking in any insight as to how he may be perceived by others. All this means that he is in exactly the right job of course, propping up the Parliamentary green benches, or rather, popping up on them even when it's wholly inappropriate. Which is most of the time, since he'll try and wrangle a quip about Europe or immigration into any debate you care to choose, however off-topic it might be. Oh, and his voice goes so far back in his throat as to take you back in time through generations of impeccable aristocratic inbreeding.

But I wouldn't be saying any of this were it not for the fact that he was rude about my coffee. And not just once. After forcing me to make him a fresh cup he made yet another dig about how he even gets a better 'cuppa' (a word that didn't quite ring true coming out of his mouth) down the greasy café in his constituency, which he is forced to visit once a year. Now, it's one thing bossing me around and taking me for granted. After all, I didn't spend a whole year of pupillage learning nothing. But criticising my coffee-making skills is just a step too far. So the third time around I dropped a bunch of UpTights's herbal 'chill pills' as she likes to call them (they are basically St John's Wort) into a nice strong 'cuppa'. Special like. Jus' for 'im. That certainly shut him up for a while. Perhaps they should adopt the same approach in the House of Commons?

As for OldSmoothie, after bringing to bear on the issue all of his innumerable (ahem) years of experience in the field of libel law, his esteemed advice was to 'fight'. As far as he was concerned, if BigMouth, his 'best friend', was telling him that the allegations were entirely manufactured and false, then that was good enough for him. He wasn't going to go through the silly formalities of testing the strength of the evidence as he would do with a normal client. No, his friend's word – even if that friend *is* an MP – is his bond. OldSmoothie is simply taking the story at face value, which means therefore that we have a case, and unless the newspaper in question (I shall call it RedTop) backs down we may well end up in court.

Bad news for the client I would have thought. Good news for the lawyers all round.

But then, who am I to say? I can't even get the coffee right.

Wednesday 10 October 2007
Year 2 (week 2): Short skirts and long looks

TheVamp had, put it this way, made an effort with her attire for the conference with BigMouth yesterday and when, later in the afternoon, she rocked up at chambers tea, HeadofChambers couldn't help but comment, and in his most judicial tones at that, 'Is it just me or are skirts getting shorter these days?'

'Yes, and men's looks are getting longer,' replied TheVamp.

'Particularly in the case of a rather well-known circuit judge I could mention,' said BusyBody who is still in chambers and now looking very heavily pregnant. No one knows whether the father-to-be is OldSmoothie or FanciesHimself, the junior clerk. The fact that she has been allowed to remain in chambers for a third six months after her original pupillage has caused suspicions that OldSmoothie may bear more responsibility than he was letting on and is trying to avoid any scandal coming out. Then she added about the judge: 'I'm sure he's getting worse. I mean, whenever I appear in front of him I feel like his eyes are undressing me.'

'Must have very big eyes then,' said OldSmoothie, somewhat ungallantly.

Thursday 11 October 2007
Year 2 (week 2): Smutton

'Wake up and smell the cash, BabyB.'

SlipperySlope, who, it turns out, is acting as BigMouth's solicitor, was as full of himself as ever when I encountered him in chambers this morning. He introduced me to an extremely glamorous partner in his firm who I can only call Smutton, not just because she was dressed in a similar style to TheVamp, despite being probably twenty-five years her senior, but also because almost everything she does and says seems to be dripping with innuendo. Imagine perhaps a filthy version of Sarah Palin or maybe a panellist on some daytime TV show for women. Someone who looks like she had a few too many brandy and Babyshams in the seventies, cocaine in the eighties and young boys in the nineties. Yet someone who also carries herself with a self-assurance and humour that despite everything is well, I'm a little ashamed to admit, kind of sexy. But this was all just my first impression and as these thoughts passed through my head she stared at me in a way that made me want to hide in a corner.

'Ah, so this is the famous little BabyB,' she purred. 'I hear you're doing a little *pro bono* for us.' Need I mention that her eyes looked me up and down as she paused on the word *bono*.

'Er, actually, er, it's on a no win, no fee,' I stammered.

'Never mind, BabyB. I've always been *pro bono* myself.'

Friday 12 October 2007
Year 2 (week 2): Letter of claim

The Vamp and I drafted a letter of claim to the publishers of RedTop today. It essentially said, 'Dear RedTop, It was very naughty of you to have been so rude about our client. We know he's an obnoxious, arrogant so-and-so of the worst kind but really, honestly, he did not and we repeat, did not, hire a prostitute.'

'Do you think he did it?' I asked The Vamp.

'Well, the fact that he invited me over for dinner in the Commons on Tuesday and boasted about the luxury pied-à-terre he gets on expenses, means I certainly don't buy the happily married rubbish in his witness statement. But as to whether he went the whole hog, so to speak . . .'

She tailed off. That really is the million-dollar question. At some point we're going to have to be given the chance to grill BigMouth a little more thoroughly. It's certainly unfortunate that we haven't been allowed to do this before the letter of claim, but there you go. It's his loss for having chosen his best friend to represent him. To make matters worse, unlike most clients who would probably be satisfied with a retraction and a prominent apology, our politician friend and his inflated ego insisted that our letter stipulated not only an apology but also half a million pounds by way of damages. Right. If I were a juror, even if the story *was* untrue, I would find it hard to put a value on BigMouth's reputation at anything more than a few pence.

But then the man did insult my coffee.

So let me explain. It's not cool, I admit it, but I still live at home, with my mum. That's right: grown-up barrister; Oxford law degree and still living with my mum. Now things might have been different if chambers had paid me just a little bit more during pupillage. Different on two fronts in fact: I could perhaps have afforded my own flat, but I might also have been able to help with the financial mess my mother has got herself into. A mess caused by debts she'd run up whilst getting me through Oxford – problems she'd kept hidden from me until last year when they started to explode like landmines. At least they did until I cut a deal with her loan shark. We agreed that he would leave my mother out of it and once I was a fully fledged, gold-plated tenant, I would take over her debts. Well now I am a tenant, and today I rang the shark to arrange swapping the payment schedule to myself. It would be a mere formality I was sure.

'Well, Sir, we do need to go over a few details before we can finalise the arrangements.'

'Of course,' I said. 'Not a problem. Any time you like.'

'Oh, and we'll need your mother to attend as well. You do understand.'

'Of course I do.'

What can there possibly be to worry about? Only the tone in his voice and the fact that the man I struck the deal with last year has mysteriously disappeared. So now I anxiously await the meeting at the end of this month.

Got a postcard from TheBoss today. Well, it didn't actually say it was from him. In *Shawshank Redemption* style, it was a little overdramatic and forced on the *mysterioso* front, which shows that he's probably still unravelling after the shock of the hearing. But thankfully there was humour rather than menace in its tone. It was a picture of a long golden beach somewhere in the Caribbean and it read simply, 'Wish you were here . . . don't you?'

Unfortunately it has conjured up the deeply unattractive image of TheBoss and his mistress BattleAxe sunning themselves for all to see. When I mentioned it in chambers tea, OldSmoothie wasted no time. 'BattleAxe. Hmm, yes. I'd call her, er, agricultural.'

To which HeadofChambers added, as if repeating something people had said about her before, 'When she stands to address the court all around are sucked down.'

Wednesday 17 October 2007
Year 2 (week 3): Double dare

SlipperySlope faxed through RedTop's response today. It was along the lines of: 'Dear Slippery, Your client is a vain, arrogant and nasty man. You know that as much as we do. If you want a fight we look forward to exhibiting him in front of a jury.'

Unfortunately, they are of course right. Nor have they helped by leaving it ambiguous as to whether the allegations are true or even as to what evidence they may have. They are clearly calling our bluff. If BigMouth tries to seek pre-action disclosure to assess the strength of his case, they would report it front page along the lines of 'BigMouth, surely you don't need us to tell you whether it's true or not?' What's worst of all is that even if they fight and lose, their circulation will rise so dramatically during the trial that it'd more than pay for any damages.

So the question now is whether BigMouth will step up to the mark in this game of dare and double dare.

Thursday 18 October 2007
Year 2 (week 3): Sue or true

'Of course he'll sue,' said OldSmoothie as we sat in conference discussing RedTop's letter.

'But nobody believes what the papers say any longer,' said TheVamp. 'Why would he take the risk with all those costs, even if it's all fabricated?'

'Because Tory MPs are the very last of a breed who still cling to the nineteenth-century notion that unless they sue, the allegations are taken to be true.'

All of which is convenient for us. Like OldSmoothie, I'm now starting to look forward to a long, high-profile trial. Win or lose, it's got to be better than the rest of my practice, which currently consists of car cases in such glamorous locations as Ilford and Slough.

Monday 22 October 2007
Year 2 (week 4): Conspiracy theories

'It's all a conspiracy,' boomed BigMouth as he stomped into OldSmoothie's room for another conference.

'Hmm. Conspiracy theories are the last bastion of the desperate or insane, if you ask me,' I thought. Thankfully, perhaps, I wasn't being asked.

'I wouldn't put anything past RedTop,' said OldSmoothie sympathetically.

'What sort of conspiracy were you thinking?' asked TheVamp gently, which made me realise that she may well be the one who can ask the difficult questions in this case and still get away with it.

'A mobile phone mast, that's what. Mobile masts this. Mobile masts that. It's killing people, you know.'

Even OldSmoothie had to take a deep breath. His friend looked as though he might be beginning to crumble before our eyes and OldSmoothie decided to break the tension.

'Let's take this one step at a time. I'm assuming you don't mean that there's a killer mobile phone mast on the loose?'

'Of course not. But there's one near their houses. It's driving them mad.'

Some form of madness was becoming apparent to us all but no one said as much.

'Who are "they"?' asked TheVamp with a look a psychiatrist might give a patient.

'The old people, that's who. Constituents. Keep on clogging up my surgeries.'

'Er, in what way?' asked OldSmoothie.

'Brain damage, that's what. It's getting into their heads and killing all the brain cells. What's left of them anyway.'

'Er, right.' OldSmoothie was beginning to struggle.

Facing a room full of raised eyebrows, BigMouth ploughed on. 'You don't believe me, do you? Nobody does.'

You don't say.

'I've got a load of people being pumped full of mobile rays and, well, how can I put it? It's affecting them. Badly. All gone potty.'

I knew that we were all now picturing BigMouth's blue-rinsed constituents. Potty was something we could believe. OldSmoothie clearly thought that his friend had also been exposing himself to too many mobile rays (well it's better than prostitutes, I guess) and wanted to steer away from this particular red herring.

'I think this is something BabyB can investigate. What do you say?'

He turned to me. What was I to say? 'You must be joking. Stop wasting my time, you mad, pompous, out of touch old fool.' Well, that would have been one response but instead all I managed was, 'Er, okay then.'

Tuesday 23 October 2007
Year 2 (week 4): Just good friends?

Got a call from Claire yesterday asking if I was free to meet for a drink this evening. From her voice it sounded a little ominous but I agreed nonetheless. I've missed her these last two weeks and despite my worries about where things might be going with us I still wanted to catch up. Unfortunately, I was so involved in working on background stuff for BigMouth's case that by the time I left the library I realised I was going to be late and called ahead. Thankfully, at least, having just been awarded a tenancy herself, Claire understands the difficulties of juggling work at the Bar with a normal life and she told me not to worry.

When I finally arrived at the restaurant, she rose from her chair, revealing a black figure-hugging, knee-length dress that made her look absolutely stunning. Being used to seeing her in her court clothes, for a moment I just stood there, speechless. She smiled and offered me a glass from the bottle of wine she had already started. Then a little more wine, as we talked about our new tenancies and caught up with each other's news. Then dinner and yet more wine and soon enough we were walking along the Embankment and over Waterloo Bridge with its stunning views of St Paul's and the river. My doubts about whether we should try and change the nature of our relationship had dissolved, and if ever there was a time to make a move this was it. I took her hand and we stopped. There was an awkward pause in which both of us stared down at the river below us, and then Claire said, 'Look BabyB, I really don't want to risk our friendship.'

My heart sank. I knew where this was going. Then she looked in my eyes and said, 'I mean, do you?'

In that moment I couldn't tell whether she was saying she just wanted to hear it from me first, or whether she simply wanted affirmation of her own decision not to take things any further. But what I did know was that there were no half measures in this, any more than a jury can ever find someone half guilty. I could either go for it and risk everything, not knowing whether she wanted the same thing, or pull back to the safe haven of our friendship.

'I guess you're right,' I replied, knowing that I had made the coward's choice. Even in that moment the irony was not lost on me that whilst at work I never hesitated to take risks when it came to Claire it just felt, well, too important to gamble and get it wrong.

She looked at me quizzically and dropped her head a little.

'I guess so.' Her voice was quiet.

Which just goes to show that even professional communicators singularly fail when it comes to crossing that unbridgeable gap between the sexes.

Wednesday 24 October 2007
Year 2 (week 4): An apple short

Today, still troubled by the outcome of my evening with Claire, I was charged with calling up BigMouth and trying to get a bit more sense out of him than OldSmoothie had managed on Monday. In truth, I think he was just embarrassed for his old friend and he didn't want to explore the whole conspiracy story in too much detail.

'Please can you elaborate on the conspiracy you suspect?' I asked, trying not to sound circumspect.

'I know what you think, young man. Old duffer's gone off the deep end. An apple short and what not. But you'd be wrong in this case. There are big commercial interests at stake here. If phone masts do the damage my people suggest then other people stand to lose billions.'

'And who are those people?' I asked.

'Well that's what I'm hoping you might be able to find out. Telecom companies, I assume. All I know is that I asked one question about phone masts in parliament and within a week I was being exposed by RedTop.'

'Maybe that's simply because they had something to expose?' I refrained from asking. Instead I followed up with, 'Er, yes, I'll see what I can do. In the meantime, what exactly do your constituents say are the effects of this exposure to the, um, rays?'

'Well, there's a group of old age pensioners all within the same neighbourhood who have suddenly started causing all sorts of trouble. A grey crime wave they're calling it locally. Turned themselves into something of a gang. At least a dozen of them have been served ASBOs already and the figures are rising by the week. It's all very peculiar.'

Well, he's certainly not wrong there. I will await the documentation and maybe I'll even get to meet this unusual bunch of oldies who have suddenly started razzing it up. It would be worth organising a conference with them in chambers just to see the reaction of a few of the more staid of the tenants.

Thursday 25 October 2007
Year 2 (week 4): Snakes and ladders

The new pupils were all standing neatly in a row at chambers tea today. OldSmoothie was the first to comment.

'Look at you. All unformed. Still finding your place in the world. One minute you'll be buzzing around feeling like a drone and the next you'll be absolutely full of your own cleverness as you get to help on some big case or other.'

'Oh but don't they look so cute,' whispered TheVamp eyeing up the two male pupils. 'All fresh-faced, clean-cut and so deliciously corruptible.'

Then, I think without realising, she actually licked her lips.

'Must be about time for the annual snakes and ladders speech,' said TheBusker, referring to the talk the pupils always get about their status now being at the very bottom of the pile just like that of new judges.

'That's all it is really, isn't it?' said UpTights, looking a little madder than usual. 'This whole thing. Life. Just one big cruel game of snakes and ladders.'

'There's certainly no shortage of snakes,' said BusyBody looking at OldSmoothie.

'Yes, and the only ladders you've ever got close to are in your tights,' he replied.

'Well, little pupil boy,' purred TheVamp into the ear of the nearest of the two she'd been admiring. 'How would you like a game of snakes and ladders?'

With which he blushed, quickly made his excuses and left.

Friday 26 October 2007
Year 2 (week 4): Humiliation

On my arrival this morning all I got from HeadClerk was a very curt nod, which was completely out of character for a person who is usually so positive and upbeat. 'What's up with HeadClerk?' I asked TheBusker as I passed him in the corridor later.

'It's not good at all,' he replied. 'As bad as it gets actually.'

'What can be that bad?' I asked innocently.

'One of OldSmoothie's solicitors rang up and demanded that HeadClerk double his fee. Said that at its current level it was making their own fees look embarrassingly high to the client.'

'That sounds great,' I replied. 'How can he be annoyed about an increase in our fees?'

'That's just it. HeadClerk prides himself on billing top dollar for all his barristers. To then have a solicitor ring up and say that what he's billed simply isn't enough . . . well, it hurts . . .'

Oh.

'They're all as mad as cheese, BabyB.' SlipperySlope had called me to talk about BigMouth's ASBO-attracting blue rinses. 'They're far more eccentric than your usual Saga louts with their recycling bins stuffed full of bottles of fine Rioja. No, these ones are quite simply mad, mad, mad and very old. But even if there's a small chance that there's something in this, we could be on to a windfall settlement just to keep the whole thing out of the press.'

'And how do you think I can help?' I asked him, somewhat confused as to what role I might play in all this.

'You're going to be doing the running, BabyB. All the important work.'

Chief dogsbody more like. But I'm not exactly in a position to argue.

'I'll provide the back-up and funding. BigMouth has asked for a two-hundred-pound backhander for every case he refers involving a mad oldie or Moldy as I like to call them. My shout on that. All tax deductible through my er, marketing budget although somehow I doubt it'll ever appear in his declaration of members' interests. You, meanwhile, my sharp-witted friend, will get to work growing our little money-making tree.' This was all delivered in a voice that reminded me of Del Boy in *Only Fools and Horses*, putting his arm around his brother's shoulder and assuring him that this time next year they would be millionaires. Oh, except Slippery already is a millionaire, several times over probably.

After that little introduction, he sent over the paperwork, which consisted of long ranting letters from each of TheMoldies but little else. No medical evidence, no real details of the legal case they are trying to make. Which means of course that we need to get them all into chambers for a nice cosy little conference in the next few days. I've deliberately booked it to coincide with chambers tea . . .

I can't pretend that I haven't been worrying about today's meeting with my mother's loan shark. The deal I'd made last year was that they wouldn't call in her debts and leave her homeless and destitute on the condition that I would agree to take over her loan next year. It all seemed so simple at the time and it is only as the months have gone by that I have started to regret not having the agreement in writing. But then, why on earth wouldn't they allow the debt to be passed to her oh-so-solvent barrister son?

Why on earth indeed? And this is the question I am now left asking as my mother and I try and recover from the bombshell that was delivered today in the form of the loan shark's new spiv. He told us that he had it from 'on high' that the loan could under no circumstances be refinanced on their books.

'It's the credit crunch I'm afraid. No exceptions. So, Mr BabyBarista, whatever you say was agreed last year, either you pay up the whole amount now or we start enforcement proceedings.'

Now there's no way, even with my new place in chambers, that I can raise anything close to the four hundred grand that is the terrifying total of all my mother's debt.

All of this was bad enough but my worries were then multiplied when I rushed back from the meeting for a drink with Claire. I had had to stop at chambers on the way, to catch up with the BigMouth case and once again I arrived late. After apologising profusely I'd explained about everything that had happened with the loan shark and she listened with an increasingly furrowed brow,

'I hate to say it, BabyB,' she said, 'but there may be more to this than just the state of the economy.'

'What do you mean?' I asked.

'Look, I'm definitely no conspiracy theorist, but if there is any truth at all in what your MP is saying about the telecom company you're thinking of suing, well they're a pretty powerful enemy to be taking on.'

'Oh.'

Then she added enigmatically, 'And I really don't know what went on between you and TopFirst, but it's pretty clear to me that he's trouble and also that he's the sort of person who would have no boundaries when it comes to wanting to hurt someone.'

'But he couldn't possibly have anything to do with this loan company.'

'Maybe you're right. But we both know that half his friends all work in finance.'

Oh.

'Listen,' she added. 'I don't know anything and I'm sure I'm just being extra paranoid because I care about you.' She paused and then added, 'But even so, what is it they say? Just because you're paranoid doesn't mean that they're not after you.'

'Do you really think so?'

'Who can tell?' With which she smiled and changed the conversation.

It left me desperately wanting to tell her about everything that happened last year. About TheBoss and his corruption, but above all about the compromises I had made myself. But on second thoughts, I'm in too deep to even start offloading now. So much for my mother's prediction that I'd never need to worry again.

CHAPTER 2

NOVEMBER: WAR

Thursday 1 November 2007
Year 2 (week 5): Flying

I was on the train to court today, haggling over the details of a claim with my opponent, TheCreep, who had plonked himself down at my table. Haggling is putting it politely. Getting harangued by him would be more accurate. Bearing in mind I've always admired the fact that arguing with TheBusker is like trying to nail jelly to a wall, I decided to go with one of his tactics by simply changing the subject.

'Yes, very interesting,' I said. 'Er, have you read any good books lately?'

But this just provoked the retort: 'Leave the Buskering to TheBusker, BabyB.'

Ouch. Once more he was back to badgering over interest calculations as if he really believed that I cared about them. Then, just as the train sped over a tall bridge, a child in the carriage who was staring out of the window shouted, 'Mummy, we're flying.'

Conversations actually stopped. Even TheCreep hesitated and for that moment, as we were all carried away from our present cares and lifted back to an innocent past where lawyers didn't exist and dreams were real, the whole carriage really was flying.

It was a fleeting moment of hope before it all started up once again.

Monday 5 November 2007
Year 2 (week 6): Declaration of war

After a weekend of unsuccessfully trying to untangle finances with my mother, the very last person I wanted to bump into this morning at court was TopFirst. Thankfully, at least, we weren't against each other and so I tried to ignore him. However, it became ever more clear that he was trying to get my attention and eventually he came over and collared me as I left the client to give my solicitor a call. He said just four words, 'How's your mother, BabyB?'

By the time I began to make sense of what he had said, he was gone. Claire had been right. TopFirst was behind the loan shark's change of tack. As my mind started to clear, an anger rose in me like I've never felt before. War had been declared and this time there would be no rules.

Tuesday 6 November 2007
Year 2 (week 6): Facebook friend

Why and how are the two questions that continue to reverberate around my head. Why would TopFirst go nuclear when I still hold the Ginny tapes that I could release any time I like? I can only assume that he's figuring on my not wanting to risk incriminating myself in setting up a honeytrap just to ruin his engagement. In this he would be right, if that was the only thing I stood to gain. As to *how*, that's something I obviously need to investigate. But above all, if TopFirst has decided to show his hand to me at this point then I also have to ask what kind of trap he's trying to set now and how I might stay one step ahead?

So for the moment there'll be no brown envelope winging its way over to TopFirst's fiancée and he can keep on guessing just how far I'm prepared to go. In the meantime I need to start gathering information and there is no better place than the lovely fiancée herself. Which is why I added her to my list of friends on Facebook today. Since we did actually meet a few times last year, I also added a note:

Hi, hope all's well with you and TopFirst and that you're still enjoying life in your new career as a management consultant. Got to be more interesting than the cases they're feeding me. Anyway, just a note to say that if you're ever in the area and at a loose end, do pop in for coffee.

Wednesday 7 November 2007
Year 2 (week 6): Rehabilitation of offenders

TheVamp was complaining today about how pointless it had been for the judge to have sent her negligent doctor client to prison.

'I mean, it's not like he's about to re-offend,' she said.

'And it probably costs more to keep a prisoner for a year than it does to train a pupil barrister,' said TheCreep.

'Yes, and all they learn is how to lie, thieve and generally live off the backs of honest, upstanding members of society,' said OldSmoothie.

'As well as the little tricks which will keep them out of trouble on some ridiculous technicality or other,' said UpTights.

'And that's before you add the shady network of contacts they get to tap into,' said OldSmoothie.

'You're so right,' said TheCreep. 'I mean, how on earth can they be expected to come out as normal, well-balanced individuals with that kind of legacy?'

'Can't be much better for those in prison,' said TheBusker with a wry smile.

Thursday 8 November 2007
Year 2 (week 6): Skeleton argument

I had told TheBusker about my frustrating time with TheCreep the other day and he suggested that I follow him to court tomorrow when his opponent will be none other than the little upstart himself. My occasional trips with TheBusker not only provide a great distraction from my other worries but they also teach me more about courtroom tactics than anything I ever learnt from my pupilmasters. Then again, TheBoss and UpTights were something of a rum bunch. The case tomorrow is an appeal and skeleton arguments have been ordered to be written. TheCreep's is hardly either a skeleton or an argument, extending as it does to some fifty-three and a half pages. The Busker only highlighted the absurdity of such a creation for a relatively small personal injury case with the following skeleton in reply: 'The appeal is misconceived since it has failed to refer to the binding authority of Davies v. Howard.'

I look forward to the fight.

Friday 9 November 2007
Year 2 (week 6): Chuckled out of court

TheBusker had already wound up TheCreep with his skeleton argument and by the time we arrived at court TheCreep was almost jumping up and down with frustration as he tried desperately to find out what TheBusker was going to say. Unfortunately for him the only response he could elicit was a low-pitched chuckle. Once in court, the chuckle continued. Not in a snide way but merely in response to the constant jibes being thrown forth by his opponent.

By way of example, TheCreep said, 'Your Honour, my learned friend has singularly failed to set out any coherent argument against each of my points and has even failed to do so when I have asked him this morning . . .'

And then when everybody looked at TheBusker for a response his shoulders started rising and falling and he just carried on chuckling to himself like he was privy to some hilarious private joke.

In the end, TheCreep cracked and started to look more and more paranoid about TheBusker's show of confidence. Then TheBusker made the killer blow by handing him a note saying, 'This Judge appeared in the case I referred to in my skeleton.'

When TheCreep read the note his face dropped and he immediately asked for a short adjournment. Once out of court he said to TheBusker, 'Why on earth didn't you tell me that beforehand?'

'It's in the report for all to see,' replied TheBusker, still chuckling.

Sure enough when TheCreep studied TheBusker's copy he found that the judge had indeed appeared and in fact successfully argued against exactly the legal point that TheCreep was now trying to make. To put him out of his misery, TheBusker made an offer that if TheCreep withdrew his appeal he wouldn't seek his costs thus far. By this point, TheCreep was in a blind panic fearing that he had in fact been negligent in not spotting the significance of the judge's identity for himself and accepted almost on the spot, before TheBusker reminded him that perhaps it might be wise to take instructions first.

It was only on the train home and after TheCreep had stropped off in a sulk after agreeing to the settlement that TheBusker gave me the full low-down.

'You know, things are rarely as they seem. I heard this judge speak at a dinner only a few weeks ago when he described that case as [and he put on a slightly pompous judicial tone] "the worst injustice I've ever caused in a long career dedicated to causing such injustices". And he went so far as to say that "If such a case ever comes before me on the bench, it's one of the very few of my wrongs I intend to right."'

All this has led me to wonder if I can apply the ChuckleBluff to a few of my own upcoming cases.

Monday 12 November 2007
Year 2 (week 7): TheMoldies

TheMadOldies or TheMoldies, as SlipperySlope has taken to calling them, arrived in chambers today. I'm not sure what the collective noun would be in this case: a cackle? Or maybe a hobble? Whatever it is, they certainly lived up to all expectations. Despite their average age being well above that of the Rolling Stones, they were certainly rock 'n' roll, baby. There were seven of them in all and apparently there are more in the background. It doesn't really bear thinking about. All of them have been served anti-social behaviour orders aimed at stopping them from causing various kinds of idiosyncratic offences. An eighty-five-year-old man called Arthur, for example, says that he can't stop doing moonies every time he sees a police car go by. Then his seventy-nine-year-old wife Ethel says she gets into moods where she feels compelled to chuck buckets of water on teenagers going past her house. Another is an eighty-one-year-old man called Stanley (a nickname he says is due to the fact that his surname is Matthews), who has recently taken to dribbling a football wherever he goes. This not only includes the local shops but it even extended as far as chambers today. Mind you, I have to admit that I enjoyed it when he dribbled into UpTights's room and kicked the ball on to her desk shouting, 'He shoots, he scores!'

Now whilst this may seem unusual behaviour, you may well ask whether these people are simply starting to suffer the terrible effects of such ageing diseases as dementia. This is no doubt the case that the other side will try to make, but the clients today were having none of it. We were told that there are dozens of them who have all been affected in similar ways within the space of six months and they all blame this on the local mobile phone mast that has recently been installed on top of a nearby little hill. They reckon that the telecom company in question has boosted its signal beyond the norm.

Well, despite it certainly proving to be a colourful conference, there is very little I can do at this stage. If we are going to get anywhere with this case we will need some evidence, a vital part of the whole process, which at the moment is lacking in almost every regard with the exception of TheMoldies' symptoms.

Either way the case isn't going away any time soon and it should provide a bit of extra interest to my practice.

Tuesday 13 November 2007
Year 2 (week 7): Soul destroying

Been thinking a lot about TheMoldies. They remind me of a poem by Roger McGough called 'Let Me Die a Youngman's Death', in which he says, 'when I'm 91 with silver hair and sitting in a barber's chair may rival gangsters with hamfisted tommyguns burst in and give me a short back and insides.'

It's incredibly sad that they are being affected by something and yet it was clear from the conference that their symptoms are something of a double-edged sword. As one of them said, 'Us oldies have never spoken out before. But there are lots of us now young man and sooner or later we're going to take back the power.'

There was a kind of breathless excitement to the whole thing. It was like they were on to something really quite big and that despite the injuries of which they were complaining, they also seemed to be treating it as the start of some great adventure. Perhaps it was the sort of adventure they wished they'd embarked upon years before. It just got me thinking. Because when I look around chambers there are so many people who have had all sense of adventure sucked out of them. It's as if the law has turned their lives to black and white. Erased the poetry.

Wednesday 14 November 2007
Year 2 (week 7): Memento mori

I talked through my thoughts on TheMoldies with OldRuin today.

'*Memento mori*, BabyB.'

I looked at him a little lost and his kindly smile appeared, as if he was actually pleased that my ignorance gave him the opportunity to pass something on.

'Reminders of our own mortality. It's what we're all running from. Sometimes so fast that we forget we are even alive.'

He paused and looked pensive. 'It's what they're doing, BabyB. Reminding us to live.'

Thursday 15 November 2007
Year 2 (week 7): A chilly 'un

OldSmoothie walked into chambers tea today on a post-court high with his 'I love myself' look even more prominent than usual. In order to collect his tea he had to pass in-between UpTights and TheVamp who were deep in conversation. As he approached, UpTights said to TheVamp, 'Do you have a Brazilian?'

To which TheVamp replied, 'A Chilean.'

'Well, I should think it would be a chilly 'un if you've got a Brazilian,' said OldSmoothie, looking very pleased with himself.

'Sorry?' said UpTights. 'What on earth are you talking about?'

Doubt suddenly flashed across OldSmoothie's face and he stumbled back with, 'Oh, er, er, what were you talking about?'

'Our cleaners, you stupid old fool.'

Oh.

Friday 16 November 2007
Year 2 (week 7): The joys of being self-employed

I haven't seen BusyBody for a few weeks but today she was spotted in chambers by TheVamp. I asked if her due date was fast approaching.

TheVamp replied with, 'Well, let's put it like this. She's on a donkey and heading to Nazareth.' Then she added, 'By the way, have you heard that HeadofChambers has now indicated that he expects her to be given a tenancy once her maternity leave and third six come to an end?'

'I hadn't heard that,' I said, reflecting on my own journey to tenancy. 'Funny how it works out.'

Later that day, I spotted BusyBody on the other side of the room as I entered chambers tea and heard UpTights muse, 'If we were lawyers, in most parts of the world we'd be working for some terrible firm of solicitors.'

'Can't think of anything worse,' said OldSmoothie.

'But you already are,' said TheBusker, breaking it to them gently.

'Oh, hmm, well, maybe so technically,' said UpTights. 'But we don't actually "work" work. We're self-employed and so we, er, deign to give them a little of our valuable time.'

'In return for cash,' said TheBusker, again looking sympathetic.

'But that's not the same as working,' said OldSmoothie. 'You know, like being employed.'

'You're right there,' said TheVamp. 'I love waiting two or three years for payment. I mean who'd want a regular pay cheque when bank loans will fill the hole?'

'And I just can't get over how good that cold, empty frightened feeling is in your stomach when your diary becomes clear, your paperwork dries up and you still have a mortgage to pay. It's the kind of thing that makes me just skip to work,' said BusyBody.

'Then there's the sick pay, company cars and pensions that we definitely wouldn't want to receive,' said TheBusker.

'Not to mention paternity pay,' BusyBody added, looking point-edly at OldSmoothie who is still the bookies' (i.e. the clerks') favourite to be revealed as the father of her child.

'My old head of chambers always used to say that if we were to succeed at the Bar we should get used to waking up unemployed every morning,' said OldRuin.

The room was silent as everyone contemplated the joys of being self-employed.

Monday 19 November 2007
Year 2 (week 8): Geriatrigation

In the last few days I've decided that I'm going to help TheMoldies whether they have a case or not. Don't start getting any ideas that this means I'm going all soft or anything. It's just that, win or lose, the David and Goliath-type story can only bring me the sort of career-enhancing publicity that most barristers never come near even once in their careers. Particularly if I can help them run the campaign. They haven't taken the fight anywhere yet but I'm figur-ing that with the whiff of adventure they'll be out on the streets if necessary.

So here's to geriatric litigation. Maybe I'll call it geriatrigation. Not quite Californication, but who knows, it might even be fun.

Tuesday 20 November 2007
Year 2 (week 8): Terms of enragement

One of my favourite instructing solicitors is ClichéClanger, a northerner whose no-nonsense approach belies a very wry sense of humour and a subtle twinkle in the eye. He also does wonders with the English language. Today I received a good example where I am still left not knowing whether he'd made a slip or a joke. They were instructions for a case involving a client who has been caus-ing him no end of grief. They began, 'Your instructing Solicitor is enraged to represent the claimant in this matter . . .' They contin-ued with, 'The claimant has been lying in London for the last ten years.'

When I mentioned it to Claire over a rushed lunch she chuckled and asked, 'Is that what they call a malapropism?'

Then before I could own up to ignorance on that subject she continued, 'Don't you just love the sound of that word? Just like mellifluous, flibbertigibbet, slubberdegullion . . .'

I certainly did when they came out of Claire's mouth, and once again I was struck by a pang of regret at not having taken the risk last month.

Then Claire added, 'BabyB, I think you've just inspired my next set of submissions in court.'

Wednesday 21 November 2007
Year 2 (week 8): Credit crunch

Still no progress on my mother's debts. So far I've been to seventeen financial advisers with a glowing letter from HeadClerk setting out the millions I can expect to earn in the future. Yet each of them has eventually had to turn me away, claiming that the credit crunch makes things just too risky. With the threat of repossession hanging over my mother's head and no contingency plans yet in place, things are all starting to feel somewhat precarious.

But in the meantime, a worldwide recession hasn't stopped the banter at chambers tea, which inappropriately enough today seemed to focus on exactly that.

'You know UpTights,' said OldSmoothie, 'every time I hear mention of toxic debts, depression and sub-prime, for some bizarre reason it makes me think of you.'

But ever since BusyBody stepped up to the mark on her behalf, UpTights has occasionally been doing the same and today she replied with, 'Well, from what I hear on the grapevine it's not just the economy that's suffering deflationary pressures, OldSmoothie.'

Then TheVamp joined in the fun. 'Yes, what with that and a shrinking endowment, you're hardly best placed to be keeping anyone's interest rates particularly high, wouldn't you say? No more FTSE or asset stripping for you. More like dead cat bounce.'

Then UpTights came in for the killer blow, 'Maybe an expansionary stimulus package might be of assistance.'

I was working late once again last night when I got a call from my mother.

'I was just wondering where you were. I've cooked a shepherd's pie and wondered if you wanted it keeping warm in the oven.'

I explained to her that I was as busy as I'd ever been and that I'd probably just end up eating a takeaway in chambers.

'Well do you have time for a little chat?' she asked.

Again I answered that I was only just keeping my head above water but I assured her that I was hoping to work something out with the finances. Unfortunately this seemed to upset her and she said, 'It's not about finances, BabyB. It's you, my son, I want to talk to. I'm just worried for you with all these long hours you've been putting in.'

I assured her that it was just something that came with the territory of being a junior tenant unfortunately and that I was sure it would calm down sometime soon. I'm not sure she was terribly reassured by this but she seemed to cheer up a little at least and ended with, 'Well please don't forget your health, BabyB. It's the most important thing you have.'

Anyway, today we received the first tranche of evidence from RedTop's lawyers which, they claim, proves that BigMouth hired a certain lady of the night, who I shall call RoundTheBlock. There were also a couple of witness statements along with mention of a birthmark in a place where the sun most certainly does not shine. The only photo they have is a grainy CCTV image of a man in a suit standing next to RoundTheBlock and leaning forward slightly, as if he is offering something in his outstretched hand – possibly cash. To be fair, it could easily be a picture of any number of backbench Tory MPs though it does at least bear a passing resemblance to BigMouth, albeit from a distance.

OldSmoothie remains in denial and refuses to grill his friend about it. I've therefore figured that the only way forward is to look at discrediting RoundTheBlock. This will necessitate a disguise and then a chat. My plan is to pass myself off as a representative of RedTop itself. So today I acquired a couple of ID cards online.

One visit to the printers later and I was the proud possessor of one National Union of Journalists identity card and a few copies of a personalised RedTop business card.

Friday 23 November 2007
Year 2 (week 8): Chinese walls and palm tree justice

UpTights was talking about her case at chambers tea today which involved a student appealing a decision by his college to expel him. 'It was a complete kangaroo court,' she said.

'I've always loved the image that conjures up,' said TheVamp. 'You know, a huge kangaroo of a judge and all the little joeys coming up before him and with none of them able to sit still for a second. All bouncing up and down on the spot trying to make their submissions.'

'It'd make it quite hard to keep their wigs on,' said TheBusker.

'It's Chinese walls which make me chuckle,' said UpTights. 'I just imagine a huge wall of takeaway boxes separating two halves of an office.'

'Palm tree justice has always done it for me,' said TheBusker. 'Makes my mind wander to hotter climes than this.'

'I always liked the idea of lawyers going on fishing expeditions,' said OldRuin. 'Always brightened up even the most dreary day in court.'

'As for skeleton arguments,' said OldSmoothie. 'They make me think of two skeletons stepping out of a closet, squaring up to each other and then one of them saying "I've got a bone to pick with you".'

Monday 26 November 2007
Year 2 (week 9): The sting

Went in search of RoundTheBlock on Saturday evening and I was delighted to find that RedTop's description of her working area was accurate. Right down to the exact street corner in fact. I found her in precisely the same place they'd described BigMouth picking her up. It seems her celebrity status hasn't gone to her head at least. Though I imagine bagging a backbench Tory MP is hardly in the same league as bringing home a story about a footballer or rock star.

She was very suspicious when I approached her and introduced myself as a representative of RedTop, all in my newly honed Scottish drawl. But then I whipped out my, er, ID and she was all ears. It's ridiculous really, given how easy it had been to fake. After that she visibly relaxed and agreed to go for a coffee in a kebab shop round the corner. Now, I admit this was a pretty big risk as all she needed to do was to call whoever she had previously dealt with and I would have been a goner. However, although she might be wise to the ways of the street, newspapers are a whole new game for her and in that I had the upper hand. The other thing I had going for me was that for RedTop this case was small beer compared to most of their stories and so I'd figured that they wouldn't have invested a great deal of time or effort protecting her from this type of situation.

I told her that RedTop wanted to run another story about her and BigMouth but that this time we needed her to embellish it a little. Perhaps mention another Tory MP who had also hired her in the past? As you might imagine, she was not happy with this at all. Until, that is, I mentioned the figure of £200,000. Then she became a little more interested. Well, she supposed she might be able to help 'just this once like'.

Just this once indeed. I had hit gold at my first strike and was out of there in a flash, video camera still rolling in the pocket of my jacket.

Tuesday 27 November 2007
Year 2 (week 9): Counting the inches

TheCreep was explaining tripping accidents caused by holes in the pavement to a couple of the pupils today.

'It all boils down to whether it's half an inch or an inch,' he said in his usual patronising little squeak.

Unfortunately for him TheVamp happened to be passing at just the wrong time. She smiled sweetly, patted him on the head and said, 'Of course it does MrCrinchyPinchy. You've got to make the most of what you've got and in your case I guess an extra half inch might make all the difference.'

Wednesday 28 November 2007
Year 2 (week 9): Leverage

Just because I was prepared to take the calculated risk in talking to
RoundTheBlock, don't think I was going to tell OldSmoothie about
it. Instead, I edited the footage and, still in my disguise, posted it up
on YouTube from an internet café in King's Cross, before sending
an anonymous email to myself with the link. I then forwarded it to
OldSmoothie explaining that a 'friend of mine' who knew I was on
this case had done some digging and come up with it.

Well, OldSmoothie, as you might imagine, was more than a little
pleased. He'd been obviously starting to worry about the case in
the last couple of days, as denial began to turn into a realisation
that he might have taken on a complete loser of a case in return for
no fee and egg on his face.

'This is great, BabyB. I don't know who your friend is and I'm
not sure I want to know. Anyway, I've spoken to BigMouth and
told him that whatever is the truth of the matter, we need to settle
if at all possible and that this might just provide us with enough
leverage. He wasn't happy but he said that he trusted my judgment.'

So, SlipperySlope will negotiate.

Friday 30 November 2007
Year 2 (week 9): See you there

Heard from TopFirst's fiancée today. She accepted my request for
friendship on Facebook and sent the following message:

Hi BabyB. Really lovely to hear from you. I don't know what
went on between you and TopFirst but I'm glad that you and
I can remain friends, at least. As it happens, I'm actually down
your neck of the woods next Thursday. If you're not in court do
you fancy lunch?

To which I of course replied simply:

Look forward to it. See you there x

CHAPTER 3
DECEMBER: SCANDALMONGER

Monday 3 December 2007
Year 2 (week 10): ScandalMonger

BigMouth's case rumbles on. Slippery wrote immediately to the other side giving them the evidence I had discreetly gathered on RoundTheBlock. This morning they replied, telling him where in particular he could stick his offer. No real surprise there given the bullish stance RedTop have been taking all along. But then Slippery asked to see me in his office this afternoon.

As we sat down he said, 'I need to have a serious talk, BabyB.'

'Of course,' I replied, a little nervously, wondering what on earth I had done wrong.

'You and I haven't worked together much in the past but it seems our paths are woven together at least for the foreseeable future, what with BigMouth's case and then TheMoldies.'

'Yes, I can't pretend the thought hadn't been worrying me, given what a lowlife, scum sucking, slime bucket we all know that you are.' Thankfully those thoughts didn't come out and I managed a diplomatic 'I guess so'.

'Well, I think now's probably a good time to explain a few home truths about how we work.'

Oh, here we go, I thought. You should be lucky for the work and all that. I'm in charge and you'd better not forget it. But instead he continued with, 'Actually, there's just one particular issue at this stage and it concerns bringing in a little outside, er, help for both of our cases.'

'Like an expert witness?' I asked innocently.

'Exactly, BabyB. Just like an expert witness.' He paused. 'Though he's not a witness.'

'And don't tell me – he's not an expert either?' I smiled.

'Well, not in the traditional sense, at least.'

'OK,' I said hesitatingly, 'you'd better tell me a little more.'

'Better still,' he said, 'I'd like to introduce you.' He then picked up the phone and asked his secretary to bring his other guest in.

I was slightly taken aback at having someone else foisted into the mix but I tried not to show it. We both stood up as an odd-looking tall man in a brown suit with a mop of wavy brown hair and thick NHS glasses walked in. But above all, what hit me most was his disproportionately large hands, which seemed to be fizzing with energy down to the tips of his fingers.

Slippery introduced him as a man I shall call ScandalMonger and as he went to shake my hand all I could think of were those huge hands that football fans hold aloft at matches. I gathered that he is one of those types whose day job is to buy and sell stories. Not any old stories, just those involving human misery in one form or another. If the misery isn't in the story itself then it follows pretty soon afterwards. He is the kind of man who believes he can bring down anything from political parties, to star strikers, to the best that middle England has to offer: a larger than life impresario who's so much of a fraud that he even believes his own lies. All in all, he is a horrible creature who would make even TopFirst seem like a modest sort of fellow. Well, that's what I took from Slippery's flattering thumbnail sketch anyway.

'So how will all this help our cases?' I asked.

'Well, BabyB, that's not all he does. What with all these clients, investigators and press contacts he also acts as a rather discreet . . . how shall I put it? Er, fixer. Or as we put it to the taxman, "corporate PR".'

'Oh.'

ScandalMonger raised his eyebrows in a particularly smug way, as if to say, 'Yes, I am the master of the universe and am able to fix anything. Little people, little problems. Easy.'

'Yes,' continued Slippery, 'we can get a little help with the planting of stories and from time to time he can even assist with the odd witness.'

'Oh.'

'So you can see why I might need to mention it?'

'Indeed.'

'It's just that I don't want to get further down the line and then for, how shall I say, "scruples" to kick in.'

'Well, quite.'

'So I just wanted to make sure that you were all OK with his involvement from the outset?'

Now the truth is that of course I wasn't 'OK' with it. Not in a million years. Witness tampering for a start. Then there was contempt of court with the press. And these were just my initial thoughts. My guess was that Slippery wasn't telling me even half of it and he was simply asking whether I was prepared to turn a blind eye. After my experience last year with TheBoss, my answer was simple. Sorry Slippery old boy, but go and slip and slide on someone else's patch. I'm just not interested. Except that after I'd explained this in about ten different ways, he eventually said, 'I'm disappointed, BabyB. Really I am. Believe it or not, you actually came on the highest recommendation from TheBoss himself. You might be surprised to hear that despite, or perhaps because of, what you did to him, he left with a very high regard for your abilities.'

'Well that's very generous of him and all but I'm afraid the answer's still no.'

'In which case, BabyB, let me sweeten the pill a little. What if I were to offer to pay off your loan shark and to refinance your mother's loan for the next twelve months in return for your, er, cooperation?'

My mouth must have dropped open since he added, 'Don't be surprised, BabyB. That's the whole point. It's our job,' at which he looked across at ScandalMonger, cueing more smug face-pulling from him, 'to know things. All things. Like the fact that a certain learned friend of yours called TopFirst is out to get you.'

They both looked at me as if they knew rather more than they were letting on.

Now I must decide.

Last night I heard a noise downstairs and when I went to investigate I found my mother sorting through her jewellery which she had strewn across the living-room floor. As I entered the room she looked up and I could see that her make-up from the day before was smudged from crying. She knelt there, with a couple of earrings in her hand, and stared at me with a look of quiet desperation on her face. Then she said, 'I just thought that perhaps these might be worth something.' Her voice tailed off.

I knelt down and hugged her and she started crying again.

'I'm so sorry, BabyB. I really don't know how I let it all get this out of hand.'

Her whole body began to shake as she sobbed. I've seen her in a bad way over the years but never quite like this and all I felt able to do was to hold her in my arms. Then I took her by the shoulders and looked her in the eyes.

'I promise you,' I said, 'that it's going to be OK. You've put everything you have on the line to get me to where I am now and I'm not going to let you down. All I ask is that you trust me.'

This seemed to calm her down and through her tears she said, 'It's not your responsibility, BabyB, but I do appreciate what you say. Thank you.'

She took a deep breath. 'You know, BabyB, you've grown up so much in the last year. If you're even a fraction as reassuring to your clients as you are to me then you're going to be an incredible barrister.'

After I'd made her a cup of tea and she'd finally gone to bed, I tried to get a little sleep myself although I slept for only a few minutes before I was woken again by the worry of what was ahead. Slippery has me in a corner and I have little choice but to make the deal. I mean, he's not asking me to actively participate in any shenanigans. Not that that would make any difference if it were to come before the Bar Standards Board. You see, that's where he's been clever. If he didn't say anything then there was always a risk I'd start making my own discoveries and in some way upset the apple cart. But by disclosing it now, he has compromised me by the very fact that from here on in I won't be able to plead ignorance. And behind all this I can't help wondering whether the whole thing might be some protracted scheme of revenge by TheBoss.

But on the other hand, I'm not going to be churlish. He's also offering to solve what is currently the biggest problem in my life: keeping the loan sharks away from my mother and for that I am grateful. So this morning I made the call and told him he had a deal.

'A wise choice, BabyB. Which means I can now speak to ScandalMonger and we can come up with a plan.'

'Quite.'

'Oh, by the way, did I mention that he's already representing RoundTheBlock in her negotiations with the press?'

'Er, no.' The penny dropped.

'Oh. Must have slipped my mind. Should come in handy, though, wouldn't you say?'

I had no answer to make and then Slippery added, 'BabyB, this could be the start of a bountiful friendship.' Which as he said it made me suddenly realise exactly where one of his employees, a certain ClichéClanger, gets both his clichés and the habit of mangling them from.

Once the deal was done I took the rest of the day off and collected my mother from work, let her go home and get changed and then took her out for a very expensive meal in Soho where I explained that I'd basically found someone who would take on the debt.

'BabyB, that's the best news you could ever have given me. I've been so very worried that by next month we'd both be out on the street.'

I told her that that would never have happened but now there was absolutely no reason to worry. I obviously failed to mention the fact of yet another compromise I've had to make.

Wednesday 5 December 2007
Year 2 (week 10): Man with a plan

'OK. So here's the plan.'

Slippery was on the phone again. 'ScandalMonger fixes RoundTheBlock to become our witness. She decides to tell a new story about how someone from RedTop came to her and offered her cash in return for making a story up about BigMouth. He sells another front-page scoop and we win the case. He then packs her off to Brazil for a couple of years and RedTop will never get round to suing her for lying to them in the first place.'

Thursday 6 December 2007
Year 2 (week 10): TopFlirt

With worries about TopFirst at the forefront of my mind, it was fitting that today was the day for my lunch with his fiancée. I figured that if she mentions it to TopFirst then at the very least it'll raise the idea of my releasing the Ginny tape to her as well as causing him a certain amount of worry as to what I might be up to. If she doesn't mention it to him then I still have the possibility of stumbling upon some useful information.

Anyway, despite the contrived nature of our meeting, I have to say that I thoroughly enjoyed the lunch, not least because, to my complete surprise, at one point I was fairly certain that she was beginning to flirt with me. Enough at least for me to give her the name TopFlirt. This not only came as a complete surprise but it has put me into all sorts of quandaries. First off, she's extremely beautiful and bright and who wouldn't be flattered by her attentions? Then there's the fact that if anything were to happen it would be the ultimate way of getting one over on TopFirst, so to speak. On the other hand, she is my enemy's fiancée and it's at least possible she's helping him to spring a trap. Also, if anything were to happen between her and me that might break up the engagement then even the tiniest hold I had over TopFirst with the Ginny tape would be gone. And finally, well, I couldn't help thinking about what Claire might say.

'It's so difficult at home, at the moment, BabyB,' TopFlirt had confided. 'TopFirst is so wrapped up in his work that he never seems to have any time for anything else.'

I gave her a sympathetic look. What could be worse than being engaged to a monster like that?

'Don't get me wrong, I know what he's like,' she continued. 'He's always been ambitious. But there's a fine line between hard-working and ambitious and completely losing sight of what's important and he's way, way over the other side of that line.'

She looked upset as she said these words, as if this were the first time she'd dared to articulate them, even to herself, and then she added, 'We used to take walks in the park and have day trips into the countryside, weekends at his parents'. These days it's back to his flat and he's straight in front of his laptop working away on whatever he works away on.'

I just kept nodding gently and offering her my ear.

'And what makes it worse, BabyB, is that he won't even talk to me about his cases. "All confidential" apparently. I mean, let's face it, you guys are hardly dealing in state secrets and I don't see why he can't share some of them with the person he supposedly wants to spend the rest of his life with. But hey, what do I know?'

Then she touched my hand which was on the table next to the wine glass and said, 'I'm sorry, BabyB. This is the last thing you want to hear, I'm sure.'

Actually, nothing could have been further from the truth on so many different levels but I simply shrugged nonchalantly and said, 'Hey, it's good to chat about these things.'

Despite all of my reservations, I am tempted to take her up on her offer of meeting up again in the new year.

Friday 7 December 2007
Year 2 (week 10): Billing clock

I got an update from Slippery this morning. ScandalMonger did his job and the story is going out in Sunday's newspapers. Meanwhile, RoundTheBlock has already booked her ticket out of the country. But that's not quite the end of it.

'I'd start working thirty hours a day on this for the next few days if I were you, BabyB. You know and I know that RedTop will fold and then we'll both collect 100 per cent uplifts. I have ten staff working round the clock on the case as we speak. You've probably got until Monday morning when if they have any sense they'll stop the billing clock immediately. Oh, and although OldSmoothie and TheVamp don't know about our friend MrScandalMonger I've indicated to both of them that settlement might be imminent so you might find that they'll also be burning the midnight oil.'

Monday 10 December 2007
Year 2 (week 11): Case settled

Having taken Slippery's advice, I certainly billed for England over the weekend and I was not surprised that Slippery was right and both OldSmoothie and TheVamp were also to be spotted skulking around chambers trying to look busy. Research, working on documents and then more research. You never know, I would argue, RedTop may still decide to go ahead. Yeah, right.

The only drawback about it was that I had to cancel a daytrip that Claire had organised to Brighton on the Saturday, after which she'd said she'd cook dinner for me at her flat. I did feel particularly bad when I rang her yesterday with the news but as she said herself, 'Don't worry, BabyB. Given that we're both in the same job, I'm perhaps one of your few friends who fully understands the difficulties we face in organising anything beyond the end of our noses, never mind a normal social life. The joys of the Bar, huh?'

Then she said with a chuckle, 'Still, it's great news that you have so much well-paid work. I mean, just think of all the dinners you'll be able to buy me off the back of it.'

Then after all the work was done, as if like clockwork at seven thirty this morning, we all received an email from RedTop telling us to stop billing immediately. We were not to add another penny to that big fat timesheet. The case was to be settled for half a million pounds plus costs. That's a thousand times more than the £500 that BigMouth apparently paid RoundTheBlock in the first place, which is quite a return even for the litigation money machine.

Tuesday 11 December 2007
Year 2 (week 11): Worrier returns

Who should I bump into at court today but a blast from my recent past. I realised it was her before I saw her by the sound of her voice asking question after question of the person she was with. Yes, it was Worrier and I was against her. Well, against her barrister anyway, as she's now crossed over the profession and is working for a firm of solicitors. He had been the one fielding all the questions. When I saw her, I caught her eye and went straight over.

'Worrier, what a pleasure.' Despite all her foibles, it really was good to see her.

'Hello, BabyB, how are you? How funny to be against you!'

'Exactly. How are you?'

'Oh. Very well. I think being a solicitor is definitely for me.'

You don't say, I thought.

'It's funny I should bump into you today,' she continued, 'since only yesterday I received a very mysterious email from TopFirst asking about you.'

'Oh, yes, what did he have to say?' I must have looked a little thrown as Worrier suddenly started shifting her gaze and mumbling that perhaps she had said too much. She changed the subject and I didn't want to push her on it any further.

Now I just have to find out what else he's up to.

Wednesday 12 December 2007
Year 2 (week 11): Ewe-turn if you want to

Everyone was discussing BigMouth's case in chambers tea today.

'I just can't believe it,' said TheCreep. 'One minute they're all guns blazing, the next they've got the white flag flying. You must have really socked it to them, OldSmoothie.'

Whilst I don't think OldSmoothie had a clue as to what had gone on behind the scenes, he wasn't about to play down his moment of victory. As far as he was concerned, helpful new evidence just happened to come to light and then just happened to end up in the Sunday papers. What with that and the natural fear his opponents must have had in facing such a formidable opponent as himself, it came as no surprise whatsoever that the case had settled. He looked extremely smug and said, 'Yes, well, it's always rather satisfying when the hard work pays off. A complete U-turn.'

TheBusker smiled at this and took up the conversation with, 'U-turns. Reminds me of the driving instructor who said to his farmer client, "Can you make a ewe turn?" To which the farmer replied, "No, but I can make its eyes water."'

After work today, BigMouth took OldSmoothie and myself out for a celebratory drink at his St. James's club. He was in mightily fine fettle as he greeted us in the bar.

'Come in, come in,' he said. 'There's lots to celebrate.'

'Yes, it was a great result,' said OldSmoothie proudly.

'I expected nothing less,' said BigMouth. 'All talk and no trousers these newspapers. Big bullies the lot of them and then the first sign that someone's actually going to stand up to them and fight they run away like cowards into a corner.'

'Er, yes,' said OldSmoothie, clearly biting his tongue.

'But that's not what I want to drink to.'

'Oh?' said OldSmoothie.

'No. That's old news,' he said just a tad ungratefully. 'It's these old people I'm now interested in.'

'Oh,' said OldSmoothie. 'That's BabyB's domain rather than mine. At least at this stage.'

'Yes, I understand that,' said BigMouth. 'But I wanted to keep you both in the loop as to quite how important this case might be for me.'

'I do realise that these people are your constituents,' said OldSmoothie, 'and they must have gone through a lot of difficulties.'

BigMouth brushed this concern away with a wave of his hand. 'That's not what I meant. No, this is the sort of case that could finally get me off the backbenches. Shining white knight taking on a big corporation and all that. You do understand, I'm sure.'

'Er, yes,' said OldSmoothie.

We both understood perfectly.

Thursday 13 December 2007
Year 2 (week 11): Silver Surfers

I popped into my old room today to say hello to OldRuin, and as is often the case he was dictating what I thought was an advice for his typist. That is until he told me exactly what he was doing. 'I've decided to enter the modern era BabyB and get on to the interweb. I've even decided to take advantage of chambers' very kind offer of an electronic mail address.'

'That's great news, OldRuin. Do tell me if you need any help working it all out.'

He looked a little sheepish and then said, 'That's a very kind offer, BabyB, but I've been using my typist now for more than forty years and I fear it would cause her great offence if I actually started typing my own correspondence at this late stage of my career. She's offered to attend a special email course for pensioners, where I believe they'll teach her how to print off the emails I receive and also to type the replies I dictate.'

'Quite right,' I said. Then I added mischievously, 'Will they also teach her to spell?'

'BabyB, she's been spelling atrociously all of her life. I've always thought it better that solicitors assumed I was dyslexic than make her feel any worse by continually pointing it out.'

'I think my favourite was when she cancelled the "Cricket outing to Lourdes" on your behalf.'

'It was a similar dilemma when she changed an invitation I had drafted from simply "RSVP" to "Please RSVP". Again I chose the possibility that people might think I didn't understand French rather than having to correct her.'

He smiled to himself.

'She tells me that we'll both be officially Silver Surfers. Apparently her grandson even has a cartoon book where the hero is a Silver Surfer.'

Friday 14 December 2007
Year 2 (week 11): New counsel

Today we received a letter from the other side's solicitors in TheMoldy cases notifying us which counsel they had taken on. Slippery and I had already speculated as to who this might be but in our wildest dreams we hadn't expected to see these names. The first was UpTights, which makes me wonder whether I should try and get OldSmoothie on board just to wind her up. For the moment I think I'll simply try and copy some of his well-honed strategies in dealing with her, although I know that really the only reason he ever succeeds is because she hates him so much. But it was the other name that elicited the most surprise: that of TopFirst himself. It makes me extremely suspicious that these appointments are far from coincidence and that TopFirst is up to something, and it certainly made Claire give me a knowing look when I mentioned it to her after work this evening. The difficulty will be in working out just exactly what it is that he's plotting.

Let the litigation games begin.

Monday 17 December 2007
Year 2 (week 12): An offer

Slippery and ScandalMonger have been making hay in the last few days and they've now set up a website, called geriatrigation.com, to bring in more of these Moldy cases. Scandal's whipping it up in the papers and Slippery's doing all the admin. In the meantime I've picked out a couple of our better cases to lead the charge and on Wednesday we will issue proceedings. It's then over to ScandalMonger to get it on to the front pages.

Unsurprisingly, then, I got a visit from UpTights this afternoon.

'You do realise that this whole thing is a complete try on?' she said.

'I presume you're talking about my case against your lovely telecom company?'

'Of course I am, BabyB. It's not like you're doing any other cases that are big enough to be against me, now is it?'

Ouch. She's going for the patronising approach, I see.

'You're right there, UpTights. Except I would have thought these are just straightforward personal injury actions, which are well below your usual size of case . . .'

I tailed off and looked at her. 'Which did make me wonder why they had instructed someone as senior as yourself. Suggests there's more to this than meets the eye, wouldn't you say?'

She was slightly thrown by her former pupil answering her back so directly and she hesitated for a second before coming back with, 'You know full well, BabyB, that if you raise such provocative issues these big companies will always take it seriously.'

'Unless of course,' I answered, 'there was nothing to them at all. In that case why would they waste their money?'

She could see she was getting nowhere.

'Enough of these puerile games. I have an offer to make. If you agree not to pursue your claims any further, then my clients will not seek any costs which have been wasted thus far.'

'But why should my clients be bothered when they're insured against your costs?'

To that, at this stage, there was no answer and after a little more bluffing and attempts at bullying, UpTights was on her way.

Tuesday 18 December 2007
Year 2 (week 12): Arthur and Ethel

Today I went off to spend a little time with the two old people whose cases will be among the first ones to be issued tomorrow. They are the wonderful couple, Arthur and Ethel, who I'd met in our earlier conference: Arthur who pulls the moonies and Ethel with her bucket of water. Arthur is a small man, hunched over with age, which does give him the perfect stance to pull off quick and unexpected moonies at the drop of a hat. But beyond this idiosyncrasy, his single concern is Ethel who I discovered today he thought he might have lost to cancer some five years ago but who has since made a full recovery. Away from the silliness and mayhem that was the last conference in chambers, it really was quite moving to sit and listen to them today and to see that the strength and the stoicism they both exude is fed by a deep, underlying love.

'We've been married fifty-seven years this April,' Arthur said proudly.

'And never a dull day,' added Ethel with a real twinkle in her eye.

'We've had our ups and downs, I'll grant you,' said Arthur, 'but I wouldn't have made it this far without her. She's the air that gives me life, you know.'

'Listen to yourself, Arthur, won't you? You'll embarrass the young man.'

'Never mind that, Ethel. Doesn't do any harm passing on a thing or two now and again.'

But above all else, what came over was their zest for life. Arthur had survived the Normandy landings and as well as her more recent troubles, Ethel had lived through the Blitz. Both had an enthusiasm you rarely come across even in children. What's more, they seemed genuinely excited to be involved in this forthcoming litigation. As Arthur said, 'It's about time us oldies had a voice and demanded a little respect.'

Then at one point in the conversation, Ethel asked me quite directly and out of context, 'What do you do in your spare time, BabyBarista?'

'Er . . .' I didn't quite know how to answer that.

'You know,' said Arthur. 'What do you do for fun? When you're not working.'

'Er, well . . .' I still felt a little awkward. 'Well it's pretty busy at the moment actually. I spend time with friends, I guess.'

They didn't press it further and we then went back to discussing the case. After my visit I had to finish going through the paperwork for the big day tomorrow, which unfortunately meant I had to once again cancel on Claire, this time for drinks, though as she'd indicated before, I knew she'd understand.

Wednesday 19 December 2007
Year 2 (week 12): Freudian slip

It was zimmer-frame city outside the High Court today. With the help of ScandalMonger, TheMoldies have set up a Facebook group in the last two days, publicising the event, and when I arrived with Slippery, who was issuing the claim form, there were at least four hundred Moldies and their supporters standing around cheering. It was, to say the least, a little surreal.

ScandalMonger had also tipped off the press and I'm happy to say that I think we're in business. Though where there's press, there is also BigMouth and sure enough he was there puffing out his chest and soaking up any reflected glory from the storm that had been created. ClichéClanger also came along for the sport and it didn't come as a great surprise to see him get rather over-excited at all the attention. At one point he held some papers in the air and shouted, 'We will wield aloft the mighty sword of Damacles and justice will be ours.'

A Freudian slip, I fear, when it comes not only to taking on a big corporation but also to courting the press so vigorously.

Thursday 20 December 2007
Year 2 (week 12): Making plans

Well, we certainly scored on the publicity front and Slippery has been inundated with more cases from people claiming to be affected by the particular telecom company that we're targeting. As I sat in a strategy meeting with Slippery and ScandalMondger, Slippery explained, 'The plan is to have these first cases paving the way and in the next two or three months we'll pick a few more as test cases. If we win on any one of those, I mean it guys, we'll all be shopping. Big settlement.'

He looked at us as if we should both be very impressed with his big words. Then he added, 'But to be fair, the main part of our plan at this stage is to embarrass the telecom company into settling by raising the fear of blanket and damaging press coverage.'

Then, as I was about to leave, Slippery looked at me and said dramatically, 'Do you feel plucky, BabyB? Well, do ya?'

Friday 21 December 2007
Year 2 (week 12): BusyBaby

BusyBody was at chambers tea this afternoon showing off her new-born girl. She seemed as full of energy as ever, which prompted TheBusker to ask, 'How are you finding the sleepless nights with the baby?'

'Oh, that's not a problem. I'm following a new online motivational course for babies and I've been specifically training her to sleep through the night from week one.'

There were a few sceptical looks from some of the more senior members of chambers but by this point HeadClerk was asking the most important question of all, 'Er, so when exactly was she born?'

He singularly failed at trying to sound nonchalant and after she gave him the answer and left the room a number of people began flicking through their diaries. They all knew that FanciesHimself, the junior clerk, is one of the two possible fathers, along with OldSmoothie, but early conclusions seem to be that it was too early for FanciesHimself to have been responsible. This squarely puts OldSmoothie in the frame and adds more weight to the theory that BusyBody is only being allowed back into chambers on the basis that she keeps quiet about the identity of the father.

All of this perhaps also explains why OldSmoothie made a point of being seen in chambers today, all 'business as usual'. Except it wasn't business as usual because everyone knows that Friday is his golf day. Everyone, that is, except his wife who apparently believes that it remains one of his regular court days.

As for chambers tea itself, aside from the cooing from the ladies and the polite grunts from some of the male members of chambers, OldSmoothie was lamenting times gone by. 'No one just emerges any longer.'

'What do you mean emerges?' I asked.

'Emerges. Just what it says. Appears in place. Emerges from nowhere to take the role.'

'And I'm imagining that you would be referring to the role of high court judge?' asked TheVamp.

'Not just them. Prime Ministers used to just emerge. Ambassadors, heads of the civil service. They'd all just emerge. But yes, since you're asking, high court judges too. It's ridiculous having an application process for such a complicated and sensitive role.'

'Yes, I hear you weren't even shortlisted following your own application, OldSmoothie. Great loss to the judicial system, I'm sure.' This sideswipe came from UpTights.

'Coming from someone who can't even judge our little games of Battleships without exploding, I hardly think you're one to talk.'

OldSmoothie was referring to the particular cases that he likes to settle with an insurer over a game of Battleships. But he wasn't to be diverted from his little reverie. 'But all I'm really saying is that it's a crying shame. No more old-fashioned consultations. Quiet words over a G and T. Now it's all just form-filling and quotas.'

'Well,' said UpTights, 'any time you want to emerge as Ambassador for Outer Mongolia, you just tell me OldSmoothie and I'll get right on to the Prime Minister myself and make absolutely sure it happens.'

'I'd support your emergence into any place but this one to be honest, OldSmoothie,' added BusyBody looking him straight in the eye.

The tag team were reunited.

'Yes,' said UpTights, 'a campaign for the emergence of OldSmoothie. Maybe a few articles in the press, a petition on the Number Ten website and of course the obligatory Facebook group.'

BusyBody smiled and said, 'I think you may just be on to something there.'

Really, I dread to think where it may now lead, what with BusyBody's rather terrifying post-birth energy and UpTights's manic moments. But the other thing that occurs to me is to question why exactly BusyBody is still being so horrible to OldSmoothie when he might be the father of her child? Maybe she just can't help herself in the face of such pomposity. Or maybe it's because he's told her that he'll have nothing to do with the baby.

Monday 24 December 2007
Year 2 (week 13): Ringers

Got a call this morning from ScandalMonger.

'Sorry to be disturbing you on Christmas Eve but I've just had a terrible thought. Well, let's put it another way. If I were running the other side's case I would have a terrible thought. Terrible, in the wicked sense. Something that is a potential weakness in our plan.'

'What's that?' I asked, finding it unlikely that ScandalMonger was suddenly going to illuminate me on the common law of torts.

'You're only going to run a very few of these claims as test cases, right?'

'Yes.'

'And if they fail, we pretty much fall by the wayside.'

'Correct.'

'So what's to stop them bringing in ringers?'

'Bringing in what?' I asked, nonplussed.

'Ringers, BabyB. Fake cases that they can control.'

'Well whoever would do that? And how?' Though it had suddenly got me thinking.

'Wake up, BabyB. You and I both know that your friend TopFirst will stop at very little to damage you and I assume, by extension, the biggest case of your career so far.'

He was of course right.

'Anyway,' he continued, 'just thought you should bear it in mind when you're going over all the new cases this Christmas.'

Just what I need to be worrying about over the festive period. Then, as if things couldn't get any worse, I had a visit from SlipperySlope at about one minute to six this evening as he personally delivered six boxes full of new Moldy cases stacked high in his black cab. He was a little over-excited and kept saying, 'Show me the cash, BabyB. Show me the cash,' whilst insisting on doing a high five, which is the sort of gesture from a middle-aged man that makes Jeremy Clarkson's jeans seem trendy. Then he said, 'The good news is we're all going to be rich, BabyB.'

There was obviously more to come, and sure enough, 'The bad news is that these cases need to be prepared within the next couple of days, ready to follow up straight after Christmas. It's the guarantee ScandalMonger gave that we'd get back within a week and the newspapers will be on us like a flash if we don't deliver on our first challenge.'

He paused and I didn't react one way or the other so he continued, 'The other bit of bad news is that I have to spend time with my family and so won't be able to do it . . .'

Go on, let me guess . . .

'But the good news is that you, my little wigged one, can do it for me.'

Tuesday 25 December 2007
Year 2 (week 13): Christmas cheer

'You've got to take a break, BabyB. It's Christmas day.' It was Claire and she'd invited my mother and me to join her family for their big Christmas lunch.

'I did take a break, Claire. But now that we've eaten, I've just got to carry on going through these files.'

'But, BabyB,' my mother said, 'I really thought all your worries would be over once you were made a tenant.'

Claire smiled as if to let me off the hook. 'Don't worry,' she said to my mother. 'We'll get him back on the straight and narrow what with the meditation course you've booked him on to, and the

64

executive stress doll and relaxing bath salts I gave him.' I guiltily thought of the presents I'd hurriedly ordered online for them only a few days ago.

I haven't told either of them about the compromise I've made in order to refinance her debts or indeed any of the others I had to make last year, though I suspect Claire wouldn't see them merely as compromises but rather steps down a very slippery slope. I really wish I could but I certainly wasn't about to start blabbing in front of Claire's parents of all people. One thing I do know: this is not why I came to the Bar.

Thursday 27 December 2007
Year 2 (week 13): Creative accounting

The few people who are around this week all seem to be getting their expenses ready for their accountants today. Let's just say that even at Christmas time when it comes to HM Treasury the spirit is far from what you might call giving and there are some pretty imaginative claims going in. There's a young member of chambers called Teflon, owing to the fact that whatever trouble he causes nothing ever seems to stick. He is 'forced' to take his best solicitor client to a lap-dancing club once a month in return for the work he is sent. Membership of said club is put under 'Specialist Bar Associations'. Then OldSmoothie has a demanding insurer client with a penchant for Bolivian marching powder who puts all of these related expenses through his accounts under 'motor fuel', which seems to be the barrister equivalent of the music industry's euphemism of 'flowers'. But best of all is TheVamp who was proud to declare last week that she puts all her hairdressing bills under 'wig maintenance' and then went on to suggest that OldSmoothie maybe put his Viagra in the bicycle section under 'hard hat and inner tube'.

Meanwhile, SlipperySlope arrived at chambers at 9 a.m. on the dot and not only took the files from me but delivered a whole new batch.

What joy.

A rather sultry-looking Vamp was in chambers this afternoon.

'Out this evening, by any chance?' I asked with a smile.

'Might be,' she said. 'Not that you'd be interested now that you've shifted your attentions to TopFlirt.'

'What?' I asked incredulously. 'What exactly is that supposed to mean?'

'I hear you had lunch with her before Christmas,' she said conspiratorially.

'How on earth did you know that?' I asked, no doubt looking slightly flustered.

'Oh, you know . . .'

'No, I don't know,' I pushed.

'Don't worry, BabyB, your secret's safe with me.'

'What secret? Why would I be worried?'

'Oh, you know . . .'

This was becoming just slightly annoying. 'No, I don't know what you're trying to say at all.'

'Well, I heard TopFirst doesn't like you very much. Got a bit of history with him it seems. Then you're spotted having what by all accounts was an extremely intimate lunch with, of all people, TopFlirt. Enough to get people talking I'd say. But as I said, don't worry, your secret's safe with me . . .'

With that, she waltzed out trying to look enigmatic but managing nothing more than what she is, a stirring, mischievous little minx.

CHAPTER 4
JANUARY: HE'S BACK!

Tuesday 1 January 2008
Year 2 (week 14): Confession . . .

What a night it was last night. New Year's Eve and a huge party in Battersea with Claire and a whole bunch of other Bar School friends. It all started off swimmingly with one round of shots inevitably leading to another, until we were stumbling around and hugging each other by midnight like it was the last time we'd see each other. Which after what followed might well be the case for Claire and me. It was about 1 a.m. and we were sitting on a sofa and surveying the scene of carnage which had once been our friend's flat.

'Claire, we need to talk.' I looked at her trying to focus. 'I've got something to tell you.'

She smiled. 'I think we've already been there and done that, BabyB. Don't worry. You don't need to go over old ground.'

'No. I want to tell you about TheBoss. About SlipperySlope. About the whole thing. I really, really want to tell you.'

At this point Claire suddenly turned on me and for the first time in my life I saw her looking angry. 'I'm sorry, BabyB, but I'm afraid I've simply had it up to here with you and your work, work, work.'

She put her palm above her head as she said it. Then she continued, 'You ruined Christmas with the parading of your files in front of the tree. I'd say you put more time and effort into just one page of those cases than you did into choosing the generic books you bought everyone from Amazon. But after that day I told myself one thing and it was this: I was not going to allow you to ruin New Year too. So leave it, will you?'

I think I must have looked pretty shocked. Then she softened.

'Look, BabyB. I love you dearly. Truly I do. But we're all so worried about you. You never have time for anyone these days, not even your mother from what she was saying when you disappeared off to work at Christmas.'

The subject was well and truly dead and any chance of confessing my sins and perhaps sharing the burden was gone forever.

'I'm sorry, Claire. It's pretty difficult at the moment, that's all.'

'It's difficult for all of us, BabyB. We're not students any longer. It's the real world and we have to make the best of it.'

With which she gave me a long hug and went off to join a couple of her friends. It was not a great start to the new year.

Wednesday 2 January 2008
Year 2 (week 14): Guess who?

No sooner have the geriatric cases started coming through the door than guess who should crawl out of the woodwork? Why, it's TheBoss, calling my mobile.

'Hello, BabyB. How's tricks? A little bird tells me you might be involved in all this oldie litigation.'

'So what if I might be?'

'Well, I think I might be able to help. Strikes me you have your solicitor in place who is complemented by a rather excellent PR man. But what you're lacking is an accident manager who can put these cases together a little more professionally. You know how I work. How about it? I act behind the scenes and you keep a healthy professional distance from the source.'

'But aren't you banned from all that?' I asked.

'I'm only banned from working as a barrister, BabyB. What else I decide to do in my own time is my business.'

'And what's in it for you?'

'Oh, you know. Job satisfaction in keeping the clients happy. The pursuit of justice. Things like that.'

'And a wodge of cash from Slippery no doubt.'

'I'm sure he'd see me right.'

All of this of course raises a few issues, not least as to how TheBoss would know about ScandalMonger's involvement. I told him I'd think about it.

Thursday 3 January 2008
Year 2 (week 14): Divorce central

Whoever said lawyers were vultures? Well, true to form Slippery's niece NurserySlope, who skis, rides and looks like a horse, has been busy rejuvenating the family law department of their firm. Today she sent out an internal memo which said:

> Gear up for Monday! It's time once again to turn those post-Christmas new year blues into little rays of financial sunshine :-)

I kid you not. Right down to the fake little smile. The sheer lack of scruples reminds me of that 'good time to bury bad news' memo after 9/11. Then after a load of motivational chat about how the credit crunch was already helping business, it ended with:

> Oh, and don't forget, please remember that with the inevitable increase in activity during January, your fee-income target is (as always) 20 per cent higher this month.

I wouldn't be surprised if they also gave an award for the most number of acrimonious disputes brought through the door. When I mentioned this memo at chambers tea OldSmoothie said, 'That's nothing, BabyB. I've heard of one firm who pays marriage guidance counsellors not only for referrals but even gives them a "success fee" when it all breaks down in acrimony. What's more, you'll never find the other side complaining about the counsellor since it benefits both sides' lawyers.'

'It's all just a symptom of the compensation culture,' said UpTights.

'I've always thought that a particularly unfortunate term myself,' said OldSmoothie. 'Makes it sound like some horrible bacteria.'

'What, you mean it makes you associate it with the very bottom of the evolutionary tree of life?' said TheBusker.

'Exactly,' said OldSmoothie.

'Sounds about right to me,' said UpTights.

Lawyers, huh? You gotta love 'em.

Friday 4 January 2008
Year 2 (week 14): He's back!

Clearly impatient to start earning some cash, TheBoss was on the phone again this morning. 'So what do you say, BabyB, are we going to work together?'

Now I know that it's a risk getting involved with him in any way and this is particularly so when there's every reason to suspect that TopFirst may well have contacted him in the last few months. However, despite this, I figure that for the moment it's probably best to keep your enemies close. Besides which, it might well not only lighten my own workload but also help Slippery's firm, who desperately need someone like TheBoss to get TheMoldies' cases in order at their end, since it's well beyond what they're used to. So eventually I answered, 'I think we might be able to do something. But before we do, I need some kind of guarantee from you.'

'Oh, come on, BabyB. After all we've been through?'

'That's exactly why I want such a guarantee.'

'And what exactly did you have in mind?'

Well, although I was trying to sound all confident and cool about the whole thing, I had absolutely no idea what sort of guarantee might be appropriate.

'One hundred thousand pounds, to be held by ClichéClanger rather than Slippery and paid to me in the event of any dirty business.'

'BabyB, you've got to start setting your sights a little higher. That's just a few settlements' worth. Anyway, you're on. I'm back in business.'

Later on, I met up with Claire for a drink. She said she wanted to meet up to apologise for her outburst.

'I'm so sorry, BabyB. I really do want to be there for you but sometimes ...' She hesitated as she looked for the right words.

'Well sometimes you do seem to become a little over-involved in your cases.'

'I'm sorry,' I said. 'I'll try to make more of an effort and I promise not to talk about work ever again.'

'That's not the point, BabyB. I want to hear about your work and to help if I can. I just don't like seeing you lose yourself to it.'

Then she smiled and with the twinkle back in her eye said, 'So come on, tell me what happened at work today.'

I told her about the return of TheBoss.

'BabyB! Are you absolutely crazy? I don't know everything that went on last year but I know you well enough to be sure that the prospect of his being back in your life is horrific. Why?'

'I thought it might be one way in which I could get back a little time from work,' I answered and then explained the guarantee I'd garnered.

'BabyB, this is a man who makes SlipperySlope seem like Atticus Finch. He'll wheedle his way out of absolutely anything you put in front of him. That's the only guarantee. Well, that and it'll all end in tears.'

Then, realising that she had started lecturing again, she made another effort at lightening the mood.

'Kind of reminds me of Jack Nicholson screaming about Johnny coming' she said.

'Or the return of Hannibal Lecter,' I agreed.

She gave a wry smile. 'When the Luftwaffe took off a few years ago for the first time since the war, one of the German headlines said simply, "We're back".'

'My favourite headline is "Fog in channel, continent stranded",' I responded, glad to get a chance to change the subject.

'Or the apocryphal "Titanic sinks. Glasgow man feared dead",' said Claire, thankfully taking the conversation completely away from TheBoss and all the potential problems he posed.

But at the end of the evening the subject was clearly still weighing on her mind and perhaps trying to avoid appearing constantly disapproving of me she said, 'I think perhaps, BabyB, we both need a little space from each other for a while. What do you think?'

The look I gave was a blank one as I struggled to take on board the suggestion. In the end I just nodded. With which we hugged and then I watched her leave the bar and hail a black cab.

Monday 7 January 2008
Year 2 (week 15): MoreFlirt

Got an email from TopFlirt this morning asking what I'm up to and mentioning that she's free in a couple of weekends' time. What to do? Could it still be a trap set by TopFirst? Seems a bit extreme to pimp his fiancée, even by his standards. But does it carry the risk that it could unleash untold wrath from the Weasel One? Perhaps, but I'd already decided what I would do and so I arranged to meet her a week on Saturday.

Tuesday 8 January 2008
Year 2 (week 15): Small is beautiful

'You will often find that the size of the bundle of papers is actually disproportionate to the size of the case itself,' said TheCreep, as he patronised a couple of the pupils who were listening politely.

'Shame that's not true in other areas, my love,' said TheVamp, as she passed by and tapped him on the head Benny Hill style just to underline his shortened stature.

'What on earth are you talking about?' asked TheCreep in a voice that was pompous even for him.

'Oh, MrCreepyWeepy, you're so touchy these days. Not getting enough attention in the lurve department are we?'

'I can always count on you to lower the tone. Even when I'm teaching them a very valuable lesson.'

'And what exactly was that lesson then, CreepsyWeepsy? That "small is beautiful", by any chance?'

Wednesday 9 January 2008
Year 2 (week 15): Scallies chasing scallies

Had a meeting with Slippery, TheBoss and ScandalMonger today. I told them that of the cases I'd reviewed there were a couple that I was concerned about because they looked just a little too perfect. My fear was that they were the ringers about which ScandalMonger had warned me. I suggested that TheBoss and ScandalMonger might be better placed to investigate this further, on the basis that the best person to catch a scally is another scally, although I didn't quite put it in those terms. It'll be interesting to see what they come up with.

Just as I was leaving Slippery's office, I bumped into Smutton and I have to admit that I blushed as she greeted me.

'Ah, BabyB. My favourite hot little barrister. I hope you got your fill of goose over the festive period.'

Then she ever so slightly adjusted her blouse as she continued with, 'I always find it so disappointing when we're forced to put away our Christmas baubles for another year. Still, won't be long until that first harbinger of spring.'

I looked at a loss and Slippery smirked in the background.

'Oh, come on, BabyB. Do join in. The swallow of course,' she said, rolling her tongue over the word as she said it.

I blushed again, much to her obvious delight.

Thursday 10 January 2008
Year 2 (week 15): Paranoia

What do you do when you overhear something you shouldn't have heard from the other side? That's the dilemma I have today after having heard UpTights gossiping about my case over lunch in hall. To be fair, she obviously didn't realise that I was sitting on the table just behind her but despite this her voice is such that I imagine even those sitting halfway across the room would probably have picked up some bits of the conversation. All I heard was, 'The insurer's getting a little shaky and is thinking of trying to settle early for say twenty thousand each and tying it up with a big confidentiality clause.'

Once I realised that she was talking about the Moldy cases, I actually sidled off, worried that if I heard any more it might in some way conflict me out of the litigation. But then when I got back to chambers I started thinking it over and although I'm fairly certain that this can't possibly conflict me – otherwise barristers would be able to get rid of their opponents at the door of court just by talking loudly to their clients – I'm not actually sure that this is the case, and the last thing I'd want is to get it wrong when TopFirst is on the other side. And of course, that also makes me wonder whether UpTights did in fact know I was there and that it is all a trap.

Friday 11 January 2008
Year 2 (week 15): Lost dreams

Having mulled over what to do with UpTights's information last night, I've decided that it's time to wheel out OldSmoothie and get him involved in the case, on the basis that he knows specifically how best to wind her up. I went over to Slippery's office to discuss it this afternoon.

'I used to know them both years ago,' he said, referring to UpTights and OldSmoothie. 'Rising stars of their generation. Picked out for great things. They even made rather a glamorous couple for all of about a week.'

'Oh.'

That was news to me.

'But now they're like a couple of old has-beens fighting over lost dreams and faded glory, BabyB. Great to watch but you know what? It's one of the few spectacles in this whole money-making world that actually makes me feel just a little bit sad.'

He paused.

'You know what I mean, BabyB. OldSmoothie with all his "I coulda been a contender" rubbish, as old colonels blow smoke up him on his golf club committees.'

I couldn't help smiling at the accuracy of that portrayal. It seemed there might be more to Slippery than his brash front suggested.

'Then poor UpTights. One minute she's all Gloria Swanson and "I'm still big, it's just the world around me got small", and the next minute she's Blanche DuBois and the kindness of strangers, lost in her own little world. These days UpTights hates the whole world, especially women and most especially OldSmoothie. He just hates himself.'

Golly. There really was no answer to that. Then he brightened up and said, 'But hey, that's why they're still in business. Complex is good in your line of work, BabyB. I mean, no case is ever black or white. Just like barristers.'

Then he paused and looked at me sympathetically and added, 'I wouldn't be a barrister for all the money in the world.'

With which he packed me off with instructions for the pompous one.

Monday 14 January 2008
Year 2 (week 16): OldSmoothie on board

OldSmoothie was delighted when I told him that he was to lead in the Moldy litigation, though the prospect of more UpTights baiting seemed to give him more pleasure than the case itself. After I'd been through the basic facts and issues this morning, I then went on to ask his advice about what I'd overheard UpTights say.

'Don't worry yourself so much, BabyB. It's her own fault for giving it away. I think the best use we can make of it at this stage is to pay our stretched friend a little visit. I suggest that we pop round to her room when she is least expecting it, say tomorrow morning.'

Meanwhile, BusyBody's back in chambers, having handed over the day care of her baby to her mother. The deal appears to be that she'll be a third six pupil until the end of March and then she will automatically be made a tenant. No further explanation has been given, which as I've already speculated suggests that a certain overweight silver fox might have had to cut a deal of some sort behind the scenes. Whatever the reasons, she certainly wasn't looking quite as energetic as she had been last month. BusyBaby, it seems, is not following orders.

'Yes, my motivational course for babies isn't quite going as planned and she still seems to wake up crying at four in the morning, every morning.'

'That sounds pretty normal,' said HeadClerk in a very knowing way.

'Well, I'm determined that there must be a way to train her,' said BusyBody. 'I've got hypnotherapy tapes playing twenty-four-seven at the moment and I'm hoping that some of it might just kick in.'

'But surely she'll struggle to understand what they're saying on the tapes,' said TheBusker.

BusyBody suddenly looked very alarmed, her tiredness clearly showing. As if she hadn't even thought of that very obvious point. Then she said, 'Still, that's why I thought I'd come back to work. Let's face it, if I'm going to be woken up at that unearthly hour, I may as well make use of it by doing a set of papers or two, don't you think?'

Tuesday 15 January 2008
Year 2 (week 16): Confrontation

'UpTights, my darling. What a lovely pleasure.'

OldSmoothie, with me in tow, had entered UpTights's room without an invitation – the same room in which I had spent the last half of my pupillage.

'And what unfortunate circumstances brings a snake like you into my room, OldSmoothie?'

'Oh, my, we did get out of bed the wrong side today? Or perhaps it was another pupil's bed instead?' he answered, referring to her brief tryst with one of my fellow pupils last year.

'Look OldSmoothie, if you have something to say, then spit it out.'

Not even OldSmoothie was going to stoop so low as to follow this up with some innuendo or other and so he said, 'You'll never guess what? We're against each other in the Moldy litigation.'

UpTights's mouth dropped. Well it opened as far as her stretched skin after all the facelifts would allow anyway, and she glared at me.

'You coward, BabyB. Couldn't stick up for yourself, is that it?'

We had rehearsed what I would say and I let her have it. 'Actually, I brought him in to help me with a professional conduct point. You see, I, along with the rest of Middle Temple Hall, couldn't help overhearing you screeching that your clients wanted to settle for twenty grand a claimant. Even a loudspeaker wouldn't have reached as many people.'

Now she looked really taken aback.

'I don't know what you're talking about,' she lied.

'A pretty serious breach of client confidentiality, I'd say,' said OldSmoothie. 'Just out of interest, what would you do in our shoes?'

'Oh, do shut up you old fool. You have no idea what you're talking about. BabyB's talking cock and bull and you know it.'

'Well, we were wondering what your own clients might think about that if we were to write to them personally, advising them that their own barrister was giving away their secrets.'

Then he went in for the kill.

'Of course, if you were to advise your insurer client to stump up fifty grand per claimant, we might not need to send that letter.'

If it were possible for steam to be coming out of her ears, then it would have happened at that moment. She looked more like a cartoon character than ever before and just when I thought that she might actually stand up and launch herself physically at OldSmoothie like some demented harpy, he left the room adding as he did so, 'Oh, and given that we're such careful souls, we might also need to check with the Bar Standards Board as to what we have to do in such a situation. I'm sure they'd be fascinated to hear all about it.'

Once out of the room, OldSmoothie whispered to me, 'Of course, she'll never take the bait and she'll be pretty sure we're just bluffing. But the very fact that I've even presented her with such an option is so offensive to everything that she stands for that it'll eat away at her for the rest of the case. When that happens, BabyB, we're halfway there.'

Wednesday 16 January 2008
Year 2 (week 16): Solicitors in wigs

Now don't get me wrong, I've got nothing against solicitors. Well, not unless you count greed, laziness, incompetence and late paying by a select few. But I certainly don't have any problem with them having an equal right to barristers to appear in court. But today, just when you thought that wigs were finally on their way out, I was against a solicitor who turned up proudly wearing a little horse-hair number.

'What chambers are you from?' I asked.

'I'm not from any chambers,' came the reply. He looked at me proudly and then pronounced, 'I'm a solicitor,' in the same tone that they say 'I'm a laydeee' on *Little Britain*.

'Oh.'

I must have looked a little quizzical because he followed up with, 'If you're wondering why I'm wearing a wig, there's a new Practice Direction says I can.'

He brandished it at me somewhat defensively.

'Oh.'

Then we were off into court, where the subject was raised again even before the judge had a chance to ask.

'Your Honour,' he said, wrongly addressing the district judge. 'I am a solicitor of the Supreme Court of England and Wales and am proud today to be wearing a wig.'

The judge stared down at the solicitor and answered only with 'Oh'.

'Yes, Your Honour, and if anyone wants to question my right so to do, I have here a copy of the recent Practice Direction on Court Dress which covers this exact issue.'

Again, 'Oh.'

The judge shifted awkwardly and looked over to me. I shrugged back, not wanting to be the one to say it. The judge sighed and said, 'Personally, I don't mind what you wear in your own time. However, haven't you wondered why neither I nor your opponent are wearing wigs today?'

The solicitor glanced around and then looked completely lost. Then the judge said, 'No one robes in small claims I'm afraid.'

To which the solicitor could only reply with 'Oh'.

Thursday 17 January 2008
Year 2 (week 16): Breach of confidence

Despite the time that the Moldy litigation has been taking up, I've still been trotting off to court most days and I guess sooner or later it was inevitable that I would end up against TopFirst. Well, I found out today that my case for a week on Wednesday is just that. What's more I have the slight difficulty that our claimant has gone AWOL. Literally skipped the country without explanation. This leaves us in something of a predicament as to whether we alert the other side to our difficulty and apply for an adjournment or simply brave it out. It mostly hinges on whether the other side are going to accept the settlement offer of some twenty thousand pounds that we made a few days ago. If there's a chance they might accept we definitely don't want to alert them to our little weakness. But if they are going to fight then the earlier we ask for an adjournment the better.

With this in mind I thought I'd chat it through with OldSmoothie and so I went over to his office and explained my predicament.

'Simple, BabyB. Watch this.'

He then looked up the number and with the phone on loud speaker rang TopFirst's chambers and asked to speak to his clerk. OldSmoothie then put on his best estuary drawl, which really didn't wash, and said that he was from a particularly big firm of solicitors who wanted to instruct TopFirst next Wednesday.

'We've heard he's the hot young thing at the Bar and want to try him out. Big trial. Insurer-backed.'

'Er, it seems he's already booked on a case at the moment but it's actually marked in the diary as likely to settle. Let me just speak to him and then give you a call back.'

A few minutes later and OldSmoothie had the answer.

'Yes. He says it's definitely going to settle. No question. He can guarantee to do your case.'

Oh.

When I got back to my room I rang TopFlirt and confirmed our dinner for this coming Saturday. She sounded quite pleased to hear from me and complained almost immediately that TopFirst was still working far too hard. Oh, and yes, she's looking forward to Saturday.

See you there.

Friday 18 January 2008
Year 2 (week 16): Carry On Cricket

OldSmoothie and HeadofChambers were on a post-settlement high at chambers tea this afternoon and they were telling their old stories like two musicians jamming to their favourite tunes. At one point talk turned from cricket to one of the female pupils who thankfully was nowhere to be seen.

'Well, I'd give her a thick edge,' said OldSmoothie.

'I'd just settle for a feel of her silly mid-off,' said HeadofChambers.

'Just pitch it up and watch her tickle it to fine leg,' chortled OldSmoothie.

'Bowl it into the rough and watch her perform a nifty little reverse sweep.'

'Around the wicket, of course.'

'Absolutely. Then all you need is good line and length.'

'To bowl a maiden over.'

'Exactly. After that you just get her to stroke it into the covers.'

'Poke it away to deep point.'

'Nudge one into the slips.'

'Slip it into the gully.'

'Tease her out of the crease.'

'Give your googlies a fine touch.'

'Pull it to long on.'

'Hook it to long leg.'

'On a full toss.'

By this point these two grown men were starting to giggle uncontrollably, which reminded me of the time when the two cricket commentators Brian Johnston and Jonathan Agnew got the giggles on air.

'Give her a long hop,' continued OldSmoothie.

'On a sticky wicket,' said HeadofChambers.

'Show her my googlies.'

'Tail-End-her.'

'York-her.'

'Straight through the gate.'

Then BusyBody stepped up to the crease and said, 'Of course, if she had any sense, she'd see your googlies coming a mile off and crack each one of them through midwicket.'

Monday 21 January 2008
Year 2 (week 17): Trouble

Met up with TopFlirt again on Saturday evening.

'I don't know what you've done to TopFirst, BabyB, but he really doesn't like you, does he?'

'Not much, I guess,' I replied with the understatement of the year. 'Maybe it's just jealousy over the whole tenancy thing.'

'Could be, although it does seem to be something more than just business. Definitely a personal edge to it although he simply won't tell me.'

'Ah, and you want to know what it is that you think he's hiding from you?'

Now this, by the way, wasn't the start of the evening but was instead after about three bottles of wine and at about twelve-thirty at night. It was also after we'd both opened up our hearts. TopFlirt about how TopFirst is still neglecting her in favour of work and me about my fear that I might have lost Claire for good. There was definite tension as we got up to leave the restaurant since I don't think either of us quite knew what would come next. But I have to admit we were both pretty drunk and when I suggested that she crash on my sofa that seemed like a pretty safe compromise. Well, when I say *my* sofa, what I really mean is my mum's, but thankfully mum was fast asleep when we arrived home.

As we sat on the sofa, TopFlirt was still complaining about her fiancé. 'I thought I was getting some progress when he started to talk about this case you're both doing about the old people. But the more I heard the more it sounded like these people might be really badly affected and yet all he seems to be interested in is impressing his big new corporate client. That and beating you.'

More chat and more booze later and we were still talking at around 5 a.m. when we both eventually fell asleep where we were. Talking, and well, having a goodnight kiss that despite caution on both our parts, led from one thing to another certainly more by accident than good judgment. So now I'm in all sorts of trouble. I've got TopFirst plotting behind my back and against me in two cases and things really do seem to be getting a little close for comfort with his fiancée.

Tuesday 22 January 2008
Year 2 (week 17): Touchy feely

Two of the pupils were chatting away at chambers tea today about the idea of solicitors wearing wigs. One was young Sharon, who had been pulled up early by OldSmoothie. The other was a tall skinny, more fresh-faced than usual young guy, who looks as if he'd completely topple over if you were even to blow in his direction. He has the sort of face that seems constantly on the verge of tears, or what OldSmoothie has described as 'an invitation to treat it to a good punching'. Worst of all in regard to his vocation as a barrister, he can't even get to the end of a sentence without raising the tone of his voice a notch so that everything he says sounds like a question. It's as though he's not sure whether what he's saying is correct and so he figures he'll ask for your reassurance each time. Maybe it's the result of too many OldSmoothies having bopped him on the nose but whatever the reason, you just can't help but feel sorry for him. His name's Giles but given his delicate nature he's been given the name FraGiles by everyone else in chambers. Today, FraGiles happened to mention where he stood on the issue of solicitors getting to wear horse hair on their heads in court.

'I feel it's no bad thing,' he said simply, his voice rising as if seeking reassurance.

'Young man,' interrupted HeadofChambers, who'd overheard what he said and has never masked his irritation at FraGiles's general demeanour. 'Psychologists feel, not barristers.'

FraGiles looked flustered and said, 'Oh, sorry, I believe—'

'Believe? Believe?' said HeadofChambers, his voice rising. 'Only priests believe. Barristers are not paid to have either feelings or beliefs. They are instead paid to give their esteemed and learned opinions.'

'Oh.'

'So from now on, no feelings, no beliefs. Got it?'

Er, right . . .

Wednesday 23 January 2008
Year 2 (week 17): Suspicions

You don't get much past TheVamp and I wondered how long it would take for her to start asking more questions about TopFlirt since she already somehow knows we went out for lunch. Today she popped into my room.

'How's it going with TopFlirt, BabyB?'

Despite the fact that she'd already mentioned it before, I still wasn't expecting such a direct approach and she caught me off guard for just a millisecond. But it was a millisecond too long and my hesitation was damning. 'Ah! I'm right. You have started seeing her.'

I composed myself and answered, 'That's how it starts, you know. The lie gets halfway around the world before the truth even has a chance to get its pants on.'

'BabyB, if the truth didn't even have its pants on, maybe it wasn't a lie after all.'

'Look, I've no idea what you're talking about,' I lied.

'Yeah, right. And don't tell me, TopFirst is your new best friend as well? You do realise that you're playing with fire, don't you? He really is a nasty piece of work.'

She said this as if she knew it first hand, which made me wonder. Although maybe she was offering it up just to get me to talk. Either way, I wasn't going to crack any more than I had already and I continued to deny all knowledge. Not that she bought it. Her parting shot was, 'Well, BabyB, enjoy it while it lasts. Just don't tell Claire.'

Thursday 24 January 2008
Year 2 (week 17): LeadingCounsel

Much chatter in the clerks room this morning due to the fact that TheBusker brought his little brown Border Terrier dog into chambers. Given that the dog was actually dragging him along on the lead, HeadClerk immediately commented, 'Ah, the dog you've been telling us about and leading counsel, I see.'

After which the dog could only be called LeadingCounsel.

'Wouldn't have been allowed in my day', said HeadofChambers.

'Oh, I don't know,' replied TheBusker. 'I'm sure most barristers had a gun dog of one form or another back in the nineteenth century.'

HeadofChambers didn't rise to the gentle banter but in the meantime UpTights looked like she was about to jump out of her stretched skin. 'If that mutt comes anywhere near my room I will put down poison,' she yapped.

'Shouldn't be too hard for you,' piped up OldSmoothie. 'I mean, take your pick. Do you want the spiteful venom which comes from your mouth or just the plain and simple botulism you inject? Come to think of it, maybe there's a connection.'

'Shut up, OldSmoothie. It's a health and safety issue. They bring in all sorts of things.'

'What, like fleas and ticks?' said TheBusker.

'Exactly. Bloodsucking parasites the lot of them.'

As the words left her mouth, everyone looked at her and smiled and let TheBusker deliver the punchline, 'I would have thought they'd get on rather well with a bunch of lawyers in that case, wouldn't you say UpTights?'

Friday 25 January 2008
Year 2 (week 17): The new iPratt

OldSmoothie spent the whole weekend emailing people from his sparkling and shiny new iPhone hoping that they'd notice 'Sent from my iPhone' at the end of every message. Unfortunately for him, what he hasn't yet realised is that BusyBody got hold of it on Friday morning when he ostentatiously and wholly 'by acci-dent' left it lying around in the clerks room with his name on it. A few clicks later and the settings were changed. The thing is, OldSmoothie has now sent so many emails that no one's got the heart to tell him that at the foot of every message he sends it says, 'Sent from my big fat barrister's bottom.'

As a result, this morning it was the main topic of conversation as OldSmoothie arrived in the clerks room once again waving around his new acquisition.

'I see you really have that little extra schwing in your step, OldSmoothie,' said TheVamp. 'How could it be that something so small could achieve so much?'

Ignoring the innuendo, he looked even more pleased with himself. BusyBody followed up with, 'You managed to find the app for pulling women yet?'

'Jealousy, my dear, will get you nowhere,' he answered.

'Don't you think he's so sexy with that in his hand?' added UpTights.

But OldSmoothie was still in the post-coital glow of his iPhone delivery and all the insults just bounced off his technological Ready Brek-like halo. 'I wouldn't expect old-school lawyers like you to understand, UpTights, but I think you'll find that it's not merely a telephone but the sort of practice tool that every self-respecting lawyer worth his salt will be carrying round very soon. Mark my words.'

'Ah, work,' said TheBusker with a smile. 'That'll mean that you're intending to put it all against tax and claim back the VAT then?'

'Of course,' said OldSmoothie still unruffled.

'Since it's exclusively for business use?' said TheVamp seeing where TheBusker was going.

'Naturally,' came the reply.

UpTights came in with the killer blow. 'So you wouldn't object to the taxman examining your user history and seeing quite how much of your online usage had been, er,' she paused for theatrical effect, 'work, then?'

He was stumped and clutched his precious device a little more tightly before leaving the room.

Monday 28 January 2008
Year 2 (week 18): Questions

Had to sit down with my mother over the weekend and explain a little more as to what's going on with her finances without admitting the full extent of my own complicity. Until now I've just reassured her that I have everything in hand. But on Saturday she said that she really wanted to talk. 'I'm worried about you, BabyB, and I fear that it's me and my problems that are making you so stressed.'

'It's definitely not you,' I assured her. 'It's just a difficult time in my career, that's all.'

'But what exactly did happen with my debts? What have you had to give in return?'

'Well, as I said, I managed to find someone who would refinance them. Someone who I work with, actually,' I added, hoping she wouldn't ask for more details.

She didn't but instead changed the subject. 'Well is it your relationship with Claire? It's just that it seems you're carrying the weight of the world on your shoulders at the moment and I can't work out what's causing it.'

At that point I dearly wished I could have told her everything. From TheBoss onwards. But I knew that'd be the selfish thing to do since it would only have off-loaded my worry on to her. So I simply answered her question about Claire. 'It's true. We're definitely having difficulties. It's just growing up I guess. Coming to terms with the real world and all that. Finding our place in it.'

My mother looked doubtful but dropped the subject more out of kindness than lack of rigour. After all, she had met TopFlirt the morning after she'd stayed the night, and my mother is no fool. But thankfully she just said, 'I guess so, BabyB. I guess so. But please. If you ever want to talk anything through. Absolutely anything you like. Please, BabyB. Just remember that I'm here.'

As for my case against TopFirst on Wednesday, there's still no news. For something that was definitely going to settle there's certainly been no indication in that direction. So this has meant that at the last minute I've had to make sure we apply for an adjournment, although I'm not holding out much hope.

Tuesday 29 January 2008
Year 2 (week 18): Octopussy

TheVamp was in chambers today looking tanned after yet another long weekend away skiing. 'How many times has she been away in the last twelve months?' asked OldSmoothie at chambers tea.

'Compared to the number of "golf" ahem "papers" days you take, I hardly think you can complain,' smiled HeadofChambers. 'And you've got to give it to her. She is pretty sporty.'

'Well she's certainly game, if that's what you mean.'

'No, seriously, apparently she stroked the Cambridge University Blues rowing team two years in a row.'

'I really don't want to know who she stroked at university or how many times,' replied OldSmoothie.

At which point TheBusker whispered with a smile, 'Though apparently they did nickname her boat Octopussy.'

'You really thought I'd fall for that old trick, BabyB? I'd have thought more even of you.'

TopFirst was looking particularly smug when I met him at court this morning. We were preparing for the case that I'd thought was going to settle.

'I have no idea what you're talking about,' I replied.

'Oh, come off it. Calling up my clerks with a made-up solicitor's name? You think I'm not going to check that up before spilling my guts to the clerks?'

'You're losing it, TopFirst.'

'Yeah, particularly as UpTights had warned me that you'd try this little trick sooner or later. Seems OldSmoothie's been using it on her for years.'

Ouch.

'Anyway, I thought I'd return the gesture and when I rang your clerks a few days ago pretending to try and book you for this afternoon, they were more than happy to tell me that the case definitely wouldn't be going ahead and I quote, "because his client's done a runner". Sloppy, BabyB.'

Oh.

'So it seems you have a little local difficulty,' he continued, really rubbing it in. 'No client, hmm?'

'Er, yes, as you know, I'll be asking for an adjournment.'

'You don't stand a chance.'

Now, I have to say that given the paucity of the evidence and instructions I tended to agree with him. But as a contingency plan I'd paid a little visit to TheBusker yesterday who'd given me some advice. 'Listen, BabyB. He's young and earnest and is bound to argue far more points than he needs to, particularly on such a simple issue. Remember, almost all cases really boil down to a single issue. So follow this script to the letter and you'll be all right.'

Sure enough, once in court, TopFirst was all full of indignation and clever arguments all over the place. I then stood up and literally read out my script. It began, 'Your Honour, my learned friend has made some fascinating points and in a most persuasive way.

But in the end, doesn't it come down to . . .' I then explained my position as instructed by TheBusker in no more than three more sentences.

The adjournment was granted, though whether the claimant will actually return by the end of next month is another matter.

CHAPTER 5
FEBRUARY: SELLING SHORT

Friday 1 February 2008
Year 2 (week 18): Test cases

Since OldSmoothie knows nothing of the involvement of either ScandalMonger or TheBoss, I had a preliminary meeting with them both today along with SlipperySlope. The purpose was to select our test cases before presenting OldSmoothie with a *fait accompli*. But before this there was much discussion about the possibility of having been fed fake claims.

'I think we have at least two definites,' said TheBoss. 'We haven't been able to pin down exactly who paid them, but it's clear from, er, a few discreet searches, that they've each had a sudden influx of cash in the last couple of months.'

'What sort of amounts are we talking?' asked Slippery.

'Tens of thousands we think,' said TheBoss.

'Too much for TopFirst on his own then,' said ScandalMonger.

'Except that from my investigations, it has his fingerprints all over it.'

'In what way?'

'Well, there's the fact that someone of his description has been seen at each of their houses.'

'But why would he take such a risk?' asked Slippery.

'That's something only BabyB can answer,' said TheBoss matter-of-factly. 'But whatever the reason, I think we've got to assume that he's at least brought someone from the telecom company into his tight little loop, even if just to get hold of the cash.'

'So at least we know to discount those two. But how do we know that none of the others aren't also fake?' asked ScandalMonger.

'We don't yet, although I hope by the time it comes to trial we'll have been able to conduct much deeper investigations into our chosen cases,' said TheBoss.

'But why not just hold our horses and sort out the investigations first off?' asked ScandalMonger.

'Look, the bottom line,' said Slippery, 'is that our chances of winning are pretty low and the longer we leave it the more time they will have to prepare what I imagine will be a formidable array of defences. Our best chance as we've discussed before is to go for the quick pitch battle early on.'

'But surely the judge will give them time to prepare?' continued ScandalMonger.

'A reasonable time, sure. But when we start shouting that they're trying to filibuster the cases until our elderly clients die and their damages claims reduce significantly, I think the judge is going to sit up and listen.'

As I listened, none of this really came as news to me as I'd already had quite lengthy discussions about it with Slippery. But I did have a suggestion to add to the pot that hadn't yet been mooted. 'Why don't we include the two ringers in our list of six test cases? It'll completely put them off guard. They'll think that they will be able to manipulate two of the cases in their favour and undoubtedly taint the others, too.'

There was absolute silence as what I was suggesting began to sink in. TheBoss was the first to speak. 'And then we drop the dodgy two at the last moment and hey presto, they've just lost their trump card.'

'Brilliant, BabyB,' said Slippery.

'I would have expected nothing less,' said TheBoss, with a wry smile in my direction.

I went through the finer details of the Moldy cases with ScandalMonger today.

'I like your style, BabyB,' he said. 'Shame more barristers can't be quite so devious.'

I shrugged this off and then he gave me a thoughtful look, put his feet up on the desk and took a deep breath. 'The thing is, BabyB, you and your friend TopFirst may have some sort of fight going and he may also have brought in the odd accomplice along the way. But my own take on these cases as a whole is that it goes much deeper than that. I don't know whether you've noticed, but the shares in the telecom company that we're suing have plummeted in the past couple of months.'

'Er, yes, I had noticed, actually.'

'I wouldn't put it past them to be fiddling the stock market in one form or another. Maybe they want you to get a case which at least looks bad just to send their share price down.'

'Why would they do that?'

'So they could then buy them back later, of course.'

'Later?'

'When they beat you in court, BabyB.'

'If,' I corrected.

'Yes, yes, of course,' he said dismissively. 'But it's also got me thinking that there may be money to be made for our part, too. You know we can pretty easily predict which way the share price is going to go when we know what evidence we're about to put into the public domain.'

I looked a little shocked at the suggestion of some sort of insider dealing.

'Not that I'd involve you, BabyB. It's just I thought I'd mention it.'

Well, thanks. You just thought you'd innocently mention it. Make me a part of your little conspiracy once again and then leave my failure to dob you in as a way to incriminate me further. This is just what I need.

Tuesday 5 February 2008
Year 2 (week 19): Phishing

With TopFirst plotting, I decided to set a little contingency plan in motion. So I bought myself a fax number and a domain name very similar to www.ukwhoswho.com, the home page for the famous dictionary of the establishment itself, *Who's Who*. I then set up forwarding from my site to the authentic one and sent TopFirst an email from 'editor@' followed by the new domain in the following terms:

Dear TopFirst,
   You have been recommended by a number of senior barristers and judges as one of the rising stars of the English Bar, and I would therefore like to invite you to submit an entry to *Who's Who* 2009. You have been allocated up to one hundred words. Please fill out the enclosed form and sign it and add your credit card details in order that we may charge you the subscription fee of £85 (+VAT). Then fax it back to the number specified.
   Yours sincerely,
   James Bowling-Hunt,
   Associate Editor, *Who's Who*

It's a long shot but it has the one advantage of playing to two of TopFirst's main weaknesses: arrogance and vanity. If he falls for it, the credit card details would have the potential to cause no end of damage online.

Wednesday 6 February 2008
Year 2 (week 19): Escalation

Whilst OldSmoothie was given no say over the choice of test cases, Slippery was telling me today that he's allowed him to choose another junior barrister to add to the mix. As he explained it to me, 'Don't worry, BabyB, it won't water down your own fees. On the contrary, the more people we have involved, the bigger and more important the case looks and the better the argument we'll have for all our fees being increased.'

I wasn't in the slightest concerned about that, although I do have to admit to hoping that he wouldn't choose TheCreep who, with all his earnest wranglings, has a rare ability to suck the humour out of any situation.

'It won't happen, BabyB. Whilst I've technically given him a choice, it was strictly on the condition that he chose TheVamp for whom I've always had a soft spot.'

I'm sure you have, you dirty old man, but for my part I was delighted to hear that nevertheless. Then he added, 'I mean, with most judges still being hoary old men it makes complete sense to have TheVamp sitting pretty? Kind of trumps UpTights, wouldn't you say?'

Not quite what they train you for at Bar School but then it's dirty dog eat dirty dog out there, and if Slippery wants to spend his days at court drooling over TheVamp then that's up to him. Apparently he's already told her but until he decides to announce it officially, OldSmoothie can prance around chambers waving a golden ticket in front of unsuspecting juniors who might be interested.

Meanwhile, we were officially informed today that UpTights has brought BusyBody into the case to assist her and TopFirst.

Oh, and TopFirst replied back to my fake email pretty much immediately with credit card details and all. Of course he did. Arrogance and vanity. My twin allies in this particular little battle. At least it's a start in my search for some sort of insurance policy against his plots.

Thursday 7 February 2008
Year 2 (week 19): OldSmoothie's number two

No sooner had word got out about the place on the team ostensibly being available than TheCreep was round first to OldSmoothie's room, then to mine and then back to his main target. 'Ooh, OldSmoothie, you're so funny. Ooh, OldSmoothie, you're so clever.' He even offered to make me a coffee for the first time ever. Must feel quite a comedown to have to be creeping up to people even more junior than him. Though I think the whole point is that he's either got the brassiest of brass necks ever or more likely he has such a complete lack of insight that he simply doesn't see what everyone else sees: that, as OldSmoothie so politely put it, 'he's an irritating and servile little cretin who when things don't go his way is also a sulky, spoilt little mummy's boy'. Not a great combination at the best of times and today I was finding him even more annoying than usual. Yet despite his professed views on TheCreep, OldSmoothie has never been one to turn down a bit of praise, however false its origin. Nor indeed did he turn down the lunch that TheCreep insisted on buying him. In return OldSmoothie rather cruelly, even for him, left TheCreep with the false impression that he would pick him as his junior with a deliberately misleading choice of words.

True to form, within about five minutes TheCreep had run around the whole of chambers like an excited child letting anyone he could find know. No more hot drinks being made for me since he, according to his own legend, was now 'Second in command of the Moldy ship' (ouch). When he did eventually pay me a visit, the nearest he got to talking about coffee was when he said at one point, 'I knew he'd pick me, BabyB. Cream always rises to the top.' (Ouch again.)

By chambers tea, he still couldn't contain himself and was blabbing away to everyone about it. TheVamp couldn't help having a bit of fun and said, 'I hear you bought OldSmoothie lunch today.'

'Er, that's right,' said TheCreep, looking a little shifty.

'Doesn't that breach the Code of Conduct? Making a gift for the purpose of soliciting work.'

TheCreep went a deep shade of red and stammered disingenuously, 'There was only one reason I bought lunch for OldSmoothie and that was due to the high regard I hold him in professionally.'

TheVamp came back with, 'Well, the acid test for these things is apparently the blush test. Would the gesture make the person blush? You and your little rosy cheeks just gave the game away MrCrushyBlushy.'

Before TheCreep could dig his hole any deeper, The Busker then said, 'I've always felt that the blush test was slightly unfair and weighted against those with, er,' he looked at The Creep and continued, 'a more nervous disposition. I mean, on that test, it's a carte blanche to TheVamp since she's never blushed at anything.'

TheVamp smiled at TheBusker taking it in the spirit in which it was intended. Then she turned to TheCreep and asked him, 'So what exactly did OldSmoothie say anyway?'

'He told me that I'd make a perfect little number two.'

His back straightened as he said it, as if somehow standing to attention just at the thought. There was a short silence as people tried to suppress laughter, some of them even looking a little awkward. Eventually, TheVamp couldn't resist and replied, 'His little number two. How very appropriate. Like acting as his right hand then?'

TheCreep was still struggling to get his head around the possibility that his status wasn't quite as elevated as he'd imagined and answered only with, 'Er . . .'

Which left him open to her parting shot of, 'If you'll all excuse me but I must dash for a number one.'

Friday 8 February 2008
Year 2 (week 19): Selling short

Had a call from ScandalMonger today.

'Hey, BabyB. Just thought I'd ring and tell you that Slippery and I have bought a few positions in relation to the telecom shares.'

'What do you mean, "positions"?' I asked, slightly confused.

'Sold short, that's what.'

'Oh, well that's much clearer now. Thanks for that. Have you bought some shares?' I asked, trying to clarify what on earth he was going on about.

'Not exactly. We just borrow them from the broker.'

'That's nice of him. So did *he* have to buy the shares?'

'Er, well, no, actually. He just borrowed them from someone else.'

Which all started to remind me of TheBusker's defence to a theft case where he argued it wasn't exactly stealing but instead, merely gleaning. But, hey, what do I know?

'BabyB, BabyB, you need to be a bit more financially savvy, the business you're in. To put it more simply, what we've done is made bets on the share price falling.'

Now *that* I could understand. Then he added, 'Oh, and we didn't want to leave you out of the profits that we're going to make, so we also bought a few just for you. Special like. Call it a gift. You just keep on doing your job and we'll all be in clover.'

Oh, how generous they are. At every turn they're splicing me further into little pieces. One compromise followed by another until it's impossible to back out. First there was having ScandalMonger on board in exchange for my mother's house. Now the shares. Here I am stuck between another rock and another hard place. To dob them in now would mean admitting complicity up to this point and also causing my mother to be evicted from her home. But not to do so will mean that I've stood by with full knowledge of what they're up to. I feel like the apocryphal frog who thinks that the cool water in the cooking pot is safe and when the temperature is slowly raised bit by bit, he only realises quite what sort of trouble he's in when the water's boiling and it's too late to do anything about it.

Monday 11 February 2008
Year 2 (week 20): Blagger

So today I did someone a favour. He's a good friend of mine from Oxford who I'll call Blagger. He's a banker who can never stop making bets even when he's not at work. This has often landed him in trouble and today was no exception. It all started when I took Blagger and some other friends to dinner in the Inner Temple Hall a few weeks ago. After I'd explained the rules about barristers needing to eat dinners to qualify, Blagger said, 'If it all comes down to eating dinners, then I'd make a fine barrister indeed.'

Someone then jokingly challenged him that he'd never get away with impersonating a barrister, kind of *Catch Me If You Can* style. But this is not something that you should do with Blagger. Make challenges you don't mean, that is, and Blagger immediately raised the stakes into a bet. Even though I knew better, I actually thought nothing of it until last night when Blagger rang me in a little bit of a panic. 'BabyB, I think I might be in trouble.'

'Why?'

'Well, I've only gone and convinced a solicitor girl I met in a bar that I'm not only a qualified barrister but a whiz at property law at that. Anyway, I need your help.'

'Oh.'

'And your wig and gown.'

'I see.'

'Listen, BabyB. I'll owe you one big time. But if I pull out now I'll be in so much trouble that I've really got to go through with this just to avoid being caught.'

Tell me about it. I know that feeling. But I simply replied, 'Oh.'

So I agreed to meet with him at 8 a.m. at court and to go through the case before the client arrived. Thankfully for both of us, it was a simple possession hearing and he had very little to do other than to stand up and read out a script that I had written for him, hand in a few documents and 'Yes, Your Honour', 'No, Your Honour' at the right time. I went along as his er, 'pupil', poked him in the back when it was time to stand up and had a cough for 'yes' and a sneeze for 'no'. Predictably he started getting the coughs and sneezes mixed up for a few of his answers until the impatience of the judge and the pokes in the back from me alerted him to his mistake.

Eventually he emerged from the court victorious and in a great state of jubilation. 'BabyB, I think I could get a liking for this court thing. Feels good.'

Great, I've created a monster. But worse was to come when he rang his solicitor with the result and returned to report that she was so pleased she has promised to send him more cases. Not a good thought. But in the meantime, I have asked for Blagger's help in looking a little more closely at this whole 'selling short' business.

Tuesday 12 February 2008
Year 2 (week 20): MockingBird

I was against one of Claire's good friends today. She's in the same chambers as Claire and there is only one name that springs to mind for her and that is MockingBird. You see she's as brassy a Northerner as you're ever likely to meet and calls all men 'lads' and ladies 'birds'. She makes a point of only drinking pints of beer and is a dab hand at darts by her own account. I guess in the nineties she might have been labelled a ladette but actually she's far too sophisticated for that. More like a walking, talking, ironic satire of a ladette. An upmarket Prada-inspired Bet Lynch, whose loyalty is such that she would fight to the death for her friends.

One thing's for sure, and it was clear today, you wouldn't want to mess with her or, for that matter, her mates.

'You're a complete fool, BabyB.'

She was straight to the point and we both knew what she was talking about. 'You could scour the earth for a thousand years and you'd never meet a better, or, for that matter, more beautiful woman than Claire and you know what, for some crazy reason she seems to like you.'

I didn't know what to say to her as I was completely thrown. My heart felt as though it was beating right in my stomach.

'If the world made any sense at all, our Claire would have been snapped up by a tall, dark handsome stranger and whisked away to somewhere more glamorous than life as we know it at the Bar. But we both know there are all sorts of little creases in the logic of the universe and this appears to be one of them. You're a complete and utter, one hundred per cent certifiable muppet, BabyB. You're what Jim Henson would have created if he'd ever turned his hand to this ridiculous profession of ours.'

At which she became distracted and said, 'Now there's a thought.'

Thankfully she gave up on me after that but when I arrived back from court, just to exacerbate the situation, I got an email from TopFlirt. She hasn't been in touch since our little get-together a few weeks ago and for my part I've felt completely indecisive as to what to do and in the end inertia won the day. Inertia and the fact that I can't help thinking about what Claire would think of it, something which is even more on my mind after MockingBird's little speech. Anyway, she's thrown the ball back into my court by suggesting we meet on Thursday evening. It's all very mysterious and without any further explanation whatsoever. Needless to say I'm going to go along but I'm back to worrying that it might be some sort of trap. Though after what happened between us, I find that extremely unlikely.

Wednesday 13 February 2008
Year 2 (week 20): I'm appalled ...

Following on from BusyBody's and UpTights's banter about OldSmoothie 'emerging' a few weeks ago, BusyBody was telling me this morning what it has prompted. 'Well, if he wants to emerge, I thought I'd give him a bit of a shove in the right direction. Raise his profile a little.'

'I shudder to think where this one's going.'

'Oh, you mock, BabyB, but all he needs is just a little leg up.'

'As opposed to over,' I said and then immediately regretted it given BusyBody's particular history with OldSmoothie.

She ignored the comment and continued, 'Anyway, what with all these late nights and early mornings with the baby, I've been spending a bit more time online and thought I'd try and increase his Google profile. You know, get a few more references to his name out on to the world wide web.'

'And how precisely have you done that?' I asked.

'Just leaving comments here and there. On some of the bigger news and comment websites. National newspapers, TV channels, that sort of thing.'

'Oh, and how many of these have you done so far?'

'Hmm, only a few hundred, I guess. It's a start, at least. Sets him off in the right direction.'

'And what do they say, exactly?'

'Oh, that's easy. I chatted it through with UpTights and we agreed that we want to create just the right profile to allow him to "emerge" as he likes to put it. So each comment starts with "I'm appalled" and then ends with "What I say is bring back hanging!" As for the content, well ... you can imagine.'

I certainly can and I'm wondering what OldSmoothie's reaction will be when he discovers an array of bigoted comments all made out in his name surfacing on the internet.

Thursday 14 February 2008
Year 2 (week 20): Silk purses and sows' ears

There was much chat around chambers today after the list of appointments to Queen's Counsel was announced. Apparently this is the second year in a row that UpTights has applied for silk and sadly for her, the second time that she has been rejected. OldSmoothie immediately got the knife in with the following email which he also copied to the rest of chambers:

Dear UpTights,

May I be the first to offer you my sincere condolences on your being rejected as a QC for the second time running. Whilst I'm sure that at your age rejection is something you have learnt to manage, I realise it must still come as somewhat of a blow to have it confirmed at such a high level. I hope very much that you will at least take comfort in the words of the official press release which says: 'If you have not been appointed that does not mean you are not a valued and perfectly competent advocate.'

Yours affectionately,
OldSmoothie

All of which would have been just mildly offensive on the OldSmoothie scale, were it not for the fact that the subject line of his email was labelled 'Silk purses and sows' ears'.

This was just too much for BusyBody who accosted him at chambers tea. 'You're a smug, fat, slimey and misogynistic dinosaur, OldSmoothie, who wouldn't even make it as a junior barrister these days and under the new appointments system the nearest you'd get to silk would be the collection of old girl-friends' knickers we all know you keep in the bottom drawer of your desk.'

OldSmoothie looked thrown by the knickers revelation and whilst he was still reeling she really hit him where it hurts. 'For all your pompous talk of large earnings and the high life, I have it on good authority that last year, out of the thirty-one tenants in chambers, you came precisely twenty-ninth in the list of earnings. Listen to the sweet sound of the market, OldSmoothie, and scurry on back to your golf club committees.'

She paused for effect before finishing with, 'But hey, we all know you can't polish a . . .'

She looked around the room at the eyebrows which were starting to rise, then smiled at OldSmoothie and said, 'Well let's just say, there are some things which can't be polished.'

I met up with TopFlirt last night and the first thing she said as we sat down was, 'I'm sorry, but it was a mistake, BabyB. A huge ugly mistake which I'm going to just have to live with.'

'I completely agree,' I said quite sincerely (although I have to admit to being a little put out by the word 'ugly'). The very last thing I need right now, what with problems at work and Claire very much on my mind, is that sort of complication, whatever the destabilising effect it might have on TopFirst.

After that, TopFlirt relaxed a little but still kept it pretty businesslike for the rest of the evening. Although as we parted company after the obligatory peck on the cheek she did say, 'I don't know whether it's just because you understand what I'm going through but I'd still like to see you again.'

Then she added quickly, 'As friends, of course.'

'Naturally,' I replied with a smile.

'By the way,' she continued. 'I'd watch your back at the moment. TopFirst's definitely up to something big. I think it's to do with the Moldy case but I also think it's going to involve you personally. He really doesn't like you, you know.'

You don't say.

'But what is it about this case in particular that's getting his goat?' I asked.

'No idea, BabyB. He wants to beat you obviously.'

'But what else?'

She thought about my question and then answered more thoughtfully, 'He has mentioned something about beating you to a red bag but I never asked anything more about it. Although I'm sure that as a fellow member of that venerable institution which is the Bar, with all its secret handshakes and funny walks, you'll know what it means.'

Now *that* was food for thought.

Monday 18 February 2008
Year 2 (week 21): Feral justice

Word has it in the robing rooms that there's a particular county town in which the district judges have all gone, what can only be described as, feral. Now, truth be told, there has always been the odd (in all senses of the word) one here and there and we've all known who they were. In fact, if you were advising your clients as to the likely outcomes, it was something that seriously had to be factored into the equation. One judge, for example, simply doesn't like women claimants and another hates anyone with a regional accent. But it is generally considered pretty bad luck to get one of these judges since even at their own courts they are only one out of four or five who are dishing out the justice.

Not so in this particular county town where every one of the district and deputy district judges have pretty much declared independence, *Passport to Pimlico* style. It started with the publication of their so-called 'Local Practice Directions' in which skeleton arguments and bundles of authorities were 'discouraged'. For that, read not merely 'frowned upon' but instead 'actively ignored'. Then there's the policy that 'personal injury cases are encouraged to settle' for which read 'if they don't settle, there'll be wasted costs against the lawyers'. Oh, and just the small matter of cross-examination and submissions for which the directions say, 'Judges may dispense with these if they deem it appropriate.' For this read 'We can't be bothered with you testing the evidence or going on too much so we'll just decide the cases our way thank you very much.'

Then, as if that's not enough they've even started offering oaths based on what they describe as the 'religion' of the local football club where they can all be found every other Saturday during the season. One of the judges has even started wearing the team's shirt under his judicial gown as part of what he considers to be an essential element of his dispensing of justice.

Tuesday 19 February 2008
Year 2 (week 21): London Counsel

I went to court in Yorkshire today with TheBusker who had managed to get me instructed as his junior. His opponent, who

I'll call Gruff, was an extremely patronising bully who spoke with a broad Yorkshire accent, something which it became clear he intended to wield against TheBusker in court. He introduced the case with: 'Your Honour, we are privileged today to be graced with the presence of London counsel. Not just any London counsel, either, Your Honour, for my very learned friend has even written a law book on the subject, which lies before you.'

The judge smiled back mischievously at Gruff and answered him in an equally broad accent: 'Yes, MrGruff, it is an honour indeed to have such esteemed Counsel in this humble county court.'

'Some might say, Your Honour,' continued Gruff, 'that bringing up such high-powered artillery for a case as small as this one is the proverbial sledgehammer to crack a nut. Others might say that it reflects a lack of confidence by the defendant's solicitors in their own case that they don't feel able to trust lowly and less-qualified local counsel to conduct the proceedings on their behalf.' He paused before going on. 'But all I would say, Your Honour, is that this is a great opportunity for us all to learn a little more about an area of law which most of us, who have practised in it for too many years to remember, have always taken to be governed simply by good old-fashioned, decent common sense.'

The judge was very much enjoying the grandstanding and kept giving indiscreet little chuckles in the direction of Gruff. Meanwhile, TheBusker sat through the performance as if he didn't have a care in the world. After Gruff finally sat down the judge said, 'Well, MrBusker, that was quite an introduction.'

TheBusker stood up. By way of background, the way he speaks isn't particularly identifiable by any marked accent although I've heard a note of his childhood West Country come out on occasions, particularly after a few glasses of wine, and today it came out in particular force. 'Your Honour, it is indeed a rare treat to return to the county of my birth. And when I talk of my birth I feel I must honour the suffering that my poor mother went through as she was driven several hundred miles after going into labour on the off-chance that one day I might be good enough to play for this great county at cricket – a sport at which, in the end, I'm afraid I was a great disappointment to my parents. This is a county that has not only produced the likes of Fred Trueman, Len Hutton and Brian Close but leaders in all fields. Politicians such as Wilson, Asquith and Wilberforce, explorers of the standing of Captain James Cook and Amy Johnson and writers like Ted Hughes and Alan Bennett. Indeed, Your Honour, such is the depth of their achievements that it might well be said that the men and women of this great county provide the golden thread through which the whole fabric of our nation has been woven. Yet there is a great and abiding sadness for all those such as myself who are exiled from this beautiful place and who are unable to do that which their ancestors have done before them: to breathe the fresh country air, to walk its beautiful dales and swim in its fast-flowing rivers and streams. And above all, Your Honour, to feel the warmth and sincerity of the people of this great county.'

With this TheBusker looked over at Gruff. 'The only consolation is that on those occasions when we return, we get to experience that same warmth and sincerity in the welcome we receive and it is this above all for which I offer my thanks to MrGruff.'

The judge by this point was positively beaming at TheBusker and this didn't really stop until the moment that he later delivered judgment in his favour and finished with the words, 'MrBusker forgot another great aspect of the Yorkshire character that doesn't seem to have been lost on him and that is a sharp wit and sense of humour. Whilst I can't comment on his cricketing ability, he does seem to have a great aptitude for hitting a sloppy ball exactly where it deserves to go and that's straight out of the ground.'

With which he stared pointedly at Gruff. It reminded me of that childhood fable where however hard the North wind huffed and puffed it still singularly failed to get the traveller to remove his cloak and thereby win the bet, whereas all the sun had to do was to shine in all its glory until the cloak was coaxed off through the warmth of its rays.

Wednesday 20 February 2008
Year 2 (week 21): Yes we can

I was against BusyBody in court today. Her hair was frizzier and curlier than ever which I took as a warning sign that her busyness had probably reached the manic stage of its cycle again. She was maybe getting even less sleep than usual perhaps?

'Hi, BabyB, all well I hope. I've been up since four o'clock this morning writing myself lists of goals I want to achieve.'

'Oh.'

'Yes, I've got a new life coach who specialises in doing working mothers, you know.'

'I'm sure he does,' I said, raising my eyebrows.

BusyBody was too intent on what she had to say to respond to the innuendo. 'He also showed me a speech by a new politician who's standing for President called Barack Obama. Great man, BabyB. He's going to win, you see.'

'Right.'

I didn't ask any questions since she was talking at about a thousand words a minute and I was already feeling exhausted just listening to her. So it wasn't until we got into court and she started opening her case that I quite realised the full extent of the influence of said life coach.

'Your Honour, I represent the claimant in this personal injury case. The defendant will be arguing that you cannot award damages for injury to feelings only. Your Honour, what I say to you is just one thing: yes we can. Just as Nelson Mandela walked free and saved a nation, I say yes we can. Just as the iron curtain collapsed and half a continent was liberated, I say yes we can. Just as the American people are realising that they can repent and start over, I say yes we can.'

She then paused before ending with, 'Your Honour, whatever technical, sniggly or even wriggly little legal arguments may be raised by my learned friend, I simply use three words that are already echoing around the world and waking us all up to the boundless possibility of the human spirit. Damages for injury to feelings? Your Honour, I say . . .' She paused dramatically and then, you guessed it, 'yes,' and she banged her hand on the lectern, 'we,' and again, 'can,' and this time the lectern tipped over with the force of her pounding and clattered to the floor.

Ignoring the distraction, BusyBody sat down. At that moment, wherever else in the world those three little words happened to be echoing, it can certainly be said that they were doing so around courtroom number two of Staines County Court.

Thursday 21 February 2008
Year 2 (week 21): Skateboards and sandcastles

ScandalMonger leaked a story to the press yesterday about TheMoldies suggesting that the telecom company are delaying settlement in the hope that our clients will start dying off. It's completely untrue but it didn't stop a number of newspapers covering it in lurid detail today. I guess he figures the telecom company are hardly going to sue and further stoke the fire of bad publicity.

One immediate effect of course is that the share price has plummeted. It also led to a phonecall from ScandalMonger asking for anything I might have to add to the press bandwagon. I told him that there was nothing so exciting happening in the real world.

Although perhaps that wasn't strictly true, because mid-afternoon I left chambers for an appointment with Arthur, Ethel and another Moldy friend of theirs, Alfred. Alfred at the age of eighty-one has not only taken up skateboarding, but insists on doing it along the main high street of their town, garnering a huge audience but also backing up the traffic for hundreds of yards in either direction. Arthur and Ethel had said they wanted to meet up and that it was important, and I'd therefore arrived suited and booted and with notebooks in hand. But when he opened the door to me Arthur said, 'We wanted to share a special afternoon, BabyB. You see, it's Ethel's eightieth birthday.'

I was quite thrown, and very touched that they'd thought to invite me although I realised I hadn't exactly come prepared.

'Oh don't worry, BabyB,' said Ethel, obviously sensing my discomfort. 'Arthur and I have always made a point of doing something special for someone else on each of our birthdays. Someone we considered particularly in need and for this one we both thought of you.'

I looked and felt completely confused. 'Er, well, a very happy birthday, Ethel. I feel privileged to be here. Truly privileged.'

I was stumbling.

'But why me?'

'BabyB, it's obvious to both of us that you've got a good heart. But you just need a little help raising your view from your work desk, to throw off the bowlines and look to the horizon,' said Arthur.

'To the horizon . . .' I mumbled, now even more confused.

'It was ever thus, BabyB,' said Ethel. 'Young people get so caught up in the details that they forget to see beyond.'

'Which is why we've also invited Alf along. You see, it's time you learnt to skateboard.'

'But . . .'

I could think of a thousand buts and yet they were having none of it.

'You wouldn't want to cause any aggravation, BabyB,' said Ethel. 'Not with our weak hearts and all.'

She smiled with a twinkle, which was reflected straight back from Arthur, as if they were some kind of elderly Bonnie and Clyde duo pulling a fast one on me.

'I'd go with the flow,' said Alfred with a smile.

'We've even bought you some skater clothes for the occasion,' said Arthur as he produced a bright orange jumpsuit which was more Guantanamo than skate park though by that point I was already starting to get into the spirit.

We set out for their local park and by early evening I'd not only learnt to skateboard and picked up a few cuts and bruises along the way, but I'd also really started to relax for the first time in the last couple of years. As I regretfully handed back my slightly tattered jumpsuit, Ethel handed me a glass and beamed at me. 'When you get to our age, BabyB, you realise it's not the things that lawyers set out in their witness statements and wills that stay with you. It's the little everyday experiences. The fun, the friendship . . .'

'And the love,' said Arthur, as he smiled at Ethel.

'Through the hard times especially,' she added.

'Yes, don't make the same mistakes as me, BabyB,' said Arthur somewhat obliquely. Then he raised his glass and said, 'To the little, nameless, unremembered acts of kindness and of love.'

It made me think of Claire. We clinked glasses and Ethel said with a proud look at Arthur, 'It's Wordsworth, you know.'

After we'd finished our drinks and cake I carried out the glasses and plates for Ethel and she followed me into the kitchen. As we left Arthur and Alfred in the sitting room Ethel said, 'I lost him for a whole twenty years, BabyB. Whilst the children were growing up. Work, work and more work. Always in the name of putting food on the table. Can't tell you how much he regrets it now.'

Back home in the evening, as I climbed stiffly into the bath, I found myself suddenly recalling a beach holiday I'd had with my parents when I was a small child when they were still together. We had spent a day building sandcastles and laughing uncontrollably as we each tried to construct higher and higher castles in a kind of seaside version of Jenga. It was so fleeting that it was more like a feeling than a memory but it has lingered with me. Yet however hard I try to really remember the details of that day, or indeed the rest of that holiday, I'm only left with a shadow of that small moment.

Friday 22 February 2008
Year 2 (week 21): Regrets

My birthday today and OldRuin very kindly took me out for a slap-up lunch to celebrate with his favourite meal: roast beef at Simpson's on the Strand.

As we leaned back in our chairs, contentedly full, he gave me a searching look. 'Tell me how you are. How you really are,' he emphasised.

'Full of fear and regret, if I'm honest,' I answered, looking away slightly as I did so.

Then I added, 'Fear of failure, I guess. Fear of being found out for being a complete fraud. I don't know. It feels like I'm always running. Maybe that's just how it's going to be.'

'And regret?' asked OldRuin.

'That I ever met TheBoss. That I stood by as my mother racked up ruinous amounts of debt and . . .' I paused. 'Claire. We've definitely drifted apart in the last few of months.'

'Such a lovely young lady, BabyB. Why is that?'

'She says she needs to give me a little space to grow and I guess I haven't challenged that.'

'Maybe she's right. Even when plants live side by side they always struggle to grow if one gets stuck in the shadow of the other.'

I didn't answer for a little while and then I decided to open up further. 'I had the most wonderful experience yesterday, OldRuin. Arthur and Ethel arranged for me to go skateboarding.'

'I see.' He raised his eyebrows with amusement.

I smiled back and said, 'The thing is. For the first time in I don't know how long I felt, well, free. Then last night I had the most vivid dream in which my mum and dad were together and we were all on a beach. I think it came from something I remembered for the first time in a long while yesterday. In the dream we were each building sandcastles and laughing and then suddenly the tide started to come in. At first we carried on laughing, thinking it would never reach as far as our castles. But then slowly, inevitably, it crept forward. My parents gave up and left me to it and I started furiously digging a moat and building huge walls made of sand. But of course they made no difference and eventually as the tide surged I tried to lift the sandcastles up with my hands. Then, just as soon as I thought I'd saved them they started to pass through my fingers and I woke up in a cold sweat.'

'Like time itself,' murmured OldRuin.

We looked at each other in silence for a little while and then he said, 'Believe it or not, BabyB, I used to be scared of so many things. Most of all that something terrible would happen to my wife.'

I looked at him and his voice dropped. 'Then the worst happened and she was taken from me. There was nothing left to fear but I found that if I wasn't careful, my fear was sometimes almost entirely replaced by regret. Regret at the time we spent apart.'

OldRuin looked really sad now and bowed his head a little. 'Regret at not being with her when she passed away. Despite my protestations, she'd insisted I go off to court that morning. Maybe she knew and wanted to protect me. I don't know. But when I arrived home in the late afternoon I found her. At peace.'

Then he looked back up at me. 'So who am I to say anything?'

He raised his eyes upwards and looked slightly wistful. 'The other day I discovered a note she had written to me many years ago. I'd never seen it before. She was always doing that. Writing love letters and then hiding them in silly places so that I'd find them, sometimes years later. Her "little love bombs into the future" she called them. She used to say they reminded her of the children's torn up letter in *Mary Poppins* which magically survived even the fire. Well, I found one of these sitting on top of a book from which we used to read to each other when we were courting. Charles Kingsley actually. But what has lingered with me in the last few days, even beyond the beautiful words of her letter, was the dust that had gathered on top of the book. Plain household dust. Which made me so terribly sad. The weight of time. Paths we never trod.'

I saw him suddenly light up, whilst at the same time his eyes became moist, as if he had been through some kind of catharsis. 'But, BabyB, that's just it. It's the sadness and regret that carve out the depth of your soul.'

He paused again. 'My old college's motto was *Garde ta foy*, BabyB, which is apparently old French for "Keep your faith", though I have to admit that as students the alternative translation of "Watch your liver" always seemed more appropriate. Keep your faith, BabyB, and cherish those regrets. They're who you are and who you want to be.'

Monday 25 February 2008
Year 2 (week 22): Moldy moves

We have reached an agreement, of sorts, in the Moldy litigation, which could lead to some fireworks in the next couple of months. It happened at a case management conference today, which was unusually low key given that UpTights and OldSmoothie were facing each other down. As OldSmoothie and myself arrived he suddenly stopped talking. UpTights was there with TopFirst and they both watched us approach. Then like some sort of old-fashioned dance, OldSmoothie approached UpTights and asked if she might like to have a chat with him at the other end of the corridor. She nodded without anything more and followed behind as he led the way.

TopFirst and I ignored each other as we watched them discuss matters in what looked like a peculiarly friendly way. Then they returned and OldSmoothie said with a big smile, 'All agreed.'

TopFirst and I stood there looking incredulous. One minute they're at each other's throats and the next they're the best of friends. Anyway, that was an end to even the possibility of any fights today and we all marched into the small courtroom and let OldSmoothie tell the Master what had been agreed. Basically, there will be a handful of cases that will proceed relatively quickly and with only three experts on either side. Whilst they won't strictly be formal test cases, they could end up being pretty determinative of the end outcome. OldSmoothie was obviously delighted with this as it means he will have to do very little work and then if all the others settle he'll probably somehow finagle a fee for each one.

However, I think the main reason the telecom company were up for this was that they are super-confident of winning and want to reassure their shareholders with a quick victory. Though I imagine another reason they were happy to agree to such expedition is that they think they control two of the cases going forward. So now all the opposing experts (neurological, psychiatric and telecom) will be chatting with their opposite number in the next week and after that it'll be set down for trial.

Needless to say that no sooner had the plan for trial been agreed than BigMouth the MP popped up on the evening news discussing the 'crusade for justice' that he was leading against the big bad telecom company on behalf of his constituents. This, despite the fact we haven't even heard from him in over two months.

Tuesday 26 February 2008
Year 2 (week 22): In your dreams

'I hate this job,' said OldSmoothie at chambers tea today. 'Seems a far cry from my childhood dreams of becoming rich and then going into politics and becoming even richer.'

'Such an idealistic youth you must have been,' said BusyBody. 'Though I have to admit that running personal injury claims is hardly the civil liberty campaigner I saw myself as either.'

'Oh, come on,' said TheBusker. 'It's not that bad. Though granted, I'd take being a novelist or maybe a professional surfer given the choice.'

'I just wanted to be captain of the England football team,' I admitted with a smile. 'Though unfortunately that was, if you can believe it, even more competitive than trying to be a barrister.'

'All I wanted to be when I was a child was a vet,' said UpTights.

Everyone looked at her with incredulity and her face stretched into a smile as she responded, 'Though as you can imagine, fainting at the sight of blood and the fact that I hate all animals except cats proved to be insurmountable obstacles.'

Then OldRuin came forward and said quietly, 'I know it might sound a little boring, but all I wanted to be was a barrister. Not a loud high-flying one or anything like that. Just a comfortably off one with a practice that could keep my family and bring me a few good friends along the way.'

That was enough to silence any more of our whingeing.

Wednesday 27 February 2008
Year 2 (week 22): On guard

Well tomorrow I'm against TopFirst in the case that was adjourned last month, and I reckon this probably has something to do with the fact that when I opened my post this morning I found 'final bills' for my gas, electricity, telephone and council tax. Someone has clearly rung up all these firms and told them I'm moving out. You'd think that they'd have needed my own personal say so and a bit of serious ID to do this, but after spending the whole morning on the telephone untangling it all, the companies confirmed that all they need is for notice to be given over the phone. Incredible. And this was all made even more difficult by the fact that I had to keep explaining why it was my name on the bills when my mother owned the house. Let's just say it was not a good morning.

Anyway, why would I possibly think that this was down to TopFirst? Could it have anything to do with the fact that come late afternoon, when I finally got the chance to open my papers for tomorrow's case, I discovered that this time it's him who has made a last-minute application for an adjournment. He's quoting all sorts of law and he blatantly wanted to keep me out of the library to check through it all for as long as possible today.

So now I have a long night ahead of me.

Thursday 28 February 2008
Year 2 (week 22): Get out of jail free card

After finally getting to bed around 2 a.m., I was then woken up at about 4 a.m. by a minicab that had parked outside my house with its music blaring at full volume. Then the driver rang my doorbell and shouted, 'Minicab for Mr BabyBarista.' Eventually I had to get up and explain that I hadn't ordered a minicab and that I could only imagine it was some sort of prank. Of course, this didn't go down at all well with the driver and finally, in order to keep the noise down, I paid him some cash to go away.

So by the time I got to court, TopFirst's little tactic of trying to unsettle me had, I'm afraid to say, succeeded. When we met, I said, 'Pretty low down and petty, TopFirst. Haven't you anything a little more stylish to throw at me?'

'I don't know what you're talking about, BabyB. Let's just stick to the case, shall we.'

The substance of which was that out of the blue, TopFirst had produced an expert's report that his client, who crashed straight into the back of our client's car, was suffering from what lawyers call 'automatism'. Or to put it another way, a Get Out of Jail Free card. Simply, the client has a huge no-claims bonus riding on the outcome and the insurance company suggests that maybe he suffered a 'blackout'? 'You know, come to think of it, maybe I did.' Then off they trot, get an expert to say, 'Guess what? I think your old client over there suffered a blackout,' and hey presto, my badly injured client gets nothing. Tough luck and all but blackouts just don't count. No one's fault. Just one of those things. Even if it wasn't a real blackout. Just how it works.

Well, I wasn't having any of it, particularly as I'd heard that this specific insurer had been taking this 'tactic' on quite a few cases recently. Not that I don't accept that they'd been arguing the blackout excuse all along. It's just that now they were suddenly producing a brand spanking new expert who wasn't umming and aahing as most experts do, but was instead categorically saying it was automatism and that he was the best expert in the world, ever. So TopFirst now wanted an adjournment in order to call his new expert and he gave all sorts of spurious arguments as to why.

But then, despite all of this, I have to admit that my client is still AWOL. Not that I plan to tell TopFirst this. So after much to-ing and fro-ing in the negotiations I eventually relented on the basis that he pay all of my costs and agreed to another adjournment.

I just hope my client eventually turns up.

CHAPTER 6
March: WhistleBlower

Monday 3 March 2008
Year 2 (week 23): WhistleBlower

Received a curious letter today relating to TheMoldy litigation. Hand-delivered to chambers. It came from someone working within the telecom company we're suing and stated among other things that, 'If you want to know exactly what the company knows about the detrimental health effects of their own higher-powered mobile signals, particularly on the elderly, then I suggest we meet.'

The proposed meeting place was the top of Chancery Lane and the date was tonight. To be absolutely frank (HeadofChambers would approve of my choice of words), without some sort of whistleblower evidence our case is pretty high risk at the moment so it'll be interesting to see what he or she has to offer. I mentioned it to Slippery who sounded excited I think, as much by the conspiratorial manner of the approach as by the potential content. So according to the instructions I'll be looking out for a man carrying a red umbrella at the top of Chancery Lane this evening.

Well, despite the fact that I was beginning to feel a little sceptical the more I thought about it, WhistleBlower did actually turn up last night. Although when I arrived at Chancery Lane at 7 p.m. as agreed, I saw no one. Then, just to add to the whole sense of intrigue, someone pulled down the window of a black cab and shouted to me to get in. There was no red umbrella and *she* was certainly not a man, but I figured she must be who I was supposed to meet because who else would possibly be looking for me there at that particular time? Once in, I got my first chance to see who exactly this WhistleBlower was. She was probably in her late forties and looked particularly stressed, which I guess added a whiff of authenticity to the proceedings.

'I'm afraid I can't give you my name,' she said, after I'd shaken her hand and introduced myself, feeling peculiarly English and formal.

'I do understand,' I replied. 'But why have you contacted me?'

'I simply won't be able to live with myself unless I hand this information to someone involved in the case.' She sighed. 'You see, my mother has Alzheimer's and if this mobile phone technology is in any way causing even a small amount of the same type of suffering to anyone else and their family, then I think people should know.'

'Well, quite,' I replied. 'That's the whole point of our case. But what information is it that you have exactly?'

'I have this,' with which she produced what I was slightly disappointed to note was a white, rather than a brown, envelope. Brown envelopes being de rigueur for these kinds of situation, or so I thought.

I took it and then pressed a little further. 'Will the contents make sense to someone who doesn't work for the company?'

'They should do,' she replied. 'But here. If you really don't get it, you can contact me on this email address.' She handed me a piece of paper with an anonymous email address printed on it.

She then stopped the cab and I was put back on to the street, more than a little thrown by the whole weird nature of the meeting. After that, I had to go to an Inner Temple dinner followed by a case this morning and so I haven't yet had a chance to read the papers she gave me. Slippery has been hounding me on the phone all day and we've agreed to meet this evening to go through the contents over a drink.

Wednesday 5 March 2008
Year 2 (week 23): Bombshell

After meeting up with Slippery and getting to grips with WhistleBlower's material, and then staying up half the night sifting through it in more detail, I really do think we might be getting somewhere. She's basically given us a bunch of accounts that show payments to a number of companies around the world. In themselves they wouldn't have meant a great deal were it not for a memo that accompanied them which suggested that these monies were ultimately reaching certain supposedly independent experts who have completed various supposedly independent reports on the safety of their particular mobile masts. Worse than that, there is another memo that explains how one of these experts had originally submitted a report suggesting that the technology was dangerous, only to 'change his mind' on the issue after the payments were made.

As you can imagine if I was able to prove any of this then it would be a bombshell. Not only would it show that the telecom company were potentially bribing the experts but it would also show that they were aware of the possible dangers of the technology and failing to warn people about it.

With the trial imminent and OldSmoothie approaching matters in his usual languid way, I've now got to track down further evidence to back up Whistleblower's claims and so I have enlisted the help of TheBoss (I know that Claire would disapprove, but needs must is what I'm telling myself). I've also got to consider how I would then use this evidence in the case itself.

Thursday 6 March 2008
Year 2 (week 23): Spending a penny

With the new evidence from WhistleBlower and the cases starting to get themselves into order, today was the day we needed to get everyone together for a case conference with two of the main

Moldy clients we think are clean: the delightful Arthur and Ethel. In other words clients who we at least hope don't have any connections with the other side. That meant that OldSmoothie, myself and TheVamp – representing the Bar – and SlipperySlope, NurserySlope, ClichéClanger and four other people – representing the other half of the profession – were all in the same room with our clients. That made ten lawyers billing out an average of perhaps £400 an hour which brought the total bill to some £4,000 an hour. Oh, and when you add VAT and then a 100 per cent uplift if we win the case, the costs were not far short of ten grand an hour. Or as Slippery pointed out this morning as we waited for the clients, 'That's more than one hundred and fifty pounds a minute. Time to make hay, BabyB! Chat about the weather: one grand. Football, another. Controversial celebrity topics should bring double. Oh, and don't forget to pause and enjoy the most expensive coffee and biscuits on the planet.'

Bearing all that in mind, I felt pretty guilty at the end of the conference when the effects of last night's curry meant I needed to slip out to the loo. I deliberately departed discreetly since I knew I might be, as they say, some time. And when I eventually emerged, around half an hour later, to find the whole conference waiting for me, I was mortified.

'I hope you don't mind that we waited whilst you spent a penny,' said Ethel. 'I just wanted to thank you personally for all your hard work'.

Which led to much guffawing after they left.

'Spending a penny,' chuckled SlipperySlope.

'More like half a million pennies,' said OldSmoothie.

Friday 7 March 2008
Year 2 (week 23): Paper trail

Had a meeting with TheBoss today. He's been researching the issues raised by the documents that WhistleBlower handed over.

'With the help of a few backhanders, I've already managed to complete the paper trail back to a couple of the experts. Should be enough to cross-examine on at least,' he said.

'And what about the original experts' report, the one that said that the effects of the masts *are* damaging?'

'No sign of it yet.'

This was pretty crucial and we both paused. Then he said, 'The person who would really be able to help is WhistleBlower herself. I haven't managed to track her down yet but I'm going to give it a try via the email she gave you.'

Monday 10 March 2008
Year 2 (week 24): OldWorrier

Boy oh boy, if you thought Worrier sounded exhausting, she's got nothing on my opponent today who I'll call OldWorrier. He was about sixty and said he'd been practising for about fifteen years. I found this out when he first called me up last week 'to discuss the case'. Well, given that it was a standard car case worth all of around £2,000 I certainly didn't expect to see the papers until late afternoon the day before and that would be if I was lucky. I told him this and he seemed much put out and then went on to lecture me about the merits of his own case for about an hour, constantly asking me what I thought. Well, what I thought was that he sounded more like a litigant in person than a barrister and so I looked him up and discovered that he was in fact a 'head of chambers'. This seemed even more peculiar until I then found out that he was the only member of this chambers and that they appeared to be run from his bedsit in Brockley.

This was all a bit odd, but nothing like as strange as his performance in court. You know, it's a peculiar thing about the Bar that we are rarely assessed in court by anyone other than our opponents and the judge. Most of the time this doesn't matter, but on occasions such as today you realise that it can allow the odd rogue to slip through the net. For neither OldWorrier nor his client seemed in the slightest bit conscious of the fact that he lost an easy case due to complete and utter incompetence. Without boring you with the facts, if he'd asked my client even the most basic of questions he would have discovered that our case was hopeless. Instead he simply harangued him with his terrible arguments. Even the judge was biting his lip in embarrassment. But you see, unless the client realises his barrister's hopeless, no one else is going to report him and so OldWorrier will have collected his brief fee and moved on to his next unknowing victim.

As lawyers would be the first to tell you: buyer beware!

Tuesday 11 March 2008
Year 2 (week 24): Local justice

I've often heard about a certain eccentric magistrate who doles out his own form of justice through imaginative forms of community service based mainly around the courthouse. But until this afternoon I'd never seen it first hand. As I approached the court building, I saw three young men in hoodies climbing ladders perched against the wall and asked the security guard at the entrance what was going on.

'Oh they're just a couple of His Worship's new window cleaners,' came back the answer.

Then as I entered the building itself, I saw three more hoodies cleaning the floor. I looked back at the security guard as if to repeat my question and he raised his eyebrows with a knowing smile and nodded as if to say, 'Three more of His Worship's cleaners.' As I entered the robing room, another hoodie asked if he could take my coat and after I passed it to him a little suspiciously, he took it and put it on the stand. Then another appeared out of nowhere and asked if I'd like a cup of coffee or tea before I made my appearance. Two more of His Worship's workers, no doubt.

This was all before I entered the courtroom itself, which was quite a spectacle. There were two hoodies in each of the four corners of the room, each standing stock still with their hands on their heads. They were clearly naughty boys who had been put in their respective naughty corners. But best of all were the two young men in hoodies standing on either side of the stipendiary magistrate, wielding huge bamboo fans, as well as another who was holding a silver platter with a jug full of iced water ready to refill his glass. Now let me be clear: it was a warm day for March at least and what's more, courtrooms are notoriously stuffy places at the best of times (in all senses of the word). But even so, it left him looking like a strange cross between a Roman emperor, a kind of Mr Kurz figure lazing around in the jungle bellowing out orders to the locals and Ricky Gervais bossing around his minions in *The Office*.

I was there with TheVamp and we were representing two of our Moldy clients in further prosecutions following on from their alleged anti-social behaviour. I say alleged but actually both of our clients admitted everything that was being put to them. In TheVamp's case that meant that eighty-two-year-old Tony admitted to regularly playing his electric guitar at full volume in his back garden at 3 a.m. In my case, the sprightly seventy-nine-year-old Dora was trying to sign people up on the main street in the middle of the day to help her undertake a heist on one of the local banks (though she'd never actually got around to undertaking the audacious robbery itself).

When TheVamp and I went to meet our clients, they were sitting with Arthur and Ethel. Ethel gave me a beaming smile whilst Arthur gave me a double thumbs up and a mischievous grin. They looked particularly animated and as we approached Arthur said, 'We'd like to start putting our bad behaviour to good use if that's OK, BabyB?'

Tony and Dora both nodded as if this was something that had already been discussed between themselves.

'What were you thinking?' I asked.

'Well, we want to be ordered to become litter-picking martyrs if that's alright with you, BabyB?' said my client Dora. 'If we're going to have to take any form of punishment then we might as well do something useful.'

Much nodding of old heads and then Arthur produced two luminous gillets for our clients to wear. One was emblazoned with 'Tony the Trash' and the other with 'Dora the Dustwoman'. They all smiled and TheVamp shrugged as if to say, 'no problem' on her account. So it was that the first of the Moldy Martyrs Litter-Picking Collective was born, with the magistrate ordering that they start with the courthouse and grounds and then move on to the high street after that.

Wednesday 12 March 2008
Year 2 (week 24): OldFilth

My opponent opened his case today with the following words, 'This is an appeal from a judgment of His Honour Judge . . .'

I won't mention his real name but suffice it to say that his nickname is OldFilth and that it has nothing to do with 'failing in London and trying Hong Kong'. It arises instead from the fact that he spends more time chasing the fairer sex than he does considering his cases. Such is his reputation that there are, allegedly, only three female QCs at the family law Bar who have not at least been propositioned by him in one form or another (a survey was once unofficially carried out at a Family Law Bar Association drinks party). 'Viagravation' they call it apparently. Anyway, let's just say that his judgments are not held in the highest regard and as soon as the judge heard that it was an appeal from one of OldFilth's cases, he was immediately able to throw out the apocryphal line, 'Yes, yes, and what are the other grounds of appeal?'

Thursday 13 March 2008
Year 2 (week 24): Middle-aged crumpet

OldSmoothie finally discovered a couple of days ago that BusyBody has been leaving reactionary comments on his behalf all over the internet. According to a Google search of his name, it's pretty clear that there have now been well over six hundred such comments and the vast majority seem to have ignited some row or other on the particular newspaper or blog where they were planted.

In order to counter this, OldSmoothie has decided to take offline measures, which might be seen by some as a tad heavy-handed. He has basically employed someone at SlipperySlope's firm of solicitors to write to all the various website owners threatening them with, among other things, defamation. Unfortunately for him, whilst this has meant that the original comments have been swiftly removed, the threats themselves have resulted in the blogs and newspaper sites being swamped with ten times as many nasty posts about OldSmoothie than BusyBody could ever have invented. But worse than this is the fact that a couple of the newspapers have retaliated to the intimidatory tactics by starting to ask around about OldSmoothie's private life. I know this not only because ScandalMonger tipped me off immediately but also because this morning I had to appear on behalf of OldSmoothie seeking an injunction to stop the printing of a story of which even the late Alan Clark MP would have been proud. Whilst the injunction was granted today, I doubt very much that a full hearing will be so successful.

But then, as HeadClerk said after the hearing, 'All publicity is good publicity, BabyBarista. It's just what you make of it that counts. We'll simply bill him as the thinking, er, middle-aged woman's bit of crumpet and get him running, well, strolling at least, around the divorce courts.'

Eek.

Friday 14 March 2008
Year 2 (week 24): Red bags and horse hair

I've been thinking about what TopFlirt meant when she said that TopFirst is obsessed with beating me to a red bag. Despite the fact that 'RedBag' is OldSmoothie's nickname for a high-profile, left-wing female judge, I can only assume that TopFlirt is referring to the red brief bag that is awarded to a junior barrister by a leader in their case if they do a particularly fine job. As beginners we both have little blue bags to carry our robes around in and it's true to say that TopFirst and I did have a passing conversation during pupillage about who would be the first of our generation to be awarded a prestigious red bag. But to hear that he's got a bee in his little horsehair wig about it is not only a curiosity but also something upon which I might be able to capitalise. For one thing, I'll just have to make sure that I beat him to it. But beyond that I need to think how I can use this against him.

Monday 17 March 2008
Year 2 (week 25): Liar, lawyer

Attended my first pupillage interview last night as the newest member of the pupillage committee. What struck me most was the enormous irony in the fact that for a profession that prides itself on honesty and integrity, its entrance interview is designed to judge people on how well they lie. The rubbish that was being spouted by the interviewees last night was incredible, and when I went for a drink with The Vamp afterwards we speculated on what the answers might have been had any of the candidates actually told the truth. Here's a few of the less rude ones we came up with:

Why the Bar?
'To become a fat cat part-timer like the rest of you.'

Why law?
'Because I just love twisting the truth and taking technical points.'

Why this chambers?
'Because you were stupid enough to offer me an interview.'

Why personal injury?
'Because it's easy and well, I like money.'

Why employment law?
'Because litigants in person are always easier to beat.'

Why landlaw and tenant?
'Because I'll enjoy doing-over impoverished tenants and hey, it's one better even than being a bailiff. Why, it's living the dream.'

According to The Vamp, the strangest question she was asked at interview was, 'What's your favourite Abba song?' Apparently she replied, 'Take A Chance On Me', followed closely by 'Money, Money, Money'. When they later offered her a pupillage she sent a note of reply stating, 'Thank you for your offer, which I am delighted to reject on the basis both of your poor choice of questions and your even worse taste in music.' She then added at the end, 'P.S. I forgot to mention: "The Winner Takes It All".'

As we talked increasing amounts of nonsense, I noticed Claire in the far corner of the bar. She was with another guy and when she saw me she smiled and gave a quick wave but then looked embarrassed and turned back to her conversation. The Vamp who has never been a fan of Claire immediately picked up on this and said, 'Hmm, Claire with an extremely handsome mystery man. Hasn't taken her long to move on I see.'

I've no idea whether she was actually aware that we'd argued, nor whether she really knew anything about the man Claire was having a drink with. I've seen him around at court but all I know is that he's a tenant in her chambers and about five years older than her. A few minutes later Claire and her friend got up to leave and she flushed as she passed our table but politely said 'hello' to us.

'Nice shoes,' said The Vamp, admiring Claire's shiny pair of high heels.

'Oh, thank you,' said Claire, looking even more embarrassed. 'They were a gift.'

With which she left and The Vamp said to me, 'Christian Louboutin, BabyB. Doesn't come any better. She's certainly taken a step up in the world.'

For my part I was thrown by, of all things, the smell of Claire's perfume which seemed to trigger a deep longing for her company. I do miss her.

Tuesday 18 March 2008
Year 2 (week 25): Take the lot

I am so very glad I'm not a solicitor. I had to spend the whole day at SlipperySlope's firm today trying to get the Moldy cases into some form of order. All in, I'd say solicitors probably put in twice as many hours as us barristers. That's not to say that we don't work hard. It's just that solicitors don't seem to get any faffing time. They're constantly being judged by how many hours they've billed.

Not that this seems to worry the Slope family who sometimes manage to bill more hours than there are in a day. Today was a good example. As I arrived, NurserySlope was talking to Slippery. 'I have the most annoying client in the world. He has minor brain damage which has turned him into a complete obsessive. To make it worse, ever since I mentioned he could claim for various types of care to help him with his injuries he's been sending me hundreds of different emails with links to different crazy products he says he would like. I must have had three hundred just last night.'

'That's sounds like the perfect client to me,' replied Slippery. 'Take the lot is what I say. One by one.'

'What do you mean?'

'Come on, Nursery. You should have learnt by now. Each email counts as a unit. That means ten emails make an hour. A hundred emails, ten hours.'

'Three hundred emails making . . . thirty hours.'

'Precisely.'

'Even if I don't read them.'

'Now you're getting it.'

Slippery smiled and then looked over at me and said, 'Time sheets never sleep, BabyB. I say show me the cash. Don't you agree?'

This even left Nursery wincing slightly as she left the office.

Wednesday 19 March 2008
Year 2 (week 25): BearMarket

So far TheBoss hasn't managed to track down the main telecoms expert who'd allegedly taken a bribe to change his report and without that killer blow ScandalMonger has been badgering me for a couple of weeks to be able to take what we've got public. In the end TheBoss handed over the documents to him. Whilst I wasn't keen to encourage him to go ahead, I have to admit that adding a bit of publicity to the mix may well help us force the telecom company into settling just to get rid of us.

Oh, and as far as ScandalMonger is concerned, this also has the added advantage of driving down the telecom company's share price even further – which is handy for him, since the period of the bet he made when he sold short is about to expire. But with ScandalMonger all set to leak the documents, and with OldSmoothie away on one of his many holidays and completely out of contact, I have had to make the decision to ask for an emergency application for the documents we *do* have so far to be admitted to the case, and this should be heard next week.

I arrived at court today and waited for two hours with my client only to be told by the usher that the judge did not have time to hear us due to [ahem] 'an emergency application'. I'm sure this had nothing to do with the fact that, as the usher let slip, he wants to get away for the Easter weekend. Of course not. So we trotted into court and had a chat with the judge as to when the case might next be listed. For my own part, I have to admit that I was rather pleased, since it meant that I avoided getting smashed around the courtroom for a whole day on a very weak case that I was fighting for an insurance company, and I still got paid my full fee. My opponent on the other hand, who was working on a no win, no fee basis, was getting just a little bit agitated and when the judge asked when might be the next convenient day for counsel and the parties (in that order), without thinking it through my opponent immediately jumped in with, 'Your Honour, might it not be possible just to hear the case tomorrow?'

The judge looked very surprised at the comment and then a hint of a smile followed. 'Young man,' he said, 'the last judge to sit on the day after Maundy Thursday was Pontius Pilate. I do not intend to follow his lead here in London.'

Had our application hearing today for the extra evidence in the Moldy litigation to be admitted. TopFirst and UpTights were there but unfortunately OldSmoothie was still on holiday abroad and so I had to step in. It was quite nerve-wracking to be against UpTights for the first time, particularly when she greeted me with, 'I assume you know what you're getting into, BabyB?'

But I simply presented the documents to the judge and said that it would be impossible to have a fair trial without them. UpTights refused to comment on the documents themselves, relying on the lateness of the application and saying that investigations still needed to be made. Eventually the judge did allow the documents in but he has adjourned the trial for a few more weeks. As we left, UpTights smirked at me and whispered, 'I hope you've passed this by OldSmoothie. For your own sake.'

Wednesday 26 March 2008
Year 2 (week 26): Trouble

Boy oh boy, was I in trouble today. OldSmoothie telephoned me in chambers wanting to know what had been going on in the case. I updated him about the extra evidence.

'You what? You've put in some random documents that some random person randomly gave you in the back of a random cab?'

'Well, it wasn't quite that bad,' I answered.

'Which bit did I get wrong?' he demanded sarcastically.

'Well, the alternative was to turn a blind eye to what may be devastating evidence for the other side, and it's not as if we've got much of a case without it.'

Eventually he calmed down but only to the extent that his parting words on the subject were, 'Well I just hope for your sake this evidence comes up trumps because otherwise I wouldn't like to think of the wasted costs you might have to pay the other side.'

What I didn't tell OldSmoothie was that this week ScandalMonger has been slowly leaking the various bits of evidence to the press. He's told me that tomorrow he'll be releasing the damning memo in which the telecom company, in effect, admits that they know their high-powered mobile signal is dangerous.

Just in time for his share-selling deadline on Friday.

Thursday 27 March 2008
Year 2 (week 26): Warning

Eight o'clock this morning and the memo was faxed from an anonymous contact of ScandalMonger's to all the major news agencies. OK, it wasn't headline stuff in itself but it was sufficient to make it newsworthy in the city and since the markets opened, the telecom company's shares have fallen by over 60 per cent. This is on top of a steady decline over the last couple of months.

By three o'clock this afternoon, I had a call from TopFirst. 'It's one thing messing with me, BabyB, and don't think you've heard the end of that. But for your information, you've just entered a whole new league, taking on a multi-billion-pound company in this way. After what I've heard from them today, all I'll say is that I wouldn't want to be in your pathetic little shoes.'

'I don't know what you mean,' I answered.

'Leaking like a sieve, BabyB.'

'If you're talking about the news story today, I can only assume that any leak as you call it came from someone in the company itself. It's certainly nothing to do with me.'

'Yeah, right. You forget: I know how you work.'

He then added as an aside, 'I wouldn't be surprised if you even had a financial angle off the back of it.'

This was perhaps the most worrying part of the conversation since tomorrow ScandalMonger is set to make a lot of money.

Friday 28 March 2008
Year 2 (week 26): Sweet FSA

Well, today was the big day for ScandalMonger's bet on the telecom company's shares. Midday to be precise, and at one minute past I received a telephone call from him saying, 'Congratulations, BabyB. You and I are now considerably richer than we were one minute ago. You just tell me where you want me to send your profits and it'll be done.'

ScandalMonger doesn't seem to have considered the fact that we are now all at risk of being reported to the Financial Services Authority for insider dealing, market manipulation or some other such financial crime. But it's certainly a worry for me. All I can hope is that TopFirst or the company itself will find ScandalMonger's paper trail too difficult to unravel. Although the fact that he was reckless enough to phone me at perhaps the most dangerous stage of the whole enterprise does not instil me with enormous amounts of confidence. In any event, I asked him to transfer any money to my friend Blagger on the basis that it was probably better to have a little control over what was going on than none at all. I'd already talked about this possibility with Blagger and we had both agreed that that way at least I would have someone I could trust to keep it at arm's length from me. It will also buy me some time to try and work out exactly what to do with the money without incriminating myself further.

The big news today was that I was informed of a complaint that has been made against me by guess who? A certain Mr TopFirst. He alleges that I am part of a conspiracy to commit illegal insider trading by aiding and abetting the selling short on shares in the telecom company. The strange thing is that rather than making the complaint to the Financial Services Authority, he instead reported it to the Bar Standards Board. My initial thoughts are that he has done this because he currently lacks sufficient evidence to get a conviction and because he hopes he might frighten me out of the woodwork with a professional complaint. I simply wrote back to the Bar Standards Board saying that it was the inappropriate forum to decide such a serious allegation. They may well get back to me asking whether I in fact deny what is being said or not, something I would prefer to avoid answering when I remain unsure as to what evidence TopFirst has in his possession.

Meanwhile, I will have to try and somehow force TopFirst to withdraw this complaint. Both he and I know full well that if the allegation were proved and it eventually did go to the FSA, it would be porridge for BabyBarista. As if this weren't enough, my other concern is that knowing TopFirst as I do, I doubt very much that this is exclusively driven by malice and revenge. I suspect it is also a ploy to distract me from whatever else he might be up to in the Moldy litigation.

CHAPTER 7
APRIL: GOTCHA!

Tuesday 1 April 2008
Year 2 (week 27): Pupil fodder

It's one year since I did my first case in court and as I sized up my opponent this morning I considered how appropriate it was that April Fools' Day should be the date set for the official release of the pupils into the wild. April, the cruellest month, delivering this one fresh from his pupilmaster's cocoon complete with sparkling white bands, unused wig and ramrod straight back, as if his mother was somehow at his shoulder reminding him not to slouch.

Actually I say pupilmaster but in fact it's *pupilmistress* because I happen to know who will be controlling his life for the next six months. My opponent was none other than the timid will-o'-the-wisp, FraGiles. Today the pupil who can't stop his voice from rising like a question whenever he opens his mouth had double reason to be afraid since not only was it his first day in court but he'd then be returning back to chambers to the loving care and supervision of UpTights.

I sympathised with him on both these counts but he seemed oblivious to anything I said today as he was so nervous he had switched into a kind of autopilot mode. Despite it being a small claim, he approached me carrying not only two huge volumes on court procedure but also a skeleton argument and a three-inch-thick bundle of authorities on car cases. He drew breath before asking, 'Do you accept that a car driver owes a common law duty of care to another when driving on one of Her Majesty's highways?'

'Er . . .'

'And do you accept that breaches of the Highway Code constitute negligence?'

'Er . . .'

He'd clearly been advised to be forceful since despite the obvious and wholly uncontroversial points he was making, I couldn't get a word in edgeways as he pretty much recited his skeleton at me. Then I spotted SlipperySlope, who was obviously here on a different case, across the other side of the waiting room, and I made my escape from FraGiles. Slippery was clearly in high spirits and as I approached he put his hands on his hips and had his chest pushed out theatrically as he declared, 'You smell that? Do you smell that? Pupils, BabyB. Nothing else in the world smells like that.' He paused and then added, 'I love the smell of pupils in the morning.'

'Er . . .'

'Smells like . . . victory.'

And in my case this turned out to be right. As I was leaving court, I noticed Claire talking to another barrister and realised immediately that it was the same guy she had been with in the bar. I was going to go and say hello but just as I started walking in her direction I saw her reach over and touch his chest as if brushing off some fluff that was caught on his jacket. In itself it was pretty innocuous but it's something she has a habit of doing to me, and until today I've never seen her do it to anyone else. Really, it's no big deal at all. Except that as I saw her do it I felt as though someone were suddenly squeezing my heart. I turned away and left the court immediately.

Wednesday 2 April 2008
Year 2 (week 27): UpTights's suppositories

UpTights was in the clerks room this morning talking about a case she lost yesterday.

'Anyway, I'm appealing,' she said.

As she was speaking, OldSmoothie walked through the door and said, 'I hardly think that's a very accurate description of reality, now, is it, UpTights? Not by anybody's standards.'

She ignored the comment and instead changed the subject to the Moldy litigation which started up one of their regular bouts of argument. At one point she said, 'Well, I suppose . . .'

OldSmoothie immediately rolled his eyes and interrupted with, 'Oh don't give me another one of your long, rambling "supposes", UpTights.'

Then TheVamp made a stage whisper to the rest of the room, 'He calls them her suppositories.'

'Why's that?' asked one of the pupils innocently.

'Because there's precisely one place I think she should stick her little theories and all I'll say is that it's somewhere the sun doesn't shine,' said OldSmoothie.

'Which complements exactly what UpTights calls your own verbal pirouettes,' said BusyBody sticking up for her friend. 'I mean, we all know that you talk out of that big fat behind of yours even if most of it's just hot air. But on the occasions when you get a little over-excited and exceed even your usual capacity for crassness, they're marked down as "OldSmoothie's embarrassing little follow-throughs".'

'This morning being a case in point,' said UpTights, as she whisked past him and out of the door.

Thursday 3 April 2008
Year 2 (week 27): Litigation for sale

The automatism case against TopFirst came back to life again today and I was a little surprised to hear that my client would be present this morning since until now he has been AWOL. When I arrived at court, SlipperySlope was there to meet me, smirking slightly, and standing next to him was a man he introduced as 'our missing client'. Yeah, right. Although I'd never met him, the medical report clearly stated that our client was twenty-five and yet this chap looked about fifty. Not only that but according to one of the file notes the client was said to be about six foot two whereas the man to whom I was introduced was about five six. Never having met the client myself I took Slippery to one side and asked, 'Are you sure this is our client? He looks shorter and somewhat older than I was expecting.'

'Mere details, BabyB. Look, here's his passport. Definitely him.'

I examined the passport and it certainly looked legitimate but I still didn't believe it. 'What's going on?' I asked.

'Oh, BabyB, don't you worry your little barrister head,' he replied.

'We'll both be worrying if I withdraw from this case and the judge orders an investigation.'

'You wouldn't dare.'

'I would unless you're straight with me. However bad, I still want to know what you're up to.'

He didn't look at all happy and hesitated for quite a while, as if coming to a decision.

'OK. But this one is definitely privileged.'

'Obviously.'

'Rent Your Client dot com. Solved many a tricky little situation. Sometimes, your client just won't survive cross-examination. Other times, like today, he actually disappears.'

'You what?'

'It fulfils a need, BabyB. We've got a hundred grand in costs riding on this case alone and all we need is someone to turn up at court, agree to the witness statements that we've already drafted and to answer a few questions about his earnings and his job prospects. Easy really and worth every penny of the ten grand it costs.'

'You what?'

'Oh, don't be so precious. You've got ten grand of your own fees riding on the success of this case. That's on top of the fact that you hate your opponent's guts and would do anything to get one over on him.'

Then he added, 'You're in too deep already to start picking fights about small matters such as this. See no evil, hear no evil, BabyB. Nelsonian knowledge. Just look the other way is all I ask.'

Well this wasn't quite accurate any longer since he'd actually given me the full details of what he was up to. But he was also right in his analysis of my own predicament and eventually I relented and we went into court. It did become a little nerve-wracking at one point when TopFirst's client started suggesting that my client wasn't the person he'd bumped his car into. But my answer was to point out that if TopFirst's client was as unconscious as he said he was then how could he possibly have known?

After much pushing and shoving inside the court, what it all boiled down to in the end was which expert the judge preferred. This is never a good thing since it leaves it even more open than usual for the judge simply to follow his own prejudices rather than the facts.

Now, the funny thing about the experts I've met so far is that without exception they all seem to have a small eccentricity that they play up, almost as if it helps you remember them. One might wear a bow tie. Another might be an ageing hippy with that long-haired, laid-back look. With TopFirst's expert today it was braces. Not the teeth kind. Stretchy ones. Stretchy and er, gold. Wide, shiny, gold braces, which when he took his jacket off in the witness box even made the judge raise an eyebrow at the barristers in front of him.

Then Slippery whispered from behind, 'Ouch. Clip-ons. That's them done for with this judge.'

'What?' I whispered back.

'I've seen this judge take against an expert in the past merely because he didn't have double cuffs. Heaven forbid that he'd have clip-on rather than button-on braces.'

Incredibly, after the build-up and the various adjournments, that was exactly how it was decided. TopFirst stropped off in a sulk as soon as the judge had left the court but our expert asked Slippery and me whether he might have a confidential word before we left.

When we had crowded into one of the little consultation rooms he looked at us a little nervously and said, 'I'm not sure if I should say something but word has it on the expert-witness grapevine, such as it is, that there are a few experts who have recently joined together and are literally charging clients to reproduce reports which those clients have in fact ghostwritten themselves. I know there's always been the odd rogue but this time it's more organised and explicit. The client pays and the expert says what the client wants him to say. Simple as.'

'Oh,' I said.

'The thing is, the expert your opponent was using today is one of those I've heard is involved.'

Slippery and I looked at each other, both seeing what this might imply. As soon as we had thanked our expert and let him leave, Slippery said, 'Well, well, BabyB. I think we'd better start investigating the other side's experts a little more closely in the Moldy litigation.'

Friday 4 April 2008
Year 2 (week 27): Gotcha!

Received some worrying photos in the post today. They have me getting into a taxi with WhistleBlower and then they show the two of us inside the taxi itself. They look as though they were taken from outside, but from quite close range.

It definitely suggests that there is some sort of set-up going on. The problem is that they were delivered with no explanation whatsoever. Obviously the first person who springs to mind is TopFirst. He is so determined to destabilise both me personally and the case as a whole. But it also makes me wonder about the authenticity of WhistleBlower. How on earth would whoever took the photos know about the meeting in the first place if they hadn't heard about it from her?

Monday 7 April 2008
Year 2 (week 28): Deadline

I told OldSmoothie about the photographs today and he was, to say the least, unamused.

'BabyB, we're committed to relying upon that evidence. If we withdraw it now, the other side will want to know why and they will rub our noses in it with the judge.'

'But what can we do?' I asked.

'Not "we", BabyB. You. What can you do? I think it's time you started earning your money. I don't care how you do it but you'd better come up with something substantive on this WhistleBlower evidence in the next few weeks. If you fail, I'm cutting you free from this case and if there is any complaint, I shall be pointing them in your direction. Count on that.'

This is just what I need on top of the insider-dealing complaint from TopFirst. Meanwhile, TopFlirt rang today to suggest meeting up for a specifically platonic lunch tomorrow. I think it's time I started leveraging my position with her, so to speak.

Tuesday 8 April 2008
Year 2 (week 28): Code of conduct

Met up with TopFlirt outside Temple tube today. She was wearing a big raincoat with a hood and when I arrived she immediately said, 'Quick, BabyB. Let's go straight down to the trains.'

I didn't have time to argue since she was already on her way and so I just followed. We both managed to get the one that was standing on the platform and when it moved away she pulled down her hood.

'I think he's got some private eye or other following you, BabyB, and the last thing I want is him catching me on candid camera meeting up with you.'

After that we went for a quiet little lunch near Victoria station.

'It's still going terribly with TopFirst, BabyB,' she said. 'He's becoming increasingly obsessed with the case the two of you are fighting, particularly since you delivered WhistleBlower's evidence.'

I wondered why she was talking so openly about the case, as well as her relationship with TopFirst, but I certainly wasn't going to stop her.

'I just wish he'd leave this case alone,' she said.

'Why do you say that?' I asked.

'Oh it's just as if it's stealing him away from me. Making him more distant. Compromising him in some way although I can't work out how.'

Then she added, 'Just be careful, BabyB. You know what he's like as well as I do.'

For my part, and emboldened by her openness about the problems in her own relationship, I told her about Claire's new boyfriend and the fact that I'd managed to let her slip through my fingers. There was a pause, and a moment when we found ourselves staring at each other for just a little too long. But then she gave a shake of her head, as if to wake herself up and said, 'I do really like you, BabyB. But whatever happens between TopFirst and me, you and I would never work out because I know it would destroy him. You know that, don't you?'

I agreed with her and TopFlirt perked up for the rest of our platonic lunch. But it was her comment about a private eye that has left me wondering. Perhaps the WhistleBlower photographs come from TopFirst? Or is TopFlirt just providing disinformation on his behalf? Though I have to say that I can't help believing what she tells me.

All of this means that it's not actually my witness who is necessarily questionable, from TopFirst's point of view, but instead it's my role in the evidence gathering that could give him ammunition. I think I might need to spend some time looking through the Code of Conduct.

Wednesday 9 April 2008
Year 2 (week 28): Witness summons

Had a meeting with OldSmoothie yesterday afternoon. He was pleased when I told him that there was no reason to believe WhistleBlower's documents weren't genuine.

'But you still need to track her down, BabyB,' he said.

As it happens, having put even more effort into trying to contact her, I did finally receive an email from WhistleBlower later that afternoon saying that she might be inclined to meet with me some time next week. When I reported this to OldSmoothie, he simply replied, 'Cutting it a bit close, BabyB. Trial starts in three weeks. Get a witness summons issued tomorrow and serve it on her the moment you meet.'

'But we don't even have her name.'

'Well sort it out one way or another.' He paused and then added, 'You know, I'm really rather looking forward to fighting UpTights. Ever since BusyBody stood up for her, she's started to get a little more feisty. Should add to the sport.'

OldSmoothie's been walking around chambers preening himself like a peacock today following a conversation he'd had with BigMouth who recently sent us a demand for an update on the Moldy cases. 'Yes,' OldSmoothie boomed at chambers tea, 'the Tories are scouting around for new talent at the moment to fill up The Other Place as soon as they win the next election.'

'Hmm. Scouting for Boys. Now where have I heard that phrase before . . .' said BusyBody sarcastically.

TheBusker smiled seeing comedy value from all angles. 'Reminds me of another childhood innuendo over the Everest pictures which said, "Edmund Hillary with Sherpa Tensing". Which one of the two was tensing and why, was something that caused no end of mirth. But sorry, OldSmoothie, you were saying. The Other Place. You don't mean. . . .'

He paused theatrically and looked towards the ceiling.

'Of course I don't,' OldSmoothie stammered impatiently. 'I mean that they're talking about making me a Peer.'

'What, like Brighton Pier?' asked BusyBody quizzically.

And before OldSmoothie was even given the chance to rise, UpTights waded in with, 'Or is it something to do with watering your horse . . . you know, like leaking the lizard, draining the dragon . . .' Then she added pensively, 'Hmm, a professional pee-er. Imagine that.'

'Lord Percy of Porcelain,' added BusyBody.

'I once knew a girl who only hung out with aristocracy,' said TheBusker getting distracted again. 'They always dragged out that old gag about the paddle steamer.'

'Ah, as in always moving from peer to peer,' said HeadofChambers waking up. 'Yes, I like that one.'

'Or TheLibrarian,' added TheBusker.

'Hmm,' said HeadofChambers, as if it were a cryptic crossword. 'Got it! Extremely fond of good titles. I like it.'

'You know Teflon's father's a peer,' said TheVamp, nodding at another junior member of chambers.

'So that makes you an Honourable,' said TheCreep, addressing Teflon.

'Which leaves the rest of us, what, dishonourable?' said BusyBody.

'It's a bit like the use of the label "love-child" for children born out of marriage,' smiled OldRuin. 'It's always left me wondering what a child born inside of marriage might be termed.'

'Do you use the title professionally?' asked TheCreep.

'I hardly think so,' said Teflon.

'I once did a piece of work for a QC whose father was a member of the House of Lords,' said TheBusker. 'He didn't change a single word of the advice I wrote on his behalf except for the addition of the word "Hon" before his name and for that one addition he billed over ten thousand pounds.'

'I've just never really seen the point of titles one way or the other,' said UpTights.

'Oh, I don't know,' said TheBusker. 'I remember once being taken out for a bangers and mash lunch by the Earl of something or other in a pub named after him. It all seemed quite fitting really.'

Friday 11 April 2008
Year 2 (week 28): Negotiation

With less than three weeks to go until trial, both sides formally met today for what might loosely be termed a settlement conference. Not that it was anything so organised as sitting around a table having a civilised chat about the issues. It was more like two huddles, with messengers being sent between them. The tone was set pretty early on when TopFirst came over from his huddle looking extremely self-important as if he was about to deliver a State of the Union address.

'Er . . .'

He got no further than this before OldSmoothie cut him dead in his tracks with, 'Get back in your box, TopFirst.' Then he raised his voice, 'You know what they say, "never hold discussions with the monkey when the organ-grinder's in the room".' He chuckled to himself and added, 'Not that UpTights gets the chance to grind many organs these days, poor darling.'

UpTights pretended to ignore this and when eventually OldSmoothie and I approached their side to make an offer,

UpTights immediately said, 'Send in the clowns.' She paused and addressed OldSmoothie. 'Krusty the clown and . . .' she looked at me, '. . . his little sidekick Bozo.'

I caught BusyBody's eye as UpTights said this and had to suppress a smile. But OldSmoothie was straight back on it. He gave her the offer we were prepared to accept and then said, 'There's so many voices in that screwed-up head of yours, UpTights, but I'm sure that hidden deep down among them there's a little voice of reason.'

With such a mood of conciliation it was perhaps no surprise that negotiations quickly faltered. Trial approaches fast.

Monday 14 April 2008
Year 2 (week 29): Nose jobs

Two of the clerks were discussing the merits of UpTights as a barrister today. 'Well, she certainly knows her job,' said HeadClerk.

At that moment, OldSmoothie walked into the clerks room and said, 'What? Another nose job for the wicked witch?'

'That's the only type of job you'd be able to get these days, OldSmoothie,' said BusyBody.

'Jobs for noses, I say,' said TheBusker quickly changing the subject. 'About time they paid their way.'

Tuesday 15 April 2008
Year 2 (week 29): Hospital pass

OldRuin was in chambers again today.

'BabyB,' he said, as we had our morning coffee. 'Do you think that I could possibly trouble you for a favour?'

Then, before I could answer, he said, 'And please don't hesitate to say no if it's in any way inconvenient. I know how busy you are building up a practice.'

'I'd be delighted to help,' I said without any reservation. 'What do you need me to do?'

'The thing is, in their wisdom the government have just decided that my small local hospital needs to be closed. Cost-cutting, they say. Well, I was approached by a couple of people in church on Sunday and asked if I might be able to help with a legal challenge.'

'Judicially reviewing the decision?'

'That's right, and I was wondering if you might be able to assist me? The problem is that there'll be no money in it and it'll involve a lot of legal research and work on documents. People might even say that it's just me tilting at windmills, although personally I've always seen any accusation towards the romantic or even quixotic as somewhat of a compliment.'

I hesitated to answer since the very last thing I wanted to do right now was to take on any other work in addition to both the Moldy litigation and the almost overwhelming flow of other cases. Unfortunately I couldn't hide this from OldRuin who said, 'I really won't mind if you feel that you are too busy already.' Then he gave me his kindly smile and said, 'Have a think about it.'

The problem is that I know he wouldn't be asking if it wasn't important, for precisely the reason that he does understand the pressures I'm under at the moment. Either way, despite my reluctance, I certainly wasn't going to refuse and I said, 'OldRuin, I'd be delighted to help.'

Wednesday 16 April 2008
Year 2 (week 29): Grumpy Old Man

'Nothing's ever simple any longer.' It was OldSmoothie in the bar after work this evening and he'd already had a few. 'The bigger picture's been lost forever and we're all just buried in details and small print.'

'And whose fault do you think that is?' said HeadClerk.

'It's got nothing to do with lawyers, obviously,' smiled TheBusker.

'Clever commercial lawyers who draft terms and conditions which allow companies to do over the little man, maybe,' he replied. 'But certainly not us good old-fashioned common lawyers.'

'Oh, listen to the champion of the little man,' said TheVamp.

'I like to think I have my moments,' he replied.

'And of course you'd never take a technical pleading point or kick a case out that had missed limitation?' said TheBusker.

'That's completely different. That's just our job,' OldSmoothie replied. 'We do what we're instructed to do.'

'If anything, surely we should be celebrating the modern world's obsession with detail?' said TheVamp. 'I mean, if it wasn't for solicitors instructing us to take the snivelly sneaky little points we'd all be out of work.'

'No, it's much bigger than that. Even at the Bar, everyone always seems to be running scared these days. Wherever I look, people are tiptoeing around worrying that they won't hit their billing targets or pay for those exorbitant school fees. Worrying that they might be sued or face a complaint. Gone are the good old days when you could trot off to court without a care. When great speeches and matters of principle were what counted. These days it's all in the detail. Whole careers are forged on finding loopholes and arguing over every little nuance.'

He was on a roll and none of us quite knew what to say. It's not like OldSmoothie and high principle are two things you'd usually put together. 'Now don't misunderstand me. There are still some of us left. I mean it's one of the very few things I love about UpTights. You can hardly call her dull. But let's face it, the more I think about it the more I realise this modern world rewards the likes of TheCreep.'

Oh, here we go.

'The man-boy, who a hundred years ago would have been bullied out of court, is now King. Ruling the roost with his sub-clauses and huge skeleton arguments. Beauty isn't truth for him. It's something to be broken down into its constituent parts and shot to pieces. You could give him a room in paradise and he'd still be arguing over the lease.'

Thursday 17 April 2008
Year 2 (week 29): Animal magic

As a tonic to TheCreep, TheBusker's dog, LeadingCounsel, was in chambers again today and he was showing off his new tricks at chambers tea.

'I'm preparing him for coming along to court and assisting me as a visual aid,' he said. 'I'm only going to wheel him out for the hopeless cases since I don't think it would be fair on my opponents the rest of the time. I mean, it's guaranteed to distract the judge and jury and I hardly think they're going to dislike it.'

'Why? What can he do that's so great?' asked BusyBody curiously.

'Oh, nothing too special really. It's just that I've tailored his usual exercises to the law as is only appropriate. So whenever I even mention the words "cross-examination", he simply rolls over,' and sure enough, the dog was on his back with his paws straight up in the air.

OldSmoothie chortled at this and said, 'I once trained a dog to do that in answer to the question "What do lady barristers do?" Always caused no end of fuss, I can tell you.'

BusyBody was enraptured by LeadingCounsel and pestered The Busker for more. Though I think we all thought that she was actually looking for tips as to how she could train BusyBaby as effectively. 'Come on, what else does he do?' she asked.

'If I say "settlement", he starts begging on his hind legs.'

Once again the dog was there.

'If I want to start making a point in court and use the word "terrible", I get a slight growl,' (which did indeed follow), 'and if I step it up a notch to "outrageous", I get a little bark,' and sure enough there was a bark to which even the grumpiest of opponents would have found it difficult to object. He continued, 'But whilst he will always respond when told to "shake hands" he will steadfastly ignore the command to "shake hands with counsel" on the basis that a barrister's dog should be no more shaking hands with his opponent than the barrister himself. If all of that's not sufficient to win the day then I've also got him a white collar with barristers' bands falling down the front and a tiny little horsehair wig to stick on his head.'

The irony is that whilst TheBusker's left a vague suggestion that he might be joking about really taking him to court, I can't see him going to all this trouble without actually doing it, just for the story value.

I managed to have a meeting with WhistleBlower last night after I'd received an email specifying the time and place. She said that she absolutely refused to give evidence at trial. The big difficulty is that without even her name, never mind her address, I'll find it impossible to force her there with a witness summons, which is why I had TheBoss get one of his investigators to photograph the meeting. Tomorrow he will send an investigator to each of the UK offices of the telecom company to try and identify her from their thousands of other employees. As he said this morning, 'About as likely as finding a needle in a haystack.' Then he gave me a pointed look and added, 'Or should I say as likely as finding an honest lawyer in the whole of this litigation.'

This afternoon I went to visit Arthur and Ethel at their home to give them an update on the cases. I hadn't been looking forward to trying to explain some of our difficulties but they really didn't seem all that interested. Ethel welcomed me with, 'BabyB, there's five or six of our group who have now received litter-picking sentences and the rest of us are joining in even though we haven't been ordered to. In fact we're about to go out now if you'd like to join us?'

'We've even got you a yellow bib with your name on it,' smiled Arthur, lifting up a luminous gillet to reveal the words 'BabyB the Binman'.

'And some gloves and a pick-up stick,' said Ethel handing them to me.

I couldn't help but be carried along by their enthusiasm, which was definitely infectious and so I put on the gillet to match their own and followed them out. A few minutes later and I was surrounded by twenty of our Moldy clients and probably the same number again of old people most of whom I didn't even recognise from the litigation. All were similarly attired and with pick-up sticks in hand. I did recognise Tony and Dora from the court case the other day. They came over and started chatting about their litter-picking experiences.

'I have to admit, there's probably a bit of hunter-gathering in it for me,' said Tony. 'But I also love the fact that wherever I go, things look a lot better behind me.'

'What is it they say, BabyB?' smiled Dora. 'We live our lives forwards but understand them backwards.'

A few more minutes and we were all marching up one of the main streets. A grey-haired army of litter pickers cleansing the streets to applause and smiles from the shoppers and grateful beeps of the horn from passing cars. I have to admit that it was inspiring to be a part of and I returned to chambers on something of a high.

Monday 21 April 2008
Year 2 (week 30): A helping hand

TheBoss has discovered that the other side have been going through the rubbish that is left outside SlipperySlope's offices. He's in full-on paranoid mode at the moment and has started investigating the private collection firm to whom they've outsourced all the shredding of confidential documents.

'You're only as strong as your weakest link,' he said at a case conference today, 'and we've probably been passing our secrets straight into the other side's lap. Stupid. Very stupid. But there we have it.'

Later in the day I bumped into OldRuin and I was pouring my heart out to him about Claire's new boyfriend. He listened very sympathetically. Later he asked about the Moldy case and I mentioned our concerns over the other side spying.

'You know, sometimes, BabyB, it doesn't do any harm to let the other side occasionally jump to the wrong conclusions. Accidentally, of course.'

He had a mischievous twinkle in his eye and didn't say any more, but I think I know what he was hinting at, and as soon as he was gone I rang Slippery and said, 'Let's use their dirty tricks to our advantage. Start feeding them a little disinformation.'

'I like where you're coming from, BabyB. Make up a memo especially for them.'

'Exactly. Let's start with giving the impression that we're massively relying on their own two fake cases. We could also mention a "bombshell" we intend to drop towards the end of the case. Should get them running in all directions.'

'Excellent,' said Slippery. 'I shall write it immediately.'

Tuesday 22 April 2008
Year 2 (week 30): Conflict of interest

So far TheBoss has had no luck trying to find WhistleBlower at the telecom company's offices and with time running out I decided last night to cross-reference our database of the many hundreds of Moldy clients who are lined up behind the current cases, against the various lists of the telecom company's employees in case something came up which might lead me to her identity. However, whilst I didn't exactly find what I was looking for, I stumbled upon one lady client who had the same surname as TopFlirt. Half an hour more of research and double-checking and it became clear that she doesn't just share the same surname; she is her mother. To put it more clearly, TopFirst's fiancée's mum is suing the telecom company and TopFirst is defending the action. There couldn't be a much greater conflict of interest, which makes me think that perhaps he knows nothing about it. It also makes me wonder whether TopFlirt is the one who pushed WhistleBlower forward in the first place using her knowledge of the case which she'd gleaned from her beloved.

Time for a chat with the flirtatious one.

Wednesday 23 April 2008
Year 2 (week 30): RedBluff

I've been mulling over what to do with the information I learnt from TopFlirt about TopFirst's obsession with beating me to a red bag. What I figure is that if it's getting to him that much then it might be worth trying to stoke the fire of his obsession even more. So I sent him this email:

Following on from our discussions about red bags last year, I hereby propose a wager that whoever is awarded one first will have the services of the other for a full week acting in the capacity of a mini-pupil.

I received an immediate reply saying:

Not that I'm at all bothered by what you do, BabyB, but if you insist on making it into a competition then for your information, I'll be having my coffee white with one sugar.

Despite the fact that I can't think of anything worse than being TopFirst's coffee-maker for a week, the truth is that it would be even more painful for him the other way round. So it's worth the risk just to add another layer of tension to the game. Oh, and I've suggested that Slippery writes another memo mentioning just how keen I am to beat TopFirst in this particular little battle. Though I asked him not to mention it to OldSmoothie since he might feel that the bet went against the whole spirit of the red bag and not award it simply on that basis.

Thursday 24 April 2008
Year 2 (week 30): Selling off Scotland

'If you ask me, the only way we're going to solve this whole credit crunch thing is to sell off Scotland.'

OldSmoothie was holding court once again at chambers tea yesterday afternoon. 'Oh, and all of its politicians as well, particularly the ones lording it over us down here. Yes, just stick it on e-bay and see what it fetches. Should be enough to pay for Northern Rock.'

'Well, a stick of Northern Rock at least,' said HeadofChambers.

BusyBody stepped into the ring. 'Turn off the broken record, OldSmoothie, or at least start playing a different tune.' Then her tone changed and she added, 'Though I'm sure the police would be interested to hear about your incitement to racial hatred in front of, hmm . . .' she counted the people in the room, '. . . twelve upstanding witnesses.'

This clearly surprised OldSmoothie and the advantage was then rammed home by UpTights who added, 'Yes, particularly if it were reported to a certain Scottish policeman who I just happen to know is based in Charing Cross Police Station . . .' she suddenly had an even madder glint than usual in her eye and her voice began to rise towards a screech '. . . and who just happens to bear a grudge against you for making a fool of him in the witness box.'

From the look that passed between UpTights and BusyBody, I shudder to think where they might take this.

Friday 25 April 2008
Year 2 (week 30): Nuclear option

Now I'm really worried. We still haven't managed to find WhistleBlower and today I discovered that TopFlirt is also inexplicably uncontactable, which I can't believe is a coincidence given our proximity to trial. If this weren't bad enough, I also received another letter from the Bar Standards Board warning me that if I was not prepared for them to hear the complaint made about the alleged insider dealing, then they would have to pass it on immediately to the FSA.

Finding myself between a rock and a hard place I have decided to take the gamble and stick to the Bar Standards. This means that I will definitely have to start implementing a little contingency plan I've been quietly cooking up, although it will remain very much a last resort 'nuclear option'. The problem is I still haven't quite figured out every detail of it yet. In the meantime, I wrote back to the Bar Standards asking them to delay the hearing until the Moldy litigation is finished, since that will allow for any issues that might be relevant to TopFirst's allegations to be decided by the judge. If the Bar Standards Board agree, then it will buy me some time with rat face.

Monday 28 April 2008
Year 2 (week 31): An offer

Despite the sabre rattling of a couple of weeks ago between OldSmoothie and UpTights, I was surprised to hear today that an offer has nonetheless been made. However, it is for £5,000 per claimant, which is tiny in comparison to the size of the claim and is clearly intended to buy off the litigation. Slippery and OldSmoothie were discussing what to do with the offer at our meeting this morning.

'Well obviously we'll reject it. Accept now and you can wave goodbye to the sort of fees we've been talking about,' OldSmoothie declared.

'My thoughts exactly,' said Slippery.

I was a little confused by this. 'But don't we have to take our clients' instructions before making this decision?'

OldSmoothie and Slippery looked at each other and smiled. Then Slippery looked back at me and said, 'BabyB, let me assure you. I know you like to have every "i" dotted and "t" crossed, but you can be certain that I have taken all the instructions I need.'

With that I was dismissed from their presence. In practical terms, what this means is that if we recover £5,000 or less per claim then we won't be getting any of the further costs that are now likely to be run up.

Tuesday 29 April 2008
Year 2 (week 31): Virtual assistants

'Get with the programme Nursery, it's all about virtual assistants these days. Don't forget, that's the answer to any cost-saving issue at the moment.'

It was SlipperySlope showing off in front of his niece because I was there.

'What are they?' I asked, politely following his lead.

Nursery turned to me, full of smug cleverness and said condescendingly, 'Don't you know? Half our work is done by them these days.'

Slippery took over, 'Help from afar, BabyB. It's globalisation working for us. We hire top PhD students from India and China at four pounds an hour and then bill out their work at two hundred and fifty pounds an hour. In fact, I'm surprised you don't have one. If I was in your shoes, I'd have them trained to do my phone hearings and to provide online back-up at court.'

Then he took a card and handed it to me. 'Any time you need some research, you just give this number a call and they'll have it done for you within the day. With that kind of service why on earth would we hire in this country?' He looked at Nursery and then added, 'That is, unless we're related of course.'

Nursery didn't quite know whether this was an insult or a fond remark, which left her screwing her face and madly smiling at the same time.

'Oh come on, Nursery,' said Slippery. 'Get yourself a sense of humour and stop grinning like a cat eating...' He paused and then said, 'Ooh, BabyB, mustn't swear in front of the more precious half of the profession, now must we? Let's just say that when the cat's finished there's no need to scoop the poop.'

Wednesday 30 April 2008
Year 2 (week 31): In my dreams

OldRuin collared me as I was walking into chambers this morning and we went for coffee together.

'BabyB, am I right in thinking that your friend Claire is becoming quite an expert in judicial review cases at the moment?'

'Definitely. She's really starting to shine.'

He paused and looked a little hesitant before saying, 'I don't wish to seem pushy at all but given how important this hospital case is, would you possibly mind if I were to ask her to get involved?'

'To replace me?' I asked.

'Er, no, actually. To work with you as my co-juniors.'

I imagine I looked a little stunned at the thought of having to talk to Claire.

'I know it might be difficult for you and I wouldn't ask if I didn't think it would help...'

'Of course, OldRuin,' I replied. 'If you think it'll help.'

'Thank you, BabyB. I really think it will.'

Then he changed the subject completely. 'What would be your dream life, BabyB?'

'I've no idea,' I replied. 'But I guess it'd have to involve having financial security for my mother. Maybe paying off her debts, getting her a bigger house.'

'And what would you be doing?'

'I don't know. I never imagined I'd be a barrister but I can't imagine doing anything else now that I'm here. It sounds sad but the security thing's the only bit I'd change.'

'Will you grant me a wish, BabyB?'

'Of course. What?'

'That you try to stop making plans and start dreaming again. Dream like you were a child once more.' He hesitated before adding, 'Boundless.'

I've no doubt that I looked more than a little perplexed and in a voice only just above a whisper he said, 'It's in the everyday that you forge your character.' Again he looked at me, this time a little wistfully before finishing with, 'But it's your dreams that give it shape.'

CHAPTER 8

MAY: BRAINWASHER

Thursday 1 May 2008
Year 2 (week 31): Trial

First day of trial today and TopFirst arrived at court this morning looking particularly smug. Unfortunately for him he doesn't understand the concept that sometimes it's actually better to play it cool.

'Looking forward to losing today, you loser?' he said.

Just to wind him up a little more I pretended to rise to his petty bait. 'I don't think I'm going to be the loser, you loser.'

'No you're the loser, loser.'

I couldn't resist just one more. 'No, you are . . . loser,' after which I walked off with a theatrical whisk of the head.

BusyBody had been watching all this from only a few yards away with a huge grin on her face.

'What's up with you?' I heard TopFirst say to her sulkily.

'You know,' she replied, knowing that I could also hear, 'I've just realised who you both remind me of: that little girl Violet in *Just William* who was always shouting, "I'll scweam and scweam and scweam until I'm sick!"'

Which was actually pretty fair, I thought, as I trundled back to OldSmoothie's huddle, where by now there was a whole gathering of both Moldy clients and supporters standing alongside BigMouth, who was conducting interviews with the press. I recognised Tony the electric guitarist and Dora the putative bank robber. Then there was Alfred with his skateboard tucked under his arm although unfortunately his wrist was in plaster. He gave me a knowing smile as if no further explanation were needed. Stanley was there with the football by his side dressed in the same Blackpool strip I had learnt was worn by Stanley Matthews in his famous 1953 FA Cup Final. Finally Arthur and Ethel came forward to greet me and I was rewarded with a big hug from Ethel and a firm handshake from Arthur. I'd never had any doubt that all of these Moldy cases were genuine but only four of them had been included in the batch of test cases which were listed for today: Arthur, Ethel, Stanley and Dora. Then there were the other two cases which we had decided were fake.

We all went into court, stood up for the judge and when he sat down, OldSmoothie remained standing. 'Your Honour, before we start I would hereby like to give notice of discontinuance on two of the six cases that are being run.' He then named the two cases and continued, 'May I humbly apologise for this late notice. It was due to, er, what we consider to be a certain amount of shenanigans and dirty tricks going on in the background.'

Loud gasps followed from the other side, although it wasn't clear whether this was indignation or simply disbelief that we'd found them out.

TheMoldies looked over at TopFirst and UpTights disapprovingly, and then Stanley lobbed his football at them and pandemonium broke out.

When the judge finally managed to regain some control of the court, and after he'd warned Stanley not to repeat that trick, OldSmoothie went on. 'However, I obviously don't want in any way to prejudice the court's view by going into them here . . .'

'No, I'm sure you don't,' the judge interrupted with a wry smile, knowing as well as the rest of us that the whole purpose of OldSmoothie's little speech was prejudice.

'As I was saying,' continued OldSmoothie, 'we are therefore prepared to accept any costs that were wasted through pursuing those two cases.'

'Very decent, I'm sure,' said the judge. 'Now, Ms UpTights, what do you have to say about this little revelation?'

Well, that was the funniest part of it. By this point, TopFirst had almost gone into a state of apoplexy, as had the solicitor behind him, which confirmed to me that they were both in on the fake cases and were furious to be losing a trump card. However, UpTights on the other hand clearly knew nothing about it and despite TopFirst poking her in the back and whispering loud enough for the whole court to hear, she steadfastly ignored him.

Instead, she rose to her feet and said, 'Your Honour, I'm delighted to hear that the cases before you are already starting to crumble even before we've opened the evidence. It's indicative in my submission of the strength of the evidence as a whole. Given that my learned friend has capitulated on the only other possible issue that might arise, that of costs, then I am delighted to consent to the discontinuance going ahead.'

Phew. Game, set and match for today. Our big concern was that they might try and insist on having the cases heard or at least want to see good reasons for withdrawing them at this stage. Whilst we figured that they had been faked, we certainly didn't have enough to constitute evidence. So if we'd told the other side about these cases even a minute before going into court, TopFirst and the solicitor would have had a chance to get to UpTights and give her clear instructions and our plan may have been thwarted.

As it was, I took particular pleasure in holding up a sheet of paper to TopFirst upon which I had written the words 'Who's the loser now, LOSER?'

Monday 5 May 2008
Year 2 (week 32): I am instructed . . .

With the trial now underway, both TopFlirt and WhistleBlower continue to be AWOL. I've tried calling TopFlirt's mobile a few times now but it's always switched off, and I obviously can't call her house with the lovely TopFirst likely to pick up at the other end. I even checked to see if there was any clue on Facebook but her last status update said simply, 'Out of the country'. This is all a big problem because although we have managed to get our expert evidence together, as I remembered from my own button on-clip-on-braces moment, that could still go either way. TheBoss has investigators looking for WhistleBlower and I've hired one specifically to try and track down TopFlirt just in case she can somehow help us get to her. However, it's becoming pretty clear that at present they are in hiding.

The big issue is the leaked documents. So far the telecom company has managed to hedge on the issue as to whether they are actually authentic or fake. They have merely stonewalled by saying that the burden of proof lies with us. My guess is that their main concern is that we'll track down WhistleBlower. If we do, then to have denied the authenticity of the documents will make their position far worse. But if it transpires that we can't find her, I imagine they will claim that the documents we have are fakes, having destroyed all other evidence of their existence.

All of this is why I emphasised how important it was for OldSmoothie to get the other side to commit to the documents one way or the other today. Needless to say, when he raised it, the other side were full of bluster about there being 'no proof whatsoever that the documents were authentic'.

'In which case,' said OldSmoothie in court this morning, 'it should be fairly easy for the other side simply to deny their authenticity.'

'Er, well, no, it's not as simple as that,' said UpTights.

'Why not, Ms UpTights? You've known about these documents now for several weeks. Plenty of time to conduct your own investigations. Are they real or fake?'

UpTights didn't look at all happy with this but she looked even more unhappy when she was given instructions from her solicitor via TopFirst.

'I am instructed . . .' she started, knowing full well that the use of these words indicated her own lack of complicity with what would follow, '. . . that . . .' she hesitated, looking distinctly uncomfortable, '. . . the documents are fake.'

She sat down with a grimace to those behind her, which suggested that the instructions she had been given left her feeling somewhat sullied. It's the same kind of face I imagine she'd pull in the unlikely event that she ever had a dog and was forced to pick up its droppings.

This certainly puts even more pressure on me now to track WhistleBlower down.

For some reason I decided to dig out our old family photo albums last night and I soon stumbled upon a picture of the day I had recalled after my skateboarding experience. It had obviously been taken by a passer-by and it showed the three of us, next to our respective creations on the beach, beaming. Well, almost. More accurately it would have showed the three of us were it not for the fact that my mother's face had been cut out of the photograph. Her hands were there around her sandcastle but the one-inch square where her face should have been was missing. Puzzled, I pulled it out and found myself wanting to keep it, even with the hole in it. Maybe I would even scan it at some point. Just at that moment my mother came into my room unannounced and looked at me and then the album and finally the mutilated photograph in my hand.

'BabyB? What on earth are you doing?'

I tried to sound nonchalant. 'Oh, I was just flicking through our old albums.'

'But why on earth are you taking the photos out? Why can't you just leave them as they are?'

Surprised at her tone, I just looked at her blankly. Then the expression on her face changed from shock to anger and she said, 'BabyB, I just don't know what's happened to you recently. You were always such a lovely child and now all you seem to care about is your oh-so-important cases and clients and, let's face it, money.'

I did not know how to respond, being both surprised at where it had come from and also knowing that there was a great deal of truth in what she said, and so I stayed silent and hung my head.

'I don't know what goes on in that head of yours any longer, but I know for sure that I don't like it and obviously Claire doesn't either. You've turned into a money-making machine, BabyB, and you've sold your soul in the process.' Her voice rose in pitch as she continued, 'A cold-hearted lawyer who doesn't give a fig for anyone or anything, least of all his friends and family. You never have any time for anyone these days unless they'll earn you some cash or further your career. You haven't just got your priorities skewed. You've become a different person. Sometimes I feel I don't even know you any longer. Or want to know you for that matter.' Then she paused, composed herself and flattened down her rumpled skirt before delivering the final blow. 'You're as bad as your old man, BabyB. I always knew it in my heart. However much I tried to believe otherwise.'

It was like being hit by a force of nature. I found myself struggling to compute what she was saying, but also painfully aware of how hurt and angry she was.

'You treat me just like one of your cases. One minute I have your complete attention and the next I'm effectively being tied in pink ribbon and sent back to the solicitors along with a bill for your time, whilst the spotlight of your attention moves on to the next task. Always compartmentalising, always emotionally detached. It's just not healthy. You've got to engage. Let the sadness in, feel regret and guilt. If you can't do that you'll never be able to feel happy or experience forgiveness either.'

Then just as quickly as the hurricane had started it came to an end and my mother collapsed in a heap, her head in her hands. She began to sob, and after a few moments, between breaths, she whispered, 'I'm so sorry, BabyB. I don't mean any of it. I just hate your father so very much. Not for what he did to me but for leaving you without him.'

Still in shock I moved towards my mother and hugged her. 'I know you don't mean it and I do understand,' I said, feeling tears springing to my own eyes.

'It was an education for me having a little boy, ' she continued. 'One day it was football, the next day it might be den-making, and your attention would duck and dive on a whim. But whatever it was would take up your complete focus for that moment. Boys are so very different to girls and in the beginning I thought it meant that you were careless. But then I realised that in fact you were just completely carefree and I wanted so very much to have just a little bit of that rub off on me.'

I smiled, and struggled to find words to say everything I was feeling.

She went on, 'But you're none of those things I've just said. I don't even know where that came from. It just kind of erupted inside me when I saw that terrible photo that I'd cut myself out of years ago in a fit of self-loathing. It was a deep visceral anger. I'm so very sorry, BabyB. The last person in the whole world I'd want to inflict that on is you.'

I hugged her more tightly. Her sobs were slowing down now.

'Honestly. It's him, not you, BabyB. You've always been so very patient and kind with me I can't believe I just said those things. I've never even thought them before, never mind believed them.'

I told her I loved her and then she looked up, grasped my shoulders and said, 'I love you too, BabyB, and I'm not in the slightest bit angry with you. In fact mostly what I feel is guilt at knowing that what you're doing is actually for me and is driven by the debts I've run up in the first place. But nevertheless, I am concerned about you.'

We let the silence fall and then she said very quietly, 'You're always rushing around, BabyB. Chopping up your life into hours, minutes, seconds. I suppose it's what you lawyers are about. But if you're not careful, you'll turn into one of them and your whole life will be lost on to some dusty, meaningless timesheet.'

I certainly wasn't going to dispute that. Then she seemed to brighten a little, shook her head and said, 'It's all my fault for not having the time to show you what's important in life. I was too wrapped up in wanting you to escape my poverty and powerlessness and I forgot to teach you to have fun. You know, your father wasn't much good for many things but he did know how to have fun.' She smiled and then said, 'Take the time to stand and stare. Smell the fresh morning air, look out your window at the cherry blossom, or watch the girls go by in the summer. I don't care what it is but just take a little bit of pleasure in being rather than doing.'

Her eyes were soft as she added, 'I do worry for you, BabyB.'

Wednesday 7 May 2008
Year 2 (week 32): Attic attack

I can't say that I slept terribly well last night as I lay there worrying not only about what my mother had said but also about the reasons that Claire and I had fallen out. The deeper I get into this mess the more I seem to be hurting the people that I'm closest to and yet I still can't see a way out. Anyway, as I arrived at court bleary eyed this morning, I was pleased to see that ScandalMonger had come along to watch since he's always guaranteed to take the attention away from anyone else. So it was today as he sat there chuckling to himself just behind SlipperySlope. When UpTights entered the court it certainly didn't look as though her mood had improved from yesterday. In fact, her whole demeanour was distinctly 'out there' even for her. Scandal was immediately on it with a loud whisper of, 'Who let Mrs Rochester out of the attic?'

I hate to admit it, but after TopFirst's petty attack over my utility bills, I've been determined to be equally petty in my response, and so for the last three days I've been lacing his water in court with strong senna-based laxatives. This has meant not only that he's been looking tired and emotional but also having to leave the court every half-hour or so. I'd mentioned this to Scandal before the hearing and he'd obviously heard me wrong because looking at UpTights's stressed-out face he whispered to me, 'Looks like those pills are really getting to her.'

To which I could only answer, 'No pills needed to make UpTights look like she's straining, I'm afraid.'

When there was a short break in the proceedings mid-morning, Scandal again piped up, this time commenting upon how many lawyers it takes to settle a small dispute. Then he added, 'You know, there have been studies that have shown that wherever you are on the planet you're never less than five yards away from a lawyer.'

Being the smart alec that he is, TopFirst immediately looked over to our side and corrected Scandal with, 'I think you'll find that that statistic refers to rats, not lawyers.'

'Well, there you go,' smiled Scandal gesturing around the court. 'The mother lode.'

TopFirst scowled as he realised that he'd fallen for one of Scandal's little jokes and as he did so, Slippery let loose with another of his misquotes, 'Ooh, grin for me, grin for me, they've all gorrit in for me.'

But despite all the high jinx, it was clear to all of us as the day dragged on that the more time that passes, the more we are losing the case itself. At one point in the afternoon, UpTights really rubbed it in when she made a comment to the judge about the weakness of our evidence, and all OldSmoothie could muster was the sort of resigned look that England cricket captains tend to give after another test match defeat. Whilst he was doing so, UpTights started up the theatrics by staring at him for just a bit longer than was polite and said, 'Look at that, Your Honour.'

The whole court turned to OldSmoothie. Then UpTights smiled and gave the knife a final few turns, 'Utterly beyond hope and he knows it.' She looked around and then added, 'Though I believe the death throes of a cockroach that has been decapitated can take several weeks to come to an end.'

Thursday 8 May 2008
Year 2 (week 32): BrainWasher

With the trial going from bad to worse and no sign of either WhistleBlower or TopFlirt, I was called into the solicitors' office today by none other than Smutton.

When I arrived I mentioned Smutton's name and was whisked up to the floor above Slippery's office. Her office was at the end of a long corridor. But unlike all the other solicitors in the firm, there was no little cubbyhole for her. Her office was more like something out of Wall Street, with views out over Tower Bridge and the Thames. As I entered, I was taken aback by a little white Jack Russell jumping up at my legs.

'Flea. Come here at once,' she said as I entered.

The dog went bounding back to its mistress and jumped up on the sofa beside her desk.

'Well, BabyB,' she purred. 'Always a pleasure to welcome an upstanding member of the other half of the profession to my humble abode.' As she said this she rolled her tongue over the words 'upstanding' and 'member'.

'The pleasure's all mine,' I lied.

'Oh, come now, BabyB. You should relax a little. It's not as if I'm going to eat you, is it? I'm perfectly harmless, really, you know.'

'I hadn't imagined you weren't,' I lied again.

Then it was down to business.

'Look, BabyB. I've taken a somewhat hands-off approach to this litigation so far. Left it to Slippery to deal with in the manner only he knows best.'

I raised my eyebrows in a knowing way.

'But his tactics seem to have failed us and so it's been passed along for me to sort out. Last chance saloon if you like.'

How appropriate, I thought. Smutton sitting alone in the last chance saloon.

'Which is why I've asked ScandalMonger if he can get one of his clients to help.'

She then went on to explain that Scandal happens to represent someone who I'll call BrainWasher, owing to the fact that he is one of the world's leading experts on manipulating people's minds through the power of suggestion. She concluded, 'Time to put him to good use on the judge's mind.' Then she added, 'Oh, and I imagine that with all the money our firm has lent your mother, not to mention the professional conduct complaint you've already got against your name, you'll be able to see your way past any professional misgivings you might have had.'

Friday 9 May 2008
Year 2 (week 32): Full moon

Arthur was giving evidence at the trial today, much to the amusement of TheMoldies and their supporters who were tittering in the back of the court.

'So what is it that your condition leads you to do exactly?' asked OldSmoothie.

'Well I pull my trousers and underpants right down and I show them my bare bottom,' said Arthur.

'And on what occasions do you do this?'

'Whenever I get the urge, to be honest,' said Arthur.

'Which would be when?'

'Oh, whenever I think someone deserves it,' Arthur replied with a smile.

'And when do you think they deserve it?' persisted OldSmoothie.

'Oh, you know . . .' answered Arthur. By now it was clear he was deliberately toying with OldSmoothie who was starting to get exasperated.

'Actually I do know, but it's for you to tell the court, not me. So perhaps you might elaborate as to when you think someone deserves to be, er . . .'

'I think the word you're looking for is "mooned",' said Arthur.

'Quite,' answered OldSmoothie.

Picking up on OldSmoothie's impatience, Arthur turned to the judge, gave a winning smile and said, 'Barristers, huh? They just ain't what they used to be.'

Barristers being the bane of this particular judge's life, Arthur had hit just the right note and the judge beamed back at him in agreement. Then just when things all seemed to be rosy, Arthur, who at this point was still facing the judge and therefore had his back to OldSmoothie, bent over and very quickly gave him a full glimpse of the dark side of the moon. TheMoldies at the back of the court signalled their rowdy approval and the judge tried to restore a little order with, 'That's enough of that for today.'

Arthur smiled again and just said, 'Sorry, my Lord. It's just he did ask what sort of thing led me to do it and all I did was show him. Now you get the full picture.'

'Well quite,' smiled the judge, nevertheless charmed by Arthur's irreverent put-down of the fat pompous one.

Monday 12 May 2008
Year 2 (week 33): Unorthodox

'Well, it's somewhat unorthodox, but I think it could be done. But tell me, BabyBarista, isn't it illegal to try and influence a judge in this way?'

BrainWasher had agreed to meet us at Slippery's office and he was voicing his concerns about Smutton's proposed campaign to bring the judge's mind around to our way of thinking. He was neat, trim and thoroughly in control but also looked as if he had a whacky side, which came out in his blue velvet jacket and loud purple shirt with a large collar which hung loose over a baggy pair of trousers. He clearly loved himself and when he wasn't rubbing his chin he was stroking his hand through his thick mop of brown hair.

'I don't think there's a precedent against it,' I replied.

'I see.'

'And it's not as if we're going to be harming the judge in any way.'

'No. Quite.'

'Merely influencing him. Through subliminal messages.'

'Yes. I see the point.'

'Though it's certainly not something I'd want the other side to find out about.'

'Hmm. I can thoroughly understand why that may be the case.'

'So, do you think you can do it?'

He thought about it for a little while and then said, 'If he sticks to the routine to and from work that you've described to me then I can certainly give it a go. I'll do some planning this week and aim to start next Monday.'

Tuesday 13 May 2008
Year 2 (week 33): Apple sauce and BlackBerry whine

'Oh no, she's off doing her BlackBerry whine again,' said OldSmoothie at court today, as he pointed over to UpTights who was looking exasperated as she talked into her BlackBerry.

'And I suppose that that means TheVamp over there is doing an Apple sauce,' said SlipperySlope, smiling as we all looked over to see her whispering her usual line in flirtatious innuendo into her iPhone.

At that moment BusyBody was walking past and she said, 'I've always thought it so appropriate that the egotistical maniac that is OldSmoothie should have chosen a telephone that is named in such a way that it almost seems to have been invented for him.'

She pointed at OldSmoothie's own iPhone and then added, 'I mean, it's definitely catchier than the "me, me, me, I'm a big fat slob phone" wouldn't you say?'

Wednesday 14 May 2008
Year 2 (week 33): Got a semi

I had a meeting with Smutton and BrainWasher today and whilst Smutton was called away to take a phonecall, I asked BrainWasher to give me some of the details he had already dug up about the judge.

'What kind of house does he have?' I asked.

As Smutton came back into the room BrainWasher glanced in her direction and then replied with, 'He's got a semi.'

Smutton was on it in an instant and looking straight at me she said, 'Oh, BabyB. You've got a semi? I know I can have an effect on young men but so early in the day? I'm flattered.'

I blushed and started stumbling to explain. But before I could splutter out any words she added, 'Though you'll have to do better than a semi, BabyB. You'll find that's about as useful as a chocolate teapot.'

Thursday 15 May 2008
Year 2 (week 33): Role play

Finally got a text from TopFlirt this afternoon saying that she apologised for disappearing and would like to meet up tomorrow evening. That is, midway through the trial. Despite the trouble she's caused and the difficulties she must know we're in, the text was actually a little flirty. But if I'm honest, maybe that's just my excuse. Because the judge had taken a break a little earlier than usual that day, and I'd been taken out for a very liquid lunch by SlipperySlope who wanted to get the full low-down on Smutton and BrainWasher and insisted on feeding me copious amounts of booze as a result. So when I arrived back at court I was already feeling a little the worse for wear. All of which might explain why I replied with a slightly fruity text saying:

Hey sexy, look forward to seeing you tomorrow evening and examining your particulars. I fear a bit of role play might be essential in teasing out all the details of the case. BB.

Which would have been bad in itself on a number of levels. But I realised it was far worse when I received a text back by return saying,

BabyBarista, I don't know whether this is some sort of litigation game on your part but I like your style. Where would you like to meet and what would you like me to wear? How about a super-hero evening? UpTights

I went straight to my sent messages and discovered that instead of sending it to TopFlirt I had mistakenly pressed the next name alphabetically in my mobile phone's address book, and that just happened to belong to the wicked witch.

Oh.

But you know what they say? Desperate times call for desperate measures and you never know what information I might be able to gather. So, girding my loins as it were, I replied to UpTights:

10 p.m. your house. As for the superhero, we could have Cat Woman or Wonder Woman but I'd prefer to see you in a skirt. How about Super Girl? Your call for me.

To which I received an immediate reply:

You've always been my little caped crusader, BabyB x

So after re-texting TopFlirt, I now have a meeting with her at 7 p.m. tomorrow evening followed by a very frightening encounter with an ageing superhero at 10 p.m.

Friday 16 May 2008
Year 2 (week 33): Service industry

'I hate clients,' said the junior tenant Teflon as he arrived back in chambers after an obviously hard day in court.

'The world would be so much easier without them,' smiled TheVamp.

'Quite right,' said OldSmoothie. 'No more whining in confer-ence, getting witness statements wrong and then complaining when they have to pay even when they've lost.'

'And that's just the solicitor clients,' said HeadofChambers with a chuckle.

'At least we don't have to deal with the lay clients day-to-day. It'd be a complete nightmare,' said TheVamp.

There was a lot of nodding and agreement on that one.

'Perish the thought,' said BusyBody sarcastically. 'Having to take phone calls and explain how the case is progressing and all. It'd be quite beneath us.'

'BusyBody,' said OldSmoothie, 'that's the most sensible thing you've said in all of your time in chambers.'

Monday 19 May 2008
Year 2 (week 34): Exposed

Well, what can I say about Friday evening? It was quite a night and that's for sure. First there was my rendezvous with TopFlirt. Thankfully she turned up and was very sensible and down to business.

'I'm sorry I just disappeared, BabyB. I suddenly started to panic that I'd got in too deep, what with TopFirst's involvement, my mother and then this big threatening corporation. I just got so scared and went to stay with a college friend who lives by the sea.'

'Yes, your mother . . .' I answered, leaving it hanging.

'I'm so sorry that I didn't tell you, BabyB. I have to admit that it was one of the reasons I originally contacted you. I hated what TopFirst was doing on the case and wanted to see if I could garner any idea from you as to how I could help.'

'But you didn't exactly hit me with particularly probing questions about the case,' I replied.

'That's because I lost my bottle from the first time we met up. I didn't expect to fancy you.'

'But why didn't you just tell me about it? I would have kept your secret.'

'I really wanted to but that would have meant you working out why I contacted you in the first place and then not trusting me at all.'

Despite the tallness of the story and my added reservations due to the fact that she is still, after all, TopFirst's fiancée, I found myself believing what she was saying.

'So what about WhistleBlower? Was that you?'

'It was. I read through TopFirst's files and found a report on a lady who they were considering sacking after she'd threatened to blow the whistle internally on the damaging effects of their mobile technology.'

'And you put her in touch with me?'

'Exactly.'

'So you can also put me back in touch with her now?'

'I can.'

She gave me her name and address, which I hope means that we are back in business trial-wise. Everything remained above board throughout our meeting and we parted with a kiss on the cheek.

After that it was time for a quick change into my Bat Man outfit in the back of a pub, and then into a cab over to UpTights's house in Islington. I didn't quite know what I was letting myself in for and felt just a bit silly as I climbed out of the cab. But silliness was more than overcome by a straightforward fear. Fear of UpTights the sexual predator. My thoughts turned in particular to the black widow spider who devours her mate after sex. Then again, there was always the chance that I would find something out about the case and, as TheBoss used to say, 'litigation is war'. It's fair to say that as I made my way to the house I was still undecided as to quite what I was going to do.

When I arrived there was a note on the door telling me to go straight in and make myself comfortable in the sitting room. Once inside there was another note saying, 'Hello, my little superhero. Why don't you slip into these and then get yourself a drink as I perform my own superhero change.' Below the note was a pair of Bat Man boxer shorts.

Well, this was already getting weird to say the least but I figured I had come this far already. In for a pound and all that. Except, as I stood there glass in hand in my new boxer shorts, it was not UpTights who came down the stairs but TopFirst. 'Wave to the camera, BabyB,' he said, as he fired off a dozen photographs of me standing there looking dumbfounded.

'What? How?'

'We're in the middle of trial, BabyB. You should have realised that I might actually be looking after UpTights's mobile whilst she was on her feet.'

Oh.

'As for this evening, all it took was for me to volunteer to house-sit UpTights's cats whilst she spends the night at her mother's in Dulwich.'

Oh.

'But look on the bright side. You can forget your own little threats against me. Now I've got a nice picture of you looking like a trespassing pervert to give to the press once my complaint against you is upheld.'

With that, he was out of the house, camera in hand, before I could even think of a reply.

Tuesday 20 May 2008
Year 2 (week 34): Old joke

I went to meet OldSmoothie in a bar after work in order to discuss the case, but found him half-cut and chortling away with HeadofChambers, who had spent the day judging and was now in full flow in his description of the lady barrister who had appeared in front of him.

'I told her to dispense with the pleadings and move on swiftly to the oral submissions.'

'Yes,' said OldSmoothie. 'Get her to show you her Part 18s and then after a cheeky *res ipsa loquitur* you could grant her the easement she sought.'

'Well quite, and since she was representing a bank I suppose I could order her to strip her assets and then after a period of inflation I could give her a good triple-A rating.'

As this went on, a lady legal executive who has been working on the Moldy cases approached OldSmoothie and he couldn't help slobbering all over her. Understandably, she didn't linger and as she left HeadofChambers, who by this point was approaching a paralytic state, slurred at OldSmoothie, 'She seems smart.'

'Well quite,' replied OldSmoothie.

'Out of ten?' said HeadofChambers.

'Oh, I'd give her half of two,' came the reply.

'Exactly. The old ones are always the best,' chortled HeadofChambers and they raised their glasses.

At this moment TheVamp came up from behind our table and having clearly overheard the previous comment said, 'Yes, I hear that's a philosophy to which BabyB also subscribes. Particularly when it comes to women. Nice photo by the way. Seems to be doing the rounds. Must have received it from at least fifteen different people today.'

Oh.

Today Ethel was on the witness stand giving evidence about her uncontrollable tendency to chuck buckets of water over groups of young people. OldSmoothie was helping her through her main evidence. He said, 'So, what is it about young people which brings on this urge?'

'Oh it's not all young people,' said Ethel. 'Only those I consider are up to no good. Ones who make threatening comments as they walk by or who I see spitting or dropping litter. I just can't help myself I'm afraid.'

'And where do you keep your bucket of water.'

'Oh I've got the hosepipe running to the end of my garden and a row of five buckets that I like to keep ready loaded at all times. Just in case.'

'And how do people react to this?' asked OldSmoothie.

'Well, actually, I've found that passers-by tend to give me a round of applause,' said Ethel. 'Although obviously the youngsters are not so keen.' She smiled and then added, 'I think they're rather frightened, truth be told.'

The evidence went on all morning and was expected to continue well into the afternoon. At around midday TopFirst rushed into court and spoke to BusyBody who then whispered to UpTights and the three of them all discreetly sidled out after politely bowing to the judge. Obviously something had arisen about which they needed to confer. Either that or they were just getting so bored that this was their excuse to slip off for an early lunch. Whatever the reason it meant that they left poor FraGiles, the pupil with the delicate disposition, as the barrister covering for their side and making sure a good note was taken. I say 'poor' FraGiles only in hindsight, because when OldSmoothie saw what was happening he clearly decided to make mischief and sped a little faster through Ethel's evidence so that he had unexpectedly finished by quarter to one. This meant that there was still a quarter of an hour left before lunch and it was now time for the other side to start Ethel's cross-examination.

The judge had clearly got out of bed the wrong side today and he had been grumpy with OldSmoothie all morning. What is more, he is a notorious bully, particularly when it comes to young counsel and FraGiles was now sitting directly in his firing line.

'So, young man, do you have any questions for this witness?'

'Er, we do, my Lord?'

Inevitably, the end of his sentence began to rise, accompanied by the judge's eyes as they rose to the ceiling whilst his tight lips revealed his impatience. He glared at FraGiles and interrupted him with, 'Are you quite sure about that? It sounds to me like you're asking me a question.'

'Yes, my Lord?'

'I'm sorry, young man, but could you just give me an answer. Maybe we should start off by you introducing yourself to the court.'

'I am Ms UpTights's pupil, my Lord, and as you know she represents the defendant in this matter?'

'Are you sure about that? Or anything else for that matter?'

FraGiles visibly wilted at this hectoring and he replied, 'Yes, my Lord, I'm very sure that I am Ms UpTights's pupil and that she represents the defendant?'

'So why are you asking me a question? Don't they teach you how to speak in Bar School these days?' said the judge.

'My Lord, I certainly didn't mean it as a question?'

'Well why are you speaking in that ridiculous namby-pamby little voice of yours then? Stop being such a wet blanket. Go on, let's see if you can say anything with any degree of confidence at all.'

Then, astonishingly, FraGiles suddenly cracked. 'My Lord, I am well aware of the impediment in my speech and have spent many years trying to correct it? Your reputation had already preceded you as a bully but even I hadn't imagined quite how accurate the caricature really was? So my Lord, let me tell you one thing with absolute confidence? This afternoon I will order a transcript of your unseemly little outburst? You will then receive notice from the Office of Judicial Supervision seeking your answer to a formal complaint, which will have been made against you? This will then give you the opportunity to reflect on what you have just said at your leisure? In the meantime, I would like to see that my clients get the fair hearing to which they are entitled in our great system of justice, and I would therefore respectfully request that the case be adjourned until Ms UpTights's return after lunch?'

I looked at FraGiles in awe as the judge was utterly silenced. What is more, now that he had been put on notice that the case would be scrutinised by the powers that be, 'on reflection and as a matter of fairness' he agreed to grant the short adjournment and we all went for lunch a little early, with pupil sport well and truly over for the day.

Perhaps best of all was the fact that even though he was on the other side, TheMoldies' sense of dignity and fair play had obviously been tweaked and after FraGiles had finished his speech, TheMoldies at the back of the court gave him a cheer and a round of applause.

Thursday 22 May 2008
Year 2 (week 34): Old friends

From the sound of the row I overheard in one of the conference rooms at court this morning, it's clear that the pressure of the trial is getting to both OldSmoothie and UpTights. From the pompous one I heard, 'The drip, drip, drip of life's little disappointments have calcified your heart, UpTights. You think you're building this great defence against the world whereas all you're really building is your own solitary prison.'

To which the stretched one replied, 'Oh get over yourself, OldSmoothie. You cower behind a wall of committees and smug innuendo as if to avoid the fact you're a complete failure in every aspect of your sad little life. But hey, we both know what you really can't handle. The fact that I rejected you all those years ago. Time to move on, old man.'

Friday 23 May 2008
Year 2 (week 34): Lemon next to the pie

As I die of shame, the only bit of good news is that BrainWasher is doing a sterling job on the judge. Apparently he's got his early morning newspaper seller wearing a T-shirt with the slogan 'Mobile Madness' and a picture of an insane-looking cartoon mobile phone character. Then he has somehow arranged for a billboard to go up just outside Temple tube with a picture of a confused-looking elderly person saying, 'Don't forget where you came from . . . or where you're going to . . .' All this is in addition to the various conversations that are being staged near him whilst he is on the tube itself.

I think BrainWasher's rather enjoying the challenge and he described this as merely 'the lemon next to the pie'. It makes me wonder what's coming next.

Monday 26 May 2008
Year 2 (week 35): Call my bluff

'Word reaches me that you paid me a visit the other day, BabyB.' It was UpTights and she was not here to discuss the Moldy cases. 'Dressed as Bat Man, I hear.'

'Er . . . well . . .'

'Very fetching you looked too in your little boxer shorts,' she added. 'That was very naughty of TopFirst. Rest assured he's been in the doghouse since I found out.' Then she added with a smirk, 'But I have to admit that it raised a little smile when I received the first of the emails. I hope it didn't distract you from the case. Couldn't have that, could we?'

I still couldn't think of anything to say that might remotely mitigate my embarrassment, and so UpTights was free to really indulge herself.

'BabyB, if you wanted to see me dressed as Super Girl, you only had to ask. Sounds rather fun. Maybe we should give it a go this weekend?'

At this I almost choked. But I was beginning to reach the end of my tether and so decided to take the high-risk approach. I rose from my chair, went over to her, leaned in very closely and whispered in her ear, 'Now there's a thing, UpTights. Maybe we should. I think perhaps my place this time. Though it's actually my mother's as I think you know. What do you say? We could video it this time, as well.'

Thankfully this did the trick and she reverted back to the UpTights of old, barking, 'Do be quiet, BabyB. You always have to take things just that little bit too far, don't you?'

With which she scuttled from the room.

Tuesday 27 May 2008
Year 2 (week 35): Tontine

'Have you ever heard of a tontine, BabyB?'

OldRuin and I were sharing an early morning coffee in chambers. I admitted that I hadn't.

'Quite simple, really. It's an agreement whereby a group of people hold assets together and as each one dies those left behind get what remains.'

'Oh, I see,' I replied, not really seeing.

'Well, the reason I ask is that I was party to a tontine with three friends from university. We had no money back then and very rarely thought about the future. But despite that, when it came to our final term we used up all our savings to buy four bottles of Chateau Mouton Rothschild 1945. Said to be possibly the greatest vintage of the last century.' He paused before continuing, 'One we drank on graduation and another after the tragically early death of one of our merry band in a skiing accident. The third was opened a couple of years ago after another passed away – a high court judge no less. Today, I have the unenviable task of opening the final bottle.'

'I'm sorry to hear that OldRuin. Very sorry indeed.'

He looked older than ever, as if he was surveying not just his own life but those of his three companions as well. Their ups and downs, loves and losses. 'Very kind of you to say, BabyB. Really never thought it would be me. I was never the sporty healthy type you see. But you never can tell. I remember when my father died many years ago that someone said that it was now my generation's turn to step up and face the artillery of time. I've dodged one or two bullets since then.'

He paused again, wistfully, before bringing forth a smile of happiness that looked as if it had suddenly been delivered up fresh from his youth. 'The whole point of the tontine, BabyB, was to be able to share it with people for whom you care and I wondered if you and Claire would like to share this bottle with me tomorrow evening?' Then he added with another smile, 'You never know but it might help me to remember my younger self and of course it could also give us our first chance to discuss the hospital case.'

As I was leaving, OldRuin looked up and said, 'BabyB, I know how busy and stressful life is for you at the moment but please, just for me, try to get there on time and to leave your work behind you. Just for one evening.'

And so that is what I will be doing tomorrow evening.

Wednesday 28 May 2008
Year 2 (week 35): A bit of work

'Did you get that work done, Ms UpTights?' asked HeadClerk this morning.

'Sags, bags and bingo wings,' said OldSmoothie. 'Can't you tell?'

'Oh yes, very funny, I'm sure,' said UpTights. 'We'll see if you're feeling as full of yourself next Tuesday when your so-called witness, WhistleBlower, is due in court.'

'Well, I think you're looking very healthy at the moment, Ms UpTights,' said HeadClerk, ever the diplomat.

'It's funny you should say that actually since I've been doing gym five times a week recently.'

At which point TheVamp entered the room and immediately enquired, 'Who's Jim?'

Thursday 29 May 2008
Year 2 (week 35): Old friends

I have to admit that I was pretty nervous about going out to drinks last night given that Claire would be coming along as well. But despite my reservations, it went very well thanks to the charm of OldRuin. After we'd arrived and sat down, he started off the proceedings by pouring a glass of his treasured wine and saying, 'I propose a toast to the importance of good friends.'

Though I didn't get a chance to talk to Claire by myself, he kept the conversation going smoothly all evening and whenever it appeared that it might be getting awkward, he took our minds off things by asking Claire about specific legal points on the hospital case. I still don't know quite what's going on with Claire and her new man but for last night at least it didn't seem to matter. When the bottle came to an end and we went on to dinner, the conversation had turned to much lighter fare and for one evening at least the cloud really did lift. Above all, I realised quite how much I'd missed Claire although it looks like I will have to resign myself to being just good friends.

Friday 30 May 2008
Year 2 (week 35): Glimmer of hope

For the first time in weeks there does at least appear to be some glimmer of hope on the horizon, albeit limited. Firstly, I heard from the Bar Standards Board today and they have agreed to adjourn the hearing until the end of the Moldy litigation. This gives me more time to work on my contingency plan of getting TopFirst to withdraw the complaint.

Then there's WhistleBlower, who TheBoss still hasn't managed to find, despite now having her address courtesy of TopFlirt. However, he remains optimistic that he will be able to use the address to track her down in the next few crucial days. Finally, there's our dear old clients TheMoldies who this week have been giving evidence about their suffering, and regardless as to how weak the substance of our case really is, the judge can't help but sympathise with their cause.

Particularly when he's also being brainwashed.

CHAPTER 9
June: JudgeFetish

Monday 2 June 2008
Year 2 (week 36): Needle in a haystack

There's a cartoon in which a very worried and tired-looking lawyer is in a room filled from floor to ceiling with law books and he says, 'The worst of it is that I know the answer's in here somewhere.' It's just how I feel today, after OldSmoothie has officially put me on WhistleBlower duty. Track her down, he says – or else. The difficulty is that it's quite possible that she's run into hiding as a result of threats from the telecom company and so she could literally be holed up anywhere. At least that *was* the difficulty until I received a text today from TopFlirt telling me that she has discovered the new whereabouts of our key witness. Finally, I thought I might be getting somewhere.

So that is why I found myself in deepest Sussex this afternoon and when I eventually located WhistleBlower I presented her with a witness summons that I had had issued after TopFlirt had finally given me her name and address. She seemed shocked that I had found her and also, I have to admit, a little frightened. I really did feel for her, particularly as she was only in the middle of this due to trying to do the right thing in the first place. I had a long chat with her and tried to reassure her that it would all work out. I also told her that if she really had serious worries as to her safety then I was sure that the police would help out. As I left I gave her a summary of about twenty of our cases in which TheMoldies are claiming injury, complete with pictures and life stories, which I hope will pull on her conscience.

It's now eight in the evening and I am just hoping that she turns up tomorrow, because without her we remain in serious difficulties.

Tuesday 3 June 2008
Year 2 (week 36): Rustling

Thankfully WhistleBlower turned up today. She did so at around two in the afternoon and far too late to get all her evidence in, but at least she made it. It seems she did indeed go to the police because she marched in with one of them in tow. As we had expected, the other side kicked up an enormous fuss, particularly given the fact that they've recently taken the line that the documents are forgeries, presumably on the basis that they felt there was no chance that WhistleBlower would ever make it into a courtroom. They immediately demanded an adjournment and the judge was looking like he was minded to grant it.

Then OldSmoothie stood up and actually earned his ridiculously large brief fee in a few sentences. 'Perhaps, we might just be able to have the evidence-in-chief this afternoon? After all, that'll allow the other side to know exactly what is being said by this witness.'

In other words, WhistleBlower could at least start her evidence today. As OldSmoothie continued to great effect, there was a huge commotion at the back of the court. A couple of executives from the telecom company were trying to make their solicitor get UpTights's attention. This is a big mistake when you're dealing with UpTights I can tell you. She resolutely ignored each one of the stage whispers being thrown in her direction until eventually the solicitor started putting Post-it notes on her back. Still she didn't turn round and within the space of about ten minutes the back of her jacket and even her hair had turned yellow.

We were eventually allowed to start WhistleBlower's evidence off and she did the business by stating that all the documents she had provided were originals and even elaborating on the cover-up that had taken place within the company.

After this, OldSmoothie got up and said, 'Given that the other side have said all along that these documents are forgeries, before we adjourn today could they indicate to us whether they will continue to peddle such a lie or not. We, too, need to be able to prepare our case for the adjourned hearing.'

Whilst the rustling behind her continued, you could see UpTights's normally ramrod straight back sag slightly. She was stumped. Even to hesitate would be to indicate to the judge that she didn't believe her own client's case. When she eventually got up and mumbled that they could not possibly know what would be the case in the face of such late evidence, the judge's eyebrows were already raised and you could tell that he was mightily unconvinced.

So her testimony that the documents were true was allowed in. Now we just have to keep WhistleBlower available to give the rest of her evidence, which the judge has set for next week. If she fails to turn up the other side will rightly claim that without being able to challenge it, her evidence won't amount to a hill of beans.

Wednesday 4 June 2008
Year 2 (week 36): The long con

HeadofChambers accosted me in the clerks room this morning. 'I assume that you don't intend to go to court like that?' he said.

'Er, yes, that's exactly what I'm about to do. Is there something wrong?'

'Is there something wrong? Hmm, where to start?' He took a deep breath and went on, 'BabyBarista, I had the benefit of having been born looking like a barrister . . .' You couldn't be more right there, I thought. He then waved his hand theatrically and continued, '. . . but you on the other hand didn't.' He gave me one of his particularly patronising smiles before continuing, 'However, fortunately for you, I intend to help.'

'Hmm, help in dressing me up like a pompous old fool stuck in the nineteenth century when, believe it or not, court hearings are now being blogged about and even the next Prime Minister knows what Converse trainers are . . .' is what I'd have liked to have said. Instead I simply replied, 'Oh.'

'Yes, I've already talked to you about getting rid of that rucksack of yours and investing in a leather pilot bag. Clients will never respect a man with a rucksack.'

'Oh.'

'Then I see that recently you've taken to wearing shirts without double cuffs.'

'It avoids the need for cufflinks,' I replied.

'That may be so but no opponent is ever going to take you seriously with cheap cuffs.'

'Oh.'

'And as for your slip-on shoes and off-the-peg suit . . .' He was at this point literally lost for words.

'BabyBarista, if you're not careful, you'll have fallen so low that people will . . .' he hesitated as if he was going to deliver a terrible blow for which somehow I needed to be braced, '. . . people will think . . .' another hesitation and then he spat out the words with an expression I imagine he has when he's just sipped a wine which has gone off, '. . . people will think, BabyBarista, that you're a solicitor.'

'What was it Mark Twain said?' smiled OldRuin, who had been listening in. 'Clothes make the man. Naked people have little or no influence on society.'

Later on I received another update from BrainWasher.

'We've decided to try and convince the judge that in fact he's suffering the effects of mobile poisoning himself,' he said.

'And how are you doing that?' I asked.

'Two pronged. First, we've set up a pressure group in his local area in Fulham campaigning against a nearby mobile mast.'

'Which at least exists, I assume?'

'Er, well, not exactly, but we're counting on him not investigating further than the headlines in the local paper, which we've also managed to manipulate by paying his local seller to provide the judge with our own fake copies of the paper.'

'But then you still need to make him think he's actually suffering.'

'That's true. Which is why we've had our people working on his journey to and from work each day. For example, the newspaper seller has again come in handy. Twice now the judge has handed over five pounds and the seller has given him change for amounts greater than that. When he's questioned him and offered the money back, the seller's sleight of hand has left the judge doubting his own mind.'

Oh.

Thursday 5 June 2008
Year 2 (week 36): QueenBee

Smutton called me over to her office again today. The more I see of this glamorous solicitor the more she brings to mind a queen bee dominating the hive around her. This is not only because she's more alpha than any male or simply because she makes the other solicitors around her appear like drones. No, it's also because, above all, she is always ready with a sting in her tail. Today it was aimed at the judge himself.

'I'd like your assistance in looking a little closer into the er, personal affairs of our good friend the judge in the Moldy litigation.'

'How can I help?' I asked.

'Well, it just so happens that I've discovered the name of the lady with whom he is having an affair. He's something of a sugar daddy to her by all accounts. She's a friend of a friend and tomorrow evening you and I will be attending a drinks party that she is hosting. Sound good?'

'Er, yes. Sure,' I replied. 'But what exactly do you want me to do?'

'Oh, BabyB. You're not quite as naïve as you like to let people believe. Let's just say I'd like you to get to know her a little better and discover if the judge has any ...' she drew breath, smiled and then continued, '... special interests. I'm sure you'll work it out.'

With which she dismissed me from her presence and left me to ponder my first meeting with SugarBaby.

All in all ... bee-witching ... (sorry).

Friday 6 June 2008
Year 2 (week 36): Virgin on the rude

'I've been examining law students today,' said OldSmoothie at chambers tea.

'Yes, I bet you have,' said BusyBody sarcastically.

'In every conceivable way, no doubt,' said UpTights.

'Intimately,' added BusyBody.

'You know, sometimes I get sick and tired of the two of you lowering the tone of every conversation with your whining and innuendo. Particularly when it concerns the people who carry the future of this great nation on their shoulders. Low-grade, petty and occasionally even potty-mouthed cant if you ask me.'

'Which is rich coming from a low-grade, petty and often potty-mouthed . . .'

BusyBody drew breath to deliver her final verdict and as she did everyone else stopped talking as they feared she might be about to go just too far. Then quick as a flash TheVamp interrupted with, '. . . runt, naturally.'

Collective sighs of relief followed and then OldSmoothie, assuming his most haughty and pompous look, said, 'Ladies, listen to yourselves carping away like the three witches in *Macbeth*. All I would offer you in reply are the fine words of Aristophanes: "To be insulted by you is to be garlanded with lilies."'

BusyBody fell quiet, as if surprised that for once she'd been included in the specific insults that are usually directed at UpTights. Then she looked at OldSmoothie and said, 'Why are you always so rude to UpTights?'

'Because she's a calcified witch,' said OldSmoothie without even blinking. 'Her heart turned to stone years ago and whatever soul she had wasn't able to survive in the bitterness and bile that pumps through her veins.'

'But you've got to admit that you just enjoy being nasty,' said TheCreep, rather uncharacteristically.

'Oh do give it up, won't you,' said OldSmoothie. 'You young ones are all the same. So full of wide-eyed hypocrisy that you don't even realise you're all headed in just the same direction. You can carp all you like but as sure as the sun goes up, and in UpTights's case down, one day in, er ...' he coughed, '... twenty years time, you'll wake up and realise that you've turned into us, whether you like it or not.'

Then he looked at TheCreep and gave a cruel smile, pointed at him and said, 'Although, that's not to say you're going to suddenly start growing, in case you're wondering.'

By now he had drawn an audience and he continued his lecture. 'You've already set your trajectory. You just don't realise it yet. You won't until it's far too late. It's like when they used to warn you about the wind changing when you were a child. Whatever might be in those oh so earnest little hearts of yours, you're never going to be a UN goodwill ambassador or win a Nobel Prize. You're never going to climb Mount Everest, or even simply live by the sea and write a novel. Instead cash will be king, your clerks will have more say over your lives than your family and you'll all have glorious careers at the great English Bar. So wake up kids and smell the stink of your lost dreams. They left town when you signed up for law school and boarded the cop-out-and-get-rich train of hypocrisy.'

There was prolonged silence and then everyone returned to their cups of tea and conversations as if nothing unusual had occurred at all. As I listened to OldSmoothie, I thought of my mum's and Claire's outbursts and of the grubby depths to which I had allowed myself to be dragged by Slippery and ScandalMonger and for a moment the bleak truth of OldSmoothie's words left me shaken.

Immediately after chambers tea I had a short conference with Arthur and Ethel in chambers and afterwards I took them along to meet OldRuin. As he poured them tea from a pot that he'd just made Ethel said, 'Hmm, we do like a good cup of Lapsang.'

OldRuin smiled and said, 'Yes, it's silly really but it's my favourite because it takes me back to the smell of the smoked tea we'd make as children as we built a fire and played by the river.'

'For me it's linseed oil on willow,' said Arthur. 'Just the slightest whiff and I'm taken back to those long lazy Summer afternoons watching the village cricket as you wait to go in to bat.'

'Which always reminds me of white-sliced cucumber sandwiches, scones and a big urn of hot tea,' said Ethel.

It was no surprise that they all got on extremely well. Before they were about to leave Arthur gave me a far more serious look than he's ever done when talking about the case and said, 'I'm afraid that whilst we were waiting earlier we overheard what OldSmoothie was saying, BabyBarista. In fact I think the whole of the Temple did for that matter.'

'Oh,' I said, looking embarrassed. 'Yes, we're all doomed to end up like him.'

'Don't you believe a word of it, young man. There's always hope. Right up to the end. Never let him tarnish those dreams with that terrible jaded cynicism, which reflects only on him.'

OldRuin smiled and said, 'It's true, BabyB. You're part of a wonderful profession which will allow you to do whatever you choose.' His voice lowered as he continued, 'Though we have to be careful to avoid it becoming all-consuming.'

Ethel smiled and Arthur's face lifted as if he'd just thought of something and he said, 'You know what, I think you need to meet my friend TheColonel. Next time you've got a case in the West Country, you must tell me.'

Monday 9 June 2008
Year 2 (week 37): JudgeFetish

So Friday evening went ahead as planned and I went along as Smutton's date to a very swanky drinks party in Holland Park; all high ceilings, waiters and girls on their gap years serving canapés. Well, girls on their gap years and er . . . Worrier. I saw her coming out of the kitchen carrying a tray and when she saw me she not only blushed but dropped the tray in shock. I helped her pick the food up.

'Oh, BabyB. I was so hoping I wouldn't see anyone I knew.'

'But why are you waitressing?' I asked. 'I thought you were working for some firm of solicitors?'

'I am, BabyB. But I'm still re-training and they're hardly paying me anything. Which on top of all the debts I racked up last year means that I've got to do a bit of moonlighting to make ends meet. Someone at work told me about this posh waitressing racket.'

'Well, I bet you get a few stories to tell with this job,' I commented cheerfully, hoping I'd help to calm her down.

She brightened up at that and said, 'Oh, BabyB, you'd never believe some of the things I've seen.'

Her wide eyes were even wider than usual and she looked really quite pleased with herself to have experienced such things, albeit vicariously. Before I could hear more I caught an irritated look from Smutton and I jumped to attention, wished Worrier the best and went back to her side. Next minute and she was swishing me over to the other side of the room (after a little grope of my bottom) and introducing me (with a sharp elbow in the ribs) to SugarBaby, a lovely looking lady in her mid-twenties.

'Er, hello,' I said rather lamely. 'I'm BabyBarista.'

'Hello,' she answered. 'I'm Susie. How lovely to see someone my own age.'

As we both looked around the room I realised it was full of very grown up banker and private equity types with their equally grown-up WAGs in tow. Well, I say WAGs but there were also plenty of banker women with their own partners in tow, though there doesn't seem to be any equivalent term for them. Maybe HATs: husbands and toyboys. The judge thankfully wasn't around this evening, which made things far easier. Actually, I was just relieved not to be standing around talking about how interesting it must be to be a barrister and listening to people asking how we manage to defend people we know are guilty. (After all, what do you expect? The guilty ones tend to pay more. It's far harder to defend someone you know is actually innocent.)

SugarBaby actually proved to be extremely good company, all the more so given the alternatives, and by the end of the evening we were still engrossed in not talking to the bankers. However, the trouble was that the more drunk I got the more I started to talk about Claire and about how I had lost any chance with her. This didn't actually go down as badly as it might have done, because SugarBaby then started to tell me all about her current beau, although as she said early on, 'I can't really tell you very much, BabyB, because he's married.'

Well I knew that already, of course, not that I was going to tell her. But I did start to wonder whether, if this was all the revelation I was going to get out of her, then perhaps the evening was going to prove somewhat fruitless. But as the party went on, more details about our judge started to emerge, albeit somewhat organically. Perhaps the juiciest of these was:

'You know, BabyB, it's weird but he's got a thing for shoes and underwear.'

'Oh yeah,' I replied drunkenly, 'don't we all?'

'No. I mean he really has a *thing* for it. For Myla underwear, even if it's just a hint of it, and Christian Louboutin shoes. That little red Louboutin sole sends him wild.' She gave a twirl of her ankle and looking down I caught a glimpse of polished leather above a scarlet sole. 'It's a complete fetish. Drives him absolutely crazy.'

Oh.

As I looked at SugarBaby's shoes I was beginning to see that JudgeFetish might have a point, and by the end of the evening there was only one place I was heading and it wasn't to Smutton's. Mind you, whilst she was busy fooling around with yours truly, SugarBaby continued to ramble on about how good her sugar daddy was to her, keeping up a constant, whispered refrain of 'this can't lead anywhere'.

All of which worked for me and it was mid-Saturday morning when I finally made the walk of shame home from her little judge-funded flat in West Kensington. I texted Smutton to organise a meeting with her this afternoon.

Tuesday 10 June 2008
Year 2 (week 37): First blush

Before we go any further, let me explain how I feel about older women. Or at least how I've recently started feeling about older women since Sarah Palin was first touted as a Vice-Presidential nominee in the States. I don't know whether it's the glasses or the Lois Lane-type appeal but she's definitely got something and it's certainly not her policies. Given that she's over twenty years older than me, this is beginning to give me cause for concern. Not only because I've inexplicably developed a crush on a politician but also, more worryingly, because she seems to have awakened what has presumably been a latent interest in older women more generally. OK, I admit that in the past JudgeJewellery has caused me to blush, but I figured that she was just a one-off, particularly as I'd been so horrified when UpTights tried it on last year. But now

SoccerMum Sarah and her sexy little pair of glasses have taken it to a whole new level.

Thus I found myself in a particularly vulnerable state yesterday afternoon when I arrived for my meeting with Smutton, an older woman who puts even TheVamp in the shade when it comes both to glamour and flirtation, not least because I knew that the conversation was likely to veer on to sex and women's underwear.

'Ah, if it isn't BabyCasanova himself,' she purred. 'First it was TopFlirt I hear and now SugarBaby. Good work, BabyB. You really are a very talented little barrister who I'm sure will go very far indeed.'

She raised an eyebrow as if to smirk 'all the way in fact' without actually saying it. I blushed because although neither 'conquest' had been part of a grand sordid plan of seduction, she was merely stating the facts.

Then she added, 'I hope some day I might get the chance to experience first hand just how good your skills really are.'

'My advocacy skills, clearly,' I said.

'Well, I was certainly thinking that your oral abilities would have a part to play . . .'

She moved over to the sofa and sat down. 'Have a seat,' she said, motioning to a chair opposite, which I sank into.

'Anyway, my little horsehair love machine,' she continued. 'Tell me what you found out.'

'He's got a thing for Myla and Christian Louboutins,' I said nonchalantly, as if I had in-depth knowledge of both.

'Ah-ha, and don't tell me, you've followed up that discovery with a little online research of your own?' she smiled. 'I bet you spent a little more time "researching" Myla than you did finding out about the shoes.'

'Anyway,' I said, ploughing on, 'it's more than just a small thing for him.'

'I bet it is,' said Smutton. 'At least when SugarBaby's around anyway.'

'More like a full-on fetish if she's to be believed,' I said.

'Not as rare as you might imagine, BabyB,' mused Smutton. 'Particularly when it comes to Her Majesty's judiciary.'

'Well, I was thinking that we might be able to use it in some way. I don't know,' I paused and shifted uncomfortably. 'Maybe you and The Vamp might perhaps, ahem, bear his preferences in mind when you dress to come to court?'

'BabyB. For one who plays such a worldly game, you're very naïve sometimes.'

I looked at her, uncomprehending.

'It's long been considered a simple matter of professional good practice,' she explained as if giving a lecture on the law of trusts, 'for female lawyers to dress in exactly the way you suggest for any court hearing involving a male judge.'

'Oh.'

Sarah Palin was starting to loom dangerously in my mind as Smutton leant back a little on the sofa and crossed her legs, revealing in the process a tantalising glimpse of suspender belt through the slit in her skirt.

'Er, so have you and The Vamp been dressing to please the judge all along?' I asked, my voice slightly raised.

'Of course we have. Didn't you notice? Every young man worth his salt should recognise the Christian Louboutin shoes.' She lifted her foot in the air to reveal the distinguishing red sole underneath.

'Oh.'

Except that's not all she revealed. After – as Smutton had correctly surmised – my extensive internet research, her Myla underwear was, let's just say, very easy to recognise.

'As for the underwear—'

'Yes, well, quite,' I interrupted. By this point my face was beginning to resemble a beetroot.

'BabyB. How sweet. You blush rather easily it seems.'

'Er, well, anyway.'

Tongue-tied was not a phrase I wanted to hand her at this stage of the conversation and so I gave up trying to find my words.

'And for what it's worth, according to The Vamp, even your oh-so-innocent little friend Claire isn't quite as clean-cut as you might imagine. The Vamp certainly spotted her out in Louboutin shoes the other evening and well, I'm sure you could enlighten me further as to her choice of underwear.'

Oh.

She continued, 'But looking beyond that, BabyB, you've actually given me another idea and it's one we need to pass by BrainWasher in the next couple of days.'

After which she brought the meeting to an abrupt end and I pretty much fled for the door.

Wednesday 11 June 2008
Year 2 (week 37): WhistleBlown out of the water

'Yes, I do have one or two questions for the witness,' said UpTights in court this morning.

Rather to our surprise, WhistleBlower had arrived on time and with no tales of having been threatened off the case, which immediately made me worry that we might have missed something. UpTights's tone as she started her cross examination this morning did nothing to allay those fears.

'Is it correct to say that in the past you have had problems with drugs?' asked UpTights.

'My Lord,' interrupted OldSmoothie, 'my learned friend has presented no evidence in support of such an assertion.'

'My Lord, the witness is under a duty to tell the truth and I do not therefore anticipate the need to produce such evidence. But if she denies the suggestion then, of course, such evidence will be forthcoming.'

'This is an outrage, my Lord. Trying to spring such an allegation without any warning.'

'My Lord, the huffing and puffing of my learned friend only suggests that he has concerns himself about this issue. Perhaps he might like to wait for the witness to answer before he jumps to any more sweeping conclusions.'

UpTights was completely wiping the floor with OldSmoothie and all he could do was 'Harrumph' and say, 'Well I don't exactly see that the question has any relevance at all, but if my learned friend insists on wasting valuable court time with such matters then so be it.'

UpTights savoured the moment and rose very slowly to her feet, smiling over at OldSmoothie before carefully saying, 'I'm sorry for that little interruption. I'll repeat my question. Is it correct to say that in the past you have had problems with drugs?'

WhistleBlower looked at the judge and said, 'Does this have any relevance? I thought I'd only have to answer questions about the documents.'

The judge looked down at WhistleBlower and said, 'I'm afraid that very much depends upon your answer, my dear. I think Ms UpTights here is attempting to question your credibility as a witness. So it might be a help if you simply answered the question that is being asked.'

Having heard the threat of further evidence being produced, WhistleBlower looked in no mood to argue the point and she answered, 'Yes, it's true, but I've been clean now for over ten years.'

'Thank you,' said UpTights. 'And is it also the case that you suffer from clinical depression?'

WhistleBlower again looked at the judge who nodded rather kindly at her, a bit like a hangman smiling at his next victim on the gallows. 'It's true that I am a sufferer. However, I take medication that keeps the symptoms under control.'

'Most of the time,' said UpTights. 'Though you have taken a number of days off work in the last few years as a result of your condition.'

'Yes, that's right.'

'Is it also right that you recently had your employment terminated with the defendant company?'

'Yes.'

'And that since then you have made a claim through your solicitors for unfair dismissal?'

'Yes.'

Strangely UpTights looked a little awkward after this answer, even for her. This raised my suspicions, particularly when her next question didn't even follow up on what she had elicited: 'Moving on to the documents that you leaked. Are they original documents or copies?'

'Photocopies.'

'Did you ever see the originals?'

'Er, no.'

So the copies you leaked were in fact photocopies of copies?'

'Er, yes.'

'And where did you find them?'

'They appeared on my desk one day.'

'So is it at all possible that these documents could have been forged and put on your desk by someone wanting to harm the defendant company?'

'Yes, I suppose it is possible.' She looked at her feet a little shiftily as she said this and I suddenly started to wonder whether she had in some way been forced to change her tune.

'Thank you, Ms WhistleBlower. You have been most ...' she turned to OldSmoothie as she said this and smiled maliciously, '... helpful. My Lord, I have no more questions.'

As she sat down, TopFirst passed me a note across the bench that said, 'Hope you've been practising your coffee skills.'

I poked OldSmoothie's back to get his attention and when he turned around I whispered, 'Ask her what happened to the employment claim.'

'I'm not going to ask her a question I don't know the answer to.'

'Look, it can't be any worse than what we've got so far. Come on, have a stab in the dark.'

He raised his eyebrows and, shrugging his shoulders, turned back to WhistleBlower. 'Ms WhistleBlower. It was mentioned that you recently made a claim for unfair dismissal. What has happened to that claim?'

WhistleBlower looked distinctly uncomfortable at this question and OldSmoothie quickly followed it up with, 'Let me put it another way. Has it recently settled?'

'Er, well, er ...'

Again she looked at the judge and again he gave her the hangman's smile.

'Er, yes, it did settle actually.'

'And what were the terms of that settlement?'

I smirked at TopFirst who was not looking quite so smug now. UpTights got to her feet to object.

'My Lord, the terms of that settlement were strictly confidential and the witness is under no obligation in this court to breach that settlement contract now.'

'Yes, quite,' said the judge. 'Thank you, Ms UpTights.'

The judge looked at WhistleBlower and gave her a reprieve. 'You don't need to answer that.'

'But, my Lord,' said OldSmoothie indignantly, 'I'd like to investigate the possibility that this witness has been paid off.'

This would have meant OldSmoothie having to declare that he suddenly wanted to treat her as what they call a hostile witness and therefore try and get permission to cross-examine her.

'I'm afraid you're somewhat hoisted by your own petard on that one, wouldn't you say? Even if you were to declare this witness to be hostile, you still wouldn't have any evidence to support such a suggestion, a point you were taking only a little while ago against the other side's new allegation.'

The judge beamed at OldSmoothie with great satisfaction. With no jury to play to, all OldSmoothie could do was answer through gritted teeth and with a resigned sigh, 'Of course, my Lord.'

Then UpTights gratuitously leapt to her feet and said with a manic cackle, 'I have a client who is an Everest mountaineer and he was telling me the other day that they have a term for people who experience feelings of utter dejectedness as a symptom of high-altitude sickness. You know, that feeling of defeat, when all ambition is spent and, more than anything in the world, all you want to do is just to go home. It's called "crump", my Lord.'

Then her mania became tinged with madness. 'Crump, crump, crump, my Lord. That's what it is. Now perhaps my most learned of friends might care to descend to the lower and more hospitable grounds of litigation with which he is far more familiar and where I'm certain he'll be much more comfortable.'

As she sat down, TopFirst looked over at me and made a gesture to indicate that he'd like a coffee and mouthed, 'White, one sugar.'

Thursday 12 June 2008
Year 2 (week 37): Hypnotism

'After yesterday's fiasco we really need to start upping the ante on our, er, other litigation strategies.'

I was in Smutton's office, sitting on the sofa with BrainWasher as she held court. She turned her gaze to him. 'Now, BabyB here might already have explained about our judge's little predilection for certain types of clothing. But it inspired me to think of taking your brainwashing to a whole new level. What do you think about hypnotism?'

'Yeah, right,' I said before BrainWasher had a chance to answer. 'So, I'll get out the stopwatch and start telling him he's falling asleep, shall I?'

But BrainWasher's interest had been piqued. 'Well, hypnotism's a little more subtle than that, BabyB.'

He then looked thoughtfully over at Smutton. 'Actually we could start by simply extending what you're already doing with the clothing.'

'In what way?' asked Smutton.

'By anchoring the things he likes around the bits of the litigation where we want to influence his view. So, if you were to give a quick flash of Myla when our witness is speaking, the judge would then associate everything that witness says with pleasure.'

'OK. But it might not be terribly subtle,' said Smutton, which I thought was a little ironic given that subtlety is not something that usually seems to concern her.

'Well we don't just have to work with underwear and shoes. After having followed his every move for the last few weeks, I can tell you, for example, that he has a particular weakness for Häagen-Dazs. He even sneaks off at lunchtime to eat a couple of small tubs in a local café.'

'So?' I asked.

'So we could maybe arrange for people to come into our side of the courtroom wearing a Häagen-Dazs T-shirt or cap whenever OldSmoothie's saying something we want the judge to like.'

'Right,' I said, remaining sceptical.

'And, I've also discovered from one of my "tube passengers" that he hates Manchester United with a passion.'

'Good man,' I said 'Blue Army all the way.'

'Er, well, yes,' said BrainWasher, slightly confused. 'So, as you can probably guess, whenever we want the judge to *dislike* something, we arrange for someone wearing a Manchester United badge or T-shirt to walk into court on our opponents' side of the room.'

Well, the idea had grabbed my imagination, if not the science behind it, so we gave him the green light. In fact as I write this he is currently auditioning people to find suitable candidates to wear the Häagen-Dazs and Manchester United T-shirts respectively.

He also told me to get our side to very subtly mirror the body language of the judge as another less specific non-verbal strategy for winning him over. Oh, and he mentioned that it might be useful if I steadily roll my bewigged head from side to side during the hearing as well . . .

Friday 13 June 2008
Year 2 (week 37): Who guards the guards?

OldRuin was in chambers today and talking to HeadClerk about police powers.

'It's the age-old problem,' he said. 'It's all very well having an independent police force but then who guards the guards?'

'We do. The people,' said HeadClerk. 'You know, through Parliament.'

'You're right, of course,' answered OldRuin. 'But who guards *them*?'

'Well, the judges do, I suppose,' said HeadClerk. 'But now you're going to ask me who guards them, I suppose?'

'It had crossed my mind.'

'Well, it's the barristers who guard the judges against the worst of their excesses. Expose their weaknesses. "Steer them away from the folly of their instincts" as HeadofChambers always likes to put it.'

'I see. So it's the Bar who actually guards the guards?'

'Well, yes, I suppose it is.'

OldRuin paused for effect, 'And who would you say guards them?'

HeadClerk beamed as he suddenly realised where OldRuin had gently led the conversation.

'Why it's the clerks of course! You're absolutely right, OldRuin. I hadn't thought of it like that before. Through a long and convoluted network of checks and balances it's ultimately the humble barrister's clerk who guards our democratic freedoms.'

'Quite so,' smiled OldRuin.

Monday 16 June 2008
Year 2 (week 38): Long shot

As well as the extra hours I've been forced to put in on the Moldy litigation, I've also had to juggle working on OldRuin's hospital case. In the last few weeks this has often meant working late into the night just to stay on top of it. It involves lots of documents concerning both the hospital and the decision-making process, and then endless amounts of case law that I'm having to read for the first time. I've been doing most of this alone because, to be fair to OldRuin, he's been quite subtle in his efforts to reconcile Claire and me and he has left us with different and discrete pieces of work to be getting on with.

But with the hearing set for August, it was finally time for us all to have a meeting with the locals in OldRuin's village today. So, around midday I found myself drinking coffee in Waterloo station with Claire and OldRuin as we waited to board the train to deepest Hampshire. OldRuin had travelled into chambers this morning under the auspices of 'needing to collect some papers' but by this point I knew full well that the real reason was so that he could help smooth the way between Claire and me. For what it's worth, it certainly seemed to be working.

After we'd boarded and taken our seats, OldRuin led the conversation. 'I love this time of year. As soon as you get off the train you'll smell the elderflowers just outside the station and then within a hundred yards you pass a little patch of woodland packed full with wild garlic.'

'Do you pick them?' I asked.

'Oh indeed yes. I very much like to have a little elderflower wine on the go and my wife always insisted that I made some cordial to complement it. As for the garlic, it's rather good in salads. You know it was so prized in the past that its location even used to appear on early maps.'

He smiled as he ruminated on country matters. 'Though I think my favourite crop of the early summer is the asparagus. I've never found it growing wild but our local grocer always seems to manage to source it from somewhere. The king of the vegetables they call it and not without reason.' Claire and I smiled at each other over our coffees.

When we finally arrived at OldRuin's village, what was most noticeable was OldRuin's high standing in the local community. A number of people mentioned to me how kind he had been to them personally and how much they admired him. The meeting today was for us to explain to everyone the timetable and also to bring together the various local groupings that would form the campaign outside of the litigation. Despite all our hard work, however, we are all well aware that at the very best it's a long shot.

On the train back, after OldRuin had waved goodbye to us from the platform, Claire and I had a moment of awkward silence. Eventually I asked her a question about a case I knew she had been working on and soon we were catching up with each other's lives as if the awkwardness had never happened. I realised once again how much I'd missed her. And although I didn't dare ask about her love life, I did at one point hesitatingly compliment her on her shoes. She looked embarrassed.

'Oh, these. Silly really. Not very practical I admit but I have a very glamorous grandmother who gave me them for my birthday and I feel guilty if I don't wear them occasionally.'

So much for TheVamp's and Smutton's great theory about Claire.

Tuesday 17 June 2008
Year 2 (week 38): Taking the ass out of harass

'Does anyone know anything about sexual harassment?' TheCreep asked this morning in the clerks room.

'OldSmoothie's the expert in that department,' replied UpTights promptly.

'And you should know by now that it's not sexual harASSment,' said HeadofChambers emphasising the second syllable. 'Harass rhymes with embarrass and embarrassment's exactly what you'll be suffering if you start throwing around that sort of Americanism in front of an English judge.'

'Though let's be fair,' said TheVamp, 'an employment tribunal isn't exactly the top of the judicial ladder.'

'Ooh, feisty!' said TheCreep, who has recently begun attempting to quote from television series such as *The Inbetweeners* in the hope that a bit of their credibility might rub off.

'And anyway, I think that you'll find that OldSmoothie has always put the stress on the ass when it comes to harassment,' added UpTights, ignoring TheCreep.

'You know,' said TheCreep earnestly breaking back in, 'I was recently invited to join a Facebook group that calls itself the "Sexual Harrassment Action Group" . . .' His voice tailed off as he noticed the silence and the smirks that followed.

'So quiet you can almost hear a penny drop,' said TheBusker with a smile.

Wednesday 18 June 2008
Year 2 (week 38): The moderniser

OldSmoothie went in for a meeting at Tory HQ yesterday, following up on BigMouth's suggestion that he might make rather a good life peer. Unfortunately for him, however, it seems BigMouth's influence doesn't quite extend as far as the leader's office and he was told that they were really looking for people who are a bit more 'with it'. Whilst the rest of chambers has no doubt that this means people who are more 'on the ball' and maybe just in touch with the real world, he's taken it to mean 'trendy'.

With this in mind he has unfortunately turned to TheCreep for lifestyle advice, after hearing him quoting from *The Inbetweeners* again. The result was that yesterday OldSmoothie was spotted strutting around in black Converse trainers ('sneaker shoes' as he calls them) and loudly answering his iPhone in the style of Nessa from *Gavin & Stacey*. Nessa as interpreted by an ageing barrister in a cut-glass English accent. It is as tragic as it sounds and living proof that in the cases of both TheCreep and OldSmoothie it's definitely how you tell them that counts. As UpTights pointed out, 'Reminds me of that line from Evelyn Waugh about the one being a Dodo and the other a petrified egg.'

Thursday 19 June 2008
Year 2 (week 38): Addressing the Chair

UpTights has recently set up a marketing committee for chambers and I attended its inaugural meeting today. She opened by saying, 'Now, before we get started I'd like to clarify exactly how I wish to be addressed.'

'What, like an envelope?' asked OldSmoothie.

UpTights ignored the remark and continued, 'I don't think the name "chairman" would be entirely appropriate.'

'How about simply "The Chair"?' asked BusyBody.

'I'm not a piece of furniture,' said UpTights indignantly.

'And she doesn't have four legs either,' added TheBusker with a smile.

OldSmoothie drew breath as if to add to that comment but then in an unusual show of restraint said, 'No, I won't say it. Such an innuendo would be beneath me.'

'I doubt that that would be possible,' retorted UpTights. 'Anyway, I would like to be addressed as "Madam Chairwoman".'

'For the avoidance of any doubt, naturally,' said OldSmoothie.

Ever the peacemaker, OldRuin then added, 'You know, whenever I'm challenged by my use of words like he, him or man, I tell them that they should be construed in the same way as those under section 6(a) of The Interpretation Act 1978, in which words importing the masculine gender are deemed to include the feminine.'

Friday 20 June 2008
Year 2 (week 38): Smutton or Slutton?

We were discussing Smutton at chambers tea today.

'She's got a certain, er, *je ne sais quoi*,' I said.

'More like *je ne sais pas* if you ask me,' said UpTights.

'Yes, she's definitely the brassy to UpTights's classy,' said HeadofChambers with a smile.

'Classy with a capital K,' said OldSmoothie.

'Well, quite,' said HeadofChambers.

'Or maybe the Smutton to UpTights's Slutton?' said OldSmoothie chortling, as usual, at his own joke.

Then BusyBody stepped in. 'You know, with the amount of hot air you two produce, you could start your very own barrister wind farm.'

'I like that idea,' said TheBusker. 'Imagine if you set up some turbines at say the High Court and also the Houses of Parliament at the same time. They'd probably generate enough power for the whole of London.'

'And I hear they can even generate electricity from sewage,' said UpTights, 'which might also be of use to OldSmoothie given that most of what he says comes out of his back end.'

As we returned to our room from tea, I happened to mention to OldRuin that I had been struggling with a little DIY for my mother last night and had decided that it wasn't something in which I excelled.

'BabyB, I've always subscribed to the philosophy that it is essential to earn enough to ensure that one never has to pick up a paint brush or screwdriver. You know about Lord Finchley, I'm sure?'

I replied that I didn't. OldRuin said, 'Hilaire Belloc I think. Now let's see if I can remember how it goes. It's been a few years.'

He paused and looked up and then slowly recited the following lines:

> '"Lord Finchley tried to mend the Electric Light
> Himself. It struck him dead: And serve him right!
> It is the business of the wealthy man
> To give employment to the artisan."'

Monday 23 June 2008
Year 2 (week 39): Barrister mating rituals

After the stitch up that was WhistleBlower's performance in court, UpTights has been rubbing our respective noses in it with the judge at every opportunity and she is very much managing to control the narrative of the trial. So much so, in fact, that even JudgeFetish has started making derogatory noises about WhistleBlower's evidence. This has not only infuriated OldSmoothie but it also means that our extra-curricular tactics are now even more of a necessity and BrainWasher has been hard at work spreading his not-so-subtle messages in the courtroom. Today it felt a little like he was putting on a circus.

First there were the T-shirts: a succession of beautiful girls wearing Häagen-Dazs T-shirts entered the courtroom each time OldSmoothie was making a point. Then, whenever UpTights got to her feet, a fat, male Manchester United fan would come in. All of this to-ing and fro-ing was set against a backdrop that included Smutton and UpTights dressed to the nines, as always, in Myla and Louboutins, a detail I was finally noticing.

Ostensibly, the subject of today's proceedings was the evidence from one of the telecom company's executives. But the real show, as is so often the case, actually belonged to the barristers. Every time one of them stood up either to interrupt or to ask a question, the other one would lob a whispered insult across the courtroom.

'You're a stretched and gabbling shrew-faced old harridan, UpTights,' whispered OldSmoothie.

At which UpTights leant back like a coiled spring before unleashing, 'Can't you do any better than that, OldSmoothie, you prattling, mangy, two-faced, fat, lickorous old git.'

'You're a dried-up plastic old scrag end,' he hissed as she stood up once again.

'And you my dear man are a maggot-pated clunch and a dirty old buck fitch,' came the reply as she sat down.

This rather threw OldSmoothie and we all heard him whisper, 'A clunch and a buck fitch?'

To which UpTights replied, 'That's right. Look it up if you have to, you crapulent piece of rotting horse hair.'

The exchange of insults that accompanied their rising to address the judge, or a witness, was like a barrister version of Torvill and Dean's *Bolero*: a carefully choreographed dance, in which each flirtatiously toyed with the other before the spotlight swung back. Meanwhile, in the background, the entrances and exits of the Häagen-Dazs girls and pie-eating blokes continued whilst we all did our best to copy the particular body language that the judge was exhibiting from moment to moment. All of which was accompanied by the rhythmic lolling of my head from side to side, as if I were a sort of hypnotic metronome.

Then without any warning, OldSmoothie's angry face suddenly broke into a huge smile and he put his arm out towards UpTights who was actually only sitting a couple of feet away. He squeezed her shoulder and said, 'I really don't know what I'd do without you, UpTights.'

She immediately pulled away from this invasion of her oh-so-important personal space, but not before whispering awkwardly and with as much of a smile as her stretched features would allow, 'Love you too, OldSmoothie.'

Nowt, as I've said before, so queer as folk. Either they're both starting to suffer Tourette's whenever they come within hearing distance of each other or they're actually madly in love, and insulting and degrading one another is just a kind of sadomasochistic mating ritual for ageing, bored and over-educated barristers. My money has always been on the latter.

As I told the story later in the clerks room, HeadClerk said, 'They'd each be nothing without the other. It's what gets them out of bed each day.'

'I've always liked the concept of entangled particles in quantum physics,' said TheBusker. 'That as one moves in one part of the universe it inextricably affects the other in a completely different part. It's just that in OldSmoothie and UpTights' case it's in a bad way.'

'Reminds me of a time when I saw so many shooting stars that I actually ran out of good wishes,' chuckled HeadClerk 'I ended up wishing bad things, which just kind of felt, well, wrong.'

'It's like OldSmoothie and UpTights got to that stage at about "hello",' I said.

'Diamonds and rust, BabyB, diamonds and rust,' said HeadClerk. 'Gives them the edge.'

Tuesday 24 June 2008
Year 2 (week 39): Sub-prime UK

HeadofChambers made an announcement in chambers tea this afternoon: 'It is with deep regret that I must announce that . . .'

At this point, the words and his sombre face led us all to think that he was about to announce the tragic death of someone close. He continued, '. . . chambers had three quarters of a million pounds invested in a property investment portfolio with a company that has just gone bankrupt and we are struggling to recover any of it.'

I should have realised. A face as serious as that could only be associated with financial loss.

OldSmoothie was the first to get stuck in. 'What? Lost? Who? How?'

UpTights took up the baton. 'How long have you known this?'

HeadofChambers shifted a little and looked at his feet before bringing his attention back to the room and putting on his QC voice. 'Er, well, er . . . I'm afraid I've been trying to sort it out given that I was the one who put the money there in the first place.'

'Yes, and you'll be the one we'll all sue if you don't recover it,' said OldSmoothie in a loud stage whisper.

TheCreep quickly spotted an opportunity to stick up for HeadofChambers and said, 'I really don't think that's called for, OldSmoothie. We're all in this together.'

'What? Are you worried that we might add you as a co-defendant or something?' replied OldSmoothie.

TheCreep backed off but HeadofChambers was already cranking out his defence. 'It was hardly foreseeable that the property market was going to collapse.'

'Ooh, foreseeable,' answered OldSmoothie. 'Getting a little defensive, are we?'

BusyBody stepped up to the mark just for the sport. 'Coming from the financial wizard that thinks hedge funds are for gardening and the credit crunch is a breakfast cereal, you're hardly one to talk.'

So much for that 'big happy family' line that chambers always uses with new recruits. Then OldSmoothie started musing, 'It's like the whole country's turning into one big toxic debt. No wonder the pound's being dumped. It's not like we produce anything any longer and the only thing we seem to be good at is racking up debt. I just can't imagine who'd still want to lend to sub-prime UK.'

'Well, quite,' said TheBusker diplomatically.

But OldSmoothie hadn't finished. 'I mean, what do we actually produce? Really? Nothing of any use whatsoever. Services they always say. We've become a country of so-called service industries.' He shook his head. 'Services? Huh, parasites more like.'

BusyBody had been quietly listening to this outburst and as she turned on her heels to leave she said over her shoulder for all to hear, 'Well at least no one can ever have accused you of being part of a service industry.'

Wednesday 25 June 2008
Year 2 (week 39): Judicial blackmail

'Got a nice little earner for you for tomorrow,' said SlipperySlope yesterday as I was leaving his office after a meeting with Smutton. 'Family case. Very simple.'

'But I don't know anything about family law,' I answered.

'Don't worry about that. You probably still know more than me and anyway, it'll settle, I promise.'

Then he added slightly mysteriously, 'The judge'll see to that.'

Thus it was that I ended up doing my first family law case today. I'd done a bit of research but was still massively out of my depth and I admit that my knees were shaking just a little as we rose for the entrance of the judge. It didn't help when he then boomed at my opponent, 'Who's paying for this complete waste of time and money?'

'Er, er . . .' My opponent didn't seem any more confident than me in this area and he was stumped. 'Er, Your Honour, may I please take instructions?'

'You certainly may. But let me warn you now. If this case is being funded by the taxpayer and it doesn't settle pretty sharpish, it's the sort of case where the papers may just end up with the Inland Revenue.'

My opponent and I both looked at the judge in astonishment and then at each other. We had just been issued with a judicial threat of blackmail: 'Settle or your respective clients' small businesses will be reported for tax evasion.' We both knew that a reference from a circuit judge would get the tax man frothing at the mouth. This was a code red to the lawyers to sort it out, or else.

Only it wasn't just the lawyers who had picked up the none-too-subtle message being handed down by the learned bench. First off, my opponent's lay client leapt to his feet and started making all sorts of noises at his solicitor, who then also jumped up, poked my opponent in the back and whispered something to him. Then I was given similar treatment from my own client. My opponent stood up.

'Er, Your Honour, it seems that a compromise may now be possible. Would you allow us a brief adjournment?'

The judge had anticipated this answer and was already halfway to his room as he turned and said, 'Ten minutes. No more.'

All I can say is that SlipperySlope was right and in fact we were back with a settlement in five.

When I arrived back in the clerks room, I discovered that I had been booked for a case in the West Country for Friday and so gave

Arthur a call, as he'd asked me to, and when there was no answer I left him a message. After about quarter of an hour he called me back.

'BabyB, I got your message about Friday and as I said before, I think it'd be nice for you to meet TheColonel. It'd mean you staying over until Saturday but I guarantee it'd be worth it.'

He was chuckling as he said this and then he passed the phone to Ethel. 'Surf's up, BabyB. Do go and see him. You're sure to have fun.'

Then she handed the phone back to Arthur. 'Anyway, I'm afraid I took the liberty of assuming that you'd be able to make it and have arranged it all. He suggested that you give him a ring after your case is finished.'

With which he gave me the number and was gone.

Thursday 26 June 2008
Year 2 (week 39): Oh, yes, yes, yes

Today was the day TheBusker had been planning for over a year. He's been especially training his dog for a court appearance. This morning he was to have his opportunity and I went along to watch. It was a relatively small theft case although big enough for a jury trial. By all accounts his client was definitely guilty and so he was grateful for anything that came his way, even TheBusker's DogCard.

Well, it all went to plan at the start. The client, wearing sunglasses, was led by the dog through the security gates, suggesting (without actually saying so) that the dog was there to guide him. Then, in court, the dog sat on the client's lap and if you looked closely you could see that he wore a mini barrister's winged collar, bands around his neck and a tiny little wig perched on his head. TheBusker had chosen this case specifically because the judge was a drinking buddy of his, and so the canine presence in court went unchallenged.

Then when TheBusker started making his points in cross-examination the dog sat bolt upright, looked at the jury and nodded his head like the Churchill dog in the television adverts. But when TheBusker's opponent started speaking the dog's ears dropped, his head went down, and he started to shake it from side to side as if in disagreement. The plan was proceeding splendidly and the jury were charmed.

That is, until TheBusker got up to give his closing speech and the dog became confused. Having sat up on cue he then dropped his head so low it would have made even an England football manager at a penalty shoot-out look optimistic. This was exacerbated further when he started slowly shaking his head in what can only be described as disappointment. The judge by this point cast a wry 'never work with animals' look at TheBusker who simply went with the flow and shrugged his shoulders at the jury in a kind of 'aw shucks' sort of way.

But just when all appeared to be lost, it became apparent that the dog's failure to toe the party line only made the jury smile even more, and in almost no time at all they returned with a verdict. As the foreman declared, 'Not Guilty,' the rest of the jury smiled first at TheBusker and then at the dog, who for the first time in a while was once again nodding his head.

All of this made me wonder whether TheBusker had actually planned every bit of the performance, employing double, triple, even quadruple bluffs. Who really knows when it comes to TheBusker?

Friday 27 June 2008
Year 2 (week 39): Bideford Bar

I was up against one of the most pompous and self-important barristers I've ever met today (which is saying something). I'll call him BigHead. It was a very small personal injury action in which a fisherman was claiming for whiplash as a result of a Russian-registered boat having accidentally knocked into his own boat. If there was any doubt as to what my opponent thought of himself, you only had to look at the italicised description that he had put of himself at the bottom of his lengthy (and almost incomprehensible) skeleton argument: 'BigHead is a world renowned expert [I'm not kidding] in private international law and in particular on shipping and the commercial matters which arise therefrom. He travels extensively throughout the world [don't we all . . . on our holidays] and also acts as an expert witness for English law in this area.'

Except that today we weren't in Monaco or Athens, but instead we were in the county court of Barnstaple and it was clear that the deputy district judge had the measure of my opponent from the moment he started addressing the judge as 'my Lord' rather than 'Sir'.

'Well, Mr BigHead, it's very nice of you to visit our humble little court here in North Devon. Must be quite a change from what you are used to.'

Without even realising that the judge was ribbing him, BigHead replied, 'Indeed, though I have to say that I find it's good for the soul to do a few of these little cases now and again and to remind one what the rest of the profession has to put up with.'

Ouch. But that wasn't the end of it.

'Well, Mr BigHead,' said the judge, 'I've read your extremely thorough skeleton argument and as I understand it your main point is that we do not have jurisdiction to hear such a weighty matter as this and that instead it should properly be heard in the Admiralty Court in London?'

'Precisely, my Lord. I have absolutely no idea why anyone would even have dreamt that such a case could be heard in a county court.'

'I see. Just for the sake of completeness, do you have any further points to add beyond the skeleton?'

'No, my Lord, I think it makes the point fully.'

'Yes, quite.'

The judge then turned to me. Now I have to admit that the question of whether or not the court was even allowed to hear the case had not been something I had even considered before arriving at court, and given that I'd only received the skeleton argument that morning I was, to say the least, a little out of my depth on this point. I waited for the judge to start grilling me.

'Now, Mr BabyBarista,' he began, 'I assume you want to rely upon section 27(1) of the County Courts Act 1984, which gives certain courts, including, I might say, this one, admiralty jurisdiction?'

'Er . . .'

I knew I was looking like a rabbit in the headlights, but as I stared at him I could actually make out that he was nodding at me as if to say that this was exactly what I wanted to be relying upon.

'Er, yes, of course, Sir. I'm very grateful. My point exactly.'

'Excellent. Well, Mr BigHead, for a shipping lawyer as important as your skeleton says you are, I'm extremely surprised that
you didn't know that a few of us coastal courts can also manage
the odd bit of shipping law on the side.'

BigHead was lost for words. Then the judge added, 'I don't know
whether you've heard of the Bideford Bar, Mr BigHead, but it's
provided more than a few shipping cases in its time, I can tell you.'

'Oh,' said BigHead. 'I'm afraid I hadn't heard of it. Does it have
a particular specialisation in shipping?'

'You might say that,' said the judge with a wry smile, before
delivering the killer blow. 'Though for your information it's a
dangerous sand bar at the end of the Taw Torridge Estuary and has
nothing to do with your own, er,' he looked directly at BigHead,
'esteemed profession.'

Monday 30 June 2008
Year 2 (week 40): TheColonel

Well I can't pretend I wasn't intrigued to meet TheColonel after
the billing he'd been given by Arthur and Ethel and it wasn't as if
I had anything planned for the weekend. I'd tried to see whether
Claire was free, but she was apparently also away for the weekend
and I hadn't dared to ask whether that was with her boyfriend or
not. So with nothing to lose I gave him a call after my case was
finished and I'd sent my client on his way.

'Ah yes,' he boomed down the line, 'Arthur said you were going
to call. Did he tell you we are cousins?'

'He didn't actually. But there was some mention of surf.'

'Quite right. Quite right. They told me that work is putting Jack
at risk of becoming a dull boy and that a session in the surf might
just be the answer.'

'Er, right. But isn't it difficult?'

'Not at all, young man. I'll explain it all over dinner this evening.'

And he certainly did, accompanied by several bottles of extremely
fine Rioja. He lives in a big house overlooking Saunton Sands in
North Devon and it was overrun with Jack Russells, a Springer
Spaniel and grandchildren. As I arrived I heard seagulls overhead
and took in the incredible view of the sand-dunes of Braunton

Burrows. Beyond that the sea stretched to the horizon and the sun looked heavy in the sky as it slowly made its descent.

'Welcome to the mad house. I'm babysitting the grandchildren this weekend. Though sometimes I wonder who's babysitting whom.'

He reminded me of the character played by Robert Duvall in *Apocalypse Now*, a man who could stand on the Vietnamese battlefield with his chest out and nose to the wind, utterly unmoved, as bombs fell on either side. A force of nature who looked like he'd spent years barking orders at his soldiers. But when I asked him later why they called him TheColonel, he replied, 'My father was a Colonel and eleven generations of senior officers before him. But it wasn't for me. Not after I'd ridden my first wave back in the sixties.'

He was great company and full of stories of mischief and mayhem. He also steadfastly refused to see my glass empty, and towards the end of the evening it was filled with port. As I got to hear more about him there was mention of a divorce although I didn't want to pry further. I also hinted that I was having my own troubles at the moment what with one thing and another.

'I assume it's over a girl,' he said. 'That tends to be what it boils down to most of the time. So what's the problem?'

I gave him a potted history of the goings-on with Claire and then mentioned the new boyfriend.

'So what's stopping you, young man? If you want something badly enough you have to fight for it.'

I nodded but was keen to change the subject. 'Talking of fights, how do you think Arthur and Ethel are holding up with all this litigation going on?' I asked.

'It cuts both ways, BabyB, truth be told. It's terrible the effect that these mobile things have been having and they're serious about wanting to put a stop to that. On the other hand the two of them seem more full of life than I've seen them in a long time. Kind of like the thrill of the fight is helping them to rediscover their youth.'

'It must have been difficult for them with Ethel's illness,' I said.

'Absolutely. But again, sometimes it takes something as extreme as that to remind us what it's all about.' He paused and then continued, 'You know, just the other day I passed the scene of an accident. Probably something you guys would see as work,' he added mischievously before going on. 'There was a moped laid flat out in the middle of the road and by its side were the rider's clothes, which had been cut from his body. The same clothes he'd have put on that morning. A life as I later heard that was brought to an end by the simplest of driving mistakes. Kind of reminds you how thin the ice is on which we all wander so blithely every day.' He took another drink before continuing, 'It's one of the things I like about riding big waves. Brings things into focus. Makes it real.'

After the port there followed sloe gin, before I eventually collapsed into a guest room. It hardly felt like I'd fallen asleep before I was rudely awoken by a shout coming from downstairs.

'Come on, young BabyBarista! It's five o'clock and time for the dawn patrol. The surf's pumping.'

Well, we all jumped into the van: TheColonel, the dogs, the grandchildren and me. With the surfboards on the roof we were soon at the beach. 'Take a deep breath, BabyB, and smell the offshore breeze. Nothing better.' He then threw me a spare wetsuit. 'Try this one for size.'

After much hilarity as I put it on the wrong way around to start with, we were eventually out in the surf. Actually that's something of an exaggeration. Following TheColonel's instructions I had pushed my board out until the water was up to my shoulders and then I'd turned it around and lain flat upon it, waiting for some waves. For the first hour or so I seemed constantly to be wiping seawater from my eyes or getting it in my nose and mouth. This was interspersed by TheColonel pointing out the audience of noisy oystercatchers on the rocks alongside a solitary shag drying its wings. But just as I was starting to flag, TheColonel shouted, 'Turn around, BabyB! You're perfectly placed.'

Then after I did so, and as the wave approached, he gave my board a little shove. I held on for dear life as the board went down the first part of the wave and then I desperately tried to scramble to my feet. Just as I did so the most incredible thing happened. Rather than toppling me over, the unbroken part of the wave suddenly opened up before me. Everything slowed down and became much more vivid. With the sun rising directly in front of me it was reflecting off the wave, and as it rolled forward the sensation was almost as if I was weightless, floating, and that the wave was peeling onwards forever. Like some sort of optical illusion. Leaving behind every possible care or worry. For a split second that seemed like a lifetime.

I started laughing uncontrollably and 'whooping' like a small child. Then just as soon as I'd started to settle into the wave it collapsed before me and I fell back into the sea, elated and giddy. I looked up and saw some of the oystercatchers chasing each other in a large circle as if they were mimicking the surfers' carefree games of their own.

TheColonel gave me a knowing smile and said, 'There's nothing a good surf can't sort out, BabyB. Washes all the worries from the mind.'

That night I dreamt once again of the sandcastles and my parents. Except the tide was receding, having stopped short of the castles we had built. Somehow my mind also seemed to deliver a vivid memory full of smells of seaweed, melting sun cream and salt and vinegar rising off hot fish and chips along with the sound of small waves breaking gently along the shoreline and gulls circling greedily overhead.

My first thought as I woke up and savoured the memory was that Arthur was right. We didn't all have to end up like OldSmoothie.

CHAPTER 10

July: Police Raid

Tuesday 1 July 2008
Year 2 (week 40): Watch-off

Had a chambers meeting today and the funniest thing occurred – there was a watch-off. It was like a kind of Mexican wave that started with TheCreep ostentatiously producing his brand-spanking new Tag Heuer watch and planting it down on the conference table in front of him so that, as he mumbled in self-justification, he could 'keep an eye on the time'. Unfortunately he was sitting next to OldSmoothie who, not to be outdone, pulled out his iPhone as though it were some kind of mini light sabre and then clicked it into 'clock' mode and sat it in front of him, on what seemed like a disproportionately large and very clearly specially designed docking station. A kind of turbo-charged phallic object waiting for take-off. This, of course, made TheVamp whisper loudly to TheBusker, 'You know what they say . . .' without actually needing to say more.

But it wasn't over yet. HeadofChambers's watch-vanity was such that he obviously thought he could bring this little game to an end by producing a big fat Omega, whilst aiming a look that clearly said, 'That's not a watch, *this* is a watch,' at TheCreep.

This act of arrogance irritated UpTights so much that she clearly felt the need to put HeadofChambers back in his box and she removed her small but extremely sparkly diamond-encrusted

Rolex, which she laid out on the table without even a look in his direction.

Unfortunately by this point, silliness was starting to take hold and everyone looked expectantly at TheBusker who was next in line. He didn't disappoint when he produced an old-school Mickey Mouse watch that looked like it had been delivered straight from the 1970s. OldRuin smiled at this and with a self-deprecating look, took off his lovely multi-coloured Swatch that I remember him proudly telling me had been given to him for his birthday by one of his grandchildren. I then followed up with my retro eighties-style black digital watch.

Finally it came to TheVamp who had been busily scribbling on a sheet of paper and who now tore a small line down the middle and then folded it up before exhibiting her brand new origami paper sun dial. She then looked at BusyBody who with perfect timing asked, 'Er, does anyone have the time?'

Wednesday 2 July 2008
Year 2 (week 40): Scales of justices

I don't think it was coincidence that I was booked to be against TopFirst today. More, I'd say it was our various clerks who have picked up on a general sense of rivalry and thought they'd amuse themselves with another face-off. The problem was that for me it was an almost unwinnable car case in which TopFirst had an independent witness backing his client's version of events. With this in mind I went to seek the advice of TheBusker.

'Everything's winnable, BabyB. It's all up for grabs once you have a real, living and above all fallible judge sitting in front of you. Maybe you'll start off chatting about the weather or a particular detail relevant only to him, such as his mother's health or son's prospering career as a solicitor. But even if the usual lines of attack fail, you should always, and I mean always, have a scales of justice speech up your sleeve. Get that right and it'll never fail.'

He then took sympathy on me, due not only to my forlorn look but also he mentioned that he knew about the superhero trick TopFirst had played on me a while back and wanted to help me get him back in court. He therefore took a look at my case and gave me a short script for the key moments as well as a bit of specific advice about the judge we were appearing in front of. So when I arrived at court, I was feeling a little better although still not terribly confident.

'First your Moldy cases start to fall apart and then they start sending you their other hopeless cases,' said TopFirst in the robing room.

'Actually, with you as my opponent, everything's winnable,' I said, although probably without a great deal of conviction.

Once we got into court, I followed TheBusker to the letter and stood up and said, 'Your Honour, might it be useful for us to decide the issue of liability as a preliminary issue?'

In itself this seemed like just an innocently helpful suggestion were it not for the sting in the tail: 'After all, if you're with us on that, all the other complicated and time-consuming issues fall away.' What this was in effect saying was that if the judge found for our side, the hearing would be cut short and we wouldn't have to waste his time with all the other tiresome issues. The judge nodded approvingly and TopFirst was already snookered, unable to object without seeming to be posturing for some tactical advantage in some way.

Then it was on to the toy cars. By way of background, most baby barristers are in the habit of using them to help witnesses describe the accident, and those looking for an angle tend to offer the toy Ferrari to the other side's witness and a nice, safe, responsible Mercedes or Volvo to their own witness. Meant to work on the judge's mind and all. So before going into court I followed TheBusker's suggestion and mentioned to TopFirst that he might want to watch it with the toy cars with this judge. Predictably sensitive to any game-playing tactics on my part, he decided that this was some sort of bluff and so when it came to cross-examination of my witness, he made a big song and dance of giving him the 'speedy little number'. As soon as he did so, he was hit with the full force of the judge's temper.

'Mr TopFirst, I am well aware that some members of the junior Bar think the judiciary so naïve that they can influence them through some sort of subliminal messages to do with the toy cars. However, I think you ought to know that not only do I find that implication offensive to the judicial office itself but I think perhaps it's only fair to tell you that I myself drive . . .' he gave a theatrical pause before finishing with, you guessed it, '. . . a Ferrari.'

Ouch. I smiled over at TopFirst and raised a sympathetic eyebrow. But I still had my trump card to play and it was one which TopFirst had clearly heard about during his pupillage in our chambers. Because when I got up for my closing submissions and started with, 'Your Honour, the scales of justice . . .' I could see his whole face change complexion as if to say, 'No! Not the scales of justice! Anything but that . . . please!' He immediately stood up to object almost as some kind of Pavlovian reaction. As TheBusker had instructed I gave him a kindly smile and sat down to allow him to speak. Which exposed the fact that in reality he had no grounds for stopping me other than stamping his foot and moaning 'it's just not fair'. I then stood up to resume the speech I had learnt by heart.

'Your Honour, the scales of justice are a finely balanced instrument which have been used down the ages to settle disputes both great and indeed small. A constant in our lives which for most of the time we simply take for granted. But very occasionally one is faced with an extraordinary decision where those scales are so finely balanced as not to be able to determine whether they are falling down on one side or the other. At those rare times it takes but . . .' I then theatrically dipped my hand into my suit pocket and as if from nowhere produced a gift from TheBusker, '. . . a small feather to tip the scales but one way or the other. Just the very smallest thing to make the difference between one side winning, or the other. Your Honour, this is one such rare case in which the scales are indeed balanced. We say one thing and the other side say something else, but if I was pushed I would have to admit that in reality we are equally matched.'

I then deliberately dropped my voice and continued. 'Thankfully, Your Honour, when the cases are so evenly matched then all we ever have to fall back on is the burden of proof and today that lies with the claimant. Sadly for him, Your Honour, in the absence of that little feather . . .' with which I dropped my own one to the ground, '. . . the case must be dismissed.'

Well, it was obvious to us all that the judge was utterly charmed by the performance. After that no amount of TopFirst trying to tell him that his independent witness counted for enough feathers to fill a whole courtroom was ever going to change his mind.

Case indeed dismissed. As we left court, I said to TopFirst, 'Maybe you just need a little more practice ...'

He didn't look at all amused, particularly when I added, '... in coffee-making, that is.'

Thursday 3 July 2008
Year 2 (week 40): BrainWashering

I had another update from BrainWasher today about his excellent work convincing the judge that he's suffering from brain damage as a result of exposure to imaginary mobile masts.

'I think we're getting somewhere, BabyB. Not only did we organise a little rally near his house, which he attended, but we also got one of the court ushers to chat to him about the problems she thinks she's been suffering because of a mobile mast near her own home.'

'Sounds great, but are you managing to actually make him think *he* might be suffering?'

'Well that's been the more difficult task I have to admit but we're certainly making progress. It's taken a large cast though.'

'In what way?'

'Well, I've already told you about the newspaper seller giving him the wrong change. Then there's been a host of fellow commuters at different times reacting to him as if he'd actually approached them and said something first.'

'Which he hadn't.'

'Precisely.'

'As for the hypnotism, BabyB, you've been doing an excellent job moving your head back and forth for the last few weeks in court.'

'Thank you very much,' I said, glad that my work was being appreciated, particularly as I'd been suffering a stiff neck for a fortnight.

'It's just that, well, I didn't really have the heart to tell you after the first couple of days ...'

'What?' I asked, confused.

'Well, you see,' he said looking a little sheepish. 'All of the other things are working wonders but well ... you see ...'

'Yes?' I said, not seeing.

'Well, I'm afraid I was only joking about the need for you to sway your head.'

Oh.

Friday 4 July 2008
Year 2 (week 40): Lawyerville

Went with Claire and OldRuin to a negotiation over the hospital case today with the other side's lawyers. They were pointing out a couple of technical deficiencies in our case, which appeared to have no merit other than us not having ticked quite the right boxes before the lawyers got involved.

'You know,' said OldRuin, 'sometimes I look at what we do and think we're no better than the prisoners in Plato's cave.'

The other side, along with Claire and I, looked a little nonplussed. OldRuin continued, 'Plato imagined that all these prisoners saw of the world were its shadows. Sometimes it reminds me of what we do. Yet, when I meet the people who will be affected by the hospital closure, it's like coming out of the cave and being blinded by the bright light of reality.'

He looked at the other side's lawyers and then turned to us and said with a smile, 'Come on you two. Sometimes I tire of the profession to which I have devoted my working life. The sun's shining outside and it's time to leave the cave.' He paused and then gave a wry smile at the other side, 'For today, at least.'

Monday 7 July 2008
Year 2 (week 41): Drink-driving

With summer holidays looming there's definitely a de-mob happy feel to chambers at the moment and today TheVamp and I went out for a lazy lunch after having agreed a very fruitful settlement for both of us (and of course our respective clients). We certainly weren't planning on returning to chambers and the beer was flowing freely. Then three pints in, TheVamp received a call from HeadClerk.

'Since you're now both free, do you think you could cover for us for two of our pupils at three o'clock in Horseferry Road Magistrates? Tiny plea in mitigation. Won't take long.'

Well, when HeadClerk calls, it's not really a request. More a thinly veiled instruction, and so the pair of us staggered back to chambers to collect our respective briefs. When TheVamp saw that it was a drink-driving case that I was prosecuting and she was defending she said, 'Have you ever played the drink-driving game at court, BabyB?'

'Er, no. What's that exactly?'

'Bit like the James Bond drinking game but instead you have to drink whenever the words "drink" or "driving" are mentioned. Both words and it's two drinks. Simple, really. Oh, and you just put vodka in a water bottle and fill your glass from that.'

Yes, quite simple and also quite extraordinarily illegal and unprofessional – which certainly wasn't going to stop us now that we were on a roll.

'And hey, the gaelic word for whiskey means "water of life" so we're following in a great tradition.'

'A fine point,' I said.

'And if we both do it,' added TheVamp, 'it still keeps the trial fair.'

'Well, quite,' I agreed.

The only mitigating feature of the whole case was that when we arrived at court TheVamp's client also stank of drink and so neither he nor anyone around her realised that she had also been drinking as well since they attributed the smell solely to him. As for me, I tiptoed into the office of the Crown Prosecution Service and quietly took the brief whilst avoiding speaking to anyone. Once in court the more we tried to make our drinking appear subtle and nonchalant, the more we failed. So much so that at one point the District Judge said to TheVamp, 'These drink-driving cases can be thirsty work, MsVamp? May I offer you an extra drink of water?'

This of course had the effect of eliciting three more gulps of vodka from the two of us. Thankfully, all I had to do was introduce the case since the man had already pleaded guilty and sentencing was all that remained. But when it came to TheVamp's submissions, they did get a little flowery.

'Shir, drink-driving [two more sips] is the bane of our soshiety and we're all aware of the shlogan, "Don't drink [one sip] and drive [and another]: accidents cause children." Indeed, accidents can alsho harm children Shir and sho for all of those reashons it ish what the authors of 1066 *and All That* would call "A very bad thing indeed" as indeed any fule kno. But despite this Shir, all I can ashk is that the court take mercy on this man's soul. Now and forever. Amen.'

With which she sat down.

Tuesday 8 July 2008
Year 2 (week 41): Victim of own success

I went to see Smutton again today.

'Ah, BabyB. Come in, come in.'

She ushered me into her office, being a little more physical about it than I would have chosen. Then she said, 'So, let's get down to brass tacks.'

I began to feel slightly frightened, but she continued, 'The Moldy litigation. I have some good news.'

'Oh, yes?' I stuttered, regaining my composure.

'A friend of mine bumped into JudgeFetish at a party over the weekend. Seems BrainWasher's starting to make real inroads. Apparently the judge is telling people that he thinks he might be suffering from brain damage caused by rampant mobile signals.'

'That's great news.'

'It is indeed. But there is also some bad news. I fear from what I hear that we risk becoming victims of our own success as he's now seriously considering withdrawing from the case. First because he thinks he's not up to giving judgment mentally. Then, even if he were, he thinks the fact that he himself is now suffering the effects might give rise to a direct conflict of interest.'

'Oh.'

'Which means, BabyB, that you'd better put that hot, hot, hot little brain of yours into action and come up with a solution. According to my friend, the judge intends to make an announcement in the next week or two so it doesn't give you much time.'

Oh again.

Chambers is currently awash with the first wave of law students on their summer holidays doing mini-pupillage.

'Mini-pupillages are a complete and utter waste of time for everyone,' said OldSmoothie.

'It is for those who get to follow you around at least,' said BusyBody. 'Although in itself that's probably a valuable insight into life at the Bar.'

'It's definitely good for the CV,' said TheCreep. 'I did twelve mini-pupillages during my time at university.'

'Now there's a surprise,' said TheVamp.

'Though you do have to ask why we reward people for just turning up in chambers, following us around and making coffee at the drop of a wig,' said TheBusker.

'Maybe it's a test to filter out those who don't have a sufficiently servile temperament to get them through pupillage,' said TheVamp.

'But you've got to admit that they're pretty annoying,' said OldSmoothie. 'I can just about live with having one Creep in chambers even if it's just to make fun of. But having a whole army of them descend each summer, it's unbearable.'

'You're talking absolute rubbish as usual, OldSmoothie,' said BusyBody. 'It opens up the place to people who otherwise might not even dream of applying and hey, they add a bit of youth and colour to an otherwise pretty arid environment.'

'And anyway, you didn't seem to mind that pretty young law student last week,' said UpTights. 'Getting her to spend two days, er, what was it? Oh yes, "arranging your Weekly Law Reports".'

'Ooh err,' said TheVamp with a smile.

'They get even worse than the midges as the summer goes on. It's exactly why so many senior barristers take August off,' said OldSmoothie soldiering on.

'I thought it was because the High Court closes then,' said TheVamp.

'What, and you really think we're going to tell the truth: that we can't stand having self-important, jumped-up and annoying oiks pawing at us all day. I hardly think so.'

'Maybe they actually choose August specifically to avoid having self-important, jumped-up and annoying silks pawing at them all day instead,' said UpTights.

Thursday 10 July 2008
Year 2 (week 41): Man with a plan

So. If I leave JudgeFetish to his own devices he'll jettison himself off the case pretty quickly and all our good work will have been to no avail. But what to do? Blackmail is clearly an option what with our knowledge of the mistress, not to mention the fact that he has fallen for BrainWasher's tricks. But it comes with manifold difficulties, not least the risk of being sent straight to jail at even the slightest whiff of such a suggestion. But what are the other alternatives? After mulling it over for the last couple of days and without coming up with anything, I decided to go and have a chat with SlipperySlope after work.

'Well, let's have a look at our options,' he said after I'd set out the problem. 'I agree that blackmail is something of a blunt instrument, particularly if we had to implement it at such short notice. Influence is always much more preferable to force. But come on, BabyB, you're better than this. Let's look at it from a different perspective. Always go back to basics. What are your primary objectives in this case?'

'To win for the clients, get paid for all our other cases . . .' Then it dawned on me '. . . and to do over TopFirst. That's it!'

'What's it?' Now Slippery was behind.

'TopFirst. It always comes back to him.'

'How?'

But after that, I decided not to say any more. If it all goes horribly wrong then the fewer people covering their own bottoms the better. But suffice it to say, I had a plan and I rang my good friend Blagger, who not only knows his stocks from his shares but is also quite an expert with computers. We will be meeting on Friday afternoon.

Friday 11 July 2008
Year 2 (week 41): Load of old bull

'Yes, I'm off to Pamplona this weekend to run with the bulls.'

OldSmoothie was talking about his most recent midlife crisis adventure. 'I've even had my secretary set up a page about it on The Facebook,' he said trying somehow to sound 'down wid de kidz' but failing miserably. 'Everyone's who's anyone does that these days, you know?'

'And I suppose you've also started "The Twitter" as well,' said BusyBody sarcastically.

'Actually, she did mention something about that. But The Facebook's the place to be at the moment,' he said with great authority.

'And you intend to actually do the run, do you?' asked TheBusker.

'He can't even run a bath,' said UpTights.

'More like a running joke,' said BusyBody.

'This week I've been out four nights running,' said TheVamp.

'What, around Hyde Park?' asked TheCreep.

'No, as I said, "out" four nights running,' said TheVamp and gave him a sympathetic look. 'On the tiles, Mr CweepyWeepy.'

'And as for catching the bulls, he couldn't even catch a bus,' added UpTights.

'More likely to catch a cold the speed he'd be going,' giggled BusyBody.

Monday 14 July 2008
Year 2 (week 42): Coming clean

Well, there's no going back now. First off, on Friday afternoon I met up with Blagger.

'It's funny you should have suggested meeting up, BabyB. Only last week I got a call from that solicitor lady wanting to instruct me on another case.'

'I hope you told her you'd retired?'

'Well, I thought that would sound a little boring so instead I told her that I'd just been appointed to be a judge. Thing is, I actually quite fancy her and want to keep this blag going until I've at least met up with her again, so I wondered if you could give me a bit of the lingo and low-down on well, judges.'

Inwardly I was actually relieved to hear that, for the moment at least, he had ceased to pretend to practise. I was therefore only too happy to dispense advice on how to impersonate a judge.

'I'd go for being a Deputy District Judge,' I said. 'They're the bottom of the pile and no one ever remembers them from one minute to the next and so you're far more likely to go under the radar. Beyond that, just act as though you know everything that it is possible to know in the whole world. Shouldn't be too difficult for you, in fact,' I reflected. 'Then don't forget to mention your "brother judges" in as pompous a voice as you can possibly muster. Again, you should find that relatively easy. Beyond that, arrogance, stupidity and a complete lack of insight should just about make you the real deal.'

'That's perfect, BabyB. Just as I imagined actually.'

Well, helping him was hardly the most ethical thing to do, but needs must when I am in need of assistance of my own.

'I'm in a spot of bother,' I said, 'and I need to make it look as if someone has sent me an email, even when they didn't.'

'Not at all easy, BabyB. You can always back-date emails and even some of the computer's records but if an expert were to get his hands on it they'd suss it out very soon.'

This was exactly what I had feared. I grilled Blagger on various aspects of computers and their records and then I saw him off and wished him luck with his solicitor.

After that I rang a lady called Ginny, who I hired last year to act as a honeytrap for TopFirst. She is a rather attractive student who does a little moonlighting on the side. This assignment, however, would be a little easier than her last.

'Ginny, I'd like to hire you to send an email from an internet café.'

'Why do you need me to do that?' she asked.

I explained that it was part of my plan to bring down TopFirst.

'What, that little toad again? BabyBarista, it'd be my pleasure.'

I then went on to explain the risks that might be involved.

'Risk is something I've become used to in my working life. One minute things can be rosy, the next you can be in all sorts of trouble. It's exactly what allows me to charge a premium. I'm sure as a lawyer you understand that concept very well.'

She was certainly right on that score. There were many parallels between her job and mine beyond them being the world's two oldest professions. Finally, I arranged for a letter to be hand-delivered to JudgeFetish at the high court. It was typed on plain paper and as far as I could tell there were no distinguishing features that could in any way lead back to me. The letter said simply:

> You have been the victim of a plot to brainwash you into thinking that you have suffered injury as a result of mobile phone waves. It is merely a ruse by the claimants' lawyers to win you over. You must find against the claimants. Do not think about withdrawing from the case because if you do then this will all come out in the press and you will have to admit how easily you were improperly influenced by one of the parties to the litigation.

Now I just have to hope that this will at least hold him off from withdrawing from the case.

Tuesday 15 July 2008
Year 2 (week 42): Crackington Haven

Oh, the important things we all get up to whilst sitting around in chambers waiting for our briefs to arrive. Yesterday afternoon a few of us were waiting in the clerks room gossiping.

'What are you up to this week?' I asked TheVamp.

'I'm going to Crackington Haven, near Bude, on Thursday for a long weekend,' she said.

'I don't know whether it's just because you're saying it, but that just sounds rude,' said TheBusker smiling, before adding, 'and now, that place will be forever etched in my mind as associated with you.'

'Don't forget it's just down the coast from Welcome Mouth, too,' said OldSmoothie.

BusyBody laughed and joined in, 'Well, I'd take Giggleswick,' given the choice.

'Or Wittering,' said TheCreep.

'Snig's End for you,' TheVamp said in response, 'or how about Mumbles or even better Little Snoring?'

'Yes and Madchute for the stretched one,' said OldSmoothie. 'Or Cockermouth, perhaps?' he added, smugly. 'Though I once visited a place called Clenchwarton. Now that really does fit, wouldn't you say?'

'You'd be something like Bishop's Itchington or Mold,' BusyBody retorted.

'More like Six Mile Bottom or Nether Wallop,' said UpTights. 'Or Lord Hereford's knob,' she added.

'Tutt's Clump, Upper Chute or Lickey End for you, UpTights. If you're lucky. Though if you're not, there's always Fiddlers Elbow.'

'The Lizard,' said UpTights in reply as the conversation plummeted.

'Isle of Dogs,' he retorted.

'Nob's Crook,' she said.

'Cock Alley,' he replied, looking extremely pleased with himself.

'Then of course there's always the infamous place in the Shetlands that sounds quite like, well, twit,' said BusyBody directing her gaze to OldSmoothie.

At which point OldRuin appeared from the other side of the room and dispersed any tension with, 'I've always liked the sound of Melbury Bubb myself. Makes me think of the most delicious kind of summer pudding.'

Wednesday 16 July 2008
Year 2 (week 42): Judges' Zoo

The more time goes on the more work I appear to be doing whilst I'm in court. Not court work that is, but anything else that needs doing. Let's face it, there's a lot of twiddling your thumbs during court hearings, which until recently was just lost time. But with the joys of the internet I now manage to go through all my emails and if it's a full day in court I also tend to draft a couple of sets of proceedings. It's much easier even than last year, when we all had to fiddle with our BlackBerrys under the table. This year someone came up with the bright idea of simply pretending to take notes of the hearing on the laptop whilst connecting it to the internet with one of those dongle things. So for anyone who's been to court recently and has wondered why the baby Bar is suddenly keenly typing notes on every small claim, now you know.

But what perhaps you don't know is that we now have over 500 barristers taking part in the online virtual reality game Second Life. We've created a world that is populated only by those barristers who are appearing in court. Very frightening what their creative minds have produced in the last few weeks. Forget about schools and hospitals. So far, we have a dodgy firm of solicitors, an ambulance-chasing accident management company and then, the one that took most people by surprise: the Judges' Zoo. Yes, believe it or not, it's already become a convention that if the judge you're appearing in front of is being particularly annoying then you just create a persona for him in Second Life and stick him in the Judges' Zoo. Although when I say zoo, think prison. It's proving to be one of the most popular tourist attractions, particularly after someone added a function whereby you are able to throw your wig at the occupants of said zoo.

I just hope the judges themselves don't start logging in.

Thursday 17 July 2008
Year 2 (week 42): Good news, bad news

The good news is that JudgeFetish has announced that he will remain on the case. The bad news is that I was paid a little visit by the local constabulary last night. That's correct. Far from cowering away at the possibility of embarrassment, JudgeFetish has come out all guns blazing and plod was immediately summoned to the doorsteps of all the lawyers involved in the case. Ouch. Except that thankfully, this was the reaction I had anticipated from a high court judge threatened in such an unsophisticated way. Which is also why I only put up token resistance to the police taking away my computer for examination after they'd helped set me up with a back-up of any files I would need in the meantime. Admittedly I mentioned client privilege and certainly used the words 'outrageous' and 'civil liberties' but even so, I eventually doffed my wig and allowed them to carry out their duties.

The fact that they might find a threatening and somewhat incriminating email on there addressed to me and purporting to be from TopFirst has of course nothing to do with it: an email, incidentally, that was sent from the same email café where the letter to the judge was printed. Oh, and the person who sent the email? Why it was Ginny the HoneyTrap of course and in the unlikely event that they actually identify her, I have plenty of email and video evidence which I could leak which inextricably links her to TopFirst.

Friday 18 July 2008
Year 2 (week 42): Punishment of Sisyphus

'With all this talk about the credit crunch and calling in the debts, I think it's about time we barristers stood up for ourselves. I'm owed a hundred and fifty grand by SlipperySlope alone and it's been outstanding for over a year.' HeadofChambers was in combative mode at chambers tea today.

'Yes, call in the debts. We've been financing solicitors for far too long,' replied OldSmoothie.

Even UpTights agreed. 'Greedy, fat-cat solicitors using all our money to jet set around the world schmoozing clients. I'm currently owed over two hundred grand by those thieving, snivelling pencil pushers.'

'That'll be the same thieving snivelling pencil pushers who put bread on your table,' smiled TheBusker.

'And botulism in your face,' piped up OldSmoothie.

'It's just not right, though,' said UpTights. 'No one in the civilised world gets treated like us barristers do, what with the late payments and last-minute briefs. No one. Not even, er . . .'

She trailed off as she realised that everyone was listening and waiting to hear what she would come up with next, and yet she was lost for a single example. Eventually HeadofChambers came to her aid with, 'Anyway, they really do have to realise that they wouldn't survive without us as well as their clients.'

'Well, technically they could always do the court cases themselves,' reminded TheBusker.

'Er, well, I don't think that's going to happen,' said HeadofChambers, his confidence sapping a little. Then in a more reflective tone he added, 'Although come to think of it, even if I was paid the hundred grand I'm owed by one firm, I'd probably have to pay their family law division a similar amount for what I owe them for my divorce.'

'But that's what a lot of this financial mess is about,' said TheBusker. 'Everyone's wanting to take from Peter to pay Paul, who then wants to spend it in paying back to Peter. Never-ending circles of credit and debt.'

'Reminds me of the special punishment reserved for the hubris of Sisyphus who thought he was cleverer even than the gods,' said OldRuin. 'His curse was to roll a huge boulder up a hill, only to watch it roll back down over and over again throughout eternity.'

After which the wind had well and truly left their collective sails.

Monday 21 July 2008
Year 2 (week 43): I couldn't possibly comment . . .

Had another visit from the police today. They have thoroughly searched my computer and are asking me to comment on an email addressed to me, apparently coming from TopFirst, which includes the following text:

> I promise you this BabyBarista: I will not only bring you down but all your mad oldies with you. What's more, you won't even know it's happening until it's too late and even then you'll never know how it was done.

They also found a few other aggressive emails which he has sent me in the past which only went to back up the picture they were forming. I told the police that whilst I was keen to help them with their enquiries, I didn't want to comment on anything that could potentially incriminate a fellow member of my honourable profession unless I was forced to do so. Naturally. They didn't push it any further, both commenting that they thoroughly understood what a difficult position I was in.

And if you believe that . . .

Poor SlipperySlope. There's always been something of the am-dram end of the pier about him but today his performance really took the biscuit. Not that there should even have been a performance. You see, we both turned up at court on a case and then just before the client arrived Slippery turned to me and said, 'Look, BabyB, I'm sorry I didn't mention it earlier but I've always dreamt of being a barrister and actually doing the performing in court and this could be my chance. The case is small enough not to matter and it's a new judge too. Why don't I just take it from here? I'll still pay you your brief fee. It's just that today ... well, I feel anything is possible.'

He seemed slightly hyper and I wondered if maybe his doctor had changed his combination of drugs. But I wasn't exactly in a position to argue. He was, literally, the boss and so I sat back and watched. At least I watched until I had to turn away, for it was just too painful to do anything else. The only name for him that springs to mind today is TheHamster, owing to his terrible ham acting that would put even a pantomime dame in the church hall at Christmas to shame. It was like he'd been watching endless re-runs of *Perry Mason* and *Ally McBeal* and decided that that was how lawyers should perform in court. Don't get me wrong, they're both great shows. But unless you are aged eighty and perhaps a former Attorney General addressing the House of Lords in the case of the decade, you do not go about addressing the court with the sorts of airs and graces you might see in those programmes and even then it'd be eccentric. But even this is to understate his performance I'm afraid.

Unfortunately, it also meant that the case lasted about ten times longer than it should have: something that became clear from the moment Slippery began to go through every page of the pleadings and evidence as his introduction to this tiny car case. To cap it all, the judge was just a bit wet behind the ears and so he didn't have the guts to put an end to Slippery's ridiculous charade.

Then when it came to the cross-examination of the other side's witness, Slippery leapt up from his seat, left the courtroom to the astonishment of us all and then burst back in, demanding of the witness, 'Now. When I left the room, with which hand did I open the door?'

To which the witness answered, 'No idea.'

'Aha,' Slippery replied. 'This obviously shows that your visual memory is unreliable, wouldn't you agree?'

Every one of us could hear the judge utter 'What rubbish' under his breath.

After this Slippery changed tack to: 'Do you accept that you were driving a lethal weapon?'

'Er, not exactly,' the witness answered a little confused. 'As you can see from my witness statement I was driving my Jaguar XJ6.'

'But do you accept that a car is a lethal weapon?'

'What, like your cross examination?' he replied sarcastically.

The judge smiled at this before forcing a stern look and saying, 'If you could just answer the questions please.'

Slippery repeated his question very slowly and with a staccato on each word as if he was punching the witness with each beat. 'Do you accept that a car is a lethal weapon?'

'No, my car is an extremely luxurious way of transporting me from A to B.'

'But do you accept that it still has just as much killing power as, say, a sawn-off shotgun?'

'Well, in those terms I'd prefer to think of it more as a classic Purdey side-by-side. But nevertheless no, I don't accept what you are suggesting.'

'Ah ha, but you accept the possibility that it might be like a Purley shotgun?'

'Purdey.'

'Exactly, Purley . . .'

And so it went on. When he eventually emerged from that particular quagmire he said to the witness, 'You say in your witness statement that my client, and I quote, "came out of nowhere". Is that correct?'

'Yes.'

'Do you still say that now?'

'Yes.'

With this revelation he almost jumped in the air like a footballer celebrating a goal as he then bellowed in the manner of Monty Python's Spanish Inquisition sketch, 'But no one comes out of nowhere, now do they?' Then he added with a smile and a wink (honestly) at the judge, 'Unless he's the invisible man of course.'

When it came to submissions on what, as I say, was nothing more than a minor car case, Slippery closed by saying, 'Sir, if you find for the other side, you may as well rip up the Highway Code.' At which point he took a copy of the Code which was sitting on the table in front of him and ripped it in half.

If this were not bad enough, the judge then turned to Slippery and said, dryly, 'That was my copy you just destroyed.'

Ouch.

It will perhaps come as no surprise to hear that despite the strength of his own evidence, he lost.

When I mentioned this later at chambers tea, TheBusker winced and said, 'He sounds like a walking talking professional negligence action who'd do well to have someone walking in front of him waving a red flag.'

TheVamp chuckled and said, 'Reminds me of one of those yellow signs the police put out after a crime has occurred which asks for witnesses. I once saw a blank one sitting on a pavement at Cambridge Circus. As if the area was so notoriously bad that the sign represented a crime waiting to happen.'

Wednesday 23 July 2008
Year 2 (week 43): Expert evidence

Obviously after the letter to the judge, BrainWasher's activities have had to stop. But this hasn't brought a halt to the proceedings, and today our main expert on the damaging effects of the mobile masts was cross-examined by UpTights. He is a consultant neurologist and everything seemed to be going swimmingly until he suddenly appeared to lose his bottle when UpTights asked, 'Isn't it correct that the research from which you have quoted doesn't specifically deal with the same type of mobile masts as those of the defendant?'

The answer we would have expected was, 'Well, technically that may be the case. But the subjects of the various studies are sufficiently similar for me to draw very clear conclusions as to the effects of this particular mast. Any differences there may have been were not such as to be relevant.'

Instead, what he gave us was a worried look and then, 'Er, my Lord, would it be possible to have a short break to visit the lavatory?'

Then, on his return, when UpTights repeated the question, he appeared to crumple. 'Er, well, yes. It's right that the studies I refer to aren't quite the same but even so, I think they're at least helpful to the court . . .'

But worse was to come. It was as if the proverbial seal had been broken and every time he was asked a difficult question he apparently felt the need to relieve himself and had to be excused to go to the gents. Even JudgeFetish commented at one point, 'I do understand. It comes to us all in time.' Which we all took to mean, 'Thank goodness I don't yet have prostate problems.' But the difficulty for us wasn't the loo breaks. It was the woolly answers he gave on his return which were doing us no favours at all.

After court I met up with Claire to discuss OldRuin's hospital case. I told her about the expert's terrible performance.

'My pupilmistress used to say that you should never trust experts. As she put it, the "x" stands for the unknown factor and the "spurt" is simply a drip under pressure.' Then she smiled and added, 'Though maybe it was nerves? After all, a neurologist can hardly avoid nerves in his line of work.'

'Just like work for an accountant must be incredibly taxing?' I replied.

'Exactly and crazy being a psychiatrist.'

'Shocking to be an electrician.'

'And foul to be a chicken farmer.'

We were giggling now.

'Backbreaking work for an orthopaedic surgeon,' I said.

'Like pulling teeth to be a dentist,' said Claire.

'A complete grind,' I replied.

'You know,' she went on, 'I once had a dentist with a great sense of humour. He lived in a house called High Pulham, had a boat named Fylmacavity and a coat of arms with the motto *Lucram per cariem*, which apparently means "prosperity through decay".'

Thursday 24 July 2008
Year 2 (week 43): Game on

Well, today I heard that TopFirst received a little visit from the police who were very interested in the threatening emails he supposedly sent to me. I know this courtesy of BusyBody in whom, ridiculously, he has confided. Anyway, I've heard on the grapevine that he admitted to sending me some of them but he denied sending the most recent particularly incriminating one. It all seems very convenient as far as they're concerned, I'm sure. But officially at this stage, he's merely 'assisting with their enquiries' apparently, and so there will no doubt be more to come.

This all continues to be rather a high-risk strategy when I've no doubt TopFirst's immediate response to the police will have been to put the blame squarely back on me. The game is well and truly on.

Friday 25 July 2008
Year 2 (week 43): Too many twits . . .

First it was the Judges' Zoo. Now OldFilth of viagravation fame has taken to using 'The Twitter' as OldSmoothie now regularly refers to it. Having checked out his page it's clear that he's posting his musings about cases whilst he's still in court. Here are just a few:

Very attractive counsel appearing before me at the moment.

Ha! They really think they can pull the wool over my eyes that easily.

Hmm. Must be almost lunchtime.

Whose side shall I pick? Attractive counsel or another bore? Difficult one :-) [Yes, even the smile]

He's currently posting anonymously but robing rooms are all, erm, a twitter [sorry!] with the gossip. Today I had the pleasure

of appearing in front of him, which made it rather easy to anticipate exactly what he was thinking. Unfortunately I lost despite
my inside track, due to the fact that my female opponent was the
above-mentioned attractive one.

Monday 28 July 2008
Year 2 (week 44): King of the pupils

With August almost upon us, the Temple has been beset by a veri-
table plague of mini-pupils. Little worker ants strutting their stuff
and cracking jokes about how stupid or thick this or that Law
Lord is to have written this or that irrelevant judgment. With all
this activity, TheCreep has spotted an opportunity to make a name
for himself by doing free lectures entitled 'TheCreep's guide to
getting ahead at the Bar' with a picture of himself in wig and gown
pointing at the camera. As he said in the clerks room this morning whilst putting up another poster advertising his lectures, 'They
may seem irrelevant now but these little fledgling legal eaglets will
be the ones passing us work when we're all QCs. It's time to invest
in our futures, BabyB.'

'Yes,' said TheVamp, 'in the Liliputian kingdom of the
mini-pupils, even the miniest of barristers is king.'

Tuesday 29 July 2008
Year 2 (week 44): Judges' intranet

OldFilth's twittering gave me an idea that I put into practice today.
I used one of Slippery's online virtual assistants in India to hack
into the internal network that all the judges log in to. I was after
a password. With that achieved surprisingly easily, this morning I
made a discreet visit to the library where I happen to know that
TopFirst does most of his research. Then it was just a matter of
waiting for him to take a ten-minute break before sitting down
at his laptop and logging his computer straight into the network.
After this I started typing searches for anything on JudgeFetish and
then I logged out again before TopFirst returned, leaving no visible
trace of what I'd done.

If I'm right, what I did should sound just enough alarm bells for the authorities to track the searches straight back to the IP address of TopFirst's computer.

Wednesday 30 July 2008
Year 2 (week 44): Time clock

OldSmoothie had a solicitor client today who was wise to his billing strategies and was extremely keen to keep the costs to a minimum. 'I didn't send any papers along as I wanted to be with you when you were going through them.'

'No problem at all,' said OldSmoothie. 'Now, would you like a coffee before we get started?'

At this the solicitor clicked his fingers and the assistant he had brought along with him especially for the purpose brought out a huge stopwatch and ostentatiously stopped the clock from running.

'You know, OldSmoothie, that's extremely kind. I'd love a coffee and I'd also be delighted to talk about the weather, football, politics or whatever else takes your fancy. Just so long as it's not on our time.'

'Er, yes, well, quite. Certainly. Yes.'

After which OldSmoothie conducted what was possibly his fastest conference since he became a QC.

Thursday 31 July 2008
Year 2 (week 44): End of the beginning

The trial officially came to an end today. Well, the evidence and submissions part of it did anyway. WhistleBlower has been left utterly discredited but even so the documents still remain in evidence. The experts disagree as to whether the mobile masts are affecting people's minds or not, albeit that our neurological expert didn't prove to be terribly robust. Ultimately it will all come down to the view the judge takes of the evidence. Now we have to wait for up to a month or two whilst he decides and then formulates his judgment.

As we left the court we were greeted by a loud call from BigMouth who then told TheMoldies that they needed to come with him for a photoshoot with one of the Sunday papers about the new 'litter-picking revolution' that he now claims to be leading. Tony and Dora looked over at me with a wry smile before I encouraged them to go for it.

CHAPTER 11
AUGUST: BLUFFING

Friday 1 August 2008
Year 2 (week 44): Triple bluff

Had another visit from the police today over the threats made to JudgeFetish. I have to say I was a little surprised, having figured that both my fake threatening email from TopFirst and then his supposed hacking into the judges' intranet would ensure that he was their prime suspect. However, I hadn't counted on TopFirst's own ingenuity and it seems he's responded by faking a couple of emails of his own, ostensibly from yours truly and also hinting at fixing the Moldy litigation. Sooner or later this game of bluff and double bluff is going to explode in one or other of our faces.

For the moment I simply denied any knowledge of these alleged emails and made my own view just a little bit clearer that TopFirst must be behind the whole thing. I mean, if I was the one trying to influence JudgeFetish, it wouldn't make sense that I'd have also alerted him to it.

The triple bluff.

Monday 4 August 2008
Year 2 (week 45): Like flies round . . .

I was against The Vamp in court today.

'Let's play the word game again, BabyB. It always brightens up a dull day in court. What word do you challenge me to get into the hearing without the judge noticing? Any animal, insect or bird.'

TheVamp was looking more than a little worse for wear after what I guessed was a heavy weekend, and the phrase rough as a badger's back end sprung to mind, and so I answered with, 'How about "badger"?'

'Thanks a lot, BabyB,' she answered, getting the reference. 'I know I'm not looking my best, but really. OK, for that you can have the word "termite".'

'Agreed and if either of us fail by lunch then it's on them.'

So it was that we spent the next hour in court trying to think of a way to try and spell out our particular words without the judge realising.

TheVamp struck first when she said, 'The other side's case is riddled with clichés, to which I have no objection except to point out that they're often just not good English. In the same way that 'Vorsprung durch Technik' is *bad Ger*man.'

She looked over at me in triumph. Just as the deadline was approaching and I was beginning to give up hope, I had an idea. I stopped in the middle of the submissions I was making and looked over at the clock. The judge and everyone else in the courtroom followed my gaze. I then turned back to the judge and said, 'Your Honour, to use the words of the late Mr Justice Car*ter, might* this be a suitable time for a break?'

After a good lunch TheVamp's hangover was clearly starting to subside and she was getting into her stride with quite a forthright cross-examination of a male witness. That is until he suddenly lost his rag and said, 'You know what your problem is, young lady. All these aggressive questions. What you really need—'

The judge interrupted at this point with, 'This case isn't about counsel. Please just answer the questions which are put to you.'

The witness apparently looked a little put out and replied, 'M'Lord, you see, the thing is, all that attention. It goes to their heads, it does. She's a tease. I saw them young lawyers in the waiting room. All gathering around her like flies round—'

Before the witness could finish his sentence, I quickly stood up and interrupted him with, 'bees . . . honeypots . . . surely?'

'Quite so,' smiled the judge.

Only a few days since their last visit and it was an inauspicious start to my morning when HeadClerk rang up to my room and told me two policemen were here for me. It sent my stomach tumbling just a little southwards. However, when I went to meet them they assured me that they were just here to deliver my hard drive back safely after supposedly examining it for the last few weeks. They then asked if they could have a little word 'in confidence'.

'Of course,' I replied, taking them into a conference room in chambers.

'Well,' said the PC who had been taking the lead, 'you see, your friend TopFirst may well be in a lot of trouble for threatening your judge, and that's before we even get to the matter of his faking emails from your good self. The problem is that we discussed the investigation with someone from the CPS yesterday and they said there was almost certainly not enough evidence to prosecute.'

'Oh,' I replied. 'So how can I help?'

'Well, we've decided that perhaps the best way to bring him out into the open is to let the case proceed, delay the judgment for a few weeks and see if he makes another attempt to influence the judge in some way. It's a long shot but you never know.'

'I see.'

'Yes. But what we want to avoid is any complaint from your side about having this particular judge on board.'

'Does the judge know about all these shenanigans yet?'

'We haven't told him whom we suspect, although he may well have his suspicions.'

They then gave me the kind of old-fashioned look that only corrupt policemen seem to be able to pull off with a straight face. That 1970s, cheeky, raised eyebrow, 'know what I mean, wink, wink' look that told me that they'd very clearly dropped enough hints to identify TopFirst as the prime suspect to the judge.

This, of course, was exactly what I'd been relying on. Though I hope they haven't been so obvious about it as to leave JudgeFetish once again with the feeling that he needs to withdraw from the case. But if his suspicions are nonetheless sufficient to prejudice him, then that will do nicely, thank you very much. Particularly if they end up not only turning him against TopFirst personally but also triggering wider concerns about a corporate conspiracy more generally.

After their little performance had ended, I assured them that I would take my clients' instructions and get back to them in due course.

Wednesday 6 August 2008
Year 2 (week 45): Happy Landings

TheBusker was telling us all this evening about a case he had down in the West Country last week. It was a small rural dispute between a local farmer and a very grande dame, the Dowager Lady Bossington, in which the farmer was claiming rent for her six-week stay at his farmhouse on the estate that used to belong to her late husband. The farmer was apparently an old-fashioned, servile type but despite this he clearly thought that he should be paid for the accommodation he had provided, whereas the Dowager Lady thought it came as her right. In the middle of the case TheBusker was cross-examining the farmer and he had asked him quite how intimately he knew Lady Bossington. To which the reply came back innocently and in a broad West Country accent, 'Well, I did have intercourse with her twice on the landing.'

Thursday 7 August 2008
Year 2 (week 45): A need to know basis

I got a call from TopFirst this morning.

'BabyB, I don't care whether you're taping this or not. You might think you're all very clever having set the police on to me like this. But I just want you to know that whatever happens from now on, it's not business. It's personal.'

Pompous to the end.

Later on I went to see OldSmoothie and told him what the police had said. My concern was how we were now going to explain this whole mess to TheMoldies.

'You'll do no such thing,' said OldSmoothie.

'But what about our duty to disclose everything to the clients?'

'Cock and bull, BabyB. You should know by now that we only tell the clients what they need to know. If they knew the full story you never know what they might start instructing us to do. Then where would that leave us?'

Er, well, quite. So the show will go on.

Friday 8 August 2008
Year 2 (week 45): OldSoak

OldSoak, the resident chambers alcoholic, was in chambers today and lecturing a couple of ridiculously earnest mini-pupils.

'You kids should all slow down', he said. 'You're all in far too much of a rush to be getting on these days. It's all work, work, work. Careers advisers and goal-setting. Why not let fate take a hand for once? Let life flow a little more easily.'

TheBusker joined in with, 'I would definitely suggest doing a few more things outside of law whilst you're at college.'

The worst of the two I'll call KeanieBeanie, because he's been pestering pretty much every member of chambers with offers of help, and he makes even TopFirst seem like a stand-up comedian. He replied earnestly, 'But how will that help my pupillage applications?'

The walking talking irony that is UpTights then waded in with, 'Don't you have a life other than the law?'

'No.'

'Well you need to get one, young man.'

'What would you suggest?'

'Well, er . . .' stumbled UpTights looking for an answer, 'I don't know. Er . . .'

It had her stumped but OldSoak piped up, 'Drinking and fornication, young man. Don't they teach you anything at Oxford these days?'

HeadofChambers added, 'I always thought the word "venery" summed up what youth should be about. The thrill of the chase in all senses of the word. Fillies, firm young limbs and the huntsman's horn.'

By this time KeanieBeanie had turned the colour of his brand new bright-red braces and had sidled over to stand next to TheCreep – the one person he's been getting on with in chambers. As they stood next to each other with their shiny faces and rosy cheeks, like a couple of cupcakes fresh from the baker's oven, TheVamp nodded at TheCreep and said, 'Me,' and then at KeanieBeanie and said, 'Mini-me,' before finishing with, 'Pure Creep heaven.'

Monday 11 August 2008
Year 2 (week 46): What larks, eh Pip?

What is it about the Temple and its inhabitants that defies the onward march of time so successfully? It is as if Old Father Time himself had just popped in a few hundred years ago and decided to perch down for a rest. 'Here you are my friend. Have a seat next to the fountain. Put your feet up. A cigar maybe? Then perhaps a stroll around the garden? Won't keep you long.'

And after all, there'd be no rush when you're Father Time himself.

'Oh, go on then. Maybe just one dinner in Hall. And my, this is rather fine wine I must say, and not bad conversation either. Maybe I'll stay just a little longer . . .'

It's easy to imagine how he might have got waylaid.

This afternoon there was a rather fine summer garden party in the grounds and it had been well publicised that a certain heart-throb actor would be in attendance. TheBusker had been unable to resist leaving a note on BusyBody's table first thing this morning, ostensibly from the Middle Temple Treasury and addressed to OldSmoothie, informing him that the distinguished thesp would also in fact be eating in Middle Temple Hall at lunch 'as well as mingling with fellow diners'. The letter ended by emphasising the importance of keeping this information to himself 'in order that the whole occasion may remain a discreet affair'.

True to form, BusyBody got to work and by half past twelve today there was a queue of very well-dressed ladies standing at the entrance to the Hall, looking each other up and down competitively. Having been tipped off by TheBusker, I went along and immediately spotted the double act of UpTights and TheVamp and, nearby, even Smutton who had rather stylishly understated her own get-up for the occasion. What I didn't realise was that TheBusker had brought OldSmoothie in on the act and that he had also hired a lookalike of the actor to turn up and have lunch with him. The fawning that followed was all captured on OldSmoothie's video phone and has been playing on a continuous loop in the chambers conference room ever since.

As I left the Hall with TheBusker, he turned to me and said in his best West Country accent, 'What larks, eh Pip? What larks!'

Tuesday 12 August 2008
Year 2 (week 46): Money-go-round

At a meeting this morning with Slippery, ScandalMonger and Smutton.

Slippery was looking in a particularly self-satisfied mood as he mused, 'I was reading a story the other day in which the world became so technologically complicated that when a glitch occurred there was no one left who knew how to fix it. They all ended up back in the stone age. You see, that's what I love about our glorious profession.'

We all looked at him blankly, wondering where this was going.

'It's simple. The harder we work at complicating everything the more essential we become to being able to fix it. A wonderful, money-making virtuous circle.'

'The first thing we'll do is kill all the lawyers,' quoted Scandal.

Smutton was not looking quite her flirtatious self today. She even seemed a little sad. She looked at Slippery and said, 'I remember so clearly when you arrived in our firm all those years ago. All bright eyes and legal ideals. What happened, Slippery? Where did it all go wrong? Was it the expensive trophy wife, the big house, the school fees, maybe? I mean, come on, don't you get the feeling that sometimes it's all so petty and meaningless?'

We all looked at her in surprise. It was as if finally after years of bearing witness to Slippery's corrupt ways, the thoughts she had always suppressed had suddenly started popping out as speech, leaking out like a gentle form of Tourette's. She finished in a quiet voice, 'Who was it that hurt you? What did they do?'

After that she left the room without another sound, leaving all of us temporarily speechless.

Wednesday 13 August 2008
Year 2 (week 46): Gross injustice

OldRuin's hospital case started in court today and what with everything else that's been going on, it's been all hands on deck. Of course this also means that I've been spending quite some time with Claire in the last couple of weeks, which has been very enjoyable indeed. I've deliberately been keeping the conversation light-hearted and have steadfastly avoided asking about her boyfriend. As for the case, neither Claire, myself nor OldRuin are terribly optimistic as to the outcome but we all believe that it's at least worth making a stand against what has become abundantly clear is a gross injustice. If the hospital closure goes ahead, a great number of people, particularly the elderly population of OldRuin's Hampshire village, will have to travel a significant distance to get to their nearest hospital. What's more, the various parts of the local economy that have built up around the hospital would also be severely affected.

So today, these and many other excellent points were put by OldRuin to the judge. The campaigners outside of the court were also having a fine time of it, owing to the high court's lack of cases in the holiday season, which in turn meant that they had a monopoly over the attention of the bored journalists hanging around outside. The case is due to finish on Friday after which we will then have to wait a few weeks for judgment.

The one piece of good news to emerge from today came from OldRuin who whispered to us that a friend of his who is a 'very senior civil servant' in the Department of Health had whispered to *him* that in the unlikely event that our court case succeeds, then the minister has indicated privately that the hospital will not close.

After the case I asked Claire if she would like to have a drink with me and was pleased when she agreed.

'I'm so very sorry,' I said after we'd finished the first bottle of wine.

'For what?' asked Claire.

'Everything, I guess. You know. Losing sight of what was important. Getting my priorities completely wrong.'

'Don't worry, BabyB, I know it's been difficult with your mother,' answered Claire, making me wonder if she knew more than I'd told her.

'You're right, but it's still no excuse. You, OldRuin, Arthur and Ethel, my mother. You've all made me realise that I've been way off the mark.'

'It's nice of you to say so, BabyB, and I do understand what you're going through. I guess we're all finding our way in this big wide world.'

After that I took a deep breath and steeled myself, 'So come on then, now that we've cleared the air, tell me about your new boyfriend.'

She looked a little shocked. 'What do you mean, BabyB?'

'Oh, er, well, I was under the impression that you had started seeing a guy in your chambers.'

'Who exactly?'

'Oh, you know, the tall, dark handsome older one. The one I saw you in the bar with that time.'

'What, James? Oh, no, BabyB. You've got the wrong end of the stick there. I've just been helping him to get through some marital problems.'

'Oh, I see,' I said, raising an eyebrow and smiling.

'Not like that,' said Claire. 'Though I admit that at one point he did want it to go further but I told him I wasn't interested in married men. Since then we've actually become very close friends and thankfully his marriage is now very much back on track.'

Oh.

Thursday 14 August 2008
Year 2 (week 46): Softening up

As I prepare for my showdown with TopFirst in the next few weeks over the Bar Standards Board complaint, I thought I'd soften him up today with a little opening salvo. It was just a short email:

My Dear TopFirst,

Could you please confirm whether one of our clients is or is not the mother of your fiancée? As I'm sure you can imagine, I would not like you to fall foul of our professional rules. Therefore, if it is indeed the case then perhaps you might explain how you have avoided a conflict of interest?

With best wishes as always,

BabyB

Now of course this is hardly a killer blow, since I can only imagine that he's been acting against TopFlirt's mother in complete innocence, and in any event there will probably be a way for him to get around it if he simply talks it through with his own clients. But this should at least serve to give him a scare and it may also start him wondering how I know so much about his fiancée.

Meanwhile, UpTights had her annual wig-fitting today. Given that she's now spent many thousands of pounds on the little horse hair numbers, she even gets a personal visit to chambers and as usual she was talking about it at chambers tea afterwards. 'It's so good to throw out the old,' she said.

'What do you do with it?' asked BusyBody.

'I cut it up and then feed it through the shredder,' she replied nonchalantly before adding, 'and then I burn it in my back garden.'

'You what? The shredder? Burning? As if somehow it might hold the secrets of your sordid little life within its tightknit curls?' said OldSmoothie.

'Well, I never even clean my wig,' said TheBusker. 'In fact, I'm afraid to admit that I don't even know where I'd go to get it done.'

People looked around the room as if to find out whether it was OK to admit that they too failed such basic standards of personal hygiene. 'I think most people take great pride in the fact that their wigs get a little dirty. It's a mark of experience,' said HeadofChambers.

'I believe they even sell distressed wigs these days,' said TheVamp.

'Distressed wigs makes me think of pupils on their first day in court,' smiled TheBusker.

'A little dirt's one thing,' said UpTights. 'But if you wear that wig five hours a day, two or three days a week for most of the year it's going to get pretty sweaty to say the least. Particularly given the lack of air-conditioning in the Summer.'

'It is perhaps a little ironic that wigs were supposedly introduced for cleanliness reasons,' said TheCreep. 'You know, to keep away the nits and their like.'

'Well I still wear the wig that belonged both to my father and to his father before him,' said OldRuin, 'and I have to admit that I've never cleaned it once. As to whether it received any particular treatment back in the day, I'll never know although I doubt it very much.'

'Perhaps that's why barristers never shake hands,' said BusyBody. 'I mean, once they've spent time adjusting their wigs, well, you can understand.'

Friday 15 August 2008
Year 2 (week 46): Slap versus tickle

Smutton has moved into action and she summoned me to her office today. Rather to my surprise, when I arrived I found that TopFlirt had also been invited. After we entered her office we both stood in front of her desk like two naughty schoolchildren. Smutton was looking her usual self again today and even in the company of the beautiful and really quite glamorous TopFlirt there was still very clearly a certain something about her.

'Well, BabyB,' she purred. 'I hope you've been enjoying the hot weather. Stripping down to the bare necessities I expect?'

'Er, actually, well . . .'

Before I could answer she pouted and said, 'Because I certainly have. But anyway, back to the grindstone,' she said, predictably emphasising the 'grind' and looking at TopFlirt as she did so. 'Ready to finish off this Moldy litigation?' she asked me.

'Certainly am,' I replied.

'Now,' she said looking at us both, 'I presume you both know why I've asked to see you?'

We glanced at each other before answering, 'No,' in tandem.

'Oh, come on,' said Smutton, 'let's not play games. I know about the little tryst between the two of you and I imagine you,' she nodded at TopFlirt, 'wouldn't want your loving fiancé to find out.'

She let that hang in the air before apparently softening her approach. 'But please, how rude of me. Take a seat and let me get you both a drink.'

She smiled, which made TopFlirt look even more nervous. Once her glass was in her hand, TopFlirt cut to the chase. 'So what do you want from me, exactly?'

'I want information, of course. Not enough to damage your beau, but certainly enough to damage his case.'

'Don't you think there's a risk that I might tell him?'

'Of course. But I've always enjoyed risk. That's why I'm a litigator. My guess is you won't. But even if you did, you'd have no proof. Remember, our security man checked you for recording equipment as you entered the building.'

'Information about what exactly?'

'You're a bright girl, TopFlirt. I'm sure you'll work it out.'

The subject was then dropped as Smutton attempted a little banter over the relative merits of a bit of slap versus tickle.

'By the way,' she said to TopFlirt as she was leaving, 'as for your two young men, having watched them both in court for weeks on end, my guess is that BabyB prefers you in Myla and TopFirst in Agent Provocateur.'

Not to be completely outdone, TopFlirt replied over her shoulder, 'And my guess is that you would prefer either of them to even your finest pair of Louboutin heels.'

As we left, TopFlirt glared at me and said sarcastically, 'By the way, thanks a lot for mentioning my mum's case. TopFirst is furious.'

Shame.

Monday 18 August 2008
Year 2 (week 47): Paying for experience

OldSmoothie was telling us all in tea today that the solicitor who'd brought someone along to time his every move and force costs down had emailed him, questioning how he could possibly justify charging £5,000 for a conference that in fact had lasted half an hour. Furthermore, he'd asked for a breakdown of said costs. OldSmoothie's reply, or rather riposte, echoed an apocryphal bill once sent by a doctor and said:

1. Conducting the conference: £250

2. Knowing the answer to your problem owing to over thirty years of legal experience: £4,750

Tuesday 19 August 2008
Year 2 (week 47): FILF or FILTH?

'I heard one of the mini-pupils describing me as a MILF today,' said BusyBody. 'Not sure if I should be flattered or offended.'

'What is a MILF?' asked OldRuin.

BusyBody looked embarrassed and TheVamp stepped in. 'It stands for "Mother I'd like to . . ." er, "do something rude to".'

She, too, looked a little sheepish although when OldRuin didn't flinch she brightened up again and said, 'I guess it could make barristers and solicitors BILFs and SILFs.'

'So as a father, would that make me a FILF?' asked OldSmoothie.

'More like just plain filth,' answered BusyBody, matter-of-factly.

Wednesday 20 August 2008
Year 2 (week 47): Expert-tampering

Had another meeting with Smutton today after she summoned me with a message that TopFlirt had come through with some results.

'Well, I now have something for you to go on. Your little belle came to see me last night and pretty much begged me not to tell TopFirst about her little thing with you.'

I blushed and was unable to object before she continued. 'Anyway, she finally spilled the beans. Seemed to suggest that your mate TopFirst is not as clean-cut as he likes to make out. She thinks he's been expert-tampering in some way. The problem is she isn't sure which expert.'

Now, expert-tampering is something I have already been looking into after my earlier case against TopFirst, but up until now I haven't discovered any link between the corrupt expert organisation and the experts TopFirst has been using. I said as much. As I did so, both Smutton and I looked at each other and saw the point at once.

'I think you might want to start examining our own experts, BabyB.'

With which I was dismissed from her presence.

Thursday 21 August 2008
Year 2 (week 47): BundleCard

With his midlife crisis blossoming into full bloom, OldSmoothie was trying to show off at chambers tea this afternoon.

'Yes, I've taken up jujitsu,' he told the whole room.

'What's that?' said BusyBody, unable to resist.

'Martial art, my dear. Physical exertion mixed with grace and skill.'

'Are you sure it's not origami?' she asked. 'Making paper aeroplanes sounds about as much exercise as you'd manage.'

UpTights, who continues to take her cue from BusyBody, moved in on the act. 'Or maybe they just sit around practising Chinese burns. That's about as sophisticated as your bullying ever gets.'

I could see TheBusker warming up to the joke at this point.

'Yes, I can see it now. Arriving at court and giving your opponent a wedgie as an opening gambit.' He smiled. 'Then you could challenge them to British bulldogs if that failed or maybe a skidding competition on the newly polished courtroom floor. But of course you'd also have the ultimate weapon, the playground nuclear option in your back pocket. I mean, just take along a pupil and a mini-pupil and you've got the potential to put an end to all resistance with a full-on bundle.'

But OldSmoothie was not done. 'Anyway,' he said, 'I've also taken up mountain climbing . . .'

'Oh, here we go,' said UpTights.

'Yes, last Sunday I rose at the crack of dawn and went up Snowdon.'

'Lord Snowdon, I presume,' said BusyBody.

'Who's Dawn?' added TheVamp.

Friday 22 August 2008
Year 2 (week 47): Getting head at the Bar

TheCreep's plan for fame in the kingdom of the mini-pupils isn't going quite as he planned. Unfortunately for him it seems that they have already sussed him out. A quick tour of the walls of the Temple will reveal that his posters have all been subtly defaced so that the first 'a' in the word 'ahead' has been deleted. Now, rather than promoting his earnest-sounding lecture – 'TheCreep's guide to getting ahead at the Bar' – it instead reads more like a kind of sex manual for wiglets. TheCreep has realised his folly but it's too late and for every poster he takes down, ten more appear in its place. Less subtly, people have also taken to sketching a brick wall over the bottom half of the poster and then adding a piece of TheCreep's anatomy, hanging over the wall in the style of an old school chad drawing. They have then added a variety of slogans ranging from the obvious, 'Wot no head?' to 'Wot no work?' and 'Wot no audience?' to perhaps the most cruel of 'Wot no friends?'

All that was left was for TheVamp to add when she saw TheCreep come into tea this afternoon, 'I see you're now doing a course on oral abilities, MrCweepyWeepy. Probably the most important skill you need as a barrister, wouldn't you agree?'

Monday 25 August 2008
Year 2 (week 48): FillyBlustering

I went to see TheBoss today to discuss the possibility of the other side having tampered with one of our experts in the Moldy litigation. I figured that if anybody's going to know about getting down and dirty it would be him.

'Get real, BabyB,' was the first thing he said. 'Of course they're going to try and get to our witnesses. The case is far too big for them not to. The problem's always been in proving anything like that.'

But the real body blow was yet to come. 'Though I'd also be careful about what that filly TopFlirt's telling you. If I were them my first tactic would be to try and prolong this case for so long that one by one our old clients die off. Not only might we lose our strongest test cases but remember that any future care or treatment claims also die with them too.'

'But we're almost ready for judgment from JudgeFetish,' I replied.

'Not if you start raising the issue of expert-tampering we're not. For the judge to investigate any such allegations could take years.'

Oh.

Tuesday 26 August 2008
Year 2 (week 48): Better than nothing . . .

The dirty old judge OldFilth was at it again tonight. He whose atavistic sex-crazed lizard brain dominates in such a way that it's as if he's evolved on his own little Galapogos Islands, where judges still exercise a form of *droit de seigneur*. There was a Middle Temple student dinner this evening, an affair that as far as OldFilth is concerned implies lambs to the slaughter, and for which he always makes himself available as the esteemed guest of honour. Only it seems he isn't terribly esteemed, even in the student community, and in fact he has become part of a running joke on Facebook with his own ironic fan page to boot.

This might explain why the student representative who was introducing OldFilth sailed rather close to the wind in his little welcome speech. He stood up and declared 'Fornication!' loudly to the assembled gathering, whilst looking directly at OldFilth. This certainly grabbed everyone's attention and it even led one of the older waitresses to drop a plate in shock. He then repeated the word a second time, garnering a quiet round of titters as he again looked at the sex-addled judge. Finally, he smiled and said, 'For an occasion such as this . . .'

Round one went to him and he wasn't finished with OldFilth just yet, since he then went on to describe him as having had 'a long and extinguished career' and pausing for effect, before pretending to pass it off as a Freudian slip. A slip that would have been worthy of ClichéClanger had it not in fact been deliberately done.

By this point OldFilth was not only very drunk but was also obviously extremely irritated, and when he stood up to give his address, he paused and cast a drunken eye over the expanse of the room before spluttering, 'I hate [and then he used the word Gordon Ramsay has done so much to popularise] students.'

Unsurprisingly, this brought the room to an abrupt silence. A silence that only deepened when he then looked directly at the prettiest student in the room and growled, 'Still, it's better than nothing, I suppose.'

After which he sat down and tucked into his crème brûlée. Speech over.

Wednesday 27 August 2008
Year 2 (week 48): Therapy

OldSmoothie was boasting last night to a couple of us in the clerks room about his latest sexual conquest. Apparently she was not only his opponent last week but she is also twenty years younger than him. UpTights walked in on the conversation and said, 'You really are a sad, lonely and dirty old man. What is it they say? Only two things are certain in life: death and a certain corpulent old barrister who'd get up on a crack on a plate.'

'That's a bit rich coming from someone who's been cocked more times than Davy Crocket's musket,' he replied.

This seemed to hit home. Her face suddenly bore a startling resemblance to a boiled fist and she started shaking with what I can only assume was pent-up rage at the pompous silver fox, who was looking particularly irritating and smug today. But for once she seemed too angry to speak, and so she just stood there stamping her foot and shaking some more.

Then OldSmoothie, with a nasty look on his face, bent down towards her and whispered, 'I had a dream the other night, UpTights. I saw a young girl building a gilded scaffold. Somewhere she could climb up and hide from the world behind her empty smile. I saw her clambering ever higher, her bony fingers stretched to the sun. Then I saw the noose tightening around her neck and heard her solitary scream as she jumped from the same scaffold she had erected to help her survive.'

UpTights had stopped shaking and was silent. Then astonishingly, she started crying, sobbing uncontrollably. OldSmoothie looked at her and as if it was the most natural thing in the world he took her in his arms and hugged her. UpTights eventually stopped sobbing, and indeed she seemed to turn almost catatonic. OldSmoothie pushed her away slightly, held her by the shoulders and gazed into her eyes. He then smiled flirtatiously and said, 'You know, I could charge good money for therapy like that.'

With which he was gone.

Thursday 28 August 2008
Year 2 (week 48): RugbyShuffle

'It's outrageous what's happening to rugby at the moment,' OldSmoothie said to me over coffee this morning.

'Why?' I asked. 'What's been going on?'

'Using fake blood to pretend they're injured and get themselves off the pitch, that's what. Been going on for years but they're becoming less and less subtle and if they're not careful they're going to get caught.'

'That sounds terrible,' I said. 'Could bring the whole game into disrepute.'

'No, that's not my complaint at all,' he answered. 'It's that they're risking the exposure of one of my best courtroom tricks for getting a witness off a sticky wicket.'

'What do you mean?' I asked.

'Oh, don't play innocent with me, BabyB. Surely with a pupil-master like TheBoss you were taught the old RugbyShuffle?'

'I'm not sure I was. What does it involve?'

'Ha. Well, I'm very surprised I'm able to teach one of TheBoss's ex-pupils anything but let me explain. Strictly between these four walls, obviously.'

Obviously.

'Well, only for trusted clients and witnesses really. Either people you've got to know pretty well or experts who know which side their bread is buttered if you know what I mean.'

I certainly did.

'All comes down to the same principle as faking a rugby injury with comedy blood. Very simple really. If the witness is on the ropes or even taking the count, then you need to get them off the stand any which way you can.'

'Right.'

'So you just warn the witness beforehand that if this should happen then a spot of migraine might not go amiss. Could buy them twenty minutes and even, very occasionally, an adjournment. If it's done well, then on their return the heat has been taken from the attack and the witness is back to fighting fitness. I've even known one barrister carry around his famous "nose-bleed hand-kerchief" for witnesses he was particularly worried about. One blow into that and the blood came pouring out.'

'Oh.'

'Can't believe you haven't been using it. And you can see why I'm annoyed about the rugby case, now?'

Well, quite.

Friday 29 August 2008
Year 2 (week 48): Trouble down mill

I was confiding to OldRuin about OldSmoothie's RugbyShuffle today. He smiled and then his face took on a more serious look.

'You know, BabyB, whilst I wouldn't presume to interfere or indeed to cast any aspersions, it might be an idea to give your own expert a little health check.'

I looked at him blankly and he gave an enigmatic smile and then left me to it. It was only later in the day that I suddenly realised the full implications of what he was saying. Of course, I'd told him about our expert's need for an unusual amount of breaks to relieve himself, something we all put down either to nerves or possibly something to do with his prostate. But I realised OldRuin wasn't only alluding to the physical health of our doctor, rather he was quietly suggesting I examine his honesty.

This signpost from OldRuin gave me added impetus to once again think about taking the investigation into our expert further. But what I certainly don't want to do is upset the apple cart and delay the whole process by years. So I'm going to have to tread carefully. I'm also going to have to move pretty fast since I imag-ine that JudgeFetish will be planning to give his judgment in the next month or so. Once that's done, other things, such as the Bar Standards Board complaint against me for insider dealing, will hove into view. Oh, and if we lose, I'll get no money from the case, and who knows what SlipperySlope will decide to do about the loan he made to me on my mother's behalf. And win or lose, there's certainly no money coming in from OldRuin's case either. Finally, to cap it all I'd end up spending a week dogsbodying for TopFirst and watching him get his red bag before me.

None of the above bodes at all well for the next month.

CHAPTER 12

September: Red Bag

Monday 1 September 2008
Year 2 (week 49): Waiting for Frodo

Awkward silences today as a chambers meeting sat waiting for TheCreep to arrive as he was scheduled to make a presentation.

After a couple of minutes of strained conversation, TheBusker said, 'A bit like *Waiting for Godot.*'

'Or as ClichéClanger always put it, "Waiting to pass go",' OldSmoothie added.

To which TheVamp replied, making reference to TheCreep's lack of height, 'Waiting for Frodo more like.'

Tuesday 2 September 2008
Year 2 (week 49): Drawn swords and driving sheep

'I hear you're about to be made a freeman of the City of London,' said UpTights today.

'Yes,' said OldSmoothie, puffing out his chest as if we were meant to be impressed. 'Should help my case for becoming a people's peer as well.'

'Yeah, right,' said BusyBody. 'Because being given some sort of masonic award for having eaten lots of dinners in an obscure City livery company is really in touch and down with the, er, people.'

'What, are you in some way suggesting that it's a meaningless, out-dated and irrelevant title given by a group of pompous nonentities to one of their own?' asked UpTights sarcastically.

'Although when you put it like that, I can see why he might draw the parallel with the Lords,' smiled TheVamp.

'But doesn't it come with all sorts of rights?' said TheCreep. 'Like driving sheep over London Bridge and going about the City with a drawn sword.'

'I'm afraid not,' said HeadofChambers. 'I once had to advise on those rights and I'm afraid they're all bunkum. Exemption from tolls on animals and a few other minor things were about your lot even back in the day.'

'Oh don't worry, Mr CreepyWeepy,' said TheVamp with mock sympathy. 'You can draw your sword for me any time you like.'

With which he went bright red and disappeared into the corner of the room.

Wednesday 3 September 2008
Year 2 (week 49): Ginny's return

With time running out I need to get something on the expert we were using in the Moldy litigation in relation to TopFirst. He's hardly going to go around confessing to any corruption at the drop of a wig, so I have decided to fall back on Ginny's services once again. This has meant my following our expert on and off since last Friday to see exactly where he hangs out at lunch and in the evenings, and then arranging for Ginny to casually bump into him.

I'd failed last night in my predictions about where he might be going, but this evening Ginny once again got her man. It was not so difficult this time, as he's a lot older than TopFirst and therefore even more prone to the flattering attentions of a beautiful young woman. This evening they simply shared some light banter over drinks in a bar. But she worked fast and on Friday they are booked in for dinner whilst his wife believes he's away at a conference. We'll see what she can get out of him then, so to speak.

FanciesHimself, the junior clerk, was negotiating a fee for one of OldRuin's cases today with a long-time solicitor friend of OldRuin. Apparently he was looking for an increase in the fee and the answer came back, 'I'll up the offer from pounds to guineas. I'm in favour of guineas and I think OldRuin should be too.'

Now this obviously caused a great deal of confusion for FanciesHimself but after he consulted OldRuin he discovered that the solicitor was right. OldRuin did indeed like guineas (and any other offer in old-school currency it seemed). He was also utterly charmed by the approach as was clear from the tone in which he told the story at chambers tea today.

'I wonder whether I should have made a counter-offer in groats, just to make him smile,' he said. 'I particularly liked HeadClerk's response which was to remind me that whatever money I wanted to negotiate in, his fee certainly wouldn't be limited to merely taking his shilling.'

'Shame it wasn't in gold sovereigns,' said HeadofChambers, then added, 'I liked it when I heard that special forces were issued with them in the first Gulf War to buy assistance from local people.'

Then TheBusker said, 'Maybe we should all start being a little more imaginative in our settlements. Captain Cook used red feathers as currency in Tahiti and then there were beaver skins in the States . . .' he paused and added, ' . . . though I suppose they wouldn't have been as convenient in your back pocket as the feathers.'

'And then after all the haggling we could all retire to the local tavern to down a few flagons of ale,' said TheVamp cheerfully.

This afternoon OldSmoothie, SlipperySlope and I had a meeting with the main Moldy litigants: Arthur, Ethel, Stanley and Dora. Tony was also there to support Dora and I get the feeling that romance might even be in the air between the two of them. They were both dressed today in their litter-picking outfits.

'We've got people doing the same thing all over the world now, BabyB,' said Dora excitedly. 'It's all about t'interweb these days and with our Tony the Trash and Dora the Dustwoman accounts we now have over a million followers on Twitter covering lots of different countries. It's really captured the imagination. We've even set up an official charity to organise everything.'

I was delighted to hear it and they were all obviously enthused by this great cause. But then we had to get down to business and in this Arthur and Ethel were clearly in charge. Indeed they had called the meeting following a discussion they'd had with the other Moldies whose cases rested on the outcome of the test cases. But before they could begin, OldSmoothie spent some time (billable, obviously) explaining where we were in the litigation and that whilst the case could go either way, there was a real risk we could lose. He then added, 'However, there still remains a chance that we may win and if this happens then you could all be due substantial damages.'

'That's what we've come to see you about,' said Arthur, finally able to get a word in.

'I see,' said OldSmoothie, clearly not seeing.

'You see,' (which he didn't), 'it's never been about the money for any of us.'

'Oh. A point of principle. Hit the big corporation hard. Of course, I understand,' said OldSmoothie, still not seeing.

'It hasn't even been about that either. All any of us have actually ever wanted from this litigation is to be acknowledged.'

'Oh,' said OldSmoothie, now seeing less and less.

'And if there's a chance for us to settle in a way in which the other side acknowledges what they've done and says sorry, then, you know, we'd all be happy with that.'

'We're realistic enough to realise that when the science is uncertain we're unlikely to force them to take down the mast,' said Ethel.

'Though we'd obviously prefer that they did and stop all these strange effects once and for all.'

'But what about the damages?' asked OldSmoothie, who was starting to look a little less certain about things.

'I don't think you understand, young man,' said Arthur. 'We don't want compensation. I don't want anyone else caring for Ethel and what good would the money do us at our age? All we all want is to live what lives we've got left, not accumulate figures in bank accounts.'

He paused and then reflected, '*Tempus fugit*, I think you'd say. I remember my Virgil from school: "Time flees irretrievably, while we wander around, prisoners of our love of detail."'

Then Ethel added with a smile, 'Although I've always preferred the phrase *festina lente*: "Make haste slowly" and all will be well.'

Arthur and Ethel grinned at each other, sharing something they had obviously repeated many times before. What was also clear was that this was something upon which all TheMoldies were in full agreement.

'And actually, young man,' Ethel continued, as OldSmoothie winced at her description, 'we don't want to bring down a big company and all the poor people and their families who rely upon it. As Arthur says, we just want to be acknowledged.'

'You see, it's like we have become invisible. People think because we're old that we somehow think or feel differently, that we don't feel hurt when we are ignored, that we don't matter any longer.'

She paused and looked at Arthur before adding, 'We just want people to stand up and say that in fact we do matter. Not just us, but all the pensioners up and down the land. We want them to have a voice.'

Arthur turned to Slippery. 'That's what we've been telling Mr Slope here from the start. Couldn't have been clearer, so it shouldn't be news to anybody now.'

They'd said their piece and a heavy silence fell upon the room. OldSmoothie looked very unhappy at the prospect of settling for a mere apology and with what may well end up as no costs, given that nominal offers had already been made by the other side and duly rejected months ago. Words were failing him but he managed, 'Well, let us have a think about this. I'm not sure whether we'll be able to get any settlement. But let me have a think.' With which he ushered TheMoldies out of the room.

On his return he said, 'You see, BabyB, that's the problem with taking clients' instructions. Now we'll have to find a way around them.'

'But there was nothing ambiguous about what they were saying. They want to settle in return for an apology.' I looked over at Slippery and added, 'And apparently that's what they've wanted right from the very beginning. So we could have settled this months ago. Now I know precisely what you meant when you told me you'd taken all the instructions you needed. All the instructions you needed to rip them off more like.'

Slippery's whole demeanour changed and he growled, 'Get real, BabyB, and don't forget which side your bread's buttered either. Or your mother's bread, at least.'

Then OldSmoothie stepped in, no doubt thinking he was being diplomatic. 'BabyB, whatever's done is done. But as for now, don't forget that there's *always* ambiguity. If the other side aren't prepared to negotiate then there'll be no settlement. Understood?'

I understood exactly what both of them were saying but I left the conference determined that however much wrong I'd done in the last couple of years, I wasn't going to let Arthur and Ethel down now. The first person I called was TheVamp who hadn't been able to make the conference because of a court appearance.

'It's a terrible situation, BabyB,' she agreed, sympathetically. 'But the problem is that the damage was done when Slippery and OldSmoothie didn't tell them about the other side's offer – and that was months ago. Not quite sure what we can do at this stage but I'll tell you if I come up with anything.'

Monday 8 September 2008
Year 2 (week 50): Mystery

Asked OldRuin out for lunch today, to solicit his advice. 'It would be my pleasure, BabyB,' he had answered.

Over lunch I couldn't quite bring myself to tell him the full extent of the compromises I'd once again made this year, but I also had the feeling that perhaps it wasn't necessary: that he understood. Instead I concentrated on outlining what Arthur and Ethel had told us on Friday and what OldSmoothie and Slippery's response had been. As has been so often the case, his reply was both oblique and yet perfect for my needs.

'I don't have any answers, BabyB. No plot nor plan that'll get you out of it. All I can tell you is to have faith and follow your heart.' He smiled at me and his eyes twinkled even more than usual. 'Mystery is better imagined than described. Whispers of the soul. Echoes of the heart. They are what we are. Poetry and music can give us the odd rare glimpse. But even then, you're left grasping at air when you actually try looking for answers. But follow those whispers and echoes and they'll guide you through the hard times of the soul.'

Then, in the middle of all this profundity, a mischievous look crossed his face and he added, 'Of course, I would never advise you to try to get the other side to bypass your illustrious colleagues.'

'No, of course not,' I replied.

'But if they just happened to make an offer at the door of court at a sufficient volume for your clients to be able to hear it, well, you could hardly blame your clients for choosing to accept it . . .'

Tuesday 9 September 2008
Year 2 (week 50): Frustration

If I'm to sort out the mess that is the Moldy litigation, then I will need two things: information from Ginny and an offer from the other side. Today I received knockbacks on both fronts. First, Ginny reported back on her Friday dinner with our expert witness. All had gone well apparently, but still no cigar, as it were, in either sense: no compromising position for him and no information for me. However, she seemed at least optimistic that he'll crack eventually and she told me that she hoped to see him again in the next few days. I reminded her that time was tight. *Tempus fugit* indeed.

As for the other side, I engineered a chance meeting with UpTights today at lunch in Middle Temple Hall and I quietly asked whether there might not still be any chance of settlement.

'Ah ha, BabyB!' she exclaimed loudly enough to attract the attention of everyone else in the lunch queue. 'I thought you'd crack at some point. Your case has been hopeless from the start and you should never have rejected the offer we made you months ago. We're certainly not going to make you another one now that all those costs have passed under the bridge.'

It's not really a surprise but it was at least worth a try.

OldSmoothie is still desperately trying any way possible to ingrati-
ate himself with the Tories in the hope that they might make him
one of their million-and-one new peers when they eventually get
into power. Hence his attempt at a publicity stunt today. He obviously feels that despite his (ahem) inherent brilliance as an advocate and his incredibly successful career, he is still not getting the
attention he deserves (actually, he is). But, refusing to be crushed
by the put-downs he regularly receives from his fellow barristers,
today he bounced (or rather, flounced) into chambers like a manic
child who has eaten too many brightly coloured chemical-satu-
rated sweets.

'I'm going to become the people's barrister,' he declared with a
grand wave of his hand.

HeadClerk raised his eyebrows and commented in a stage whisper, 'Ouch. I shudder to think what medication has brought this
one on.'

Then when OldSmoothie frowned at him impatiently
he enquired politely, 'And how are you going to do that,
OldSmoothie?'

Still almost breathless with excitement OldSmoothie said, 'My
new robes, that's how. Want to see?'

Then, without waiting for an answer he scuttled into a side
room. By this time, he had attracted something of an audience,
including several clients who had arrived to meet their barristers.
After about a minute he reappeared in a white gown emblazoned
with the red cross of St George and a little horsehair wig, painted
with the same insignia.

'More Lord Sutch than Lord Smoothie wouldn't you say?' said
BusyBody dryly.

'Oh, you can mock now,' he declared, 'but I think you'll change
your tune when you see how patriotic a jury can be, particularly
when England have their World Cup Qualifying game this evening
against Croatia.'

To which HeadClerk responded almost apologetically, 'Er,
OldSmoothie, may I introduce you to your client for today's
trial?'

OldSmoothie spun around and strode over to the man standing next to HeadClerk, with his hand extended in greeting and wearing an enormous smug grin.

'OldSmoothie, this is Vedran. He's from Croatia.'

Thursday 11 September 2008
Year 2 (week 50): Blaggered

'I was against a friend of yours yesterday, BabyB,' said BusyBody today.

She then told me his name and I realised it had been Blagger.

'Didn't quite catch which chambers he was in but he said he'd been at Oxford with you.'

'Er, yes, that's right. How did he get on, I ventured?'

'Well, he told me that it was his first personal injury case since he usually did possession actions.'

'Yes, I'm sure it was,' I said wryly.

'Well, I made him an offer to settle and he seemed mightily relieved to accept, I have to say. Particularly because he had looked so shocked when I had landed him with a bundle of authorities.'

'I can imagine,' I said, thinking just how much of an understatement that was.

As soon as BusyBody had left I gave Blagger a call. 'I hear you were against BusyBody yesterday,' I said.

'Oh, BabyB. I got into all sorts of trouble. You see I met up with the solicitor I mentioned and she pretty quickly worked out that I was neither a judge nor a barrister. But she also decided that it would be quite fun to continue the blag for a little longer and so gave me some papers on what she said was "a very simple personal injury case". But what she didn't warn me about was your friend BusyBody. Scared the living daylights out of me, I can tell you. Thankfully she made an offer my solicitor friend said was at least "half-decent". For my part I'd have tried to persuade the client to settle even if she'd only offered five pence. It's certainly put me off doing any more legal impersonating.'

Overheard TheBusker telling HeadClerk this morning about a parking fine he'd been given.

'Yes, I was parked about an inch over the edge of the parking bay and only because the first car had already encroached into my own.'

'So what did you do?' asked HeadClerk.

'Just not worth the time even considering an appeal so I sent off the money with a little note saying that I was not going to dispute the fine. Then I added that the traffic department had seven days to come to my house and clean off the glue that the ticket had left on my windscreen or else I would not only report them for criminal damage but I would also be issuing civil proceedings for trespass to property as well as hiring a very expensive contract cleaner to do the job.'

'And how did they react?'

'They'd obviously never had anyone raise this before and within two days of my letter being sent I not only had the traffic warden himself, but also his boss, knocking at my door at 8 a.m. with a bucket of hot water and a cloth.'

HeadClerk smiled and TheBusker, who now had the attention of the rest of the clerks room, warmed to his theme. 'I know we can't all choose what we do for a living but there's no need for anyone to be a jobsworth. I mean, who'd choose to be a traffic warden, anyway?'

'Reminds me of that Harry Enfield sketch,' said HeadClerk, 'where a child was taking his belongings out of a doll's house and then looked up at his parents and said, "When I grow up I want to be a bailiff."'

'Well, given how ruthlessly efficient they all are, I can't say I was surprised to hear it was a Westminster traffic warden who discovered the car bomb outside that London night club,' continued TheBusker. 'Maybe that's the solution to the war on terror? Just fill the security services with armies of commission-based traffic wardens.'

Monday 15 September 2008
Year 2 (week 51): Tomorrow never comes

I went to a 'Sub-Prime' party with Claire on Saturday night where the dress code was 'bring the best of your worst or the worst of your best', which basically meant it was full of shiny tracksuits and very tattered old dinner jackets.

'So what do all the papers mean when they keep describing things as sub-prime anyway?' asked Claire.

'No idea,' I answered drunkenly.

'Sub-prime shops, sub-prime clothes, even sub-prime people. It's just another way for the condescending, snotty-nosed media to call people chavs.'

I'm sure she's right but in the meantime we were all following the instructions on the 'Sub-Prime' invite which was to 'live like there's no tomorrow'.

Which means that like all good sub-prime schemes I am now suffering an almighty hangover, since despite the promises, tomorrow really did come and I still have one or two pretty enormous problems to sort out.

Tuesday 16 September 2008
Year 2 (week 51): Vultures

With the collapse of Lehman brothers yesterday it was no surprise to find that an emergency chambers meeting had been called this evening at very short notice. The topic was one that is probably being discussed in boardrooms up and down the country. Pretty standard you might think. Except for the fact that in *our* boardroom, the single agenda item was listed rather tactlessly as 'How can chambers benefit from the present banking crisis?'

This didn't stop at least half of chambers from attending and HeadClerk kicked off with, 'With all this talk of recession, what we must not forget is that wherever there is hardship there is opportunity, specifically in the areas of insolvency, property, employment and divorce.'

'Do you mean bankrupting, repossessing, sacking and er, sacking?' said TheVamp.

'Well, that's another way of putting it, I suppose,' he said.

'Or vultures, might be another way,' said BusyBody.

'Do you think we're some kind of free-living hippy, justice-for-all, do-gooding girls brigade?' said OldSmoothie angrily.

He had been offensive on so many levels that for once BusyBody was actually silent for a moment as her mind clocked all of the different insults he had thrown. Fortunately UpTights stepped in. 'Maybe not. But a bit of self respect and decorum when the rest of the world is suffering wouldn't go amiss.'

'That's a little ironic coming from you, don't you think?' OldSmoothie replied.

HeadClerk ignored them all and concluded without any hint of irony, 'So I want everyone to get out there and talk to the media about how terrible this whole recession is and how the only people who are going to benefit are the lawyers.'

Welcome to the age of prosperity (for lawyers, at least).

Wednesday 17 September 2008
Year 2 (week 51): Twits

With tenancy decisions for FraGiles, Sharon and their fellow pupils approaching, it all brings back terrible memories of last year and my initial fights with TopFirst. Although I've been more than a little pre-occupied with my own problems in the last few months, I have noticed one pupil in particular who is starting to make her mark. Mind you, when I say 'make her mark', this is not necessarily a positive thing. It seems that she has got herself on to Facebook and Twitter and has been evangelising around chambers about how this is the new way to bring in work, and that if you're not plugged in, as it were, then you're doomed. This has inspired a worrying number of the senior members of chambers to sign themselves up to various social networking sites. Or rather, taking OldRuin's lead when he started using email a little while back, it's inspired them to get their secretaries to sign up on their behalf.

What this has meant is that this pupil now has about half of chambers avidly following her status updates to see how on earth they should go about doing it themselves. The result is that Twitter (the only name that fits when you hear her haughty tones) has gone into update overdrive. So much so that not only do we (for I have of course also signed up) hear about pretty much every detail of her life from what she has for breakfast to the times she passes wind, but she has also started speaking in real life in the form of a series of staccato status updates. Even BusyBody, who pretty much does this kind of communication naturally, has spotted it after she appeared against her in court and realised that Twitter was addressing the judge in exactly the same way.

I mentioned this to Claire over a beer last night and questioned half-seriously whether this was the future of our cherished language.

'You joke, BabyB, but I have to admit that on the very odd occasion when anything interesting actually happens to me, the first thing I think of is how it will sound on my Facebook update to my friends.'

Maybe we're all doomed.

Thursday 18 September 2008
Year 2 (week 51): Bingo!

Finally, I got a call from Ginny today telling me that she's achieved success with the expert witness I've had her stalking. She managed to get him on to boasting about his 'extra' sources of income and the Moldy cases came up as an example. Sure enough, I was right. TopFirst and one of the in-house lawyers at the telecom company quite specifically paid him off – not to be completely biased their way, of course (that would have been too obvious), but instead to do the more subtle job of not performing terribly well in the witness box. So, whenever he started to go off-message, TopFirst would give him the sign and he'd fake the need to relieve himself, leave the courtroom and then start receiving instructions from TopFirst by text.

Ginny had done a sterling job, particularly because it seems she taped the whole conversation. But she held back the best news until last: her absolute *pièce de résistance*. Having borrowed his phone to pretend to make a call, she then 'accidentally' dropped it and told him she had lost it in the crush of the bar they were in. Whereas in fact she had hidden the phone, which she duly handed to me along with a DVD of her video recording. She said with some excitement, 'I nailed it, BabyB. Every single text that that little weasel TopFirst sent is on here.'

From her tone it sounded as though this job were no longer just business but rather something more personal. When I suggested this she replied, 'It's rare that any of my jobs ever get to me but there was just something about TopFirst that really got under my skin. Not just his smug arrogance and conceited ways, something deeper and more hateful. Something that I guess, if truth be told, slightly scared me.'

'Tell me about it,' I answered, as I pocketed the evidence and handed over the fee she had earned ten times over.

Friday 19 September 2008
Year 2 (week 51): Nuclear option

'So what do you want, you snivelling little creep?' asked TopFirst, with his usual charm. It was 8 a.m. and we were meeting in a café on Fleet Street after I'd phoned to tell him that he might find it in his interests to be there.

'Well, I wanted to thank you for dropping us both in it with the Bar Standards Board.'

'I don't think so, my friend,' he said sarcastically. 'This time you are well and truly going down. Should be only a few more days now before the case finishes and the Board sets in motion your final downfall.'

'That would be funny, if it weren't for the fact that I happen to know a certain Mr TopFirst sold short on the telecom company at exactly the time you have alleged that I was doing so.'

He looked confused.

'Strange that,' I said. 'Maybe you're trying to take the heat off yourself. Is that it?'

Now he was looking a little concerned. 'You're bluffing. You couldn't . . . you wouldn't . . .'

Slowly it started to dawn on him that it might indeed have been possible for someone to contrive to make it look like he had taken a bet on the same shares himself. He just couldn't work out how.

'. . . it's not possible . . .' he continued.

Well, I'm certainly not going to be the one who tells him that I have his bank account details courtesy of his desire to get into *Who's Who*, nor how easy it was to call in the favour with my friend Blagger and to get him to sell short on the telecom company in TopFirst's name.

So that's the first part of the story and I thought I'd let him stew on it for a little while. Although I admit I hadn't anticipated that TopFirst would immediately retort by telling me where I could stick my little set-ups and double bluffs. However, this wasn't all I had up my sleeve, and whilst I knew this, he didn't. So I let him rant on a little longer before interrupting his flow. 'All of which, TopFirst, would be serious enough. But just consider the double whammy of being caught out in not only insider dealing but also expert-tampering.'

This really stoked the fire and he leapt to his feet and started striding around the café, shouting obscenities and pointing at me, before sitting back down, taking a deep breath and saying, 'I don't have the faintest idea what you're talking about, BabyB, and even if I did, you wouldn't be able to even begin to prove such a baseless and scurrilous allegation.'

'Now that's just where you're wrong.'

He sat up straight as I produced a mini-DVD player and started to play the expert's little love-nest confession. TopFirst's first reaction was to say, 'What's Ginny doing there? You . . .'

But he couldn't find the words and I said, 'I think you'd better listen to the whole thing, TopFirst. Might make you reconsider your strategy for all sorts of things.'

He did so in silence and this silence continued even after the video had finished. Then he glared at me sullenly. 'So what do you want?'

'Your hide, truth be told.'

'Yeah, right. That's why you're showing this to me.'

'Ooh, very clever, TopFirst. My, we are growing up into a smarty-pants little lawyer, aren't we?' I answered.

I then went on to explain to him in roundabout terms that all TheMoldies who had registered claims with us would settle for an apology, five thousand pounds each and no costs for either side, and that in the light of the scandalous evidence I'd just showed him, he might just want to consider it. Oh, and they could also take down the mobile mast that TheMoldies had been complaining about. What's more, he might find that it's in both our interests to withdraw the complaint he'd made against me to the Bar Standards Board. And finally, any offer should be made direct to TheMoldies themselves at the door of court, thereby sidelining Slippery and OldSmoothie and without any reference to me whatsoever.

TopFirst told me to go stuff myself but then he added begrudgingly as he was leaving that he would consider it. He'll now have to talk to the in-house lawyer for the telecom company who was also in on the expert-tampering and get him to instruct UpTights in no uncertain terms as to exactly what to do.

Tuesday 23 September 2008
Year 2 (week 52): Pyrrhic victory

I received a call from TopFirst today.

'You have yourself a deal, BabyB, but on one condition.'

'What's that?' I asked.

'That you never again contact TopFlirt.'

'Agreed.'

As if he's going to be able to enforce that one, and hey, it doesn't stop her contacting me. Mind you, I'm not exactly seeking those sorts of complications any longer. His tone sounded very annoyed but there was a tiny bit of smugness smouldering away in the background and by the next sentence it was beginning to blaze through.

'But you know, BabyB, it'll be a Pyrrhic victory at best since not only will you fail to recover your costs but OldSmoothie will be so annoyed with you that your red bag's as good as lost.'

This I already knew. Then to rub it in further he said, 'And for your information, it didn't actually take much to sell the idea to UpTights, and after all of the kind things the in-house lawyer has said about me in the process I find it pretty unlikely that she won't be giving me mine.'

This I had also guessed.

'So until I welcome you into chambers as my official dogsbody, it's *hasta la vista*, BabyB.'

Then he hung up. Now I have to wait until judgment day on Thursday for the offer formally to be made.

Later, I gave Blagger a call. 'Listen. You know the money from the short-selling on the shares that were bought in my name and that of TopFirst?'

'Certainly do, BabyB. It's all currently getting itchy feet in a couple of client accounts. What do you want me to do with it?'

'Well, I know you're not going to approve but I want you to donate it all directly to a particular charity. Anonymously. Apart from TopFirst's original stake, that is, which you can send straight back to his account in a couple of weeks.'

I then gave him the details for the litter-picking charity that Tony and Dora had set up. Tempting as it might have been to keep it, whatever difficulties I'm in and whatever levels to which I've stooped this year, I will hardly make amends by spending the proceeds of crime on fixing my own problems.

Thursday 25 September 2008
Year 2 (week 52): Judgment day

Judgment day today and it started pretty well with a letter from the Bar Standards Board informing me that TopFirst had withdrawn his complaint. However, the letter had a sting in its tail informing me that this does not in fact put an end to matters because the Board will still have to consider whether or not to proceed, even in the absence of TopFirst's complaint. This is all pretty worrying because although the threat has diminished somewhat without TopFirst's accusation driving it, there is clearly a risk that an investigation may well ultimately lead back to me. The letter went on to say that a decision as to whether they would proceed or not would be made in the next few days.

In the meantime, I went off to court to discover that TheMoldies had organised a flash mob through Facebook and Twitter, thanks in particular to the popularity of Tony and Dora.

'You'll never guess what?' Tony announced.

'What?' I asked innocently.

'Our charity just received a massive pledge from an anonymous donor.'

'That's great news,' I said, faking surprise.

'Now we'll really be able to clean up Britain,' said Dora, 'as well as harnessing the power of so very many people who usually go unheard.'

The case had also made the front pages of a number of national newspapers – thanks to ScandalMonger – so there were probably well over a thousand pensioners standing outside of the courthouse waving placards and singing, 'We'll meet again' and 'We'll gather lilacs in the spring again', as if they were ready to fight the Second World War all over again.

As I'd arranged the previous night, Arthur and Ethel were both waiting at the entrance to the court and I suggested that we should perhaps go for a little breath of fresh air before we went in.

'Of course, BabyB,' said Ethel, as we set off along the street, 'only so long as you tell us what you've got up your sleeve.'

I smiled.

'We knew there was something,' said Arthur. 'As soon as you suggested the meeting.'

'And just so you know,' said Ethel, 'we can keep a secret.'

'Well, there's only one thing I really need to say,' I replied. 'And that's to wish you the very best of luck with the case. I'm sure it'll all turn out just as you hoped.' Then I paused before adding, 'Though I would suggest that you keep within earshot of UpTights and OldSmoothie at all times. Oh, and you might want to have the others gathered and primed to make any decisions. Should a decision become necessary, that is.'

They looked at each other and grinned. 'We've known all along that you'd sort it all out, BabyB. You're a good one at heart. We could tell that from the off.'

We then walked back to the court and met up with the others outside the courtroom. Then, just as we were all ready to enter and collect the judgment, UpTights came over and stood in front of Arthur and Ethel, and before OldSmoothie was able to shepherd her away, she made them the offer in exactly the terms I had demanded of TopFirst. To the letter and making it clear that the financial part was a repeat of a previous offer. All at full volume, too, so that even those Moldies whose hearing wasn't quite as good as it used to be would have been able to hear her loud and clear. As you might imagine, OldSmoothie went ballistic and Slippery followed suit. But by this point Arthur had taken charge and gathered the troops and they turned as one to face the two greedy ones, as Arthur said in no uncertain terms, 'We'd like to accept the offer.'

OldSmoothie began to bluster, but Arthur interrupted him. 'An offer it seems that had already been made some time ago.'

Well, that shut them both up. Their arms fell to their sides and like two naughty schoolboys they marched into court as if they were about to hand themselves over to the headmaster.

After the deal was done there was much celebrating outside of court. Ethel gave me a big hug and Arthur a shake of the hand and a pat on the back. Ethel said, 'I'm so pleased you made them take down the mast, BabyB.'

Arthur smiled and then made way for Tony who was holding a pick-up stick in one hand and Dora's hand in the other. They were both wearing their yellow litter-picking bibs as, I now realised, were a large number of the other Moldies.

'We've got older people following our lead everywhere now,' said Tony, proudly.

'Cleaning their high streets the length and breadth of the country,' added Dora.

'But best of all,' said Tony, 'is that this whole thing has brought the most wonderful woman in the world into my life.' At which they beamed at each other.

Stanley was also there with his football under his arm. As I stood there, smiling, I suddenly saw TheColonel marching through the crowd towards me with his Springer Spaniel on a lead.

'Well done, BabyB,' he boomed. 'You've made Arthur and Ethel happier than I've seen them in a long time. I just wanted to tell you that I've shaped you a surfboard in anticipation of your winning today. I've just dropped it off with your very confused-looking clerks and I hope to see you in the sea very soon.'

He shook my hand and gave me a hearty pat on the back and I thanked him profusely. I was beginning to feel a little overwhelmed. Then, with the cameras rolling, who should appear out of nowhere but BigMouth the Tory MP – the man who had introduced us to TheMoldies in the first place. He strode over to Arthur, who was leading the Moldy group in the interviews, and put a proprietorial arm around his shoulders. Then he muscled into the interview, giving the following little speech:

'Today we can celebrate English justice at its very best. This has been a tale of David and Goliath, in which the little people have emerged victorious. And I am proud to have been the one to lead them in these efforts.'

Honestly. Those were exactly his words, and he delivered them without even a flinch. OldRuin had come along to watch and he smiled at me in a way that suggested both congratulations on our result and also weary irony at the brassiest of brass neckedness certain politicians excel at. Then he whispered to me, 'Let him have his moment, BabyB. Pride's the biggest weakness of them all and hubris its most dangerous side. Remember what someone once said about all political careers ending in failure, and when you live by the sword . . .'

At this point he was interrupted by BigMouth himself, who had finished his interviews and now came over to throw his arm around *my* shoulders. 'Not bad for one day, BabyB. I save TheMoldies before lunchtime and also receive a letter from the expenses office confirming that I can avoid paying a single penny of tax on the sale of my second home. It seems I can simply flip it around to my first home. Who knew? Think I might go out and celebrate.'

As BigMouth sauntered down the courtroom steps, OldRuin smiled again and murmured enigmatically, 'You remember what I just said about ending in failure? Well that end may come sooner than he thinks.'

Then he turned to me and said, 'Well done, BabyB. I'm proud of you. You keep on following your heart and you'll never go far wrong.'

He looked over at TheMoldies who were still celebrating and added, 'Look at them, BabyB. They're not teaching us how to die but how to live.'

OldRuin and I were joined by Claire and my mother, who had also turned up to hear the judgment, and we all slipped away from the crowd to celebrate over a quiet lunch. Whilst we were eating, I did just have one more work-related thing to share. 'TopFirst will be smarting in a few weeks when he discovers that he didn't quite get the small print right on our agreement.'

'What do you mean?' asked Claire.

'Well, we settled all the claims that were registered with us. But it turns out that Tony never actually officially got around to signing up his own claim at the same time as the others. He just tagged along with Dora. But now he's leading a movement of Moldy litter-pickers who suddenly have some quite serious financial backing.'

I hoped no one noticed as I shifted a little uncomfortably in my seat as I said this. I continued, 'And from what he told me today he'll be delighted to start a new action of his own. After all, Whistleblower's documents still point to the fact that the mobile phone masts are seriously damaging to people's health. What's more he thinks there'll be many more litigants who will come forward once the publicity kicks in.'

'You crafty young fellow,' said OldRuin with a glint in his eye.

'Oh, and he asked me if I could recommend any honest lawyers and of course, I just happened to mention you and Claire.'

As we made our way home that evening my mother commented, 'I'm really proud of you, BabyB. Not just for doing the right thing by your lovely clients in this case, but also for all the work you've put in on OldRuin's hospital case. Despite everything I've said about your father, I always loved the fact that at the first whiff of injustice he would step up to the mark and you've got that quality in spades.'

Friday 26 September 2008
Year 2 (week 52): RedBags

'I don't know what went on yesterday morning, BabyB, but you need to know that I'm not pleased. Not pleased at all.'

OldSmoothie emphasised each word ominously. 'And as for your little bet over a red bag with TopFirst . . .'

I looked at him wide-eyed, astonished that he knew anything about it.

'What? You think I didn't know. Come on, BabyB, this profession's too small for secrets. You should know that by now.'

Oh. I figured Slippery must have let, er, slip, or maybe UpTights made some passing remark after having been tipped off by the memo.

OldSmoothie continued, 'Anyway, with a trick like the one you pulled off yesterday, you know where you can stick your little red bag? Stuff it right up there and forget you even dreamt of getting one, BabyB.'

'But the clients were happy,' I protested. 'We got them what they wanted.'

'That's *never* the point, BabyB. We didn't get what *I* wanted, which was a big fat pay cheque to help me finance my increasingly expensive wife and the *SS School Fees* that she launched out into the ocean some years ago, and which seems to become more expensive to keep afloat every year that goes by.'

Oh again.

As if to prove OldSmoothie's point about the place being too small for secrets, I received a call from TopFirst within an hour.

'My condolences, BabyB, on your failure. Just thought I'd add to your news with a little of my own. I've been told by a good source that UpTights intends to award me my own red bag at our celebration dinner on Tuesday evening. I look forward to seeing you at the start of October, BabyB. Make sure you arrive looking smart, as I wouldn't want you dragging down the standards in my chambers. Come to think of it, I think I'll have you start by shining my shoes. That is, after you've made me coffee, naturally.'

Monday 29 September 2008
Year 2 (week 53): Loan Ranger

With the Bar Standards Board complaint remaining live and the fact that I'll be dogsbodying for TopFirst next week, the last thing I needed this morning was a showdown with SlipperySlope over the Moldy case and my mother's debts. But he'd summoned me in and so that was what I was going to get.

'BabyB, I don't for a minute believe that you weren't involved in fixing that settlement. I don't know how you did it but just for the record, you should be aware that I know it was you.'

I didn't reply, not wanting to dig my hole any deeper than it already was.

'Which brings me nicely on to the subject of your mother's loan.'

Ouch. This was not a good introduction to that particular subject.

'You know, BabyB, despite what I see as a betrayal, I can still understand why you did it. Believe it or not, we're not impermeable hard-nosed monsters and both Arthur and Ethel and indeed you yourself have, I have to admit, made me sit up. Only a little mind, before you start thinking I'm going soft. What I'm trying to say is that whilst you lost me some money on this, you and TheMoldies have actually made me a lot more money by giving our firm a whole new area of specialisation through the geriatrigation cases that have been coming in. They've already massively increased our client base and, of course, where TheMoldies boldly go, their children and grandchildren have also followed. And for what it's worth, sheer audacity and inge- nuity are skills that are both rare at the Bar and highly prized by myself and ScandalMonger.'

He paused for breath, clearly not comfortable with this touchy- feely approach. 'So the bottom line is: I think you're basically a good thing and I'm going to extend the period of the loan on your mother's debts.'

I think I must have looked a little shocked at this turnaround in events.

Then he added, 'And in case you're concerned, she'll be safe with me, BabyB. I can assure you of that. You're on the team to stay after your performance this year.'

Then he smiled and, with a far off look in his eye, declared, 'So, BabyB, the Loan Ranger rides again.'

'And what was it Garbo said?' I asked with a grin.

He looked at me quizzically, and then said, 'That's it, BabyB. Now you're really getting into the spirit. "I want to be a loan." Love it!'

After which he shook my hand, patted me awkwardly on the shoulder, clearly wondering whether to give me a hug or not, and then left.

Tuesday 30 September 2008
Year 2 (week 53): High tea

So, this evening TopFirst will be awarded his red bag by UpTights at dinner. He couldn't resist calling me this morning to crow.

'Shame you had to lose, BabyB. Remember, it's white, one sugar. Starting tomorrow.'

Later, Claire and I were invited out to afternoon tea at The Savoy by OldRuin as a thank you for helping him with the hospital case. When we arrived, he was looking surprisingly furtive and he had a real twinkle in his eye. After a lavish and extremely enjoyable high tea and just as he was preparing to leave to catch his train home, I was able to resist no longer. I asked him if he had any news.

'It's funny you should ask, BabyB. I do as a matter of fact.'

He paused, smiling.

'He's teasing you, BabyB,' said Claire also smiling. She seemed to be in on whatever it was he knew.

'OK,' I said, 'what have I done now?'

'You've both kept the hospital open, BabyB, that's what you've done,' said OldRuin beaming.

'What? How do you know?'

'The judge sent both sides an advance copy of the judgment this morning.'

I looked at Claire and said, 'And you knew about this, too?'

She looked sheepish. 'Well, OldRuin might have mentioned something . . .'

Then OldRuin bent down beside the table and pulled up a bag containing what looked like a book. 'This is for you, BabyB,' he said.

I opened the bag and took out its contents. It was indeed a book. An old book, and when I opened it up I saw that the author was none other than Charles Kingsley. Then when I saw the original inscription inside it my mouth dropped as I realised this was OldRuin's very own copy, inscribed by his wife over sixty years ago.

'I wanted you to have it, BabyB.'

Claire looked at the spine and saw the name of the author and exclaimed, 'What a wonderful choice, OldRuin. I love this book.'

He looked at me and then said to both of us, 'I thought that might be the case.'

'I even learnt some of the lines when I was a child,' Claire added. Then, in a very gentle, quiet voice, she quoted:

> When all the world is old, lad,
> And all the trees are brown;
> And all the sport is stale, lad,
> And all the wheels run down:

> Creep home and take your place there,
> The spent and maimed among:
> God grant you find one face there,
> You loved when all was young.

Claire smiled at me as she finished and then turned to OldRuin, who for his part had to do no more than slightly raise his eyebrow at me to express all that he thought. Then just as I was recovering from the various surprises, I finally noticed the bag in which the book had been wrapped. It was a very distinctive red cloth bag. I looked at OldRuin enquiringly.

'It's my own red bag, BabyB and I can't think of anyone more appropriate to whom I should award it now.'

'I . . . I don't know what to say, OldRuin. I am deeply honoured.'

He then turned to Claire. 'I'd also be so pleased if you'd do me the honour of also accepting a red bag for all your very generous hard work on the case.' He pulled another one out of his briefcase and handed it to her, adding, 'This actually belonged to my father and has been gathering dust for years. I'm so pleased to be able to pass it on to a worthy recipient.'

Claire was equally taken aback by OldRuin's gift and she stammered out her thanks. OldRuin by this point was obviously becoming rather embarrassed, so he swiftly said his goodbyes to us both. As he did so, Claire put her hand in mine and OldRuin beamed.

'Look after this young lady, BabyB.'

Then he took a last look at the book he had given me and said, '*Memento mori*, BabyB. Teaches us all. Every day of our lives.'

He brought out a final gift, which he passed to Claire. 'And I thought you both might like to share this bottle of elderflower wine I made a few years ago. My wife helped me pick the flowers for this particular vintage and like good poetry, it has aged rather well.'

As he left, Claire turned to me and said, 'I think you have a bet to call in. Tell him you like your coffee iced and shaken, not stirred.'

After I'd made the call, Claire took my hand again and suggested we walk along the river. As we did so, we could both still feel the reverberations of anger emanating from TopFirst, who, like a kind of Hooded Claw, had screamed, 'Mark my words, I'll get you, BabyB . . .'

My telephone then rang again and this time it was the Bar Standards Board. 'I'm ringing to inform you Mr BabyBarista that in the light of Mr TopFirst withdrawing his complaint we will proceed no further. However . . .'

Oh no, not more, I thought.

'. . . there is one thing I should add. This decision was not arrived at lightly and I think you should know that initially the Board was set on proceeding against you in any event. But then Mr OldRuin asked permission to address the board personally and he explained not only the selfless hard work you had done for him but also a few of the difficulties that you have faced in the last year or two. It was this that changed their minds.'

I melted not only with relief but with gratitude for OldRuin's constant and unconditional love. I thanked the caller very much and then told Claire the good news. We hugged for a long time and I took her hand and held it in mine. Then we walked on, still holding hands, until at one point we passed a large television screen next to the door of a café and saw BigMouth revelling in his 'great victory' for TheMoldies and speaking about the terrible corruption within the telecom company. It made me ponder OldRuin's prediction that BigMouth's downfall 'may come sooner than he thinks'.

As we walked over Westminster Bridge and watched the Thames flowing beneath us I found myself hoping fervently that OldRuin was right.

Acknowledgements

I'd like to thank the following people in particular for their invaluable help in the making of *Law and Peace*: my agent Euan Thorneycroft of AM Heath; Helen Garnons-Williams, Erica Jarnes, Alexandra Pringle, Richard Charkin, Jude Drake and Laura Brooke at Bloomsbury; Penelope Beech; cartoonist Alex Williams for his wonderful illustrations; Mark Warby QC for his insights, humour and hospitality; Alison and Sean Derrig; Louise Dobson; Jenny Parrott; Maya Wolfe-Robinson, Afua Hirsch, Ros Taylor, Steve Wing, Janine Gibson and Alan Rusbridger at *The Guardian*; Dean Norton and everyone at 1 Temple Gardens; writers Mark Evans, Andy Martin, Tom Anderson and James Woolf; Sir Ian Burnett; barristers Daniel Barnett, Mark Sefton, Dominic Adamson, Aidan Ellis, Anthony Johnson, John Bate-Williams, Marcus Grant, Joe Rich, Melanie Winter, Jacob Dean, Anne Faul and Katie Langdon; Garry Wright at Law Brief Publishing; Jo Pye and Kath Gardner at CPD Webinars; the creative team of Paul Irwin (Goat) and Dr Miranda Coberman; Mike Semple-Piggott, David A. Giacalone and the community of 'blawgers'; readers of the blog at *The Guardian*; Frances Gibb and Alex Spence at *The Times*; Sophie Ashcroft; Madeleine Potter and Michael J Daly; Bob Moss at Clerksroom Magazine; Mrs K.E. Sechiari; Andrew 'Clanger' Clancey; Charlotte Woolven-Brown; Professor Geoffrey M. Beresford Hartwell; Rev. Anne Thorne, Rev. Bill Long and Rev. Dr John Stott; Lady Calcutt; Rachel Kyle, Tim Heyland at Tiki, Gus, Ross, Claire and Lisa Thomson at Saltrock, Dr Rob Casserley, Richard Waddams, Jay Stirzaker, Fiona Sturrock, Jamie Bott, Geoffrey and Susanna Stanford, Dan and Sunny Rudman, Rick Yeo, James Yeo, Stuart (Max Steele) and Maggie de la Roche, Gareth and Jane Harrison, Simon Skelton, Doug and Tamsin

Powell, Jim and Kath Gardner, Jon and Kat Curtis, Chris and Rachel Preston, Tony Baker, John McCrow, Rev David Rudman, David Squire, Ian 'Scratch' Wright, Kieron Davies, Andrew Cotton, Mike Elsom, Mikey and Rita Corker, Dr Basil Singer and Steve Pye; Angie Day, Steve Hole and Craig at the Black Horse; Andy and Simon Murfet and Jay at the White Lion and Emma and Andy at the Corner Bistro; Chris Martindale; Dr Jeff and Mrs Anne Mills; Mark and Luke von Herkomer, Jon Gilbert, Michael Pritchett, Ben Finn, Valerio Massimo, Pam Sharrock, Richard and Hannah Pool-Jones, Toby and Lucy Backhouse, Simon Nixon, Taffa Nice, Caroline and Keith Lister, Rollo and Caroline Clifford, Jo and Dave Williams, Jan and Phil Hall, Amy and Mike Krazizky, Marion Howard, Victoria Woodward, Rachel Murray, Tom Lister, Kevin Nicholson, Jo Howard, Jeremy Eggleton, Phil the Cat, John, Julia, Lewis, Josie and Joan Kliem and the Best family; Alan, Julie and Martine Dobson; Miranda Barnett and Peach Wright; Neil Ferguson and John Coward; remembering Lorna Wilson, Sir David Calcutt QC, Dr Roger Morris and His Honour Judge Paul Clark; Robin Kevan, Sue Chambers, Tina Kevan, Bob Chambers, Lucy, Nick, Toby and Dominic Hawkins, Anna Kevan, Bruce Wilson, Sophie Kevan and all my family; and once again to Dr Michelle Tempest for helping to start it all off.

A NOTE ON THE TYPE

The text of this book is set in Linotype Sabon, named after the type founder, Jacques Sabon. It was designed by Jan Tschichold and jointly developed by Linotype, Monotype and Stempel, in response to a need for a typeface to be available in identical form for mechanical hot metal composition and hand composition using foundry type.

Tschichold based his design for Sabon roman on a font engraved by Garamond, and Sabon italic on a font by Granjon. It was first used in 1966 and has proved an enduring modern classic.

LAW & DISORDER

CONFESSIONS OF A PUPIL BARRISTER

It is BabyBarista's first day as a pupil barrister. He has just one year to win, by foul means or fair, the sought-after prize of a tenancy in chambers. Competition is fierce: there's TopFirst, who has a prize-winning CV and an ego to match; BusyBody, a human whirlwind on a husband hunt; and wide-eyed Worrier, buckling under the weight of the world. Armed with a copy of Sun Tzu's *The Art of War*, BabyBarista launches a no-holds barred fight to the death of double-dealing, dirty tricks and a healthy dose of back-stabbing. Part Rumpole, part Flashman, BabyBarista opens a window onto the Machiavellian and frequently absurd ways of working life.

'It is a wonderful, racing read – well-drawn, smartly plotted and laugh out loud'
JEREMY VINE

'This is "The Legal Apprentice", a high concept TV show disguised as a smart book'
THE TIMES

'Blogger Tim Kevan's diary of a trainee barrister desperate to win a job is fascinating, subversive and pretty much impossible to put down'
SCOTSMAN